D0004193

"Unquestionably an awe-inspiring romance!"
—*Reader to Reader Reviews*

"Not just another romantic read . . . it's a powerful experience!"
—*The Best Reviews*

"A unique romance—it truly stands on its own!"
—Sherrilyn Kenyon, *New York Times* bestselling author

and the sensuous historical romances by Kresley Cole

IF YOU DARE

"Filled with heated passion and wonderful repartee."
—*Romantic Times* Magazine
(Reviewers' Choice Award Winner)

"Cole's voice is powerful and gripping, and *If You Dare* is her steamiest yet!"
—*New York Times* bestselling author Linda Lael Miller

"A deliciously entertaining read that kept the sexual tension high!"
—Romance Designs

"[A] classic romantic adventure that will leave you breathless!"
—*New York Times* bestselling author Julia Quinn

THE PRICE OF PLEASURE

"A splendid read! The sexual tension grips you from beginning to end."
— *New York Times* bestselling author Virginia Henley

"Sexy and original! Sensual island heat that is not to be missed."
— *New York Times* bestselling author Heather Graham

"Savor this marvelous, unforgettable, highly romantic novel by a fresh voice."
— *Romantic Times* Magazine (Top Pick)

THE CAPTAIN OF ALL PLEASURES

"An exciting, sensuous story that will thrill you at every turn of the page."
— *Reader to Reader Reviews*

"Electrifying. . . . Kresley Cole captures the danger and passion of the high seas."
— *New York Times* bestselling author Joan Johnston

"Fast-paced action, heady sexual tension, steamy passion. . . . Exhilarating energy emanates from the pages of this very smart and sassy debut."
— *Romantic Times* Magazine
(Reviewers' Choice Award Winner)

Books by Kresley Cole

The Sutherland Series
The Captain of All Pleasures
The Price of Pleasure

The MacCarrick Brothers Series
If You Dare
If You Desire
If You Deceive

The Immortals After Dark Series
A Hunger Like No Other
No Rest for the Wicked
Wicked Deeds on a Winter's Night

KRESLEY COLE

WICKED DEEDS ON A WINTER'S NIGHT

THE IMMORTALS AFTER DARK SERIES

POCKET STAR BOOKS

New York London Toronto Sydney

Pocket Star Books
A Division of Simon & Schuster, Inc.
1230 Avenue of the Americas
New York, NY 10020

This book is a work of fiction. Names, characters, places, and incidents either are products of the author's imagination or are used fictitiously. Any resemblance to actual events or locales or persons, living or dead, is entirely coincidental.

First Pocket Books paperback edition November 2007

POCKET STAR BOOKS and colophon are registered trademarks of Simon & Schuster, Inc.

For information about special discounts for bulk purchases, please contact Simon & Schuster Special Sales at 1-800-456-6798 or business@simonandschuster.com.

Cover illustration by Vince Natelie

Manufactured in the United States of America

10 9 8 7 6 5 4 3 2 1

ISBN-13: 978-1-4165-4703-7
ISBN-10:   1-4165-4703-7

*This book is dedicated to the warm, witty, and amazing
Beth Kendrick, because we're good enough friends to say,
"Isn't it about time you dedicated a book to me?"
and "How 'bout that book dedication?"*

Acknowledgments

I would like to acknowledge the wonderful short poem "The Witch in the Glass" by Sarah Morgan Bryan Piatt (1836–1919), which I use within this book, and which inspired the character of Mariketa the Awaited, as well as her unique talents.

Glossary of Terms from the *Living Book of Lore*

❧❦❧

The Lore
". . . and those sentient creatures that are not human shall be united in one stratum, coexisting with, yet secret from, man's."

The Lykae Clan
"A proud, strapping warrior of the Keltoi People (or Hidden People, later known as Celts) was taken in his prime by a maddened wolf. The warrior rose from the dead, now an immortal, with the spirit of the beast latent within him. He displayed the wolf's traits: the need for touch, an intense loyalty to its kind, an animal craving for the delights of the flesh. Sometimes the beast rises. . . ."

- Also called werewolves, war-wolds.
- Enemies of the Vampire Horde.

The Talisman's Hie

"*A treacherous and grueling scavenger's hunt for magickal talismans, amulets, and other mystical riches over the entire world.*"

- The rules forbid killing—until the final round. Any other trickery or violence is encouraged.
- Held every two hundred fifty years.
- Hosted by Riora, the goddess of impossibility.

The House of Witches

"*. . . immortal possessors of magickal talents, practitioners of good and evil.*"

- Mystical mercenaries who sell their spells.
- Separated into five castes: warrior, healer, enchantress, conjurer, and seeress.
- Led by Mariketa the Awaited

The Valkyrie

"*When a maiden warrior screams for courage as she dies in battle, Wóden and Freya heed her call. The two gods give up lightning to strike her, rescuing her to their hall, and preserving her courage forever in the form of the maiden's immortal Valkyrie daughter.*"

- Take sustenance from the electrical energy of the earth, sharing it in one collective power, and give it back with their emotions in the form of lightning.

- Possess preternatural strength and speed.
- Without training, they can be mesmerized by shining objects and jewels.
- Also called Swan Maidens, Shield Maidens.
- Enemies of the Vampire Horde.

The Vampires

Two warring factions, the Horde and the Forbearer Army.

- Each vampire seeks his *Bride*, his eternal wife, and walks as the living dead until he finds her.
- A Bride will render his body fully alive, giving him breath and making his heart beat, a process known as *blooding*.
- *Tracing* is teleporting, the vampires' means of travel. A vampire can only trace to destinations he's previously been.

The Horde

"In the first chaos of the Lore, a brotherhood of vampires dominated, by relying on their cold nature, worship of logic, and absence of mercy. They sprang from the harsh steppes of Dacia and migrated to Russia, though some say a secret enclave, the Daci, live in Dacia still."

- Distinguished by their red eyes, a side effect of drinking victims to death.
- Enemies of most factions in the Lore.

The Forbearers

" . . . *his crown stolen, Kristoff, the rightful Horde king, stalked the battlefields of antiquity seeking the strongest, most valiant human warriors as they died, earning him the name of Gravewalker. He offered eternal life in exchange for eternal fealty to him and his growing army.*"

- An army of vampires consisting of turned humans, who do not drink blood directly from the flesh.
- Kristoff was raised as a human and then lived among them. He and his army know little of the Lore.
- Enemies of the Horde.

The Demonarchies

"*The demons are as varied as the bands of man. . . .*"

- A collection of demon dynasties. Some kingdoms ally with the Horde.
- Most demon breeds can *trace* like vampires.

The Furiae

"*If you do evil, beg for punishment—before they come. . . .*"

- Ruthless she-warriors bent on delivering justice to evil men when they escape it elsewhere.
- Led by Alecta the Unyielding One.
- Also called Furies, Erinyes.

Berserkers

"A berserker's lonely life is filled with naught but battle rage and bloodlust. . . ."

- A cadre of warriors who swore allegiance to Wóden, known for their merciless brutality.
- Though some are immortal through resurrection, most are mortal—one of the few human orders to be recognized and accepted by the Lore.
- Able to conjure the spirit of the bear, and channel its ferocity.

The Wraiths

". . . their origin unknown, their presence chilling."

- Spectral, howling beings. Undefeatable and, for the most part, uncontrollable.
- Also called the Ancient Scourge.

The Turning

"Only through death can one become an 'other.'"

- Some beings, like the Lykae, vampires, and demons, can turn a human or even other Lore creatures into their kind through differing means, but the catalyst for change is always death, and success is not guaranteed.

The Accession

"And a time shall pass that all immortal beings in the Lore, from the Valkyrie, vampire, Lykae, and demon factions, to the phantoms, shifters, fey, and sirens . . . must fight and destroy each other."

- A kind of mystical checks-and-balances system for an ever-growing population of immortals.
- Occurs every five hundred years. Or right now . . .

Love spells are a lot like platform diving. Once you start the process, there's no going back, and the end will be fugly if you don't know what the hell you're doing.
—Mariketa the Awaited
Mercenary of the Wiccae,
Future Leader of the House of Witches

Witches are good for one thing and only one thing. Tinder.
—Bowen Graeme MacRieve
Third in line for the Lykae throne

Prologue

~~∞~~

The Forest of Three Bridges
Winter 1827

It wants to mark my flesh. . . . The full moon beat light down on a canvas of snow and barren trees, making Mariah's hunter green dress glow as distinctly as a beacon for the beast pursuing her.

Mark me with its teeth, she thought wildly as she leapt across an icy rivulet. When the beast's frenzied roar echoed through the forest, she stumbled at the embankment. Frantically scrambling up, she continued her flight for home.

Birch branches clawed at her hair and raked her cold-numbed face. As she twisted from their grasp, snow began to fall once more, blurring her vision. Another bellow in the dark silenced night creatures; the sound of her ragged breaths became deafening.

Bowen, the man she'd loved since she was a girl, had warned her of the full moon, preparing her: "I will change, Mariah. I canna control it. And you are vulnerable to harm still. . . ."

She'd insisted on meeting him this night, because she'd

known how critical this time was for him—and because she was anxious to make up for denying his desires again and again. But then, at this last hour, her courage failed her. She'd looked upon the face of her beloved, and the moon had revealed a monster in his place.

It had known she was horrified. Its eyes, glowing ice blue, had been filled with an animal-like yearning until they narrowed with comprehension. "Run . . . Mariah," it had grated in an unfamiliar rasp. "Get to the . . . castle. Lock yourself away . . . from me."

She could hear him crashing toward her, ever nearer, but she was almost there. Reaching the edge of the forest, she saw her home in the snowy plain below her—a castle towering amidst the confluence of their kingdom's three great rivers. *So close.*

Mariah raced for the familiar winding path that would lead her down. As soon as she alighted upon it, movement exploded before her eyes. Suddenly the air teemed with ravens, shooting up all around her, wings batting her numbed face. Swinging at them blindly, she stumbled and lost her footing on the icy, root-strewn path.

Weightlessness . . . falling . . . tumbling down the side of the ravine . . . The impact wrenched the breath from her lungs and made her sight darken. Falling still . . .

When she landed at the bottom, it was to a sickening wet sound as some force punched through her stomach. Unimaginable pain erupted through her. She gaped in incomprehension at the sharp stump jutting up from her body. *No . . . No . . . cannot be.*

As the pain dimmed to only a chilling sensation of pressure within her, she weakly grasped the remains of an axed-down birch, felled by one of her kingdom's woodsmen.

With each breath, blood bubbled from her mouth. It dripped from her face into the snow, as softly as tears.

Mariah of the Three Bridges would die in the moon's shadow of her own home.

In a daze, staring at the sky, she listened while the beast crashed toward her impossibly faster, as if scenting the blood. Before it could reach Mariah, she recognized she was no longer alone.

Just after she spied more ravens circling overhead, icy lips met hers. Emptiness and chaos seeped through her like a disease. As she writhed futilely, a voice inside Mariah's head spoke of this night, a wintry eve brimming with purpose.

"*Die,*" the voice whispered against Mariah's bloody mouth. Immediately, she perceived the stillness of her heart. Her lungs ceased their labors and the mask of pain on her face slackened.

The presence faded, replaced by another. Mariah's last sight was the beast, roaring in agony to the moon, clawing at its chest with wild sorrow.

1

Present day
Tomb of the Incubi, the jungles of Guatemala
Day 3 of the Talisman's Hie
Prize: Four Mayan sacrificial headdresses,
each worth seven points

"Stalking me, Mr. MacRieve?" Mariketa the Awaited asked the Lykae behind her without turning around. In the dark of a corridor leading to a burial chamber, Bowen MacRieve had been following her silently. But she'd *felt* him staring at her—just as she had at the Talisman's Hie assembly three nights ago.

"No' likely, witch." How could such a rumbling Scots' burr sound so menacing? "I only stalk what I want to catch."

Mari did turn to slant him a glance at that, even knowing he couldn't see her face under the hood of the scarlet cloak she always wore. But by the light of her lantern hanging over her shoulder, she could see his, and used the cover to disguise her long, appreciative look.

She inwardly sighed. Lykae males were notoriously good-looking, and the few she'd seen had lived up to their reputation, but this one was heart-poundingly sexy.

He had black hair, stick straight and thick, reaching to the collar of his obviously expensive shirt. His body—which she'd found herself thinking about frequently over the past few days—was sublime. He stood a good bit over six feet tall, and though the corridor was wide enough for two normal-size people to pass, his broad shoulders and big, rangy build filled the space.

But even with all his many attractions, his eyes were what made him so unique. They were the color of rich, warm amber, and yet there was a kind of sinister light to them, which she liked.

She was a little sinister, too.

"Look your fill?" he asked, his tone scathing. Yes, he was sexy, but unfortunately, his dislike of witches was well known.

"I'm done with you," she answered, and meant it. She didn't have time to pine after brusque werewolf warriors if she planned to be the first of her kind ever to win the Hie, an immortal scavenger hunt à la *The Amazing Race*.

With an inward shrug, she continued on toward yet another burial chamber. This was the tenth she'd investigated over the hours she and several other competitors had been down deep inside this never-ending Mayan tomb.

She might have surprised him with her curt dismissal because a moment passed before he followed her. The only sounds in the echoing space were his heavy footfalls, which he no longer bothered to muffle. The silence between them was grueling.

"Who opened the stone slab to the tomb?" he finally asked, trailing far too closely behind her.

"The three elven archers and a couple of demons." The archers, two males and a female, were deadly shooters with lightning-quick speed, and the male rage demons were incredibly powerful—second in physical strength only to the Lykae. Yet even for them, the stone portcullis sealing the tomb's entrance had been nearly impossible to budge.

They'd realized the entire pyramidal structure had shifted from time and earthquakes and now rested on the portcullis, making it weigh tons. Raising it had taken all of the others cooperating—with the two demons lifting it and the archers shoving an enormous boulder under it to prop it open.

"And they just let you enter after their effort?"

She stopped and faced him again. "What should they have done, Mr. MacRieve?" The others had not only allowed her to enter. Though she barely knew any of them, they had wanted to work together since there were four prizes. Cade, one of the demons, had even helped her climb down the dozen feet from the outer entrance into the first anteroom. Then they'd all split up to cover the maze of chambers and vowed to the Lore to alert the others of a find.

MacRieve's smile was a cruel twist of his lips. "I know exactly what I would have done."

"I know exactly how I would have retaliated." He seemed surprised that she didn't fear him, but the truth was that she didn't spook easily—when not faced with heights or unnecessarily large insects. And she was well aware of how vicious the Hie competitors could be as they raced around the world for prizes.

This ruthlessness in the Hie was why Mari had been sent by the House of Witches to compete, even though she was only twenty-three and hailed from the shady New Orleans coven, the slacker Animal House of witches. And even though she had not yet made the turn from mortal to immortal.

But Mari was not above trickery, and unlike many witches, she would not hesitate to use magick to harm another if they deserved it—and if she could manage it with her volatile powers.

MacRieve closed in until nearly seven feet of seething werewolf male loomed over her. He was at least a foot taller than she was and hundreds of times stronger, but she forced herself to stand her ground.

"Watch your step, little witch. You doona wish to anger one such as me."

The grand prize for the Hie was an object called Thrane's Key, a key that allowed its possessor to go back in time—not just once, but *twice*. For a tool like that, she knew he was ready to take her out of the contest. So she had to convince him that it was impossible for him to do so.

"Likewise, you shouldn't anger me." Her voice was steady as she looked up at him. "Remember that I could turn your blood to acid as an afterthought," she said, baldly lying.

"Aye, I've heard rumors of your power." He narrowed his eyes. "Curious, though, that you dinna open the tomb with one flick of your finger."

Yes, she might have managed to lift the portcullis— with concentration, an unprecedented bout of luck, and the absence of a hangover. Oh, and if she were in mortal danger.

Unfortunately, her power was adrenaline-based, making it as infinite as it was uncontrollable.

"You think I should use magick like mine to open a

tomb?" Mari asked in a scoffing tone. *Mistress of bluffing, working it here.* "That'd be like calling you in to lift a feather."

He tilted his head, sizing her up. After what seemed like an hour, he began walking again.

Mari gave an inward sigh of relief. If anyone in the Lore found out how vulnerable she really was, she'd be doomed. She knew this, but no matter how hard she worked, whenever she manifested and unleashed significant power, things ended up *exploding*.

As her befuddled mentor Elianna explained, "Horses have powerful legs—but that doesn't mean they're prima ballerinas." The ancient Elianna trained with Mari daily to control the destructive nature of her spells, because she believed the subtle magicks invoked the most fear in their enemies.

And the House of Witches brokered in fear.

The corridor finally ended at a broad, high wall, covered in carvings of ghoulish faces and animals. Mari lifted her lantern high and the reliefs seemed to move in shadow. They'd apparently been put there to guard a small tunnel opening near the floor, which itself was made out like a gaping mouth with fangs dropping down.

She waved the Lykae forward. "Age before beauty, Mr. MacRieve." She sized him up again, then studied the small opening, which couldn't be more than three feet square. "If you think you can fit."

He stood motionless, clearly not about to be directed. "Only humans call me Mr. MacRieve."

She shrugged. "I'm not a human." Her mother was a fey druidess, and her late father had been a warlock of questionable repute. So Mari was a fey witch or a "weylock," as her buddies teased. "So would you like me to call you Bowen, or Bowe for short?"

"Bowe is what my friends call me, so you doona."

What an ass. . . . "No problem. I have a slew of other more fitting names for you. Most of them end in *er*."

He ignored her comment. "You in the tunnel first."

"Don't you think it'd be unbecoming for me to be on my hands and knees in front of you? Besides, you don't need my lantern to see in the dark, and if you go first, you'll be sure to lose me and get to the prize first."

"I doona like anything, or anyone, at my back." He crossed his arms over his chest and leaned a shoulder against a snarling visage on the stone wall. She'd never seen a Lykae turn into its towering werewolf form, but knew from those who had that this male could be as frightening as any monster, real or imagined. "And you'll have your little red cloak on," he continued, "so I will no' be able to see anything about you that might be . . . unbecoming."

"Twisting my words? I'll have you know that I am criminally cute—"

"Then why hide behind a cloak?"

"I'm not *hiding*." In fact, that was precisely what she was doing. "And I like to wear it." She *hated* it.

Even before her birth, she'd been predicted to be the Awaited One, the most powerful born to the House of Witches in centuries—but four years ago, it was also foretold that a male from the Lore would recognize her as his own and claim her. He would seek to lock her away, guarding her with a ferocity that no magicks could defeat, thus robbing the House of her powers.

Since the prediction, she'd been forced to cover herself

every single time she set foot outside her home. Needless to say, the robust dating life of her late teens had taken a hit.

She sported the cloak—a red one because she was a Scarlet Letter-type rebel at heart—and as a backup, she also hid behind a magickal glamour that disguised her looks, the tone of her voice, and her scent.

If a male like MacRieve did see her, he would perceive a brunette with blue eyes—when in fact she was a redhead with gray eyes—and he would have difficulty recalling anything that *was* the same, like her features, her figure, or the length of her hair. The glamour was so second nature that she hardly thought about it anymore.

Even with all these precautions, it followed that unattached males in the Lore were to be avoided. Yet Mari had heard at the Hie assembly—a gossip fest if she'd ever seen one—that MacRieve had already found his mate and lost her more than a century ago.

Mari had felt sympathy for him. A Lykae's entire existence centered around his mate, and in his long immortal life, he would get only one—just one—chance in an eternity to find happiness.

When she saw he wasn't budging, she muttered, "Fine. Beauty before age." She unlooped her lantern strap and crawled in. The space was tighter than she'd imagined, but she didn't have time to rethink her decision because he climbed in directly after her. Resigned, she exhaled and held her lantern up to light her way.

The stone was cool and moist and she was glad for her cloak—until she caught her knee on the end, and the tie around her neck yanked her head down. When it happened again, she shimmied, working the material back so that it flowed behind her as she made progress forward. *There. Better.*

Five seconds later: "MacRieve, you're on my cloak. Let up—"

Before she could react, he reached between her knees and then up against her chest to slice the tie at her neck with one claw. Her eyes went wide and she dropped her light to snatch fistfuls of cloth, but he jerked the cloak out of her grasp.

"Give it back!"

"It was slowing you—and therefore me—down."

She gritted her teeth, struggling to control her temper. "If *you* had gone first—"

"I dinna. If you want it, why no' use magick to take it from me?"

Did he suspect how volatile her power was? Was he sussing out her weaknesses? "You really do not want me to do that."

"You really must no' want your cloak back. Come then, witchling, just take it from me."

Glamour or not, she had grown used to the physical security of the garment. And when she realized she wasn't getting it back from him, Mari just checked the urge to rub her bared arms. All at once, she became very much aware of how high her hiking shorts were on her thighs and how her tank top was riding up, about to reveal the mark on her lower back.

She steeled herself and made her tone nonchalant. "Keep the cloak." Though she knew he was ogling her, she forced herself to put one knee in front of the other. "It'll be worth money one day."

After a few moments, he said, "Doona fret, witch.

You're no' so unbecoming from my angle. Bit scrawny where it counts, but no' *too* bad."

Yep, ogling. Many adjectives could be used to describe her ass, but scrawny was not among them. *He's just making these comments and brushing up against you to unnerve you.* Knowing that didn't make his efforts less effective! "Scrawny where it counts, MacRieve? Funny, I'd heard the same about you."

He gave a kind of humorless half chuckle and finally followed. "No' likely. Maybe you're just too young to have heard the rumors about Lykae males. Tender wee ears and such."

No, she'd heard. And over the last couple of days, she had wondered about that rumor and if it applied to him.

How long was this damned tunnel—

"*Still, lass,*" he grated. Her eyes widened again when she felt his hot palm lying flat against the back of her thigh. "There's a scorpion tangled up in all that hair of yours."

"Get your hand off me, MacRieve! You think I can't see what you're doing? I've been scanning every inch of this tunnel—I would have seen a scorpion." When she started again, he squeezed her leg. His thumb claw pressed against her skin, high on her inner thigh, sending an unexpected shot of pleasure through her. She had to stifle a shiver.

It was only after she felt a whisper of touch over her hair that she got her wits again. "Like I'm supposed to believe there's a scorpion and it just happens to be in the tunnel we're crawling in and then in my hair? Any other creature-feature props you'd like to reference? Is there a mummy's hand tangled up in there? I'm really surprised you didn't go with 'classic tarantula.'"

His arm shot out between her legs—again—jostling against the front of her body as he tossed something in front of her. Something with *mass*. She held her lantern farther forward—

The sight of a scorpion as big as her hand had her scrambling back . . . wedging herself firmly against MacRieve—a very awkward position to be in with anyone, but especially with a werewolf.

He stiffened all around her. Every inch of him. She felt his arms bulging over her shoulders and his chiseled abs taut over her back.

His growing erection strained thick against her backside. *So the rumors about werewolf males are true,* she thought dazedly. *Exhibit A is quite insistent.*

"*Move forward,*" he said, grating the words. He was breathing heavily right over her ear.

"No way. Kind of between a scorpion and a hard place here." She bit her lip, wishing one of her friends had heard her say that.

He eased back from her. "I killed it," he said between breaths. "You can pass, just doona let it touch you."

"Why do you care?" She frowned to find herself feeling chilled without him over her.

"Doona. A sting will slow you down. And I'm behind you, remember?"

"Like I'm going to forget that anytime soon." Then his callous words sunk in. "Hey, werewolf, aren't you supposed to gnaw on your prey or play with it with shuffling paws or something? Want me to save it for you?"

"I could put it back where I found it, witch."

"I could turn you into a toad." Maybe an exploded toad.

Without warning, he fingered the small, black tattoo on her lower back. "What does this script mean?"

She did gasp then, as much from the shock of his touch there as from her visceral reaction to it. She wanted to arch up to his hand and couldn't understand why. She snapped, "*Are you done groping me?*"

"Canna say. Tell me what the marking means."

Mari had no idea. She'd had it ever since she could remember. All she knew was that her mother used to write out that mysterious lettering in all of her correspondence. Or, at least her mother had before she'd abandoned Mari in New Orleans to go on her two-hundred-year-long druid sabbatical—

He tapped her there, impatiently awaiting an answer.

"It means 'drunk and lost a bet.' Now keep your hands to yourself unless you want to be an amphibian." When the opening emerged ahead, she crawled heedlessly for it and scrambled out with her lantern swinging wildly. She'd taken only three steps into the new chamber before he'd caught her wrist, spinning her around.

As his gaze raked over her, he reached forward and pulled a lock of her long hair over her shoulder. He seemed unaware that he was languidly rubbing his thumb over the curl. "Why hide this face behind a cloak?" he murmured, cocking his head to the side as he studied her. "No' a damn thing's wrong with you that I can tell. But you look fey. Explains the name."

"How can I resist these suave compliments?" He was right about the name though. Many of the fey had names beginning in Mari or Kari.

She gave his light hold on her hair a pointed look, and

he dropped it like it was hot, then scowled at her as if she were to blame.

"Right now you're working your spells, are you no'?" He actually leaned in to *scent* her.

"No, not at all. Believe me, you'd know."

As if he hadn't heard her, he continued, "Aye, you are." His expression was growing more savage by the instant. "Just as you were born to do."

But for some reason she wasn't afraid. She was . . . excited. He must have seen something in her eyes that he didn't like, because he abruptly turned from her.

As he surveyed their surroundings, she scrutinized him, searching for a single thing about his appearance that she didn't find sexy—and failing.

All immortals were "frozen" into their immortality when they reached the peak of their strength and were best able to survive. But MacRieve had turned later than other males she'd seen in the Lore. He appeared as though he'd aged to be at least thirty-five. And, damn, it was a good look for him.

His clothes were well made but raffish. A small, ancient-looking medallion hung from a short length of leather around his neck, and a large hunting knife was strapped to his belt. He made Indiana Jones look like a poser pretty boy.

MacRieve also wore a whip at his side, no doubt to be prepared for an encounter with the vampire who'd entered the Hie. Like many demons, vampires could teleport—or trace—making them impossible to vanquish. Mari knew that some younger vampires could be trapped with a whip, preventing them from tracing and making them easier to kill.

That night at the assembly, MacRieve had clashed against the vampire in a bloody, vicious brawl, yet never had Mari seen anything so beautiful as the way he'd moved. The fight had been broken up by a Valkyrie, but Mari could have watched him for hours. . . .

When MacRieve visibly tensed, she followed his gaze. There, toward the back wall was a sarcophagus, the first she'd seen. A headdress would have to be within!

They both raced forward, colliding right before it.

With a growl he grabbed her arms to toss her away, his gaze already back on the crypt, but then he did a double take, frowning at her. He faced her fully as his grip eased on her. "You actually think to play with me?" His hands skimmed down her arms, then rested on her hips.

She exhaled a shaky breath. "Why do you assume I'm working spells?" She might have the requisite adrenaline flowing, but knew she couldn't focus it. Especially not since she could feel the heat of his rough hands through the material of her shorts.

"For one hundred and eighty years I've no' touched another." He leaned in closer to her. "Have never even given a woman a second look. But now I canna seem to keep my hands off a slip of a *witch*," he rasped at her ear. "A witch who has me feeling like I'll die if I doona find out what it'd be like to kiss her." He drew back, his face a mask of rage. "*O' course it's a goddamned spell.*"

He wanted to kiss her now? Why now? He'd been faithful to his dead mate all this time? The idea softened something inside her—even as alarm trickled in.

What if she *was* working a spell? Elianna had once advised Mari to be careful what she wished for. When Mari had nodded at the old truism, Elianna had added, "No.

Really. Be careful. We don't know the extent of your powers, and many witches can effect their desires with a mere thought."

Did Mari want to kiss Bowen MacRieve so badly that she was enthralling him?

When he lifted her onto the sarcophagus and wedged his hips between her legs, she suspected she might. She swallowed. "I take it you plan to find out what it'd be like?"

The battle raging inside him was clear on his face. "*Stop this, Marileta.*" The way he rumbled her name with his accent made her melt. He removed his hands from her, but when he rested them beside her hips, his fingers curled until his dark claws dug into the stone. "Can you no' ken why I'm in this contest? I seek *her* again and wish to be true."

He wanted his mate back. Of course. He wanted to use Thrane's Key to go back in time and prevent her death. Surprisingly, Mari resented the woman who'd engendered such loyalty in this warrior for so many years. "I'm not . . . or I don't mean to be . . . doing anything to you," Mari whispered, but the way she was reacting to his scent, his mesmerizing eyes, and his hard body between her thighs belied the words.

There was an aura about him that was staggering to her, making it difficult to think. It wasn't mere male heat and sensuality. It was raw sexuality, animalistic in its intensity—and she was starving for it.

Ah, gods, she *did* want him to kiss her. Wanted it with everything that she was and willed him to do so. *Want me as fiercely as I want you . . . desire me as you've never desired another.*

He cupped the back of her neck, staring down at her. As

she gazed up in fascination, the amber of his eyes turned to ice blue. He seemed desperate to recognize something in her, and when he clearly didn't find it, his hand on her began to shake. "Damn you, witch, I doona want another."

She suddenly knew two things: He was about to kiss her so fiercely she would never be the same again.

And he would hate himself for it afterward and despise her forever. . . .

2

The witch *seethed* with power. Spells and magicks swirled about her. Bowe could sense them, could perceive them tangling around him, binding him to her—because she was beckoning him to kiss her. . . .

No, he couldn't get distracted from his aim! He wouldn't. So much was at stake with this competition. His past, his future. He knew this—knew what he was fighting for—so why couldn't he drag his eyes away from the witch's face?

As she gazed up at him, her features seemed to shift. Her irises briefly flickered from an ordinary blue to a stormy, intense gray. She licked her lips, and right before him they turned from pink to the deepest, most enticing red. His shaft throbbed harder, straining against his pants.

Yes, he had to taste her. To walk away without knowing what those glistening lips promised . . . ? Impossible. Not after beholding the body she'd concealed beneath her cloak. She was lush, surprisingly curvy with high, plump breasts. And in that tunnel, when he'd gazed upon her crawling in front of him, the allure of her generous hips and arse had been as strong as a siren's call to him. He'd have followed her for miles, hard as rock, heart thundering in anticipation.

Then to be wedged against her in that position? Hell, he'd just stopped himself from thrusting uncontrollably against her—

"*Bowen . . .*" she whispered, an edge of need in her voice.

The witch wanted; he was helpless not to give.

His first kiss in nearly two centuries.

Pulling her closer with his hand at her nape, he leaned down and took her mouth with his. The merest contact rocked him. From the first touch, he felt how giving her lips were, parting in welcome. She gave a cry against him, and her palms traced up his chest to rest at his neck, her fingers twining in his hair.

He slipped his tongue into her mouth, and she met it with her own, with slow, wicked laps that made him inhale sharply to groan against her. His free hand grasped her waist to hold her as he deepened the kiss, and she moaned her approval, going soft against him.

She was the one enthralling him, so why did she seem to be going out of her head with desire? She seemed . . . *lost* for him. When would she pull back? Surely he couldn't be expected to. She would tell him to stop, and he would somehow manage to relinquish what he desired, as he had hundreds of times before.

But she didn't tell him. Between licks, she whispered, "*Yes, Bowen, yes.*" Instead of checking his lust, she urged him on, as if she wanted him, a Lykae, to lose control.

He clutched her neck hard. For over a thousand years, he'd unwaveringly scorned witches. Yet now he was savoring the wanton, drugging kiss of one—a soft, ruby-lipped witch who, he feared, could make all his sexual dreams come true. Having been without sex for so long, Bowe dreamed about it *constantly*.

To be lost after so long . . . *Follow her into oblivion. Follow her down.*

At last Mari sensed him letting go, growing more aggressive, turning as fierce as she'd expected.

His kiss was hard and heated as he claimed her mouth. And she was more than ready to match his need. She found herself going up on her knees, brazenly pressing her body into his, feeling his unyielding erection against her belly.

She would become an immortal soon, she sensed it, and everyone had told her the flood of desires she'd experience leading up to the change would be strong. So far it had proved *overwhelming.* Was that what was happening here? Was she enjoying her first taste of lust between two immortals?

He was the most sinful kisser she'd ever had, and she knew she wasn't going to get another chance with him ever. So she gripped his head, kissing him as if her life depended on it.

When she'd made love in the past, Mari had felt that something vital was missing, something she'd feared she couldn't do without for much longer. Now she knew what she'd missed. *Intensity.* That hectic passion so strong it made good sense—made thought itself—fade to nothing but feeling. He could give that to her.

With the hand gripping her waist, he rubbed his thumb up and down her torso. When he made contact with the small ring at her navel, he drew a quick, surprised breath against her lips.

His shaking hand finally trailed lower. . . .

Aching to touch him as well, she ran her fingers down

his broad chest. Just as she reached the waist of his jeans, he began working his fingers into her shorts. Their kiss grew more desperate.

When she thought about them touching each other like this, pleasuring each other, she couldn't prevent her hips from rocking up to his hand. But when her curious fingertips dipped down, and she brushed the broad, slick head of his erection, he jerked as if in shock at the touch, as if she'd seared him.

He grabbed her wrist, seeming to decide if he should pull her hand away or press it against him. "*Need this,*" he finally rasped, forcing her hand into the heat of his jeans to grip his thick shaft. "*So damned much.*"

"Yes!" she cried, feeling him stroking at the lace edge of her panties.

He groaned and reached lower. When he cupped the wet flesh between her legs, he shuddered, thrusting himself into her fist.

Just when she had no doubt they were about indulge in each other, he stilled. Even as his erection throbbed in her grip, and his breaths were ragged, he withdrew his hand from her and shook his head hard. "But canna have it."

Suddenly, he snatched her hand from him, squeezing her wrist so tightly, magick began building in her palm in reflex. His ghostly blue eyes flickered over the light. Then, as if reminded of what she was, he looked disgusted with her. His voice low, he said, "Quit the Hie, witch."

She slowly shook her head. "Not on your life, Mac-Rieve." Not after everything she'd done to get here. And not when the next Hie wouldn't be for another two hundred and fifty years.

His lips were subtly drawing back to bare his lengthening fangs. "Vow you'll quit, or I swear I will make it so you do no' distract me again."

"I wasn't trying to distract you—"

"Bullshite!" He shoved aside the sarcophagus cover she was perched on, jarring her. His hand rooted down, and he plucked out the headdress—a stunning gold and jade piece. "You could almost make me forget what I *really* want." Fisting his fingers around it, he cast her a menacing smile. They both knew that all he had to do was lift the prize above his heart, and it would travel to Riora, the goddess of the Hie. He raised it, and the headdress disappeared; for a second afterward, Mari felt the magick, clear and true, and smelled the goddess's forest temple halfway around the world.

So easily, Mari had just lost those points—or had had them *taken* from her.

"Do you really think you can defeat me?" he demanded. "And if no' me, then the Valkyrie or the vampire?"

"A seer predicted Kaderin will lose the Hie for once. This is anyone's game."

He eyed her. "You know why I will win. What do you seek?"

To show everyone! "It's personal," she said instead. "Look, we could team up. The key works twice."

"Team with you? What could you possibly offer me?" The expression he gave her said he was *amused* by her statement. Her eyes narrowed. He shouldn't be amused.

"I'm not without skills, MacRieve. I won the first two tasks I undertook." Mari could be surprisingly effective for someone who rarely put herself in challenging situations. When she did decide to work for something, she worked *hard.* In the Hie, she had to work harder merely because she was a mortal. "And I do believe I beat *you* here."

"Do you have any idea how much I despise witches?"

Many Lorekind did. Witches were feared and mistrusted, used only for their purchased spells. And that disdain had never bothered her so much as it did now. "No, that fact escaped me when you were sticking your tongue in my mouth."

The reminder seemed to enrage him. "You will no' take yourself from the hunt? Then I'll take the hunt from you." He twisted away from her, then charged for the tunnel.

Suspecting what he planned to do, she felt panic—and magick—rising up within her. After a sharp shake of her head, she hurried after him. "Wait, MacRieve!" When she got to the tunnel, he was already climbing out the other end. A concentration of magick built in her palm, and she threw a beam of it at him. Didn't know what she expected. . . .

Though it shot straight as a laser, it just missed him. Once the tunnel was cleared of everything but aftersparks and residual power flares, he leaned down to give her a black look, then disappeared.

Snatching up her lantern, she crawled through that awful space, breaths panicked and sharp, magick cloying about her. Once freed of the tunnel, she dashed down corridors, finally reaching the first anteroom.

The tomb's entryway was at least twelve feet above this chamber's floor. She arrived in time to see him leap the distance, easily clearing it.

As he gazed down at her from the opening, his eyes looked crazed, and she saw he was turning more fully. An image of a furious beast flickered over him. He ducked down, positioning himself under the portcullis. When he raised his hands above him to grip it, she said, "Don't do this, MacRieve."

He hefted the weight—with difficulty, but by himself. Two demons had labored with that feat. And the colossal stone that the three archers had struggled to shove under it? MacRieve simply kicked it away, toppling it from the ledge into the space near Mari.

As if her thoughts of them brought the other competitors, the archers entered the outer chamber, their easy smiles lit in the glow of their lanterns. When the three saw her, they appeared shocked that she wasn't in her cloak. Each gaze locked on her pointed ears. "Mariketa, you're *fey*, like us?" Tera, the female asked. "It was rumored at the assembly . . ."

Tera trailed off when Mari nervously jerked her chin in MacRieve's direction. The archers eased farther inside. In a heartbeat, they'd swung three nocked bows up at him, yet they knew if they shot, he'd drop his burden, sealing them in.

But he's going to do it anyway.

The demons arrived then, quickly comprehending the situation. Their fangs lengthened as they began to turn into their own enraged demon shape.

Their eyes grew black as their skin darkened into a deep red. Their elegantly turned horns, which usually curved out from just past their temples to run along the sides of their heads, now straightened and sharpened into deadly points, the normally shell-like color blackening.

Rydstrom, the older demon grated, "Bowen, think on what you plan." The two obviously knew each other.

Tera murmured to Mari, "Can you get a call out, Mariketa?"

Mari raised her right palm, intending to send a psychic message to her coven. Nothing came. She shoved her palm out again.

When she failed once more, MacRieve *laughed* at her. His voice sounding like a beast's, he grated, "No' quite so powerful, witch."

Enough. Fury churned in her like she'd rarely known before. She wanted to hurt him, *needed* to, and suddenly a rare focus came to her wrath, control to her power.

She put her left hand behind her back, and a spine of red light rose up from her palm, taking shape like a dagger. Tera must have seen what she was doing because she sidled up to her and raised her lantern to camouflage the magick's glow.

Building . . . building . . .

In a flash, Mari threw the dagger of light overhand. MacRieve appeared shocked at the speed and twisted to dodge it, but it exploded into painless fragments over his heart.

Bull's-eye. Subtle-like.

With a glance down, he smirked, thinking himself safe. "Keep your daggers to yourself, witchling, till they get some bite."

He calmly took one step back . . . then dropped the stone. As it slammed shut with a deafening boom, a volley of arrows sank into it, too late. Air, rock, and sand rushed over Mari's face, gritting into her eyes. She heard the elven males yelling with rage as they rushed forward and banged on the wall.

When Mari wiped the sand from her eyes, she blinked,

disbelieving what she saw. The elves backed away in silence. Once, long ago, something had leapt up, desperately seeking release from this place.

Deep claw marks scored the back of the portcullis in frenzied stripes.

3

⁣⁣❧ ∗ ❧

As Bowe slowly backed from the tomb, he was met with silence. He knew that inside they were cursing him, but he wouldn't be able to hear. Much of the pyramidal steps were coated with thick soil and draped with roots and towering trees.

Yet even the jungles surrounding this square perimeter of ruins were quiet.

He continued to gaze at the edifice, finding himself unaccountably reluctant to leave. Part of him wanted to charge back in there and vent more of his rancor at the witch. To his shame, part of him was burning to retrieve her and finish what they'd started together.

He thought back to that moment when the witch had comprehended he was going to seal them in. She'd seemed *hurt*, and her glamour had flickered.

In that instant, Cade's predatory gaze had darted to her, even in the midst of his killing rage. Divested of her cloak, comely Mariketa had seized the demon's attention. His brother Rydstrom, too, had done a double take.

Bowe had been surprised to find that the two demons Mariketa had mentioned were ones he knew. He had a history with the brothers—they'd fought side by side centuries ago—and had noticed them at the assembly, vaguely, when he could drag his eyes from the witch.

He recalled that the demons had been extremely popular with females.

Why in the hell did the idea of either brother with her sit so ill with him? *They can have her.* . . . With a final look, he turned, loping away to his truck.

Bowe was not immune to a Lykae's marked sense of curiosity, and when he came across the line of the others' vehicles, he decided to investigate the interiors.

Empty bottles of a local beer and crushed cans of Red Bull littered the demons' truck. The archers had water bottles, protein bars, and electronic gadgetry in theirs.

Then came the witch's Jeep. She'd driven these demanding mountain roads—mud coated all the way up to the soft top—alone. And she'd driven them through a hotbed of political unrest and danger. This densely jungled region had been simmering with the threat of war between two human armies—a turf war between an established drug cartel and a sizable band of narco-terrorists. The conflict surely would erupt soon.

What in the hell had she been thinking? The fact that she'd somehow arrived at the same time as the others—and before Bowe himself—didn't matter.

She'd left two maps spread over the passenger seat, both with highlights and copious notes scrawled on them. Four research books lay in the backseat—among them *Pyramids & Palaces, Monsters & Masks: The Golden Age of Maya Architecture*. Many of the pages were systematically flagged with colored paper clips.

Beside the books, she had a well-worn camouflage backpack. A muddy machete hung from one side of the pack with an incongruous bright pink iPod on the other.

A pink iPod with *stickers of cats* on it, for all the gods' sakes.

Exactly how young was she? It was possible she'd only recently become immortal, possibly wasn't even over a hundred.

Whatever her age, she obviously was too young and too foolish not to know better than to toy with a powerful, twelve-hundred-year-old Lykae.

And she had toyed with him, had enthralled him to kiss her. Bowen MacRieve despised witches; he did not go out of his mind with *desire* for them.

His own father had been a victim of one's machinations. Bowe remembered his father's eyes were haunted, even centuries later, as he'd recounted his meeting with a raven-haired witch of incredible beauty—and unspeakable evil.

Angus MacRieve had come upon her at a snowy crossroads in the old country. She'd been wearing a jet black ermine stole and a white gown and had been the most lovely female he'd ever imagined. She'd told him that she'd grant him a wish if he would direct her to a neighboring town. Angus was just seventeen and had wished what he always did: to be the strongest of his older brothers, who picked on him good-naturedly but unmercifully.

The next day, three of them had been crossing a frozen lake they traversed daily. In the dead of winter, the ice had broken and they'd drowned. The day after that, two more brothers had fallen ill with some kind of fever. They'd quickly passed away, though they'd been hale, braw lads.

In the end, the evil witch had granted his wish. Angus was indeed the strongest of them.

Bowe's father would never outlive his debilitating guilt. Because of his actions—inadvertent though they might have been—only two of the Lykae king's seven sons would survive, Angus, and a much younger brother.

Worse, Angus had been sickened to realize he was now the heir, and readily abdicated the position.

That witch had *delighted* in ruining a mere lad who was not an enemy and hadn't yet raised a sword in anger or aggression.

Witches had no purpose but to spread discord, to engender hatred. To plant destructive seeds in a once-proud family.

To enthrall a male to be untrue for the first time.

Rage engulfed Bowe when he comprehended what he'd just done—with a bloody witch.

He roared, the sound echoing through the jungle, then stabbed his claws into the side of her Jeep, slashing down the length. After puncturing the thick tires and plucking the engine from the chassis, Bowe set to all of their trucks, mangling them until they were useless.

Out of breath, covered in metal slivers, he scowled down at his hands. He could claw through a half-foot plate of steel like it was tinfoil without feeling it.

Yet now he felt . . . *pain*. Unfathomable pain.

4

⚬⚭⚬

"Witch, he's not coming back," the demon Rydstrom told Mari. "Don't waste your time waiting for him."

The others had been casing the perimeter of the antechamber, testing the strength of the stone floor and walls, but Mari continued to stare at the entrance, bewildered, unable to believe that MacRieve had sealed her in this forbidding place—or that she'd retaliated with one of the cruelest spells a witch could cast on an immortal.

Cade asked Mari, "What did you do to the Lykae anyway?"

She absently murmured, "*I've killed him.*"

Mari glanced away from the entrance when met with silence. "He won't regenerate from injuries," she explained. "Unless he returns to me to have it reversed, the hex will eventually destroy him."

Tierney, who looked to be Tera's younger brother, said, "You made him *mortal?*"

They all seemed shocked at her viciousness, except for Cade, who as far as she could tell from his demonic countenance, appeared admiring. "Remind me not to piss you off, witch," he said.

She'd heard of Cade the Kingmaker before and knew he was a ruthless mercenary. The soldier of fortune had waged so much war that it was said he could take any throne.

Except the one his older brother had lost.

"So you are as powerful as rumored," Rydstrom said, his features beginning to lose their demon sharpness, returning to normal—yet normal for him was a handsome face marred by a long scar carving across his forehead and down his temple to his cheek. His black irises reverted to a green so intense they'd startled her the first time she'd seen them. Though he was across the room, she still had to raise her head to meet his gaze. Rydstrom was nearing seven feet tall—with all the muscle to match.

"Powerful," Cade said, "and a mercenary like me." He looked her up and down with eyes as green as his brother's, alerting her to the fact that not only was she bare of her cloak, her glamour was faltering. But she just didn't have the energy or desire to resume it. Being recognized as an immortal warrior's mate right now might not be a bad thing. "Fascinating," Cade added in a rough voice.

The two brothers resembled each other very much, except for Rydstrom's scar, and his horns, which had been damaged somehow. Yet their accents were dissimilar. Both had degrees of a British colonial accent, but Cade's sounded lower class. And his bearing was altogether different from Rydstrom's—as if he hadn't been raised a demon royal, or even a noble.

In short, Rydstrom acted like a stalwart king but looked like a ruthless mercenary, and Cade was just the opposite.

Tera angrily adjusted the bow and quiver at her back. "MacRieve must have known Mariketa would use magick to escape, and that you demons would just teleport yourselves outside. With the entryway so high, the three of us can't even try to lift the slab."

Without the ability to lever themselves against the ground, there was no way even the demons, much less the elves, could raise it. As it was, they couldn't even reach it without leaping up.

Tierney looked enraged, his pointed ears flattening back against his blond head. "He must have sought to trap only our kind!"

Rydstrom said, "If I could trace, I would take you from this tomb—I would make sure you were out of the Hie for good, but not by leaving you in this place."

Cade unsheathed and studied his sword—clearly he wouldn't have done the same.

Hild, the quiet third archer, asked, "Why did you say *if* you could trace?"

"There's a binding placed on Cade and me that makes it impossible to teleport."

Just as Mari decided she shouldn't ask why they'd been bound, Rydstrom smiled gravely. "A coup that didn't quite take, as it were. We were reprimanded for it." His eyes flickered black as he shot a glance at Cade. "Severely."

So that was what they sought in this competition—to go back in time and keep Rydstrom's crown.

"My brother might have been willing to help others," Cade began, "but after seeing what Mariketa did to the Lykae, I bet the witchling will leave us here to rot."

"Is that true?" Rydstrom asked Mari.

Possibly.

"Of course it's not," Tera answered for her. "Mariketa wouldn't leave us any more than we would desert her. She's part fey. Look at her ears. The Hie be damned—somewhere in time, her ancestors are our ancestors."

"Oh, then by that reasoning, she won't leave me

either," Cade said, sarcasm in his voice. "She and I are both mercenaries. There's a code there."

"It's incidental if I would leave anyone behind," Mari finally said. "I don't know that I could lift it."

"What do you mean?" Rydstrom said. "You're strong. I can feel your power even now."

"I . . . I blow things up," she admitted. "And I mostly don't mean to. Mostly."

Cade shook his head. "The entire structure's resting on the portcullis. If you explode that stone, the tomb would come down like a house of cards."

Rydstrom said, "Let's look at odds and make a rational decision—exactly how often do you accidentally blow things up?"

"The times I can get my magick to work?" she said. "Ninety-nine out of a hundred."

As Tierney swore under his breath, Cade said, "So we look for another way out. Did anyone find an exit in any of the chambers?"

"There aren't going to be any exits," Tera said, her attention riveted to a frieze above the portcullis. Intricate animal signs and hieroglyphics were carved into the stone.

"Why do you say that?" Rydstrom asked.

Tera squinted up at the carvings, seeming to somehow make sense of the animal and geometrically shaped glyphs. "Because this is . . . *a jail.*"

"You've deciphered those marks?" Mari asked Tera.

Tierney answered for her, "She knows *all* languages."

Tera translated for them. "It says this tomb is a jail holding six demon essence stealers—incubi—for their unnatural crimes against the daughter of a powerful sorcerer."

"They probably all seduced her, then pops gets pissed," Tierney said. "Locks them away here."

Tera nodded. "The Mayans were custodians for them, of a sort. Kept them locked up—and fed periodically."

"That explains the sacrificial headdresses," Cade said. "Mayan females were offered up."

Tera continued, "They're cursed never to leave this place—short of death. According to these calendrics, they have been here for eleven hundred and eleven years."

"Well, that can't be right," Mari said. "No one's home—"

Claws scrabbled over stone somewhere in the shadows. Everyone glanced around uneasily.

They weren't alone. . . .

"We left the front door open for hours," Tierney said. "Why would they remain here?"

Tera said, "They probably are bound to the tomb, unable to cross the threshold."

"If they are still here, it shouldn't be a problem," Mari said, even as she backed her way to Rydstrom and Cade. "Right? Especially if Tera can speak their language."

The incubi that Mari had known were all charming and hot. Finding one in your bed was supposed to be a good problem to have.

So why were the tiny hairs of her nape standing up? Gazing up at Rydstrom, she murmured, "Mind if I stick around you, big guy?"

In answer, he briefly laid his massive hand on the top of her head in a strangely comforting way.

Suddenly, the scent of rotting flesh pervaded the crypt. Mari felt evil all around them—*old* evil—circling.

As her eyes darted around, she unconsciously began to build magick again.

A drop of something . . . *viscous* hit her bare shoulder. In the unnatural lantern light, she slowly raised her face. Her lips parted, her mind unable to comprehend.

"Mariketa," Tera whispered, as she crossed to her. "Your face has gone white. What could—?" Her words died in her throat as she followed Mari's gaze. Tera's bow and arrow shot up again.

But arrows couldn't kill what was already dead.

"The incubi!" one of the others yelled as shadowy beings swarmed the area, diving and flying all around them. Cade and Rydstrom drew their swords. Just when Mari was praying to Hekate that these people she hardly knew would protect her, Rydstrom used one hand to shove her behind him.

At the first crazed attack, the demons' swords struck and deflected. The archers shot wildly. The twang of bow and the clash of steel were deafening in the echoing space.

Yet the incubi seemed to be focusing their attacks on Rydstrom—and trying to get *to her*.

All at once, Rydstrom was besieged. Without his guard, Mari was knocked down, landing on her front so hard her teeth clattered. Blood from a wound somewhere on her head tracked down her cheeks. Power-laden blue light cast erratically from her hands and eyes but struck nothing.

"Cade!" Rydstrom yelled, struggling to ward off the onslaught. "Over here!"

His brother battled his way over.

"They want the witch—"

With a cry, she scrambled up only to be knocked to the ground once more. When she dimly realized the incubi were steadily separating her from the group, she stayed down.

"Why her?" Cade looked from Mari to Rydstrom. In the back of her mind, she recognized that Cade probably wouldn't have any interest in helping her—especially not at the expense of helping himself and his brother.

"*Why do you think?*" Rydstrom snapped, even as his sword slashed up.

Cade's eyes narrowed. "Oh, fuck that!" he roared, redoubling his fight—

Fangs sank into Mari's ankles. As she cried out in pain, her body began to . . . move.

Cade was closest to her and lunged for her, yelling, "Tierney!" With supernatural speed, the archer covered him with a torrent of arrows, but there were too many incubi diving right at them.

Blood sprayed up from Cade's body, and he bellowed with fury.

As she screamed, something dragged her back in frenzied yanks. Mari clawed at the stones, shrieking as it snatched her into the darkness.

5

*Pit of the Fyre Dragán, Yélsérk, Hungary
Finale of the Talisman's Hie
Prize: The blade of the blind mystic Honorius to win*

Tonight he would have Mariah back.

One last contest. One last struggle to put his wasted body through. Then his reward.

As he loped through a sweltering tunnel toward the Fyre Dragán's pit of flames, Bowe felt a sense of expectation, an almost light-headed anticipation that warred with the pain from his many injuries—*injuries that weren't healing.*

The Hie had been as cutthroat as he'd expected—and as he'd been prepared to be—but the witch had had the last laugh.

The spell from the tomb that he'd believed was harmless had actually taken hold of his body. Creeping through him like the strongest roots, day by day it leached away his immortality. No longer did he have the ability to regenerate, and for the first time in twelve hundred years, he felt that he was aging. In fact, he'd barely made it to the finals of this competition.

There could be no worse timing to lose his strength than in the Hie.

When the prize would bring back his Mariah.

For one hundred and eighty years, since the night he'd found her—with her thin body gored and her green cloak spread out in the blood-soaked snow—he'd searched relentlessly for a way to resurrect her.

Lingering on in a kind of half life, not dying but not really living, he'd continued to believe he could bring her back to him, when most Lykae would have found a way to die if they'd lost their mates. Others in his clan thought him mad, wondering why he continued to exist in that miserable twilight. Even his cousins, Lachlain and Garreth, who were like brothers to him, couldn't understand him.

But he would show them all, because after searching so long, a mad Valkyrie soothsayer, of all people, had alerted him to this competition—and had told him it was the means of reaching his mate. Desperate to try anything, he'd entered. When he'd learned the ultimate prize of the Hie was a key to go back in time, everything had made sense.

Bowe hadn't foolishly been hoping for something that could never be. The chance to bring Mariah back was within his grasp, and he'd fought mercilessly for that key.

Yet so had his two main competitors: the Valkyrie Kaderin the Coldhearted and Sebastian Wroth, a vampire soldier. Just two nights ago in a minefield in Cambodia, they'd forced Bowe into an explosion that had threaded a rusted length of shrapnel between his ribs and had blown away his left eye and part of his forehead.

Because of the witch's curse, those gruesome injuries remained.

Now, half blind and weak beyond measure, Bowe was

only confident of winning because just two competitors vied in this last round, and the other finalist was Kaderin. Yes, the Valkyrie was a single-minded competitor, but in the end she was still a female.

He slowed, struggling to detect if she was already here. During this final part of the Hie, killing was allowed. On this night, would Bowe kill a female to bring Mariah back? He had no doubts that if given the chance, the Valkyrie would take her assassin's sword and slice him crotch to collar without blinking her cold, emotionless eyes.

One thing Bowe did know was that if he lost, he would definitely kill the witch for weakening him so much.

A roar sounded deeper in the earth, and the cavern quaked, sending rock and dust falling over him. The Fyre Dragán—rumored to be a serpentlike beast, as large as a basilisk but with a body of fire—must be sensing Bowe's trespass.

This place was known in the Lore as *where immortals go to die*. Most immortals could die only by beheading—an unwieldy suicide option—or by total immolation in a pit of otherworldly heat like this. Yet in the ages that had passed, the location of this place had become virtually lost in the Lore. Until now. . . .

Another roar, another violent shake. Boulders began to rain down from the cavern ceiling. As he loped on, dodging them, the injury in his side screamed in protest. But the pain in his body was forgotten as he imagined what he'd do after reuniting with Mariah.

Together, they would start a new life, and he would spoil her with all the wealth he'd accumulated. They could live at his grand estate in Scotland or at the Lykae compound in Louisiana. The clan's property there was vast with miles of swamps and forests to run. There was a central, main lodge for gatherings, and then separate, large hunting cabins were spread throughout.

Louisiana intrigued Bowe. Lazy fans always seemed to be overhead. Unusual food scents and the strains of music continually carried on the breeze. Surely Mariah would love it as he did.

And when he had her back with him, he would seduce away her fears of him so he could finally claim her, at last having her completely.

Gods, he needed her beneath him. Since that night in the jungle tomb, his long-neglected desires had come blazing to life. Even with his body battered, each day he'd needed to take relief from the throbbing ache in his shaft.

Though it shamed him, his mind would wander to the witch as he stroked himself in bed. His usual fantasies of laying Mariah down and gently claiming her were replaced by ones of Mariketa, even though her glamour made memories of her hazy.

He could recall being so damned pleased and aroused by the witch's body but not remembering why. More clearly, he recalled the small tattoo on her lower back—he'd imagined rubbing his face against that mark. Even the remembered feel of the back of her leg against his palm could put him into a lather; he would shudder at mere thoughts of her soft, giving thigh under his thumb claw.

Fantasizing about tasting the wet flesh he'd cupped would make him spend so hard his eyes rolled back in his head.

Once he'd taken his release, a bitter shame would set in. But each night, shame turned to determination to win.

When the tunnel opened up into a soaring cavern

chamber, filled with smoke and wafting ash, Bowe hurried inside—and spotted Sebastian Wroth at the edge of a pit of lava, his arm trapped under a huge boulder.

The vampire? When Kaderin should be here tonight? "What's happened here?"

"A quake . . . rocks," Wroth grated with difficulty.

"Where's the Valkyrie? She ought to be here, not you."

"I'm here in her stead."

Bowe had suspected that Wroth was newly turned—relatively—but now he knew it. An older, more powerful vampire could have traced out from under the rock.

"You can't reach the prize," the vampire told him in his accented English. "It's on the other side of the pit . . . and the cable across it snapped."

Bowe surveyed the area and saw the coiled remains of a thin cable hanging loose from the opposite wall. He had rope in his truck but couldn't spy a single place in the sheer rock face to lash it to. Besides, the truck was aboveground several miles away, and with every minute that passed, the curse was siphoning off more of his strength.

He knew the vampire could trace them across with a blink of his eye, but to free him would be a great risk. Yet, though Bowe was weak, Wroth looked much more so. And Wroth didn't want the prize as badly as Bowe—he used this contest only to win over Kaderin.

The vampire was pale as death, blood pooling all around him. If Bowe left him to gear up to cross the pit on his own and failed, would Wroth even be conscious when he returned?

Decided. "I could free you to trace me across. Then, an open contest to take it."

"I could double-cross you."

Bowe narrowed his one eye. "No' if I've got ahold of your good arm."

After a hesitation, the vampire said, "Do it."

Bowe crossed to the boulder and shoved at it. Though he was constantly reminded of how weak he'd grown, he was still confounded to be unable to move a single boulder. He muttered, "*Bloody, goddamned witches*." Putting his back into it, he asked, "Where exactly are you tracing us?"

"Below the cable, there's a lava tube, another cavern."

"I doona see anything," Bowe gritted out.

"It's there. You want the prize? Then you're just going to have to trust a vampire—"

The boulder toppled over. Before Wroth could trace, Bowe lunged to grab Wroth's left arm, then whistled low at what remained of the vampire's right—pulverized bone and severed sinews of muscle. "That's *got* tae hurt," he said with a sneer.

"Have you looked in the mirror lately?" Wroth snapped.

"Aye." Bowe hauled him up. "And I plan to kill you for that. After this competition. Right now, I doona have all day."

The vampire seemed to just prevent himself from rocking on his feet. He blinked as though struggling to focus.

Bowe jostled him. "Are you even going to be able to do this—"

Without warning, the vampire traced.

Instantly, they were in a new tunnel. Though Wroth looked disoriented, somehow he'd done it. The smoke and steam were thicker here and flames seemed to sprout from barren rock.

Bowe caught sight of a reflection on the ceiling of the cave. He spied the source deeper within—a shining blade on a waist-high column of rock at the very end of the cavern. Bowe shot forward, sprinting for it. Wroth traced and got there first. He snatched the blade with his good hand and tensed to disappear.

But Bowe had already freed his whip. With a crack, he had the length coiled around Wroth's wrist and yanked down, preventing the vampire from tracing. "I'll be takin' that now."

Wroth transferred the blade to his right hand to raise it and claim the victory. But that ruined arm hung lifeless.

"Canna quite make it to your heart, then?"

The vampire bared his fangs. "I'll gut you before you get this."

"That equals the life of my mate."

"I've the same on my mind," Wroth bit out.

"The Valkyrie died?" That was why Wroth was here instead of Kaderin?

"Not for long."

The look in his eyes gave Bowe pause. He'd seen that level of unyielding determination in his own gaze in the mirror. "We could share it, vampire," he said, disbelieving what he was offering—especially when he had the advantage. "The key works twice."

"I need both of those times . . . for her." Suddenly, the vampire's wasted arm shot up. Impossible— The blade rose as if by its own accord and struck viciously.

Blood spurted from Bowe's wrist; searing pain erupted as his severed hand dropped. Freed from the whip, the vampire traced the distance across the pit, decisively out of Bowe's reach.

Bowe sank to his knees, staring dumbly at the blood streaming from his body. *How?* He gaped at his lost hand, still clenching the whip handle. How had that blade risen?

I've . . . lost? His body shuddered violently at the realization. "I will fucking kill you for this, vampire!" he roared.

Bowe had lost. He wouldn't be able to go back and save Mariah—*save her from himself.*

He'd lost her. Again.

"*I will eat your goddamned heart!*" But the vampire was already gone, leaving Bowe trapped in a cavern of fire where immortals went to die.

6

*J*ump, Mariketa! I'll catch you."

Mari crawled on her belly inch by inch among the rancid corpses of the incubi slumbering all around her. In the last two weeks, this was the closest that she'd made it to the edge of their lair without waking them.

The night of the first attack, one had dragged her into the shadows, then lifted her into the air by her ankles, feet over her head, though she'd kicked and thrashed to be free. As the incubus had flown ever upward, her body had swung loosely like a rag doll. When her head had knocked against a shelf of carved stone, blackness dotted her vision. She'd awakened here on this ledge, somewhere high in the tomb.

Almost there. When she raised herself up on her elbows, she shook so wildly her head bobbed. *You can do this, Mari.* One elbow in front of the other. Finally . . . finally, she reached the edge—and barely stifled a gasp. She'd known she was high up, but didn't realize it was this bad. They were at least a hundred feet in the air.

Heights. Just ducky.

When Tera saw Mari peeking over the side, she politely turned up her lantern. Though the other immortals could see in the dark to varying degrees, Mari couldn't, not yet. "Mariketa, are you okay?"

Mari nodded weakly.

"Come, then. I promise I'll catch you," Rydstrom said once more in his deep baritone voice.

During the days, Mari had heard the five of them debating plans of defense or arguing about their escape, and she'd learned their voices and personalities. She liked Rydstrom the best, and not just because he was so stalwart and handsome. For the most part, he was coolheaded, especially for a rage demon, and remained rational even as hour upon hour lagged by.

Yet Cade seemed to be able to provoke him as no other, and the brothers sometimes fought in the heat of the day. "Still acting like a king!" Cade had snapped. "But you're not. No longer."

Rydstrom had answered, "And whose fault is that, *brother?*"

The two had, in fact, entered the Hie for the means to reclaim their kingdom—lost because of some act by Cade.

As for the archers, Tera was indeed sister to the hotheaded Tierney. And Mari suspected the pretty, brunette elf was also an object of great interest to the second male archer, Hild. Hild was normally silent, but when he spoke the others listened. Mari hadn't discovered if those three had had a specific agenda in entering.

"Come on, Mari! Rydstrom won't let you fall," Cade said, and the others nodded with encouragement. "Just jump!"

Yeah, I'll get right on that. Ge-fucking-ronimo, bitches.

Her expression must have betrayed her thoughts

because Tera asked, "If you can't jump, then can you work any magick?"

Over the last two weeks on this ledge, each failed attempt had angered the incubi and drained her even more. She couldn't even produce illumination to break up the inky blackness surrounding her.

Mari shook her head. She was simply too weak. She drew away, collapsing onto her back. She wasn't a puss in most circumstances, but she'd been born and raised in an area situated below sea level. She'd never even seen a mountain in person until she'd flown in white-knuckled awe over the Guatemalan countryside with its volcano silhouettes and jungle-covered peaks.

Kiddie Ferris wheels could wig her out—diving from the height of nearly half a football field wasn't forthcoming.

Oddly enough, she had gotten past her other great phobia—the very unwitchly one of large insects. Once she'd become too weary to continue swatting them away, they'd crawled over her in abandon, and she'd simply grown accustomed to them with repeated exposure. If they didn't bite her, she wouldn't bite them. . . .

As she lay there, staring up blankly into the dark, the incubi began to stir once more.

Starved for centuries but unable to die, these beings truly were the living dead. They were maddened from their never-ending captivity and deprivation, yet they retained their brutal strength.

Soon they would rise and continue their nightly attacks on the five below—striving to stamp out the immortals as if they were foreign, thieving trespassers who'd broken into the incubi's home, intending to steal their precious sacrificial headdresses.

And what of her? She'd feared they would try more "unnatural crimes," but so far, other than sinking their teeth or claws into her legs to drag her out of their way, or forcing her to eat and drink things she couldn't even contemplate without retching, the incubi had kept their hands off her.

It wasn't time for a swan dive just yet.

Though she couldn't communicate with them—if they opened the yawning blackness of their mouths, nothing came out but screams or worms—Mari somehow comprehended things about them, like what they expected from her.

They kept her alive, because they wanted to die.

Once beautiful demons, born to seduce sexual energy from females, they'd been rendered into monsters.

And Mari had realized that they *knew* they were.

On that ledge in the blackness, she'd truly recognized for the first time in her life that some creatures who went bump in the night might hate that they did.

The incubi had sensed great power in her, and believed she could destroy them, but if she could speak their language, she'd tell them they had the wrong girl. Mari was what was known as an *underachiever*, which even an underachiever knew was sociology code for "overfailer."

She was famous in the Lore for the simple fact that one day she might be worth being famous. All hype—no substance. That was Mari.

Everyone in the covens expected her to do something epic and always kept an eye on her. They wanted her to be worth "awaiting." Even other factions in the Lore monitored her with anticipation because, while most witches possessed the strengths of one, two, or very rarely, three of the five castes of witches, Mari was the only witch ever to possess the strengths of *all of them*.

In theory, Mari was a witch warrior, healer, conjurer, seeress, *and* an enchantress.

A potential perfect storm of badassness.

In reality, Mari had lost her college scholarship, couldn't manage even the simplest spells, and kept blowing things up. She couldn't even balance her checkbook.

Had competing in the Hie been a *shaking her raised fist, I'll show you* attempt at redemption? Well . . . yes.

Now she was paying for it. The incubi could never free her—not when they themselves were prisoners for eternity. If her coven hadn't scryed her by now, they never would. The jungles around the tomb were teeming with humans, guerilla armies, but they fought and shot all around the temple without ever attempting to enter. How ironic. They had no idea what battle erupted inside each night.

And Mari knew the werewolf would never return. How could she have desired someone so cruel that he would leave them all to wither away here? Some in the Lore whispered that, at heart, the Lykae were nothing more than ravening beasts from nightmares.

Bowen MacRieve must be. Why else wouldn't he come? Or at least send someone?

Perhaps he was already dead from her spell. If he somehow still lived by the time she got out of this, she was going to kill him. She didn't know how she'd do it, just that it would be *slow*.

When the incubi began to rise all around her, she squeezed her eyes shut and tried to lose herself in dreams of making the Lykae pay.

* * *

Bowe sat propped against the scalding wall of the cavern, cradling his arm. Though barely able to remain upright, he was determined not to give in to the temptation to lie down.

Through the haze of agonizing heat, he stared at the Fyre Dragán slithering back and forth through the lava, waiting for him.

When sweat dripped into Bowe's remaining eye, he moved to wipe it away, but his hand was gone. He knew it was, endured the pain constantly, and still he tried to use it.

The beast that lived inside him desperately wanted to live, but as for Bowe himself, he could take a bloody hint. For over two weeks, he'd been trapped, unable to discover a way out or a way across the pit. He'd never anticipated that this cavern would end without another exit.

If he couldn't escape, as an immortal he could waste away here, never dying, becoming a shadow of himself. And Bowe knew no one was coming for him. Not even resourceful Lachlain, his cousin and king, could find this place. The coordinates here were known only in esoteric corners of the Lore—or by the vampire, and Sebastian Wroth would probably relish knowing Bowe suffered.

His body was wracked, his will gone. He should step down into the fire. Struggling to live on under these circumstances seemed even more cowardly than ending it.

Hell, for nearly two centuries, his clan had been expecting him to step down in some way.

I'd wanted oblivion. This would be the way to get it.

But he'd vowed revenge against that vampire. And he longed to make the witch pay for his unbearable defeat. As far as he was concerned, she'd ensured he lost the competition. The Valkyrie and vampire had only capitalized on weaknesses Mariketa had provided.

Bowe suspected she and the other five had long since escaped the tomb; now he was the one trapped. He consoled himself by recalling the nasty surprise they'd been in for. Before he'd left he'd destroyed not only their vehicles but their CBs and sat-phones as well.

Yet stranding the witch in the jungle wasn't nearly enough retribution for what she'd done. He'd *failed*. Because of her.

He felt like he'd lost Mariah all over again. He'd allowed himself to have a glimmer of hope, to envision his mate back by his side. And he'd been smug about winning.

Until Mariketa had cast her spells over him. . . .

The bloody witch invaded his thoughts. He would try to remember Mariah and instead would see glimpses of stormy gray eyes and red lips. He hated the witch for that, hated that he couldn't picture his mate's face. When he slept, he dreamed only of Mariketa.

Bowe had been untrue to his mate in thought—and deed.

The fire serpent roared, as if impatient for Bowe to make up his mind. After several attempts, Bowe managed to rise, swaying at the precipice of the pit.

End it now. It was cowardly to live on.

He felt an unexpected flare of guilt. *Mariketa lives still.* . . .

Why in the hell would he be concerned about his enemy?

Recognition hammered home. When he'd been gazing into her eyes, he'd known she was enthralling him. But he hadn't known how deeply she'd done it or how permanently.

He wasn't suffering the effects of only one spell.

Bowe worried for her as if she was his *mate*. He dreamed of her as if she was. He thought of her as his—*because she'd forced him to with one of her disgusting hexes*.

Perhaps that bloody witch should learn to be careful what she wished for.

He knew his expression was pure evil when he took a step back from the edge.

7

~~❦~~

The lack of sunlight and real food had begun to take its toll. Mari was getting sicker, was even now beset with fever.

Rydstrom and the others continued to encourage her to jump. Maybe if the five were asking her to swim across a crocodile-infested river or walk a low tightrope over a bed of swords, she could make herself do it, but not heights.

Ignoring them was becoming easier as each day she grew more delirious. Sometimes she would find herself smiling or crying blindly in the dark as she thought of her friends or her home.

In a feverish haze, she pictured Andoain, her coven's estate just outside of New Orleans. She'd never thought she'd miss the creepy place so badly, but now she'd give anything to go back.

To most, Andoain looked like a millionaire's stately fortress, adorned with colorful landscaping that attracted butterflies. The wrought-iron fencing surrounding the entire property was painted glossy black, perfectly matching the shutters. Apple trees—either laden with fruit or dotted with blossoms—grew in profusion.

Without the estate's glamour, however, the structure was a decrepit old manor complete with snakes coiling along the rotting railings. The apple trees remained, but for every one butterfly in the glamour, multiple spiders and frogs lived in bliss. Reed-filled puddles dotted the property, bubbling up odorous fumes.

Deep within the groaning manor, her disparate room was wallpapered pink, with lace curtains and her cheer-leading pom-poms on the floor. A spell at her doorway kept out anything shorter than the coven's obligatory black cats and dogs.

But Andoain hadn't always been her home. For most of her childhood, Mari had lived with her fey mother, Jillian, in a bright, modest beach cottage on the Gulf Coast. They'd been content there, just the two of them, since Mari's warlock dad had abandoned them with nothing but a jolly promise to be back soon.

Yet on Mari's twelfth birthday, Jillian had packed up their cottage and had taken her to Andoain. There she'd opened her arms wide and pronounced it Mari's "new home." Rendered slack-jawed, Mari had run in the opposite direction faster than even her most hell-bent pursuits of ice-cream trucks.

For two days, her mother had remained with her there. Then she'd peeled Mari off her to leave her behind, bawling on the front porch. To go on *sabbatical*, to a secret druid island somewhere in Europe. Over the years, Mari had received sporadic letters, supposedly from her mother, but she suspected Elianna was actually penning them.

Without Elianna and her best friend, Carrow, the coven bad girl, Mari didn't think she would have made it past those first months she was abruptly immersed in nothing but witchery. Gods, she missed her friends now. . . .

Beautiful, raven-haired Carrow thought being a witch

was the best thing in the world. Whenever other Lore creatures like the nymphs and satyrs turned their noses up at the "hex-hacks," Carrow would raise both her hands in the rock-on horns gesture and shout, *"Double, double, toil and trouble, muthafuckas! You just got cursed!"*

Then she actually *would* curse them.

Carrow was one of those rare three-caste witches, though she was mainly a warrior—with an incongruous specialty in love spells. Fierce Carrow was supposed to have entered the Hie with Mari, but then she got arrested at the last Mardi Gras for public indecency again. All poor Carrow had done was to invoke a little-known fashion rule—*It's not streaking if you're wearing beads*—but the covens had vowed earlier that they wouldn't fix her next offense for her.

Carrow was presently in County. Or probably out by now.

And Mari longed to see Elianna, who'd been the best substitute mother she could ever ask for. Though Elianna had received the gift of immortality from her witch mother, her father's humanity ensured she continued to age. Kindhearted, occasionally befuddled Elianna was over four hundred years old, and without her glamour, she looked every minute of it. She liked to joke that "all the exercise in the world can't help a sunbather."

Mari hoped they didn't worry about her too much—

"Mariketa, it's time." Rydstrom's voice carried up to her, cutting through her thoughts. "You need to do this *now*."

Bowe's sole eye slid open when he had the vaguest impression that he wasn't alone. That for the first time in weeks it was no longer only him and the serpent.

"Lachlain?" he rasped, blinking for focus.

"Aye, Bowe, it's me," his cousin said as he knelt beside him, his gaze flickering over Bowe's injuries. Bowe knew he was shocked, but Lachlain hid it well and simply said, "I'm taking you home," then helped him to his feet.

Bowe's sense of smell was wrecked, nearly burned away in the heat and oppressive smoke, but he could still scent a vampire. He tore from Lachlain's grasp and lunged for the shadowy figure behind them.

Wroth, that cold bastard, simply traced to the side, sending Bowe reeling to the ground. All his medley of wounds reopened in a fresh wave of blood.

Lachlain reached for him once more. "Damn it, Bowe, do you wish to die? He's brought me here to retrieve you."

Bowe tried to break from Lachlain's iron grip. "He put me here!"

"I hold no ill will against you, Lykae," Wroth said in a measured tone.

"Because you fucking won!"

"This is so," the vampire answered easily.

"How?" Bowe spat the word. "How did you raise that blade?"

"It was blessed never to miss its mark," Wroth explained. "I had only to picture a target." The vampire wouldn't be calm like this if he'd lost Kaderin for good.

"You brought the Valkyrie back from the dead?"

"I did."

The key had worked! Bowe felt a flare of hope and swallowed before he asked, "Did you use it . . . both times?"

"Yes."

Bowe lowered his head. He couldn't hear this—that his

enemy had managed to do what Bowe himself could not. The shame of his failure ate at him.

"We retrieved Kaderin's two blood sisters, who'd died long ago," Wroth said.

"Talk of this later," Lachlain said, eyeing the fire. "I see no reason to be here any longer." Bowe understood Lachlain's uneasiness. For over a hundred years, the Vampire Horde had tortured Lachlain in a never-ending fire. Each day he'd been burned alive but could never quite die. He'd only escaped recently, and merely being here must be excruciating for him.

That reminded Bowe . . . "Lachlain, how can you, of all people, trust this vampire?"

"He's no' of the Horde. And his brother did save Emma's life." Emma, Lachlain's beloved mate and queen, was a half-vampire, half-Valkyrie waif.

"Aye, he helped Emma—for a price. So why'd this one bring you here? What did he demand?"

"For Emma to meet with Kristoff, the king of the rebel vampires," Lachlain admitted. "Kristoff's her first cousin."

Bowe shook his head. "Too dangerous. I will no' have Emma take that step for me."

"She wants to meet him. Besides, we dinna have a lot of choice. Just as you are the only one who knows how to locate that tomb in Central America, Wroth and Kaderin are the only ones who knew how to find this place."

Bowe was suffering from blood loss and two weeks of food and water deprivation, and he grew confused by Lachlain's words. Why had he mentioned that tomb?

"If you want to leave this place, you have to accept his help," Lachlain said, then added to Wroth, "Get one arm."

Wroth gave a short nod and stepped forward.

"Doona touch me, vampire," Bowe snapped. "I'll bloody stand on my own." As he struggled to rise, he gritted out, "Why would anyone want to find that tomb?"

Wroth answered, "Because the players you trapped there, Lykae, never returned."

"*What?*" Bowe rasped as he indeed made it to his feet by himself. Just before he lost consciousness.

8

"What the hell are you doing?" Lachlain snapped when he saw Bowe struggling to sit up in bed. It'd been a mere day since he'd been delivered back to the Lykae compound in Louisiana.

"Got somewhere I need to be," Bowe answered. His tone was weary, and yet there seemed to be some kind of underlying excitement in his demeanor.

"You're no' ready to go anywhere yet." Yesterday, before Bowe had come to, Lachlain had seen to it that all his injuries were debrided and dressed as best as was possible. The amount of damage done to Bowe had been staggering. Besides missing a hand and an eye, his torso had been pierced with some kind of rusted metal, tearing the bottom of his lung. "You're in no shape to be moving around so soon."

"Does no' matter."

"You'll reopen your wounds." The idea that Bowe had been able to keep fighting on in this condition was astonishing—if one didn't know what he'd fought for. But after such trials and then such a loss, Lachlain couldn't understand why Bowe hadn't stepped into that pit. If Lachlain had lost his mate, Emma, not once but, in essence, twice, he'd have dived in within a heartbeat's time. Why hadn't

Bowe? What drove him? The subject was one of great conjecture among the clan.

"Stop analyzing me, cousin."

Lachlain exhaled. "I doona understand you sometimes."

Bowe eased his legs over the side of the bed, then gritted his teeth against an obvious stab of pain. "If you have no' after twelve hundred years, then you never will."

Lachlain knew he was right. But then Bowe had always been singular among the clan.

Like most Lykae, Bowe was impatient and hotheaded, yet he'd also been known to spend hour after hour patiently teaching bairns the fundamentals of rugby, his favorite sport before Americans had come up with their own "football." Though Bowe was always the first into a fight, eager to punish slights, once the battle was over he was also the first to forgive those slights.

In the north of Scotland, winters could be harsh, with spring eagerly awaited by the clan, but Bowe always regretted seeing winter, his favorite season, fade. Lachlain supposed he'd enjoyed it because it was stark like him.

At least Bowe had enjoyed it until he'd lost his Mariah in the dead of winter. . . .

"What's so important that you canna rest more or eat?" Lachlain waved at the gel packs of food and strange-smelling mineral replacement drinks beside his bed. Bowe was supposed to partake of them, having just come off such a long interval without food and water, but had scarcely touched them. "Is this about revenge against Wroth?"

Bowe said nothing, just seemed to be preparing to rise, planting his feet wide on the wooden floor.

"If so, I ask you to reconsider that action. And no' only because of the debt I owe his brother." If not for Nikolai

Wroth, Emma would have . . . died. At the mere thought, suddenly Lachlain needed to see her, to feel her, even when he knew she waited for him just twenty minutes away with her fierce Valkyrie family. He'd left her safe at Val Hall behind thick curtains, protected from the sun, and happily playing video games. "Bowe, you have to remember that it *was* a contest. And the reports we received all said 'the Lykae competitor' was proving ruthless—and that he played dirtier than Kaderin had in three previous Hies."

Bowe shrugged.

"We heard you mesmerized Kaderin with a glittering object so you could barricade her behind a rock slide. Did you no' trap her alone with three hungry basilisks?"

A flicker of something arose in Bowe's eyes—or eye— that Lachlain suspected was satisfaction. "And we also heard that when you were on a task in the Congo, you whaled a shovel across Sebastian Wroth's face. Knocked him out and then threw him into a raging river. At *high noon* in *Africa*."

His cousin had obviously taken a savage thrill in that act—and still did.

"This is no' about Wroth," Bowe said. "No' yet."

"Then are your thoughts occupied with the witch?"

At last, Bowe turned to him with interest. "What have you heard?"

"I know about the curse. And that you can actually die from these wounds."

Bowe didn't appear to be concerned about that in the least. "That witch and I have much unfinished business. I'm going to retrieve her from the tomb, since no one else has been able to. Though I doona understand how none could locate that place. In that round of the Hie, the coordinates were given to *all* the competitors."

"I'm told the goddess Riora erased them with each round," Lachlain explained. "No one took note of that location if they dinna plan to journey there. You trapped anyone who did."

Bowe scowled at that. "I was sure they'd eventually escape."

"And what is the witch to you?" Emma actually knew this Mariketa fairly well because the witch often visited the more rowdy Valkyrie at Val Hall. That didn't surprise Lachlain—nearly every time he'd been to Val Hall he'd spotted intoxicated witches laughing and staggering about the place.

Bowe hesitated, then said, "She put another spell on me besides the weakening one. A spell to make me feel things for her. I think it's triggered me to think of her as . . . my mate."

"You are sure it's a spell?" Lachlain hastily asked. "What if it's real?" He could only hope. Emma had told him that aside from a bit of a wild streak and a pinch of a witch's natural deviousness, Mariketa had a good heart.

Lachlain didn't know if he could say the same for Bowe's mate from before. He'd met Mariah on occasion when he and Bowe had traveled to convene with her father, the king of a large faction of fey. Lachlain had always found Mariah to be a spoiled sort, and though she'd been beautiful, tall and blond, she'd seemed to show disdain for all the elementals that the Lykae celebrated—food, touch, sex. But Bowe had been content with her, so Lachlain had remained silent about his misgivings. Yet now . . . "Bowe, it could be that you were given two."

"Have you ever heard of that happening?" he asked, his tone growing frustrated.

"Well, no, but—"

"In five thousand years of the clan's record keeping, there's never been an instance of it. Five millennia, Lachlain. I know because I took half a decade to comb through every line of every single record. Every bloody one."

Lachlain knew Bowe had been dogged in finding a way to have Mariah back, but he hadn't realized he'd sifted through all those records.

Bowe added, "The witch put one spell on me—why would I no' think she'd hex me twice?"

"But *why* would she do it?"

He ran his remaining hand over the back of his neck. "There was a short window of time when she . . . when she wanted me for herself. She made me kiss her—"

"Made you?" Lachlain raised his eyebrows.

"*Enthralled* me to do it."

"How can you be sure you didn't merely desire her?"

"Because I could feel it happening. And I have been true to Mariah all these years . . . until that witch toyed with me."

The fact that Bowe hadn't bedded another for so long didn't shock Lachlain. Though the Lykae were notorious for their insatiable appetites, their kind revered few things above loyalty. "Emma knows the witch and has seen her without her cloak. She says Mariketa is a beautiful girl. Did you no' find her so?"

"She had a glamour on. I canna recall her looks clearly."

"What did the Instinct tell you?" A guiding force with which all Lykae are born, the Instinct was like a voice in the mind directing the individual toward what would be best for him, as well as for the collective clan.

Bowe hesitated before admitting, "The Instinct has long been quiet in me."

Lachlain glanced away. The idea that his cousin had been denied the comforting presence of the Instinct was painful for Lachlain, but he didn't want Bowe to think he pitied him. Even when Lachlain had been tortured, the Instinct had never forsaken him.

Bowe added, "The bottom line is that the gods could no' be so cruel as to pair *me* with a witch."

This was a good point. All Lykae mistrusted witches—the Instinct cautioned continually—but Bowe's dislike had always been more marked than others'. Ever since he was a lad he'd had a pronounced aversion to them, even before Bowe had learned of his father's tragic encounter with one.

Still Lachlain said, "I was given a half-vampire, half-Valkyrie as mate, and I could no' cherish her more."

"I could handle anything . . . just no' a bloody witch, Lachlain."

Lachlain let that rest for now. "You canna travel until you've built up some strength. And think, if you do in fact recognize her as your mate, for whatever reason, you canna go for her yet. Today's Wednesday—the full moon's on Friday night." And all mated Lykae turned in the heat of the moon.

"Christ. When I change I might pursue her as my mate and claim her."

Bowe made the comment as if this was a scenario to be avoided at all costs, yet Lachlain had seen a flash of pure anticipation in him at the imagined prospect. His entire body had tensed. Lachlain hadn't seen excitement like that in his cousin in nearly two centuries.

"You'll have to wait."

Bowe shook his head. "I'll get her to remove the spell before then."

"And if she refuses?"

"I'll throttle her."

"Damn it, Bowe, I'm going in your stead."

"When the full moon nears? You'd be away from your female?"

Bowe didn't know that Lachlain had just missed the last one with Emma because she'd been on the other side of the world holding vigil with her family for Kaderin. Being without Emma had been grueling for Lachlain, and he dreaded the repeat prospect, but he'd not see his cousin walk into a trap. "There will be more. Emma will understand."

"And why would you no' send Munro or Uilliam?"

The Lykae twin brothers were among Lachlain's most trusted soldiers. "They have no' returned from the last task I sent them on."

"And Garreth?"

Lachlain's younger brother had called just two days ago. "He still pursues Lucia, his Valkyrie huntress. She's proving to be elusive quarry, even for him. And there's no one else I'd trust to do this. I'm going. This is my final word on the subject."

Bowe's expression darkened. Lachlain was so used to giving orders that he sometimes overlooked the fact that Bowe was an alpha himself—a strong one who was far more comfortable giving orders than receiving them. Not to mention the unspoken fact that Lachlain was king only because Bowe's father had ceded his heirdom.

"I'm no' off to fight the goddamned Hydra, Lachlain. I

fly, I drive, I collect a witch. Do you truly believe I'm incapable of this?"

Lachlain had not only angered Bowe but offended him. He exhaled. "No, of course no'. Just . . . just let me know if I can help you."

Bowe nodded. "Before I go I want to know why that Valkyrie soothsayer told me I would get my mate back through the Hie. Can you call Emma and get her to find Nïx—"

Lachlain's new pager went off and he started, still uncomfortable with the technology of this age. Emma had gotten this contraption for him and tried to teach him how to work it, but he'd been gone that entire day without seeing her, and the only thing he'd been interested in was ripping off her red negligee with his teeth. . . . He hadn't yet told her that red was an attractant to Lykae males, much less mated males.

He tossed the pager to Bowe. "Tell me what it says. And if you canna work it with one hand, then you sure as hell canna drive a stick shift down in Guatemala."

Bowe glowered, then fiddled with it. "It says, 'Dim the room. xoxo.'"

"Bugger me!" Lachlain lunged for the drapes, yanking them closed.

Just as he was finishing the second window, Emma traced inside the scant light of the bedroom and smiled softly at him, her expression proud. "See? The system works."

"What're you doin' here, lass?"

Casting Bowe a sympathetic glance, she said, "I had to come when I heard all the commotion at Val Hall."

"Commotion?"

"I had better let my aunt Nïx explain it." Emma's beautiful blue eyes grew troubled. "She's on her way here. Said Bowe was going to want to speak with her now?"

Bowe scowled. "Eerie, bloody foresight. I'm weary of it, and of magick—and of the whole bloody Lore!"

9

When Nïx blithely entered the room minutes later, Bowe said, "You told me that if I entered the Hie I would get my mate back. What reason would you have to deceive me?"

Ignoring his question, she unabashedly crawled onto the foot of Bowe's bed. Her T-shirt read: *It'll only hurt for a second. Promise. . . .* Weird bloody Valkyries—and she was one of the weirdest. As the firstborn of her kind, she was likely over three thousand years old, though she looked not old enough to buy liquor in the States.

Other males saw Nïx as exceedingly comely; all Bowe saw was a powerful being made mad as a hatter from her foresight.

She lay on her side, bending her elbow to casually prop her head in her hand. With a sigh she said, "Bowen, I took you on as my pet project because I like to *ogle* you. Due to your rowr factor." Her distracted gaze flickered over his face and the bandaged end of his arm. "If you're not going to keep yourself up, well—"

"Answer me."

"Soooooorry, I didn't see that you'd be enthralled to love another, or, more correctly, *ensorcelled*—"

"I knew it!" Bowe cast a look at Lachlain.

"You're aware of it, then?" Nïx asked.

Bowe annunciated, "*Brutally.*"

"Mariketa will remove it from you, you know, in time," Nïx continued. "As well as that pesky mortality spell. Which is convenient since you must go for her and return her to her coven."

"Return her to the witches?" Bowe gave a humorless laugh. He'd had his suspicions confirmed, and now he really wanted to throttle Mariketa—not do her a sodding favor. "After I force her to fix me, I might just strand her in the jungle for this."

Nïx shook her head. "Not quite possible. There's a contingent on their way here. Regin the Radiant is in a . . . snit. She and several of Mari's witch friends—including the ever-vicious Carrow—arrive forthwith."

Bowe let her see exactly how bored he was with this news. Regin was a young Valkyrie he could take even in his present condition. And no witch would dare cross onto Lykae territory without permission.

Emma said, "Nïx, can't you stall Regin?"

When Nïx shook her head, Bowe asked, "What did I do to that glowing little freak anyway?"

Nïx answered, "Because of your cousin Garreth, Lucia is gone. Everyone knows she's Regin's BFF, fellow hoodlum, partner in crimes both foreign and domestic—"

"Yes, yes, we get it," Emma interrupted.

"But then for *Mari* to disappear on top of that?" Nïx asked. "She, too, is one of Regin's friends. They're poker buddies, sisters of the *Wii*, and Mari is a vaunted member of the karaoke contingent. Regin has long acted as the witches' designated driver."

"BFF?" Lachlain asked, brows drawn. "Sisters of the what?"

Emma supplied, "Best friend forever and a video game."

Lachlain muttered to Emma, "Your relatives are just no' *right*."

Emma blinked at him. "Lachlain, I thought we were going to agree to disagree about this."

Bowe snapped, "She's *no*' friends with a Valkyrie. I heard her at the Hie assembly asking the most basic questions about your kind."

"Was she doing it for someone else's benefit?" Nïx asked.

Bowe thought back. . . . The vampire had in fact been eavesdropping on her at the time. She'd bloody known it and had been feeding him information about the Valkyrie—about *Kaderin*! "Your *friend* Mariketa willfully sicced a vampire on your half sister Kaderin during the Hie. Still so ready to champion the devious little witch?"

"Please," Nïx scoffed. "Kad would have plucked Mari's knees from her legs to slow her down. All in good fun. Besides, it's not just Regin and her cohorts you have to worry about. There are others concerned that you took out the future leader of the House of Witches, one of the largest factions of the Lore." She tilted her head at Bowe and said softly, "My pet, you had to know there would be ramifications from your actions."

Nïx had begun calling him her pet and thinking of him as such, and he'd let her because she helped him on occasion—yet another indignity he'd endured to get to his mate. "If Mariketa is so sodding powerful, then why has she no' used her magick to escape?"

"She lacks control over her volatile powers—and there are so many of them. We keep watching and waiting, but she's just too young to harness them."

Bowe's patience was nearing its limit. "Then the witch should no' have entered the Hie in the first place!"

"Regardless . . . The House demands Mariketa be delivered safely—or your head. The Lykae won't give up your head, so that means war. In that conflict, the Valkyrie will show allegiance to the House. And that means our allies must pony up some ill will toward you as well. The wraiths will happily, of course. The rebel Forbearer vampires will be pleased for a chance to show their loyalty to the Valkyrie—as will several Demonarchies, who coincidentally aren't thrilled that you've entombed the true king of the rage demons, *as well as his sole heir.*"

Bowe was well aware that Rydstrom was the true king, but damn it, he'd thought they'd find *some* way out.

"Four mighty wizards and thirty-seven covens of witches unite and arrive here this week." Her tone grew grave. "A nest of a dozen furies rise from sleep for this," she added, making Emma swallow nervously. "Don't even get me started on who the elven archers know—let's just put it this way: Their daddy's bigger than your daddy."

"They *all* ally with those witch mercenaries?"

She nodded. "Naughty Lykae, creating an interspecies incident like this. *Six* immortals you trapped. This is a Charlie Foxtrot of epic proportions."

At Lachlain's irritated look, Emma supplied, "Charlie Foxtrot is code for, well, a cluster fuck."

"Why dinna you tell me this was developing?" Lachlain asked Emma.

"I only knew about Regin and some growing rumblings

within the House. I'm friends with the witches, but they're very secretive and keep their plans close until they're ready to act."

"There's no need for this to escalate," Lachlain said, his tone calm. Bowe knew Lachlain would never reveal that he was concerned about the repercussions of Bowe's actions, but in his position he must be. "Bowe can tell me where the witch is. I'll free the six and bring Mariketa back."

Bowe exhaled. Lachlain was still trying to protect him, always cleaning up after him. If he had a dollar for every time Lachlain said, "Ach, Bowe, you've fucked up this time."

But then Lachlain had never bailed him out of something like this.

"No, I've told you. This is my problem." Bowe unsteadily stood, growing dizzy just from that. "I'll deal with it."

Lachlain shook his head. "How are you going to defend yourself against six verra irate immortals?"

"They should be grateful that I returned." When Lachlain raised his brows, he added, "I'll make them vow to the Lore no' to attack before I will agree to open the tomb."

"Then at least eat and rest until after the full moon."

Nïx clucked her tongue. "The House says Mari must call in *before* the next full moon to avert this. Besides, this town isn't big enough to hold so many factions. They all might be allies of the witches or Valkyrie, but *none* are allies with each other. Any much longer with them bumping elbows, and something will happen."

Bowe swung a glare at Nïx. "Are you no' overstating all this, Valkyrie—"

From outside: "You wanna fuck over *my* witch? Like

playing your games? Then play catch!" Something whistled overhead; the house shook—they all ducked as plaster splattered down from the ceiling.

"*What the bloody hell was that?*" Bowe yelled.

"That was Regin," Nïx answered serenely. "She threw a car over us to land on the main Lykae lodge. Lucky thing the lodge is empty. Bowen, she thought the vehicle was yours. But it's really . . . *his*." She pointed delicately at Lachlain, who scowled before flashing a meaningful look at Emma.

Bowe grated, "She's throwing bloody *cars?*"

"See? Not overstating." Nïx rose, smoothly slipped behind the curtains, then shouted out the window, "Bad form, Regin! Wrong car."

Immediately after, the house shook again. "Oh, much better!" Nïx assured them. "That was Bowen's!"

Another violent shake of the manor. Nïx peeked out from the curtains, wearing them like a nun's habit. "Who drives a seventy-eight, Chevelle-looking—"

"Nïx!" Emma said.

She withdrew from the window. "The timing of all this is impeccable," Nïx said in an abruptly grave tone. "The Accession has really arrived."

Emma and Lachlain shared a look. All Lorekind dreaded the Accession. Occurring every five centuries, it was a kind of mystical cull that killed off immortals. Though there wasn't necessarily a great war or determining battle, fate seemed to seed conflicts, pitting factions against each other. Bowe's father had told him fate would sow some families by bringing together mates—yet would reap from most others.

"Why all this?" Bowe took uneven steps toward his

closet to dress, and had to clench his jaw against a wave of pain in his ribs. "Do you no' think that a Lore war is a wee bit much for a witch having a three-week hiatus?"

"A hiatus . . . with *whom?*" Nïx asked. "My pet, you've trapped a beautiful, nubile young woman with a school of incubi. Though Regin swears it's not a *school* of incubi, but a *pod*—"

"Nïx, stay focused!" Emma said, and Nïx gave her a halfhearted hiss.

"Incubi?" Bowe rasped, a finger of dread running up his spine. "The tomb was empty, long deserted." There weren't living incubi in there. There couldn't be.

Sadness flashed in Nïx's confused eyes. "The witch fares ill after three weeks inside that lightless crypt." In a confessional tone, she added, "Seems you forgot to leave her any food or water."

"I scented nothing, *sensed* nothing. . . ." At Nïx's implacable expression, Bowe shook himself—he didn't need to be thinking about the implications; he needed to be doing something about them.

"Lachlain, can you help me arrange transportation?" He dug for clothes, battling dizziness. "If I leave within the hour I can get there today before sunset."

"Aye, then." Lachlain exhaled. "Of course, I'll help you with anything you need."

Though Bowe had made it sound like a routine task, freeing and squiring Mariketa back to the States would not be without numerous difficulties.

On his last trip, the "roads" had been difficult to navigate. Now that the rainy season had fully arrived, they might be impassable. Especially since Bowe would be forced to drive a stick shift with one hand and a stump.

And now that he was weakened, it was possible the human soldiers teeming the area could subdue and actually contain a Lykae, even when he was fully turned. Bowe would have to evade them until he had the mortality spell removed.

Raising the tomb's portcullis had been nearly impossible even when he'd had all his strength and both of his hands . . . but now? "I'm going to need to bring something like a pneumatic lift to help me get into the tomb."

When Lachlain nodded, Emma said, "I can get you a satellite phone, too, so Mari can call at the earliest opportunity."

"Aye, and I'll need more of that stuff they've been trying to feed me. The drinks and gel packs. And some kind of med kit just in case."

Nïx clapped with excitement at the activity, looking as addled as ever. "I can help, I can help! I can get you a rhyme for Mariketa!"

Lachlain, Emma, and Bowe briefly paused to glare at her.

"You can't leave home without it!"

"*Anyway* . . ." Bowe continued, "I just went two weeks without food or water. Three will no' kill her."

"Incorrect."

Bowe glanced back at Nïx. His voice broke an octave lower when he asked, "Why incorrect?"

She squinted at him and momentarily appeared puzzled at where she was. "What's incorrect? Am I incorrect?" She buffed her nails. "I so rarely am."

Barely stifling the urge to throttle the weird being, Bowe grated, "You told me I was incorrect when I said three weeks will no' kill the witch."

"Oh, yes, *that*. How am I supposed to remember conversations from last year? I can't see inside that crypt—bad voodoo and major mojo keeps prying eyes out—but common sense says Mariketa is likely dying."

"*Dying? How?*" he rasped, knowing Lachlain was studying his harsh reaction.

"Because, pet, young Mariketa the Awaited has not yet turned. She is still . . . *mortal*."

Another car whistled overhead.

10

Bowe's machete hacked through a braid of woody liana vines as he pushed forward through the brush. The trail to the tomb that had been cleared just weeks ago had already grown over.

As he'd predicted his last time here, the conflict between the two human armies had since erupted. Bowe had had to ditch his truck miles from the tomb because soldiers were planting mines all along the roadways.

He burned with urgency to get to Mariketa, but his body could do only so much in this state and burdened with his pack—which weighed over three hundred pounds with the gear he'd been forced to bring.

Earlier, the action of gathering supplies and hastily readying for the trip had helped Bowe keep his mind occupied, but during the flight down, he'd wanted to claw the walls of the plane in frustration. From his bag, he'd snatched Nïx's missive addressed to "Mari the Awaited." He'd ignored the Valkyrie when she'd insisted repeatedly that he bring it, until she'd become so furious that lightning had begun to spear down all around them. It had grown so violent that even Regin and the witches had backed off, spooked.

Alone on the plane, he'd ripped open Nïx's black wax seal and read the bizarre contents—a rhyme about mirrors and whispering and secrets. The words had inexplicably given him chills.

And reading it had only killed moments of the wait. With nothing to do but think, he'd wavered between hating Mariketa and fearing for her life. Bowe despised what she'd done to him—and what she was—but he did not want her to die.

Another blister gave way against the machete handle, but Bowe ignored it. Wasn't like he could switch hands.

The odds were against her being alive, yet Bowe had hope. The scarred demon Rydstrom was a brutal warrior, but he was also honorable. And Bowe knew Rydstrom and Cade had younger sisters. If Rydstrom had decided to protect the witch, she might have a chance of surviving starvation—and the incubi.

And then there had been the unsettling interest that had flickered in Cade's eyes. The mercenary might be moved to protect her . . . because he wanted her.

The thought made Bowe swing the machete harder than necessary, slicing clean through a sapling.

Damn it, what in the hell had that little mortal been thinking to enter the Hie?

Even as he'd cursed the idiocy of her actions, he'd marveled at her courage, especially since she was so young. He'd suspected she was, but Bowe had since found out that Mariketa was an astonishing twenty-three years of age—*chronologically*. Not only hadn't she made the transition into immortality, she hadn't passed even a third of an average mortal life.

If Bowe had thought Emma, at eighty chronologically, was too young for Lachlain, then Mariketa was a damned bairn.

And a witch—

Ear-piercing screams sounded. *From the tomb?*

Bowe sprinted as fast as his wounds would allow, leaping over fallen trees. He ran headlong through the brush instead of cutting, ignoring the pain as vines snagged his neck and arms and abraded till they burned.

When he finally crashed through the tree line surrounding the perimeter of the tomb, he heard what sounded like a war inside.

White light glinted up through new cracks in the stone. The entire edifice rumbled. He heard Rydstrom roar with pain while the female archer shrieked. Bowe didn't hear the witch.

Was it already too late?

How the fuck was he going to *quickly* raise the stone portcullis? To set up the lift with one hand . . . too much time. Could he possibly raise it himself? He was a thousand times weaker than before. He didn't have a propping stone to lift from.

He didn't have two hands.

No way—

Bowe finally heard Mariketa's cry—weak, reedy. There was no time to analyze the consuming sense of relief he felt that she still lived. He knew she was badly hurt, knew she needed protection.

Bugger the lift.

He shoved his hand under the edge of the portcullis, claws digging down, wedging under for a good grip. When he heard another of her cries, he strained every muscle in his body.

Nothing.

Damn it, if she'd truly been his mate, he would have

been able to lift it. Which meant it was still *possible* even when she wasn't his—he could do this!

No longer did he hear her. Sharp fear stabbed at him . . . he heaved with all his might, yelling out. The stone began to budge. An inch higher, then two . . .

He'd lifted it only a foot when a limp body was shoved out from the fray.

Mariketa? Yes, though he scarcely recognized her without her glamour to cloak her looks.

As Bowe grappled against the weight, he jerked in surprise when the Instinct rang inside his head, strong and clear.

—*Yours.*—

Why would it return now, after so long? Why would it make him feel as though he recognized her as his own?

No, this was merely her spell, tricking him. Even knowing this, he had to fight panic when he comprehended how battered her body was. He focused his hearing on her heartbeat and found it erratic. Her lips were pale and chapped, her cheeks hollowed. Blood tracked from the corners of her mouth.

Just as it had on Mariah when she'd lain dead in the snow.

He couldn't hold the stone much longer . . . needed to drop it . . . but the witch's leg was in the way. As he struggled to reach his boot to the side to shuffle her out of the way, the battle continued inside.

"Duck!"

"Bloody *shoot* them!"

"I'm out of arrows!" Out of arrows? The archers had mystical quivers, said never to empty.

"Me as well— *Run!*"

The female elf screamed for Cade to help her. A second later, she was launched from the interior, her bloody bow strapped to her back.

Then claws scrabbled up as Cade and Rydstrom crawled out. They didn't acknowledge Bowe, just dropped their swords and weakly attempted to keep the stone raised until the last two archers shimmied out.

The strings on their bows were stained by blood from where they'd pulled them again and again. What exactly had they faced?

As if in answer, just as Bowe was about to drop his burden, a hand shot out from the tomb as some being with matted gray skin, *dead* skin, reached blindly but unerringly to the witch. Its claws sank into her ankle—she didn't react.

Another hand darted out from the tomb, its fingers clenched around . . . *one of the gold headdresses?*

"*Drop it,*" Bowe yelled, and the three released the stone, severing the hands. As Bowe fell back against the sealed entrance, struggling to breathe, Cade lunged to Mariketa to pry the claws from her ankle. Her skin there was bloodied, marked again and again. Bowe knew in an instant that she'd been dragged like that repeatedly.

He squinted his eye at the other gruesome hand. Why offer a headdress?

Once Bowe raised his gaze, he faced the killing looks of five powerful immortals, promising retribution.

"Forget him for now!" The female archer hurried to cradle Mariketa's head. "She's in shock." The others gathered around her, except for one of the archers, who twitched his pointed ears, then raced from the clearing.

When the witch began to shudder, Bowe dropped to his knees beside her.

"Water!" the female elf screamed at him. "We're losing her!"

He hastily unwound the canteen over his shoulder and handed it over. "What's happened to her?"

They all ignored him.

"Damn it, tell me what's happened!"

The witch went still beside him, seemingly at his raised voice. Her eyes opened dazedly as she moaned; white light flashed from them into the sky and boiled up from her limp palms. Her lips parted around her ragged breaths.

Without warning, she was on her feet, her eyes glittering with fury, and riveted to Bowe. As though in a tempest, her red hair swirled all around her bloodied face. Leaves and sand circled her body. *"You."*

"I—"

With one flick of her hand in his direction, she tossed Bowe back against the tomb, crushing the contents of his pack. She pinned him there by his neck as he futilely writhed and fought for breath. In the midst of his struggles, he realized the toes of her boots were turned down—because she was no longer touching the ground.

Her body was too frail . . . too small to conduct this power—*unimaginable* power. Never in his long life . . . never had he seen anything like this.

The witch smiled with ghostly lips. "You came back," she purred as the pressure increased around his neck. She was horrible. She was awing.

And he knew he was about to die.

11

⚬⚭⚬

"Mariketa, no!" Rydstrom bellowed. "Let me deal with him!"

Mari could barely hear him. Magick tolled in her ears and danced through her veins, pure and perfect for the first time in her life.

It feels delicious.

She tightened her hold around MacRieve's throat once more, vaguely noticing his missing hand, the bandages on his face.

"Give him to me!" Tierney had drawn his blade. Cade and Tera closed in on MacRieve, each wanting the pleasure of killing the Lykae for what he'd done.

Mari wouldn't give up her catch. Not until his head had left his body—

A sharp pop like a gunshot sounded in the near distance. She heard it even over the din inside her head.

"Mariketa," Tera began in a wary tone, "drop him and run. Now."

Wary? After what they'd just lived through? More pops—definitely gunfire.

She'd sensed Hild had raced from the clearing, and now he returned. "Two guerilla armies engaging in the brush a mile to the west," he reported between breaths. "Each with at least two hundred humans. They've got rockets, mortar. We actually might have to consider them in our decisions."

Bowe saw it all unfolding but could do nothing. Frustration welled in him, matching the torture of her strangling grip. The force was pinning his back against his bag, pulverizing the contents.

Then the witch's eyes changed, becoming a shade of silver—one color, unbroken—shining brilliantly. As he stared in incomprehension, he could see . . . could see they were . . . *mirrors*. Nïx's strange rhyme flashed in his mind, even as Mariketa was killing him.

With her other hand, the witch emitted a pulse of energy at Bowe—a beam that made him feel as if he'd had a transfusion of acid. *Turn your blood to acid*, she'd told him.

Rydstrom grabbed her wrists and moved to draw her magick from Bowe's direction, then frowned that he hadn't budged her thin arms. With both hands, he heaved back and finally got her to aim away from Bowe—toward the tomb.

Freed of her hold and the scalding pain, Bowe sucked in air, scrambling away. As he rubbed circulation back into his throat, her beam battered the stones. The entire structure trembled. The first rumble shook the trees growing over it. The second rattled them, stripping bare their swaying branches.

The witch's eyes, so brilliant, appeared fascinated.

Rydstrom yelled, "*It's going to blow!*" He yanked Mariketa up to his side. The light from her ceased, and she fell limp.

But it was too late.

The tomb exploded with atomic force—even the great

foundation stones erupted into the sky—leaving nothing but a gaping crater behind. Whatever lived inside had been annihilated.

With the witch in his arms, Rydstrom sprinted, following the others as they darted for cover from the plummeting stones. Though Bowe dashed off right behind them, for some reason, he lunged down and plucked the gold headpiece from the severed hand, then worked the heavy prize into his pack.

Just before Rydstrom reached the tree line, an immense stone landed on his leg, trapping him. The demon kept his hold on Mariketa, struggling to protect her head.

Bowe sensed what was about to happen, even before the towering hardwoods of the jungle began to bend and rock toward the crater where the tomb had once existed. "Give her to me!"

Rydstrom gritted out, "Directly after . . . she was about to *kill* you?"

Bowe didn't have time to explain, so he simply snapped, "I vow I'll get her to safety."

"You don't understand, MacRieve! She can fucking *die*—"

"Aye, mortal, now release her!" When Rydstrom still hesitated, Bowe said, "You doona know what's coming?" The tomb had been a place of power. Extinguished power created a vacuum.

Rydstrom glanced back. He shook his head hard, and his grip on Mariketa eased. He eyed Bowe. "Another scratch on her, and I will take your head, Lykae."

Mari came to with a moan, blinking open her eyes to find herself firmly strapped over some male's brawny shoulder—

and looking straight down the side of a mountain. Hundreds of feet below, trees and earth poured into a vacuous chasm that used to be the tomb.

Shaking violently, she drew a breath to scream, but a rasping voice said, "Hold your shrieks, and hold on to me. And doona dare try anything like before, witch—no' if you want to get out of this alive."

MacRieve. Hadn't she killed him? She clutched at his broad back for a hold. "Wh-where are the others?"

"Scrambling for safety below us."

"Why d-did you go *up*?" Faced with her worst fear and forced to trust her life to this Lykae.

"Doona like heights, then? I went up because the humans canna."

He was ascending by climbing *a vine*? "You'll drop us—you only have one freaking hand!" He'd been yanking down on the vine and catching it higher, propelling them up inch by inch.

"Aye, and I'll be havin' it back. Along with my eye. Now. Remove your curse and heal me."

"Never. I hope you die from it," she hissed.

"Then also hope my hand does no' slip any more on this slick vine. We go much farther down and that vacuum will catch us for sure. Ach, I can feel the pull on my feet already. And now it's starting to rain."

She raised her head in disbelief. Fat drops of water beaned her in the face.

He deliberately let go, allowing them to plunge several feet before he snatched the vine back, jouncing her over his back as her hands frantically fisted in his shirt.

"Stop that! Ah, gods, stop that!"

"Give me my hand back!"

Think! She did believe she could successfully remove the curse, even as weak as she was. Removing spells wasn't as difficult as placing them, she reminded herself. Elianna always said, "A toddler can't inscribe calligraphy but can easily erase it."

Silently vowing to stick a new, worse curse on him at the earliest opportunity, she laid her flat hand on his back, then drew it outward, pulling at the hex.

Nothing. Gritting her teeth, she returned her hand and attempted once more. This time her hand met resistance, as though she'd laid her palm in a pool of glue. She had a grip on the hex!

Mari drew her hand back again. Stretching . . . pulling . . .

His hand began to regenerate—growing, bulging in his bloody bandage until his new claws ripped through the cloth.

As he stared at his healing hand, he murmured, "You've almost done it." He sounded partly mystified and partly disgusted.

"I'm too weak."

"More of it, witch!"

She shook her head against his back. "I'm going to pass out again."

"Doona care."

"I do! Vow to the Lore that you'll get me safely to Rydstrom."

"To Rydstrom, then?" he snapped in a strange tone. "Do this and I'll vow it."

Inhaling a deep breath, she made another shaking attempt, growing dizzier with each second.

"That's it." His hand appeared restored, and still he demanded in a husky voice, "*More.*"

She gritted between her teeth, "Doing everything . . . I *can* . . ."

With his new hand, he ripped at the bandage on his head and raised his bared face to the rain. "Good girl. Now only one more spell to go—"

Was that *her* strangled cry? And the world went black once more.

12

∽৩৫∾

As the witch's slight body grew limp over him, Bowe's strength came surging back. He blinked his eyes, flexed his hand, and inhaled deeply. After inwardly cataloging his many smaller injuries he realized he was completely healed—whole again. No pain, no wrenching agony in his ribs with each breath. She'd done it.

Bowe recognized that he felt better than he had in memory.

Now he easily climbed the vine, and even leapt the twenty feet to the top of the mountainside shelf he'd sought. Earlier from below, he'd scented that somewhere at this elevation there was a source of spring water in case it stopped raining. He'd also noted the musty odor of a sheltering cave in case it didn't. As soon as he'd claimed her from Rydstrom, Bowe had made for the mountain.

The cave was about a half mile away through thick hardwoods, so he decided to get food and drink into the witch at once, now that the immediate danger had passed. He stalked a small, square area of the plateau, surveying for poisonous plants or animals. With his keen eyesight restored, he spied none—only rain-matted, leafy vines. Yes, this place would work.

Once he laid Mariketa on the bed of thick foliage, the

light rain began to wash away the blood on her face and smoothed her hair back from her pointed ears. With one of her slender arms limp at her side and the other curled beside her head, she merely looked like a delicate, vulnerable female—not the witch of unspeakable power he'd just witnessed. And not the killer she'd proven herself to be.

He had indistinct memories of her rather ordinary looks—nothing special or standout, which was no doubt exactly what she'd intended with her glamour. Now her pale skin was stark against the leaves. Her wee ears pointed sharply, beautifully. The small top she wore was wet and nearly transparent against her generous breasts.

Even dirty and injured, she was so damned striking. . . .

—*Yours.*—

When the Instinct whispered soothingly, he closed his eyes. He hadn't mistaken it earlier, hadn't imagined it. Gods, how he'd missed it—he wanted to roar with pleasure from its return.

When he gazed back down at her, for the briefest instant he thought, *Keep the bloody spell, keep the Instinct, keep the beauty offered up before me. Why no'?*

He shook his head hard. Guilt set in, and anger began to build. He was actually contemplating becoming a mindless slave to a witch's will? A witch that had been so savage just moments before? His father must be turning over in his grave right now.

Bowe removed his pack, dropping it beside her, and easily opened the previously plaguing ties now that he had both hands. Kneeling down, he dug for drink—only two of the bottles hadn't been crushed. At least the gel packs were intact.

He looped his arm under her neck and lifted her, but

even unconscious, she feebly resisted him. With repeated attempts, he made her drink half a bottle and swallow some of the gel.

Satisfied with that for now, he swept his gaze over her body. Hazy recollections of her appearance from before began to crystallize in his mind, and he realized that she didn't seem to have lost a good deal of weight. Somehow, she *hadn't* starved. But his relief was short-lived.

Had those things gotten ahold of her?

With his heart in his throat, he laid her back to examine her injuries, washing from her arms and legs the worst of the dirt and blood in the light rain.

If they'd taken her, he'd expect her shorts to be ripped, but they weren't. He'd expect to see bruises consistent with the grip of fingers, but he found none at her neck or on her pale thighs.

After tugging down her shirt, Bowe gazed at her plump breasts, plainly visible through her transparent bra. No bruises marred the creamy flesh there either. There was a chance she'd been protected from the worst attacks of those incubi.

He tried to turn away then, but her deep pink nipples were growing harder as drops of rain hit her breasts. He hissed an oath. No witch should ever be as fine as this.

She was perfect and lovely, and his mouth watered to suckle those jutting nipples. Unable to help himself, he brushed the backs of his fingers over one, and she shivered.

This is madness. He'd just pulled her top back when movement rustled the leaves all around her. Claws bared, his hands shot down, thinking an animal approached, yet then . . . *vines* began to creep up over her body, twining over her in profusion, as if protectively.

Eyes wide, he snapped, "Ah, bugger me!" and just prevented himself from lunging back. Magick. Right bloody here. When he reached for her, briars jabbed and tore at his skin. Even with his strength, he couldn't rip them from her.

Yet he didn't sense danger to her.

Her blowing up the tomb was bad enough, but this eerie, insidious magick unnerved him far more. He stood and paced back and forth, glancing uneasily at her, raking his fingers through his hair.

There in the cage of greenery, right before his eyes, her skin began to pinken, her lips reddening and plumping once more. As she slept, as natural as if she'd been born there, her scrapes and bruises faded, leaving behind only smooth, porcelain skin. He found her so damned attractive—even as the magick made his stomach roil.

Was this another charm? Not a healing spell but another enchantment? Was this even what she truly looked like? Bloody hell, he hoped not. To be pitted against both the unnatural spell *and* her natural beauty?

He forced himself to recall her visage as she'd delighted in strangling him. That was what she truly was.

Below them, the vacuum began to slow, sated at last. He heard the others climbing long before they'd reached the plateau. Once Rydstrom had cleared the edge, his gaze flickered over Bowe's hand and eye. "She healed you?"

"Aye. And herself. But now she's trapped in those vines."

Rydstrom nodded, seeming unconcerned with his leg injury. "We need to get her somewhere dry." He limped over to her. "None of us are in any condition to navigate our way out of here tonight."

Bowe saw that the five were gaunt, their lips chapped

and eyes sunken. Now that she'd worked her magicks, the mortal appeared to be in better shape than the immortals.

"And what about the Scot?" one of the male archers asked.

Bowe answered, "The *Scot* goes wherever that witch goes."

Cade said, "I think Tierney meant *now* can we grease this Lykae?"

Once Rydstrom reached the witch, he bent down for her. The briars parted for him, allowing him to lift her. When Rydstrom cradled her in his arms, Bowe felt his lips drawing back, his fangs lengthening.

—*That male takes your place . . . takes what's yours.*—

No, damn it, not his. She was a means to an end to get the curse lifted, a means he didn't want to let out of his sight. But he knew they couldn't get far from him. He was strong again, he reminded himself. No one could prevent him from taking her back.

"The explosion will draw the humans' attention," Rydstrom said as he handed her to Cade. "Best get her out of sight. I scent a cave nearby."

The one where Bowe had planned to bed Mariketa and himself down for the night.

Cade took her but hesitated to leave, plainly hankering for a fight.

"I'll handle this," Rydstrom assured him. "My old friend Bowen and I are going to have a talk."

A talk? Bowe gave a humorless laugh. Then why were his horns straightening and blackening? Bowe's own beast stirred, ready to battle the demon if it came to that. Bowe hoped otherwise. He needed to question Rydstrom—not kill him.

"I'll get a fire started," Cade finally said, gazing down at her. "Try to scavenge some food." When Cade started off, Bowe battled the nearly irresistible urge to retrieve her. He checked it, but followed the sight of her hair swaying over Cade's arm for long moments.

The archers cast Bowe menacing looks, then eventually trailed after Cade, leaving Bowe and Rydstrom alone.

"You're lucky I owed you a blood debt, MacRieve, or I'd get retribution for the stunt you pulled."

When Rydstrom had been king, he'd allied with Bowe's army—back when there were enough Lykae for Bowe to be a general of his own men. In one battle against the Vampire Horde, Rydstrom and Cade's youngest sister had sneaked into the fray. Bowe had saved her life.

"Yet that doesn't mean I'll be able to hold off the others from trying," Rydstrom said.

Bowe couldn't care less about them. Now that he was strong, they posed no real threat to him.

In fact, the only one who did was the witch.

"And Cade will not be bothered by the debt if Mariketa doesn't recover fully. Or if she asks him to kill you."

"What is she to him?" Bowe demanded. "What's his interest?"

Rydstrom shrugged. "He probably wants to attempt her."

Bowe felt his fists clench, claws digging into his palms. Whereas Lykae could recognize their mates by scent or even sight, many demon breed males could only determine if a female was his by mating her. Demons called this investigation *attempting*.

"Why don't you tell me what she is to you?" Rydstrom said, his tone stern. "That you're *still* glancing over my shoulder in her direction, and your hands are bleeding?"

"She cursed me, and I need her to remove it."

"But you're healed."

"The witch did no' just hex me with mortality—she hexed me to believe she's my mate."

Rydstrom raised his brows, but before he could ask for details, Bowe said, "Now tell me—what in the hell happened to her in there?"

"The better question would be what *didn't* happen to her." Bowe scowled, but Rydstrom said, "What did you expect? You left a beautiful female in a tomb with at least a half dozen crazed incubi."

"There were no bruises consistent with that." Bowe stubbornly shook his head. "She dinna appear to have been hurt that way."

"No, I don't believe so. But you have to know that she's been through hell and back for weeks."

"Believe so? What do you mean *believe* so? You were no' with her?"

"They took her shortly after you sealed the tomb. We suspect they'd just been waiting for the chance to snatch her."

"Why did you no' steal her back?" Bowe closed in on Rydstrom, ready to tear out his throat. "Because she's a witch?"

"You might be eaten up with that prejudice, but all I saw was a defenseless young mortal. I didn't succeed in stealing her back because they took her to their lair, over a hundred feet above us. And any time we tried to scale the walls— the inverted walls—they attacked with a viciousness I have seen in few battles in all my years."

"Then how the hell did you get her tonight?"

"Each day I tried to convince her to jump, but she's

terrified of heights. Then, while the incubi slept this afternoon, she finally said she'd do it. It's as if she knew you were coming," he said, clearly thinking back. "I had just caught her and checked her over—she'd been sick—when they attacked again. You returned right as we were having our asses handed to us." Frowning at Bowe, he said, "You know, I'd been uneasy when I learned that Mariketa had cursed you, but now I see that if she hadn't, we'd still be in that hell."

"I didn't return only to have her spells removed," Bowe said. "More is at stake."

"What?"

"War. My faction, yours, the Valkyrie, the House of Witches. I've been given till the full moon to get her to call in and assure her coven that she's all right."

"You have a sat-phone in your pack?"

"Aye," Bowe answered. "That was smashed when the witch slammed me against that wall."

He shrugged. "I have one in our truck."

"No. No, you doona. I trashed your cars, CBs and phones."

Rydstrom narrowed his eyes. "Then you did anticipate that we would get free?"

Now Bowe shrugged.

"That will help with the others' anger."

"Doona give a damn about them. But for your sake, know that I was especially confident of your escaping since the witch led me to believe she could lift the stone as easily as she lifted me tonight."

Rydstrom glanced in her direction. "She has little control over her powers and was immediately weakened—they took her swiftly and violently. All the way up to their lair, they bashed her skull against the stones, knocking her unconscious." At Bowe's expression, he said, "If it's hard to hear, imagine how it felt seeing it happen and not being able to do a goddamned thing." He grew quiet, no doubt reliving the sight. Facing Bowe once more, he said, "Now, why don't you tell me why we can't take her back west?"

"How did you know?"

"Because you didn't simply carry her to your truck and drive away while I was pinned."

"I came past the armies on the way in. The conflict's exploded since I was last here."

"I see. Obviously, you lost the Hie. Who won?"

"The vampire."

"A *vampire* beat you? And a witch cursed you? Damn, Scot, seems you're having a fuck-all month."

13

❦

When Mari woke again, she squinted her eyes. She was in a cave? Yes, and Cade was just before her, putting wood on a new fire, his sword lying within easy reach.

She frowned to find he was shirtless, until she realized her head was on his bunched-up shirt. When the flames grew, shadows began to creep up the dusky walls. The light glinted off the wide gold band on his huge bicep and burnished his proud horns.

Mari had always found a demon's horns so pleasing. There were worse sights to wake up to.

As if he felt her eyes on him, he turned and gave her a grin. "Remind me not to piss you off, witch," he said, repeating his words from the first night in the tomb.

Hild, Tierney, and Tera entered then, their arms laden with green bananas and another kind of small, round fruit that smelled like melon.

"Look who's awake," Tera said, pushing her nut brown hair from her face. It was as matted and tangled as Mari knew hers was.

Though the others were obviously strung out with exhaustion and hunger, they were typical immortals, shrugging off the past and looking forward, gamely getting back to their lives.

Would Mari ever possess that talent? She felt like she'd been caught in a twister and left spinning. "What happened?"

"You blew up the tomb, got snatched by the werewolf, then healed yourself," Tera answered.

Healed? Her injuries were gone, the dizziness and exhaustion she'd suffered for weeks . . . faded. She slowly eased herself up to sit against a dank wall. From tomb to cave she'd gone. And she now had to tick off ten hours till dawn before she could see the sun again.

She hugged her knees to her chest and tried to make sense of everything that had just happened. All she knew was that too much had.

Questions hammered at her. *How* had she blown up the entire tomb? Yes, demolition seemed to be her specialty, but the structure had been the size of a small stadium. Never before had she unleashed that kind of power.

She also contemplated if she would have continued killing MacRieve if Rydstrom hadn't stopped her. And did she want to try killing MacRieve a little again?

As she lifted a hand to her face and patted for injuries, she wondered how she had been completely restored from the damage over the last weeks. "Are you sure I healed *myself?*"

Tera nodded. "MacRieve said these vines covered you and that you were mended within them."

"Vines?"

"It all seemed very . . . Wicca-earthy."

Mari had never been able to heal herself before. She couldn't even rid herself of a hangover with four Advil and a prepaid magick wand.

Of course, she hadn't been able to see into the future

before either. Yet just before dusk, she'd woken from a dead sleep, and somehow she'd known she had to get down. She'd finally taken that swan dive, because she'd known MacRieve had returned at last. But how?

"Where's MacRieve now?"

Cade answered, "Rydstrom's questioning him."

"Did you catch the look in the Lykae's eyes when she had him pinned?" Tierney said around bites of fruit. "He'd known she was going to kill him." He frowned at Mari. "It's hard to see you now and think you're the one that destroyed the tomb." Like the others, Tierney was regarding her as if she was a curiosity—with a mix of admiration and wariness. "You weren't kidding when you said you blow things up, were you?"

"Leave her alone." Tera sat beside Mari and stroked her tangled hair. "Can't you tell Mariketa's shell-shocked?"

Shell-shocked, confused, and disgusted by how filthy she was. She could smell the incubi on her and knew she reeked even after being doused in the pouring rain. She was also wondering what the plan was now—

MacRieve and Rydstrom entered the cave. Everyone but Mari scrambled to their feet.

"What the hell is he doing in here?" Cade demanded, his hand shooting to his sword hilt.

"Cade, I'll talk with you outside," Rydstrom said, his tone brooking no argument. So kingly. "All of you. I've news I want to discuss."

Tera cast a scathing expression in MacRieve's direction. "And MacRieve?"

"Leave him."

"What if the Lykae tries something with Mariketa?" Tierney asked.

Without looking up, Mari answered in a soft tone, "If the Lykae tries something with Mariketa, she'll finish what she started before."

Rydstrom raised his eyebrows at that, then turned for the cave entrance. The others reluctantly followed.

Alone with her, MacRieve paced, glancing at her repeatedly and muttering in Gaelic. She understood a bit of the language—her mother was a druid, after all—and knew enough curse words and the term for *witch* to pick up the general thrust of his thoughts.

Over MacRieve's muttering, she could hear the others' conversation outside. Rydstrom began by explaining what would happen if Mari didn't call her coven before the full moon and how MacRieve had been handed the task of escorting her back.

The others decided that they would be the ones to see her home for myriad reasons. First, they planned to kill MacRieve directly and so didn't see him available for the role of escort. Secondly, *they* wanted to protect "the little mortal"— the archers, because the three saw her as one among the fey, and Cade, because, as he said, "I bloody feel like it."

In that case, Rydstrom wanted them to spare the Lykae to allow him to be an extra sword. They would need him, he reasoned, to protect Mari on the journey to civilization because it was more perilous now than when she'd come on her own. The human armies were on the move and posed a real threat to her.

But the others despised MacRieve, couldn't trust him, and all agreed that "Bowen the Bitter doesn't exactly *play well with others*."

Bowen the Bitter? How appropriate.

They also agreed that they didn't know a more brutal,

ruthless, and underhanded immortal than Bowen MacRieve.

MacRieve scowled in their direction, then turned back to her, as if he hoped she hadn't heard that. He opened his mouth to speak but closed it. What did he want to say to her? What could he say? "Oh, *my* bad for setting you up for torture and terror, and I know you will never be the same again, *but* . . ."

"I thought you would be able to get free," he finally said. "I never intended for you to be trapped so long."

She ignored him, staring at the far wall of the cave.

"And I could no' return sooner because I was trapped somewhere as well. With no food or water either."

Good. When she gave him no acknowledgment, his frustration became palpable. He ran his new hand over his face, seeming surprised to find it restored. Then, as if he couldn't stop himself, he actually sank down beside her.

There they sat in the firelight. Enemies. He'd almost destroyed her. She'd nearly murdered him. And for some reason, this moment felt the most surreal of the entire crazed night—because she recognized that on some level his presence . . . *comforted.*

"You've got to lift this curse from me, Mariketa."

She finally faced him with her brows drawn. "I *did.*"

"Aye, you did lift one, but I know you hexed me more than once."

She pinched her forehead between her thumb and forefinger. "What are you talking about?"

"Sometime when we kissed, you enthralled me. You've made it so . . . so that I feel that you're my mate."

"Why do you think I've done this?" she asked, trying to recall that hazy night.

"Because you've shown you're no' shy about casting

spells on me. And the Valkyrie Nïx confirmed it—she also said you would remove it for me."

Mari swallowed. She knew Nïx and trusted her.

He studied her expression. "Do you deny this?"

Want me as fiercely as I want you. . . . She just prevented her eyes from widening. Oh, Hekate, had she made him want her? To the degree that he would believe she was his mate? She flushed guiltily.

Then her lips parted. *The prediction.*

It began with the obligatory "*It shall come to pass . . . ,*" then basically said that if an immortal warrior recognized the Awaited One as his, he would steal her away from the House of Witches. No magick would be strong enough to defeat his hold on her.

Was it *MacRieve* in the prediction?

An immortal? Check. A warrior? Check. Who'd recognized her as his mate? Damn.

Could she have brought this about with her erratic powers? Apparently so.

"If you dinna do this, then just deny it. Vow to the Lore that you dinna, and then we will figure out what is happening."

She couldn't say she'd done it, but she certainly couldn't deny it outright either.

"You're probably too weak to remove the second spell right now. I ken that. But I press for this for your own good as well. The need to treat you as my mate is strong in me. Nigh overwhelming."

"You have got to be kidding!" She scrambled away from him, casting him a horrified look.

"No, no, it's no' like that." He raised his palms when she still edged away from him.

"I wouldn't have sex with you if you were the last immortal on earth!"

He scowled. "There's far more to being a mate than just that."

She gave him a disbelieving expression.

"Just tell me you'll remove it after you rest. Then I will no' even have to explain my meaning." He stood and began pacing again. "We will no' ever have to speak to each other again. I know you want that as much as I do."

"You have *no* idea."

"I am grasping for patience when I'm no' known for it whatsoever. I ken you've been through hell, but I dinna intend to harm you so badly. You *did* intend to with me. Now, do I have to put us in a similar situation as during the first spell removal?"

"*Similar situation?*" she cried. "Like the one where you put me in fear for my life, then let go of that damned vine to heartlessly build my fear?" The callous bastard! "Mac-Rieve, I hope I enthralled you. Then you can rot wanting me to be yours."

Something frightening flashed in his eyes. "You say that so easily when you've no comprehension of the damage you've already done with your tricks."

"Like what?"

"I was inches from the means to go back for my true mate—to prevent her death—and believed it would be so. Yet because I was so injured and no' regenerating, I was forced to make a decision that cost me the Hie. Because of you, Mariketa, I canna save an innocent young woman's life. I will *never* have her—which means you've robbed her of life and me of a future, a family, or any kind of meaningful existence."

Mari realized the others outside had fallen silent and were likely eavesdropping.

"So are you still glad that you'll continue to torment me with your spell? Because you canna hurt me worse than when I lost my mate—no' once, but two goddamned times!"

Fury suffused her, and she stood as well. "And what about how you've hurt me?" she asked in a low, seething tone. "Day after day I was forced to lie amid the incubi's putrid corpses, where I went without seeing *daylight* for three weeks. And each time they seized me in the dark and forced me to swallow blood to keep me alive, I got through it by imagining how I would make you pay." His jaws and fists clenched as his anger built, but she was beyond caring. "You sealed me in that vile place to die without a backward glance and only returned because you wanted something from me!"

He stalked closer, forcing her to crane her neck up to face him. "You convinced me that you could open the tomb, and I believed you would escape eventually. And I dinna know that the crypt was *occupied*—or that you were a bloody *mortal*!" He clutched her shoulders.

She tried to twist from his grip, but he held firm. Gods, she wanted to throw him across the cave—and with the same strength as when she'd pinned him earlier!

"What in the hell were you thinking to enter a competition like the Hie?" He gave her shoulders a jostle. "You knew what you were getting into, and you still signed up. You could have *died*!" he roared, shaking her hard.

She raised her hands to shove against his chest; he flew across the cavern, as though tossed against the far wall.

When he landed, he looked as dumbfounded as she felt.

MacRieve was like a lightning rod for her powers. Whenever she wanted to use them against him, they worked *perfectly*.

As he made it back to his feet, an expression of such pure menace twisted his face that she thought he could kill her.

Fitting—since she was about to kill him. "By that same token, MacRieve, you knew what you were getting into as well!" she yelled. "So quit *whining* about any curse I put on you! If you enter a deadly competition against a witch, you should expect I'll use the weapons allotted me."

He pointed at her, opening his mouth and then closing it, knowing she was right. "I dinna intend this to happen to you! You struck out at me with malice."

"Only when you were about to seal us in!"

"Which I did because you put your filthy spell on me!"

"Just as you didn't intend for me to be trapped and have all these horrible things happen to me, I didn't intend for you to lose your mate, and I wouldn't wish that on anyone, even you. So you have a lot of nerve to say that *my* nightmare was *unintentional*, then to blame me directly for your troubles. Over a three-week period you lost the Hie, and because you lost the Hie, you lost your mate, so it's all *my* fault! You might try blaming the person who ultimately defeated you—I'm sure they didn't do it politely. Or you might try blaming the person responsible for her death in the first place!"

"*I* was responsible," he grated, his eyes suddenly so bleak they staggered her. "*Me*. And the gods know I do." Then he stormed from the cave, knocking their speechless audience out of the way.

14

That little, bloody *witch!*" Bowe snapped as he stormed to the plateau. What was she thinking to scream at him like that? To bloody *throw* him?

Just as Bowe put his fist through a tree, Rydstrom appeared. "Got under your skin, then?"

"What do you want?"

"To tell you what we've decided to do."

"What *you've* decided? The witch is my charge."

Rydstrom ignored him. "Hild will begin the journey tonight, heading back into the conflict. He'll move more quickly alone and will be able to sneak past the armies to get the word to the factions as soon as possible. Cade, Tera, Tierney, and myself will travel east with her and get her back to the States."

Bowe flexed his bloody fist. "And what do you propose for me?"

"We want you gone. Your presence is obviously upsetting for her."

"Oh, aye, the poor, wee lass—who tossed me like a skipping stone. You want me gone, and believe me, I want to be as well. But you forget—it's my head if she does no' arrive in one piece. Considering that this just turned into a game of 'protect the mortal' through the jungle, I think I'll stay and ensure that she lives."

"Your job's over. Hild will inform everyone that I take full responsibility for Mariketa. If anything happens to her, it's my problem, not yours." When Bowe was unmoved, Rydstrom said, "We think that if you stay, the two of you will kill each other."

Likely. "I canna leave until she undoes this second curse. Understand me, I *will* no'."

"And I'm sure she's keen to do anything you ask right now. Bowen, what were you thinking?"

"Was no'."

"You know women better than this."

"I know *women*—no' witches. And believe me, demon, there's a difference."

"I've never seen you lose your temper like that. And I've seen your wrath many a time," Rydstrom said, his tone becoming musing. "I hope you're certain she's not your mate reincarnated."

Bowe froze. The thought had crossed his mind, of course, but there were dozens of reasons to discount the idea. *Still* . . . "Why do you say that?"

Rydstrom limped to a fallen tree and dropped his giant frame down onto the trunk. "What if Mariketa didn't enchant you? If you accept the belief that no one in the Lore gets a second mate, then reincarnation is the only other explanation for you to think of her as yours."

Bowe knew Rydstrom's curiosity could rival any Lykae's, and he enjoyed solving mysteries and fixing problems. Rydstrom had obviously deemed this situation one or the other, or both. He got that analytical air about him, so contrary to his demon state when reason was lost—even worse than Bowe in his werewolf form.

And therein resided the problem with Rydstrom. When he went demonic, he *really* went.

He continued, "Reincarnates are extremely rare, true, but they do exist."

"No, the witch did enchant me," Bowe insisted. "The Valkyrie soothsayer confirmed what I'd already felt. She even told me Mariketa would eventually remove it for me."

"Valkyrie soothsayer?" Rydstrom's brows drew together. "You don't mean Nïx? What was it that they called her?"

Nucking Futs Nïx.

"Shame a beauty like that is so soft in the head. But why would you trust that mad creature on something this important?"

"Everyone I trust in the world trusts her," Bowe said. "That's good enough for me." But was it, really? Damn it, Mariah and Mariketa, aside from the similar fey names and pointed ears, were complete opposites. Mariah had been so ethereal and innocent, the witch so sensual and devious, and so . . . *brave*. No. Mariketa could not be her. Simply impossible.

Rydstrom studied Bowe. "Wouldn't matter now if Mariketa was her anyway."

"What does that mean?"

"Animosity has probably already turned to hatred in that one. And there's nothing like boiling hatred to dampen a female's acceptance of her mate. Especially when he's not of her kind." Rydstrom ignored Bowe's scowl and said, "I just wonder if the witch actually could have cast such an intricate spell on you. Think about it—this couldn't be a simple love spell to trigger this kind of reaction in you."

One thing Bowe was unequivocally certain of was that he didn't love her. He desired her, had overriding urges to protect her—and to bed her. *Gods, how I want to bed her.*

But he didn't even *like* her. Which followed. Considering that she'd just attacked him. *Twice.*

"Though her power's great," Rydstrom continued, "it's volatile, and she's clumsy with magicks. Yet to do this to you, she would have had to affect the Lykae's Instinct in you. And not merely to *tamper* with it. Somehow she would have had to *trick* a force that has been honed over hundreds of thousands of years. Then, say she'd managed that, instead of accidentally blowing you up—which she admitted to us that she does ninety-nine out of a hundred times. Do you think she could have removed just one of her spells from you tonight, leaving the other? And in her condition?"

Bowe felt sweat dotting his brow. What if . . . what if Mariketa the Awaited actually was . . . *his*? His female, returned to him? His to claim, to protect—to *claim.* He felt a savage thrill at the idea of possessing her and bending her strong will to his.

What if fate had finally taken pity on him after all these wretched years?

He shook his head hard. "My ability to heal was honed over the same amount of time as well, but she managed to tamper with *that.*"

"Someone would have taught her that mortality spell, but do you think they'd have taught her how to affect a Lykae's Instinct?" Rydstrom said. "Let me ask you, isn't there some way you can prove without a doubt that she's yours?"

Bowe hesitated to answer before muttering, "If I can get her with bairns."

"Are you bloody jesting?" Rydstrom snapped, then narrowing his eyes, he added, "That's right! I recall this now."

Bowe ran his palm over the back of his neck.

"Since that's how to get the proof you need, I know what I'd be aiming for, and a pleasanter endeavor I can't imagine."

"Doona be imagining that at all, or I'll be tearing your throat out!"

Rydstrom raised his brows.

"So if you were me, you'd just go along with the Instinct, treat her as yours for possibly years until you decided for certain?"

"If it meant I got to enjoy the curvy redhead in that cave for possibly years, then yes."

"Damn it, doona bloody talk about her like that!"

Rydstrom gave him an expression that said Bowe was proving his point. Again.

"And then say I eventually determined it was an enchantment?" Bowe asked. "What if after so long, I canna quit her?"

"If she couldn't quit you either, then would it be so bad?" Rydstrom said. "Some men would take happiness where they found it." There was something like sympathy in his eyes. Rydstrom, too, had gone long without finding his destined demoness. "Especially when they have absolutely no promise of it anywhere else." He rose to leave. "Whatever you do, make a decision about her, Bowen, one way or the other, and stick to it."

"You're helping me with her? Though Cade wants her? Do you do this because of an old friendship or to thwart him?"

If the latter, Cade had it coming.

The relationship between the two demons was complicated. Not only were their personalities averse—if Rydstrom would take a scalpel to a problem to systematically cut through it, Cade would take a hammer and swing wildly—there was also the matter of Cade's losing Rydstrom's crown.

Rydstrom answered, "Either would work for you, would it not?"

"True." If the demons' history was complicated, Bowe and Cade's was contentious. They were too much alike—both killers in service to kings, leaders compelled by fortune to follow another. Bowe followed Lachlain because he was like a brother and was worthy to serve. Cade followed Rydstrom because, in his own violent, misguided way, he strived to make up for the loss. "So which is it?"

"My brother thinks he wants Mariketa because she's beautiful—"

"Did he find her so when she was in that bloodthirsty witch state, strangling me?" Bowe snapped. "Or when she was blowing up that tomb and all its occupants."

"The girl was merely doing her job with the latter."

"What does that mean?"

"Witches are mercenaries—that's just a fact of life—and I think the incubi *wanted* her to kill them. I believe that's why they were shaking her when she was unconscious outside the entrance and why they were trying to give her that gold headdress. They wanted to pay her. Desperately."

To pay her with the gold piece that Bowe currently had in his pack.

"Anyway, Cade probably did think her beautiful in that state. Unlike you, he likes that there's something dangerous about her and that she has the potential for some serious destruction. Still, she's not the one for him. Cade's already seen the female that will be his, yet is in denial. Long story, but suffice it to say that the first time he spied her, he lost the power of speech for some moments."

"Cade will seize on the witch just to get even with me," Bowe said.

Seven hundred years ago, Cade had decided to *attempt* a bonny barmaid. He'd been hopeful. Instead, she'd crawled into Bowe's bed. After a night of mead, Bowe hadn't recalled that she was the prospective barmaid.

In a dry tone, Rydstrom said, "Yes, naturally to get even. Obviously there could be no other enticement to want Mariketa." Before he turned to go, he said, "Remember, make a decision. You would begin things with her with far fewer chances at forgiveness. And something tells me your witch isn't the type to abide the indecision of a Lykae, one who can't seem to conclude if he wants her or not."

When Bowe was alone once more, he found his heart pounding. Could he give himself up to the Instinct? To let his body and soul guide him, while ignoring what his mind told him?

Could he ignore his past with Mariketa's kind?

What if he wasn't contemplating giving up his will to the witch, but merely investigating every possibility as he had tirelessly for eighteen decades? Aside from Nïx's prediction about the Hie, this was the most promising lead he'd ever had.

His brows drew together as he recalled exactly what the Valkyrie had told him. "Through the Hie, you'll have your mate." Not that his mate would be *returned* to him or that Bowe would *retrieve* her. And she'd never actually said that

Mariketa had cast an enchantment—only that she would remove it.

Bowe swallowed. It was . . . *possible*.

Hell, Rydstrom could be right—it could be too late. What if too much damage had already been done?

No, Bowe knew females could be forgiving creatures. Lachlain had admitted to Bowe that in the crazed days after he'd been freed from torture, he'd treated Emma badly, and she'd been able to forgive him.

Of course Lachlain had never *entombed* Emma.

But Bowe had to believe that Mariketa could be coaxed to move past that. After all, she wasn't immune to him, or she hadn't been during their first encounter. When he remembered her body's response to him, how wet she'd been as her hips rocked to his hand, he hissed an oath and palmed the front of his jeans.

So how to exploit her weakness? He was sorely out of practice wooing. Since Mariah's death, his only interaction with available females had been a sneer if they'd had the nerve to approach him. Yet he'd used to be called charming by females. Hadn't he? He could scarcely remember women before Mariah.

The sense of urgency that lashed him constantly over these long years now redoubled. He couldn't quite wrap his mind around the idea that there was even the remotest chance that his mate was less than a mile from him—though in the form of an enemy who wanted him dead.

Now that he had his strength back after weeks of being weakened, he wanted to run the night, but would never stray far from the prize he intended to take. Instead, he climbed to the mountain's peak, surveying the surrounding area.

From this vantage, he spied river after river unfolding to the east, then caught the scent of salt water. The Belizean coast wasn't too far out of reach in that direction. To the west, he could see humans in fatigues swarming over the land like ants, continuing to riddle the countryside with mines.

Mariketa definitely had to travel east. Bowe had been able to survive a mine blast, but he knew he couldn't risk a mortal's being within a mile of one—a mortal who was possibly *his*. The trek would be longer, but it would prove safer for her in the end.

Unless they didn't make it out before the full moon. . . .

He immediately stifled that thought. No, they'd reach the coast by Friday.

Directly below him lay the bomb blast site, reminding him of what Mariketa was and the power she possessed, filling him with doubt about her. Even if he knew for certain that she was his mate, could he accept a witch as his own? Present her to the clan as his female?

Again he imagined her trembling and wanton beneath him, and his body quickened for her.

I'll bloody figure something out.

A few miles away from the new crater, Bowe spied the line of their ruined vehicles. Her belongings would likely still be within. And in her present situation, even the smallest comfort would be treasured.

He could go out into this night, retrieve her things, and hunt for her. He could use his strength and skill to provide for a female, a female who needed him. The idea made him shake with anticipation.

—*Protect. Provide.*—

The Instinct was guiding him once more. Ready to obey, Bowe plunged into the jungle.

For the next hour, he hunted in the intermittent rain, hitting the mountainside and streams with a renewed ferocity. At last, after a lifetime of waiting, he was doing what he'd been born to do, and he wanted to howl to the sky with satisfaction.

Yes, Bowe knew all this could be false. With his body and soul, he felt one thing, even as his mind feared the truth. But for so long, he'd known nothing but misery and yearning.

Even Mariah would have understood the witch's pull was just too great to resist—

The clouds briefly dissipated then, revealing the waxing moon. He raised his face to the light that commanded his kind alone, and the power of it filled him with awe, just as it had over all his years. Yet now the coming moon made both dread and eagerness war within him as well.

When he lowered his face, he narrowed his eyes in Mariketa's direction.

If she truly belonged to him . . . the witch would do well to fear what he was.

15

After Hild had set off, plainly loath to leave Tera—though she seemed oblivious to his attraction—the remaining five had eaten as much unripened fruit as they could tolerate, then taken places around the fire to pass out.

Cade had moved to sleep beside Mari, and she was good with that plan, but Rydstrom had said something sharp in Demonish that made Cade scowl at the entrance to the cave, then turn away from her.

As the others drifted off to sleep one by one, Mari remained wide awake and still chilled and hungry. Though they were in a jungle, this cave sat at a higher elevation. The night air inside was moist and cool, and her long hair hadn't dried.

Rydstrom remained awake as well, and after placing more wood on the fire, he limped over to where she lay.

"How's your leg?" she asked.

"Healing rapidly."

"I'm glad to hear it," she said, reminded again of everything he'd done for her. "Listen, Rydstrom, thank you for helping me tonight. For all your help."

"It was nothing." When he sat beside her, her attention wandered to his damaged horns. One had a piece gouged out, and the other had at least four inches missing from the end.

Mari's first—and only—long-term boyfriend, Acton, had been a storm demon. After dating him for years, she knew how important a demon's horns were to a male. Even females were vain about their tiny, downy ones that looked more like cool hair accessories.

And for rage demons, when their horns straightened and sharpened, the points emitted a deadly poison. Their kind didn't often get jumped from behind. To lose an end would be handicapping for a warrior. "What happened here?" She just prevented herself from reaching out and skimming her finger over one—which would have been totally taboo. "Did it hurt?"

"Like hell. I fought a bit when I was younger."

"I'll bet you did with Cade."

He shook his head. "We didn't live in the same household growing up. The heir is always separated out."

That explained the differences in their accents and bearings.

In an obvious bid to change the subject, he said, "You know, something struck me as odd tonight."

"Only *one* thing struck you as odd?"

He raised an eyebrow, then continued, "Earlier, when I mentioned that I'd told the Lykae to leave us, I thought you would have been more pleased." Why was Rydstrom studying her reaction like that?

"I was thoroughly pleased." Utterly. "Good riddance, I say."

"If I didn't know better, I'd think that even now you're wishing he'd come back."

"Oh, but you *do* know better. MacRieve's rabid, and

needs to be put down. Though maybe I shouldn't say anything bad about him since you're obviously friends with him. You saved him tonight, from me."

"I did that for you as well. I didn't want you to regret taking his head."

"I'm a witch—I'm sure I would have found a way to carry on." She tilted her head at him. "And you really stuck up for MacRieve with the others."

He nodded. "Bowen and I fought together for many years. And in one battle he saved my youngest sister's life."

"MacRieve did?" At Rydstrom's grave nod, she asked, "Then how could he trap you in the first place?"

Rydstrom shrugged. "I think he was a shade shocked to see me inside, but honestly, I'd have done the same to him. It was a competition, and he desperately wanted that key."

In an uninterested tone, she said, "I suppose he must have loved his mate very much."

"I can't say for certain. I never had the opportunity to be around him and Mariah together. They were only together for a few weeks before she died."

"*Mariah?* She was fey?"

"Yes. A princess of the fey. Very beautiful, by all accounts."

Princess? Mari thought, running a hand over her matted hair. *Beautiful?*

Puzzling, but her Pig Pen appearance bothered her more than it had a moment earlier. Her hand shot down when Rydstrom regarded her quizzically. "How did she die?"

"I'd heard it was an accident in the woods."

"Then what did he mean when he said he was responsible for her death?"

"He was with her and blames himself."

"There's got to be more to the story than that."

"I'm sorry, Mariketa, but it's not my story to tell. And unfortunately, I can't recommend asking him about it either."

"Oh. Well, it's not like I'm going to stay up nights thinking about this."

"No? You seem curious about him."

"He's my enemy. It's a good idea to learn about him."

"You are right, of course. I will answer any questions I can."

She hesitated, then couldn't keep herself from asking, "What's he usually like? When not fighting for something?"

"He once was jovial, but he always did his own thing. Since his mate's death, he's been dying slowly, turning cold and indifferent. Some say crazed, even. I will admit he can be coarse, saying exactly what's on his mind, but the others were wrong tonight—he's never been needlessly cruel."

"Why does he hate witches so much?"

"I don't know the specifics, but I think his family was grievously hurt by one in some way. Besides, all Lykae mistrust witches. And I think they instinctively fear them a little."

"I can't see MacRieve fearing anything."

"True, he was always on the front line in battle, the first to meet the enemy. But with your kind . . ." He trailed off and lowered his voice. "I've seen him unconsciously ease across the street to give even a fortune-teller a wide berth. He was wholly unaware of it."

"No way!" When someone mumbled in sleep, she softened her tone to say, "So my attack tonight must have completely thrown him—pun intended."

He grinned, flashing his even white teeth and short fangs. "Yes, but that's the thing about Bowen—he'll shrug it off soon enough."

As she thought over what she'd learned, Rydstrom said, "There's one thing you should remember if you ever do happen upon him or another Lykae. If you want the key to understand them, know that they truly are *like wolves*. If you're around them enough, you can see it clearly."

"What do you mean?"

"Have you ever heard of the Lykae Instinct?"

She nodded. "They have a wolf spirit inside them or something. Makes them howl at the moon, bite their bed partners, scratch inappropriately, blah, blah."

He seemed pleased by her flippant answer for some reason. "It's a bit more complicated than that. But we'll talk some more tomorrow." He lay on his side and shut his eyes. "Get some sleep. The upcoming journey will be arduous. . . ."

Hours later, Mari was still awake, hungrier and now shivering. Though she was abjectly miserable, she'd thought she would sleep through anything—

"*Come tae me*," she heard from a distance.

She shot upright, squinting into the shadows. At the entrance of the cave, warm amber eyes glowed in the darkness. He'd come back!

"Ah, you're excited about my return, then," he murmured. "Your heart sped up at the verra sound of my voice."

The nerve! "Only because I'm eager to throw you around some more. That'll *never* get old."

"You're cold and still soaked through."

"Nothing escapes you."

"I've something for you to eat."

At the thought of more gel packs or green bananas, she almost retched, but then the scent of something cooked, something *heavenly*, assailed her. "What is that smell?" she asked just as the others awakened one by one.

"Food for you, Mariketa," he answered. "A feast of it." Beside his spot at the edge of the cave, she spied what looked like grilled fish and crayfish, as well as some kind of roasted meat laid out on a smooth flank of wood. Succulent fruits lay in abundant piles, with not a green banana among them.

As her mouth watered, Rydstrom muttered, "Methinks your Lykae is trying to impress you. What he can't take, he'll tempt."

"Shut it, demon," she said, and he gave a half laugh.

"There's food enough for everyone, and I will bargain for it," MacRieve said.

"What do you want?" Tera asked, rubbing her eyes.

"As you likely overheard, it seems the wee witch might have cast more than one spell over me, a spell that makes me think of her as my mate. So I'm no' letting her out of my sight—I *will* be accompanying her on the trek out of the jungle and will fight anyone who tries to stand in my way. When I settle my plans for her and she agrees to them, you'll abide by them as well. No interfering."

"What plans for me?" Mari demanded, crossing her arms over her chest.

"You've three options, Mariketa. First, deny you cast the spell. Second, admit the truth and remove it. Or third, for the duration of our adventure here you'll vow no' to use magick near—or at—me again and you'll prepare to have yourself a mate."

"What exactly does that mean?"

"Long and short—I'll provide food for you, I'll protect you, and you'll do whatever I tell you." As she sputtered, he said, "I think once you've experienced what it's like to have me—an overpowering, commanding Lykae—ordering you about, you'll do whatever's necessary to get rid of me."

"I *already* want to get rid of you!" she cried. "I'd take a freaking incubus over you, and I'd take him with a cheery smile and hello kiss."

"Ach, you wound, witchling," he said, sounding not the least wounded.

"Even had I done what you're accusing me of, I don't know how to reverse it. You've seen firsthand how little control I have over my powers."

"Necessity is the mother of invention. If you get sick enough of me, I'm sure you'll figure something out. Or you can simply deny that you've done this."

"Mari, just tell him you didn't do it," Tera said.

She couldn't! "I don't believe I did. But I . . . I can't make a vow to that."

"Then you've only two other options. Decide." To Rydstrom, he said, "You gain a feast and another male to guard her—if you do no' interfere when I treat her as mine."

Mari glanced around the cave. *They're considering it!* All but Cade, who had a calculating, unsettling look in his eyes. "You people have all gone mad. I despise him." She met MacRieve's eyes and snapped, "If you think I'll sleep with you, you're cracked, deranged."

"I have no need to *compel* you to sleep with me," he interrupted, his tone so smug. "That is no' part of this deal."

"I will never agree to this. Never—"

"Before you decide," MacRieve interrupted, "know that

if you were my mate, I'd make sure you had whatever you needed to be comfortable." Her lips parted when he pulled *her bag* from behind him and proceeded to dig through it. "Like your toothbrush." He held up her pink toothbrush.

He'd retrieved her things from her car? And rooted through her personal possessions.

She'd seen MacRieve's ferocity, and now she was getting a good glimpse of his sly side, his tricksy side. She could see what Rydstrom had been talking about. MacRieve seemed . . . *wolfish.*

Then she remembered what else she had in her bag. *Oh, great Hekate.* Dread settled in the pit of her stomach. Mari had private things in there—rocket of the pocket–type private things. Like a tube of lipstick that wasn't really one.

"Or this." He carelessly flicked her birth control patch. "Doona know what it does, but I ken that people who use patches for whatever reason might be eager for a new one." He displayed her iPod next. "It's my understanding that females your age canna go long without listening to music or they become irrational and impossible to deal with. And how long's it been for you, then?" He drew out a blue-labeled bottle and shook it. "You had several bottles of Orangina in your Jeep. Must like it, do you no'?"

Not the Orangina! Her mouth watered even more.

"And here's your bit of Mayan gold that you're probably keen to hold on to." He held up the weighty headdress. *Stunning.*

She hazily remembered seeing it in the severed hand of an incubus, as if in offer, but she'd thought the piece had been lost into that crater. If MacRieve gave the incubi's headdress to her, it would be her first payment as a mystical mercenary.

No, resist him! To act like his mate? To follow his orders? She could resist the food and the Orangina. She could even resist *gold*, but there he went digging once more.

He'd find *it*. But maybe he wouldn't know what it really was—

"And your *lipstick*," he said with a wicked glint in his eyes. Oh, no, he knew, and he was playing with her. She was going to die of mortification!

Her face grew hot when he added, "You must be in sore need of this after three weeks without."

Playing with me . . . "Put my things back," she said between gritted teeth. "Now!"

"Come tae me, agree to my plans, and I will. It'll take us till Friday to reach civilization. Until then, I'll treat you as mine."

Food, dry clothes, a toothbrush, the absence of scalding humiliation . . .

"One day," she countered.

His tone firm, he repeated, "Till Friday."

As she hesitated for long moments, his demeanor seemed uncaring and aloof, as though he'd merely shrug if she said no. But when she studied him closely as he waited, she detected more.

Bowen MacRieve was holding his breath.

Whether she used magick against him or not, she wasn't going to be powerless in this exchange. For whatever reason, he wanted this arrangement badly. She could use that.

When she forced herself to rise, Cade asked her, "You're not really willing to go along with this? Sleep with him for some fish? Because if that's the case, wait half an hour for me to return with my catch."

"I've said sex is no' part of this deal," MacRieve grated.

"Now, Cade, why would I bargain to get a female in my bed when I can scarcely keep them out of it?"

Mari raised her brows, knowing she was catching only the very surface of this conversation. She also sensed Cade was merely waiting for the time to strike.

As she crossed to MacRieve, he put her things back in her bag and smugly patted the ground beside him. She sank down farther away than indicated, but he simply dragged her closer. "She's accepted her lot," he told the others as he handed Mari a broad leaf covered in flaking fish. "Agree you will no' interfere on our journey." A rich, sliced avocado followed.

"Mariketa, you don't have to do this," Tera said, even as she kept eyeing the food.

Mari put her chin up. "No. I'll do it. If I survived something so distasteful as confinement with the incubi, I should be able to tolerate even a Lykae for a couple of days."

Tierney said, "Well, I'm not waiting for an engraved invitation." When he and Tera attacked the offering, Cade strode from the cave, looking murderous.

"I'll get back at you for this," Mari whispered to MacRieve. "I don't have to use magick to make you sorry for trying to humiliate me."

"I thought your 'tube of lipstick' might bring you round. And I dinna even have to turn it on."

Her cheeks burned anew. "Are you done?"

"Canna say." Moments passed, then he leaned down near her ear to murmur, "After you eat, I'm going to enjoy giving you a nice, long bath. . . ."

16

I still don't see why we couldn't sleep in that cave," Mari said as MacRieve led her out into the night.

"Because my cave's better than their cave."

"You know, that really figures." After the rain, the din of cicadas and frogs resounded in the underbrush all around them, forcing her to raise her voice. "Is it far?" When he shook his head, she said, "Then why do I have to hold your hand through the jungle? This path looks like a tractor busted through here."

"I went back this way while you ate to make sure everything was clear. Brought your things here, too," he said as he steered her toward a lit cave entrance.

When they crossed the threshold, wings flapped in the shadows, building to a furor before settling. Inside, a fire burned. Beside it, she saw he'd unpacked some of his things, and had made up *one* pallet. "Well, no one can call you a pessimist, MacRieve." She yanked her hand from his. "*Deluded* fits, though."

He merely leaned back against the wall, seeming content to watch her as she explored on her own. She'd read about this part of Guatemala and knew that here limestone caverns spread out underground like a vast web.

Above them a cathedral ceiling soared, with stalactites jutting down. "What's so special about this cave?"

"Mine has bats."

She breathed, "If I stick with you, I'll have *nothing* but the best."

"Bats mean fewer mosquitoes. And then there's also the bathtub for you to enjoy." He waved her attention to an area deeper within. A subterranean stream with a sandy beach meandered through the cavern. Her eyes widened. A small pool sat off to the side, not much larger than an oversize Jacuzzi, and laid out along its edge were her toiletries, her washcloth, and her towel. Her bag—filled with all of her clean clothes—was off just to the side.

Mari cried out at the sight, doubling over to yank at her bootlaces. Freed of her boots, she hopped forward on one foot then the other as she snatched off her socks. She didn't pause until she was about to start on the button fly of her shorts.

She glanced up to find him watching her with a gleam of expectation in his eyes. "You will be leaving, of course."

"Or I could help you."

"I've had a bit of practice bathing myself and think I can stumble my way through this."

"But you're tired. Why no' let me help? Now that I've two hands again, I'm eager to use them."

"You give me privacy or I go without."

"Verra well." He shrugged. "I'll leave—because your going without is *no'* an option. Call me if you need me."

Too easy. She knew he'd capitulated readily, but the call of the water was irresistible. She stripped, throwing her shorts, underthings, tank top, and used-up patch all into a pile to be put on the fire later. Then she stepped in, moaning with bliss.

The water wasn't hot, but it was lukewarm and felt delicious in the humid air of the cave. She ducked under, then swam up to the edge. He'd thought of everything—toothbrush, toothpaste, her shampoo and conditioner. She loaded her toothbrush, then brushed, lavishing every tooth.

After that, she poured lotion soap into her washcloth and scrubbed it over every inch of her body. She'd just finished the second wash and rinse of her hair when MacRieve strolled in, barefoot and wearing nothing but a worn pair of jeans and the medallion at his neck.

She ducked down until the water hit her neck. "You said I'd have privacy!" she sputtered. "You promised." She was by no means a shy person, but she also didn't see any reason to tease him with the goods he would never be getting.

"Aye, and I kept my promise." In the firelight, she saw his chest was massive and sculpted, dusted with the lightest smattering of golden hair against his tanned skin. "There's no way the others will be able to see you."

"You know I meant privacy from you."

He frowned, as if she spoke nonsense. "Mates have a different concept of privacy," he said, smoothly stripping himself of his jeans, leaving that spectacular body completely unclothed.

Dumbstruck, she was unable to do anything but stare at the expanse of skin and rippling muscles. Her gaze dipped lower, past his chiseled torso to the trail of darker hair below his navel. In a kind of daze, she found her eyes following it down to his huge erection.

She'd felt how large he was but was still unprepared to

witness his size. With every second she gaped, his penis grew harder, distending before her eyes. His breaths were coming faster, yet she couldn't seem to look away.

The broad head that she'd once briefly stroked grew slick, and the sight called forth an answering clenching between her thighs, so powerful she nearly cried out. . . .

She knew what was happening—she was suffering from the immortal phenomenon of *overstimulation*.

The transition from mortal to immortal was a time of uncomfortable adjustment. Eyesight and sense of smell improved exponentially, and even tactile awareness increased, yet it took time for transitioning mortals to get accustomed to the difference.

In short, her senses were bombarding her, and that was a problem.

Because superhuman senses meant superhuman lust.

"Gods, Mariketa," he rasped, "I can *feel* your eyes on it."

She finally forced herself to drag her gaze away. As soon as she turned from him, she heard him enter the water. With a gasp, she lunged for the side to get out, but he caught her with an arm looped around her waist.

"Let me go!" she demanded, struggling against him, briefly stunned by the rock hardness prodding her.

"I'm enjoying your squirming, but no' your kicking so much. Ach, watch that you doona hit me in the ballocks! We're both going to need those in working order."

Galling! "You bastard—stop poking me with . . . with *that*!"

"You keep squirming, witch, and I'm no' goin' to be able to keep my hips still either."

She froze, out of breath and realizing she couldn't fight him anyway. He was breathing hard, too, but not from exertion. She felt his warm exhalations on her neck and ear and shivered, her nipples hardening against his arm.

"You need my help in here—even if you doona want to admit it."

"You think I can't clean myself?"

"You brushed your teeth for a good ten minutes, and you've washed your hair twice and you'd probably do it again for good measure, but your arms are likely getting tired."

"They're not!" They *were*. "I'm fine."

"Oh? Then let me see your hands."

She rolled her eyes and raised her hands. At his tsking sound, she glanced down. Her nails were dirty! Her face flushed wildly. *Damn him!*

When he spun her around, she draped her arm over her breasts. Glaring at the ceiling, she allowed him to wash one hand at a time. Using the lather, he massaged each finger from base to tip.

Her eyelids began to grow heavy as he firmly pressed his thumbs into her palms, one then the other. "Your hands are so small," he said, his voice pleasingly low and rumbly. "But pretty." She just stifled a shiver.

He finally let her go, and embarrassingly, she swayed. Once she opened her eyes, mustering up the energy to lay into him again, she found him running his thumb claw against the limestone. "What are you doing that for?"

"Dulling the verra edges. Give me those wee hands again." More massaging followed until the fight in her was blissed away. When he began carefully running his dulled claw under each of her nails, she watched his face. His brows were drawn in concentration while he painstakingly went about the task, as if this was very important for him.

"There," he said when finished. "Now for all that hair of yours." He eased her around again.

Still rendered relaxed and cooperating, she let him tend to her. With his claws retracted, he massaged her head thoroughly until she felt she was the consistency of a puddle. And she knew he was wearing that look of concentration as he did it, because he wanted to get this right. What she didn't know was why.

If this was meant to torture her and make her miserable enough to remove the spell, then he was doing a shoddy job of it.

But MacRieve couldn't truly believe she was his. Could he?

17

As he worked shampoo into her long hair, he said, "See, Mariketa, this is no' so bad. If you'd known you'd be treated like this, I probably would no' even have had to blackmail you."

"You had no right to go through my things like that."

"I'd warned you that you'd find me overbearing. Strange, though, when I investigated your belongings, more questions were raised than answered. What is the patch for, the one in your bag?"

She shrugged. "Birth control."

"A *contraceptive?*" he hastily asked. Bloody perfect.

"Yeah, so?" She stiffened. "Do you think I'm easy now?"

"Sensitive about this, Mariketa?"

"Most guys my age would look at the tattoo on my back and the patch on my arm as tramp stamps."

"Tramp . . . ? Oh, I see."

"I'm not. A tramp."

"O' course no'," he agreed, trying to keep amusement out of his tone. "Most 'guys your age' just *hope* that you are one. And would no' know what to do with you even if you were."

"And exactly how old are you, MacRieve?"

"Twelve hundred, give or take."

She glanced back at him, as though gauging if he was jesting. When he raised his brows, she said, "Great Hekate, you're a *relic*. Don't you have a museum exhibit to be in somewhere?"

He ignored her comments. "Another mystery—I dinna find a razor in your bag, but your legs and under your arms are smooth."

"I was lasered," she said, then added, "I can *hear* your frown, Father Time," surprising him because he was.

She didn't explain more, but he didn't miss a beat. "Makes a man recall where else you're so well groomed." She shivered from a mere murmur in her ear. "I'm lookin' forward tae touchin' you there again."

"Ha! Why would you think that I would *ever* let you?"

"I happen to ken that you're a lusty one. And I've taken away your wee alternative. Tossed it into a river." As she gasped, he said, "Took me a minute to figure out what it was—a minute more to believe you actually had it. Then imagining you using it? Had me in such a state, I could scarcely run without tripping over my own feet."

"You're trying to embarrass me again. Give it up. I'm not going to be ashamed because I'm like every other girl my age."

"I doona want you to be ashamed—never in matters like that. And I ken you're to turn immortal soon, know the need must be overwhelming. In fact, most females get confused by all their new lustiness," he said. "Best to have a firm hand to guide them into immortal sex."

"And I'll just bet that you're happy to volunteer."

Making his tone aggrieved, he sighed, "If I must . . . Now lean back so I can rinse your hair."

She hesitated, then finally did. He rewarded her by

using the water he'd warmed in his canteen. "*Ooh*," she softly moaned, making his shaft throb harder.

"So responsive." Once he'd rinsed her hair clean, he lowered his voice to say, "If you were no' so tired, I'd make you come a few times."

She jerked upright, her hair whipping across her chin and neck. "That won't happen! I learned my lesson about you." She backed away from him. "The bloom is definitely off that rose."

"How's that?"

"Got lost in a kiss—got locked in a tomb with an ancient evil bent on making me drink blood. It's all about causality. The bottom line is that you are bad news."

"I'll make you believe differently in the time you've given me."

"And how do you expect to do that?" she asked, her tone scoffing. "By bathing me really, really good?"

"No, I plan to use my roguish charm to seduce you."

"But you're not charming."

He gave an arrogant half laugh, though he had been worried on that exact score. "I've no' even begun to try with you. Now come back here—you're to bathe me."

Mari frowned at him. She didn't like this new flirty side of MacRieve because, damn him, he did have a certain rough charm. "Like that's going to happen. I'm getting out, and I don't want you to look."

He gave her a brows-drawn look of disappointment, as if she'd taken away a toy—and for no good reason.

"It really is the least you could do."

When he finally turned his broad back to her, she found herself again getting caught up staring at the damp skin and muscles. With a hard shake of her head, she hurried from the water, then bent for the towel he'd laid out, covering herself.

Kneeling beside her bag, she rifled through it, searching for something to sleep in. She'd had a roomy T-shirt in there. Where was it? *Wait . . .* She narrowed her eyes in his direction and found him running a shaking hand over his face, his eyelids heavy.

"You watched me get out, didn't you?" she asked absently, realizing that she could not see his right hand below the water—and that the muscles in that arm were moving.

"*O' course*, I did," he replied with no shame. "And I'd describe the sight as life changing. It's also made me ponder if a male can have a cockstand that's so hard, it canna be tamed."

She glared at the ceiling, irritated that he was getting to her like this. "Did you take the sleep shirt from my bag?"

"Aye. Found some silks in there that I want you to wear for me." Shameless, tricksy wolf.

Mari bit her lip as she surveyed the three underwear sets he'd seen—and probably felt, and who knew what else: *recovering nymphomaniac*, *hooker*, and *playful hooker*. Just ducky. The last time she'd *ever* go lingerie shopping with Carrow.

She stood, marched over to his bag, and rummaged inside for the largest shirt she could find. When she pulled one out, she spied a folded letter with a broken wax seal. The script had faintly bled through and was feminine.

What female was writing him letters? And why was it so special that he would bring it with him on this trip?

She thought he was climbing out, so she closed his bag.

Behind her, she heard him shaking his hair out, wolflike, and felt a few drops of water hit her as she stood.

With her back to him, she maneuvered the towel, endeavoring to dress without revealing anything.

"Though I could watch this all night, you should no' bother with it, witchling. I've seen every inch of you by now."

She glanced over her shoulder, not knowing if she was pleased or disappointed that he'd slung on his jeans. "How's that?"

"I'm tall enough that when I was behind you, I could see straight over you. And my eyesight's strong enough to easily see through the water."

She wasn't modest, and this hiding her body like a blushing virgin wasn't her front anyway. "In that case . . ." she said, dropping the towel.

He hissed in a breath. As she set about dressing as usual, he grated, "*No' a bashful one, then?*"

Bashful? She and her friends made *Girls Gone Wild* look like a quilting circle. "Just being charitable to aging werewolves."

18

Pert, plump arse, smooth thighs, slim back and waist . . .

Bowe had never seen such a tantalizing figure in all his life. And he'd lived a long, long time. He was well aware that he'd been rendered speechless by the body of a twenty-three-year-old witch.

And when she'd bent over naked for her towel? If he hadn't been braced for what he'd known was going to be a heart-stopping vision, he'd have drowned, thunderstruck.

Now, as he watched her slip into her wicked silk underwear and bra, he just stifled a groan and instead observed, "I never thought the saying 'bounce a quarter off her arse' could be literal."

"I didn't think you cared for my ass. I believe you said I was scrawny where it counts."

"You said the same about me. *Obviously*, we were both mistaken. And I care for your arse verra much. My affection for it grows by the minute."

She shot him a glare, then dressed in his shirt, rolling up the sleeves because it swallowed her. He frowned when she drew out that second patch, applying it to a spot on the inside of her elbow. He'd had no idea what it was for or he'd have thrown it out in an instant.

Contraception in a patch. And the damned thing seemed to be taunting him.

After putting more wood on the fire, he sat beside it on the pallet, coaxing her to join him there. "Come, witchling, I'll dry your hair."

"I can do it myself."

"This is still part of the deal, the deal you agreed to."

With a sigh, she joined him. Outside, the rain started up once more and began to pound all the broad leaves. Inside, the fire crackled, burnishing her long red hair with gold as he sifted it through his fingers, drying it into big curls. Now that he'd bathed her, the scent of her hair and skin was sublime, filling his senses.

Yes, she could have done this herself, but he didn't want to give up tasks like these. They pleased him in new ways, soothing the constant yearning he'd battled for years. At last, he didn't suffer from that strangling sense of urgency—to find the means to bring his mate back to him.

He felt his lids grow heavy, not only with desire, but with *satisfaction*. He'd almost forgotten what it was like to be content. The need to have her was still pressing, yet he savored even that. He'd rather endure unfulfilled lust, with the hope of slaking it, than the hopelessness he'd suffered for so long.

He found he was able to push aside his reservations and just enjoy this, feeling as if he was exactly where he was supposed to be. He grew so comfortable that he didn't believe his eyes when tears began to stream down her face.

"Bloody hell, Mariketa. Why do you cry?"

She swiped at her cheeks. "I'm your enemy. It should please you to see me miserable."

"Should. But it does no'." She was . . . *miserable?* He racked his brain for what else she could possibly want. He'd thought he was making progress with her. "What do you need, then? To no' be unhappy?"

She jerked back from him, and he just unthreaded his fingers from her hair in time not to hurt her. "I can't do this! This gentleness from you . . . you confuse me, and I'm so tired and I *hate* you so much." Tears continued to track down her face.

"Damn you, stop this cryin', Mariketa."

At that, she went up on her knees and punched his shoulder. Her expression said she'd found that hit surprisingly satisfying, so she did it again and again, slapping and punching. "You left me in there!" His eyes narrowed as he took the blows, but he didn't stop her. "And the only reason you came back was to get well again."

"Had I that night to do over again, I'd act differently."

She finally ran out of energy, gave a halfhearted slap, then sank down onto her bottom. In a stunned tone, she murmured, "You just . . . *left* me."

The witch had her swagger and wasn't shy about using her powers—his neck still hurt from her attack. Yet had she experienced a moment of astonished disbelief like this when the stone had dropped, not only because of her predicament but because he'd done it to her?

"You were the one who told me I could no' complain because this was a competition. You said all's fair."

"It is all fair. However, this doesn't mean I want to be seduced by the man who hurt me. You looked me in the eyes and trapped me, setting me up for hell. Do you possibly think I'd want to wake up next to you? Or see you staring down at me when we had sex?" She rested her forehead in her palm, and he suspected she was too exhausted to guard her words. "I'd thought you were different."

"Regret for my actions with you weighs on me. And take pleasure in knowing that your weakening spell hit me hard." He exhaled a long breath. "I was in a minefield competing against the vampire and the Valkyrie. That bloody vampire made it so a mine was triggered just beneath me. I lost my eye, had half my face seared away. A length of shrapnel pierced my torso. I accumulated injury after injury that I could no' heal from. This information should please you."

She continued to cry, sniffling as she repeated his words: "Should. But it doesn't."

Bloody hell, this is unbearable. He had no idea what to say, no experience comforting a female away from her tears. So in the end he said nothing, just eased her down onto the pallet, his palm covering her entire shoulder.

As she stared dazedly into the fire, he sat up behind her, using his whole hand to smooth her hair back from her face, his other thumb to brush away tears. When he grazed the tip of her pointed ear, it twitched in reaction.

Eventually her eyelids grew heavy. Yet even when her eyes closed, tears continued to fall. Under his breath, he muttered, "*Damn it, witch, doona . . . hurt.*"

When her breathing grew deep and even, and he knew she was asleep, he gazed down at her, studying her. Her small, pixie nose had the lightest dusting of freckles, and her chin was delicately stubborn. That silky red hair curled about her finely boned face.

Her ruby lips were slightly parted as she slept. An exquisite, if small, female.

And, gods help me, she might be . . . mine.

Unable to stop himself, he eased down behind her. When he wrapped his arms around her and pulled her soft, wee body against his, she sighed. As a test, he nuzzled her neck. Her ear twitched again, and she curled into him closer. Even in sleep she responded to him as if she were his.

Two things he knew: Taking her would be like nothing he'd ever imagined. And second, he had to be certain of her, which meant getting that patch off her at the earliest opportunity.

19

Mari woke sometime in the night, compelled for some reason to read the letter in his bag. She feared that even after everything, the reason was jealousy.

She suspected he'd awakened when she'd left the pallet, but he said nothing as she went through his things. Really, what could he say after he'd gone through hers?

Once more, she eased the letter out and opened it, frowning to find it was from the Valkyrie Nïx, and intended *for Mari*. Why hadn't MacRieve given it to her? Instead the bastard had broken the seal and read it!

After a glare in his direction, she skimmed the lines.

> *Mariketa,*
> *Happy Accession! Behold, a gift. A skeleton*
> *key of sorts . . . a piece of the puzzle for the*
> *Witch in the Glass.*
>
> > *Fondly as ever,*
> > *Lady Nïx,*
> > *Proto-Valkyrie*

> *My mother says I must not pass*
> *Too near that glass;*
> *She is afraid that I will see*

> *A little witch that looks like me,*
> *With a red, red mouth to whisper low*
> *The very thing I should not know!*

PS: *You still owe me fifty bucks.*

What—the—hell?

What glass? Was the mother Mari's own? Why would Nïx think Mari would need this?

Mari had known Nïx all her life, and she was aware that, as confused as Nïx always seemed, the Valkyrie did not do things without reason. In fact, Mari had been around her enough to know that *everything* she did—no matter how seemingly inconsequential or crazed-sounding—was done with purpose, from a stray word to an absent touch.

With that in mind, Mari took the letter and padded past MacRieve and the fire toward the water. At the pool, she knelt down and peered at the smooth surface, wondering if the words could be an incantation.

Mari's spell casting was hit-or-miss at best, and witches were most vulnerable to another's spells when they cast their own. Spells opened the gates, and anything could get in.

As Elianna taught, "Reach for power, leave your power vulnerable."

Mari's uncontrollable, near *useless* power. What was there to lose, truly? Besides the ability to send MacRieve airborne?

Decided, she began to murmur the words, once, twice . . . on the third recitation, her reflection began to shift as if the pool had been disturbed. Then she saw something she never expected. Her eyes looked like mirrors and her hair swirled about her head, though Mari felt her hair heavy down her back in the windless cave. It was her in the water, but it wasn't.

"What . . . what is this?" she whispered.

The reflection *spoke*, answering, "*A conjuration.*"

Mari was actually conjuring? "Who *are* you?" she breathed in amazement.

"*You,*" the reflection replied.

"But how?"

"*You are the Mirror Witch. Reflections conduct your powers to you.*" The voice was Mari's own, but distorted—the way wind sounded different sieving through misted leaves.

"I can divine by mirror?" She knew of a few witches who could do this, and it was a handy talent to have.

"*You are a true captromancer.*"

Whoa. Not just a handy talent. Captromancers were extremely rare. They were said to be able not only to divine by mirrors, as astromancers did with stars, but to use them as focusing tools, protective talismans—and even as portals for travel. "But I don't understand. I've never used a mirror to aid my magick."

"*Come with me—I'll show you.*"

Mari pulled back, fear like ice building inside her veins. "In there?"

"*Are you ready, Mari?*"

"R-ready for what?" She felt danger warring with allure, her compulsion battling her aversion. This could be a trick by a sorceress, a spell to divert Mari's powers from her. She shook her head wildly. "No, I'm not ready . . . not ready . . ."

When a pale hand broke the surface of the water, Mari wanted to lunge back, to escape this, but was transfixed by the glistening apple offered in the nearly transparent palm. In that sighing voice, the reflection coaxed, *"Just have a taste . . ."*

20

⚉

Bowe swallowed, rubbing his eyes in disbelief. . . .

Yet Mariketa still was there, reaching forward to accept an apple from a ghostly wet hand.

Shooting to his feet, charging for her, he roared, "*Doona touch it!*"

His bellow echoed again and again. In the shadows all around them, the bats erupted into flight. As he sprinted past the water, out of the corner of his eye he saw the reflection of the witch—but *it didn't match her*. Mariketa hadn't glanced up at him; the woman in the water kept her brilliant eyes on him.

He lunged for Mariketa, snatching the apple from her hand, then throwing it against the wall so hard it disintegrated. Just as the bats swarmed them, he pressed her down, rolling atop her to protect her head and body.

Minutes passed. When the throng settled at last, she opened her eyes—and they reflected *him*, before gradually clearing.

"You vowed to me you would no' do magick around me!"

"I-I figured you would be asleep."

"Even worse!" Bowe had woken to find his arms empty of warm, curvy witch and had been displeased about that to a surprising degree. He'd heard her rummaging through his bag and had thought she might be searching his things for the same reason he'd done hers—because she was itching with curiosity about him. Instead she'd been intent on getting to that chilling letter. "You went through my bag."

"You went through mine! Why didn't you give me the letter? It was for me!"

"Because I bloody knew something like this would happen. The thing in the water came about because of that rhyme, did it no'? And just what in the hell *was* that thing?"

"I don't know."

"It looked like you." In a diabolical way. "If you doona know what it is, then how do you know it will no' harm you?"

She attempted a shrug.

He exhaled. "How am I to protect you if you do things like this?" That was one of the reasons he detested magick so much—it was an enemy he couldn't see, couldn't understand, and couldn't defend against. He comprehended nothing about that rhyme, or why he himself had reacted so strongly to it. "I doona suppose you have any idea about what you canna know?"

"No. No idea." Her gaze flickered over his face.

When her eyes didn't appear witchy, they were so damned lovely. Fringed with thick black lashes, they were gray like fierce storm clouds—and as intense as everything else about her. He felt as if she was *supposed* to look up at him like this. The pull of the Instinct was strong, making him feel he'd done right to protect her and now was rewarded by having her safe in his arms.

The need to kiss her suddenly became critical. . . .

"Oh, not again!" She tried to wriggle out from under

him, which only made his erection grow harder. When her lips parted on a breath, he knew she'd felt it pulse against her.

"I'll put you across the cave, MacRieve."

In a flash, he pinned her wrists behind her back. "I doona believe you can, no' with your hands like this." He eased to her side and used his free hand to begin slowly unbuttoning the shirt.

"What do you think you're do—" She broke off with a little moan when he raised his knee and firmly pressed his thigh between hers, languidly moving it against her sex.

With an openmouthed kiss on her collarbone, he pulled the shirt open, one side then the other, but he fumbled at unclasping her transparent bra from the front. This was partly because he had no experience with modern female undergarments, but also because he couldn't stop staring as her nipples budded right before his eyes, jutting against the gauzy material.

He finally sliced the front clasp with his claw. By the time he brushed the material over the tight peaks, her breathing had grown hectic, making that bared flesh rise and fall so temptingly.

Just when he was about to touch her, she struggled again, and her breasts quivered. His voice rough, he said, "Ah, beauty, now you're just showin' off."

She stilled, her face and chest flushing hotly.

Leaning down to her nipple, he said, "I've heard rumors about bedding witches, heard that if you can close your lips around one of these, the witch will be slave to your hands."

"I'm not a sla— oooh." She arched her back sharply when he licked and sucked at her.

He moved to her other breast, flicking the tip with his

tongue. When he saw she hadn't closed her eyes but was raptly watching him, he groaned against her.

Though he burned to rip off her panties and plunge between her thighs, he forced himself to slow his touch, gentling her. Her piercing caught his eye, and he brushed the backs of his fingers over it, making her jerk in reaction. "I've thought of this often over the past weeks. Kissing you all around it, flicking it with my tongue." He knew his words were arousing her even more, could scent how wet she was for him.

"I don't want this," she said with a shiver, her eyes heavy-lidded.

He rubbed his hand up her side and she flexed to it. "You're saying these words, but your body's telling me something altogether different."

"You're wrong."

"I have no' had sex in nearly two centuries, nor any kind of release in three weeks. And the last time I handled myself, I was dreaming about your body beneath mine in just this way. This would be enough to madden a male, but then to know you're aroused for me, too?"

"I am *so* not turned on for you."

"Lie about other things, but no' about this. You forget I'm a Lykae—I can scent you're aroused, and it's making me crazed. If I stroked you between your thighs, I'd find you wet, would I no'? You *ache* to be sated."

"Maybe. But not by you, MacRieve." She shook her head hard, and her eyes narrowed. "*Never* by you." She appeared utterly unflinching. "Get off me, or I'll scream."

Apparently, the young witch could deny her desire for her enemy.

At that moment, he wished he had that talent.

21

MacRieve ran his hand over his mouth. At length, he drew away from her, sitting back against the cavern wall, one knee raised.

Pulling the shirt back together, she sat up as well, then waited long moments until he finally said, "I am weary, Mariketa. So damned weary. I've suffered for long enough without this added torment from you."

"Oh, I'm tormenting you because I won't sleep with you?"

"I've got a force inside me—a strong one—screaming that you're mine. Just tell me, are you making me want you like this?"

She bit her lip—she didn't know! "You really think there's a chance I could be your . . . mate? You only get one."

"There might be ways around that," he said in an impassive tone. "I will no' be angry if you admit to any trickery now." At her expression, he amended, "I'll be ireful, but it will blow over. I doona hold grudges."

When she looked away without answering, he exhaled. "Mariketa, have you ever felt your way was lost? So bewildered you dinna know up from down any longer?"

Right now. She was bewildered by this sudden change in his demeanor, and found herself nodding.

"I have no'. *Ever*. My path has always been clear to me. Everything in black or white. Now, nothing is as it was."

"Like what?"

"Like how I was dreaming of you every night and fantasizing about you in the days I was out there fighting to get my mate back." Seeming ashamed, he glanced away, and the firelight cast his profile in shadow. "The pain from my injuries was nothing compared to my guilt." He gave a bitter laugh. "*Always* the bloody guilt. You canna understand what it's like to feel *nothing*—nothing but that."

He stood and paced. Almost to himself, he said, "Or what it's like to know you're no' whole and never will be." He ran his fingers through his hair, then stopped to meet her eyes. "Then with you, everything looks different—feels different—and I . . . damn it, Mariketa, I *want* it. So bloody much."

He crossed to her, clasped her upper arms, and pulled her to her feet. Gazing down at her, his voice breaking low, he said, "Doona bring me back to life only to destroy me once more."

The depth of pain and confusion in his expression shook her. And even after everything, she felt sympathy for him. "Look, what if I tell you everything that I know—only the truth—and you can decide what's going on? I'll lay it all out there for you, because I don't understand it."

He gave her a quick nod, then released her arms to lead her back by the fire. As if he was her host, he waved her to sit on the pallet. When she did, he eased his towering frame down, sitting to face her.

"Okay, MacRieve, I can vow to the Lore that I did not consciously set out to make you believe I'm your mate. I have *never* enchanted anyone. My friends could work over their teachers from the first grade on, but I never had that ability."

He began to have a hopeful light in his eyes, so she hastily added, "But then I was never a seeress until the tomb either." At his questioning look, she explained, "In any coven, there are members from each of the five castes of witches. That's why we stick together, because the collective whole is so strong. Well, I'm supposed to have powers from all five castes—the powers of a warrior, conjurer, seeress, enchantress, and healer—but I haven't been able to tap into or harness any of them. Then tonight, I somehow knew you were coming. So there's the seeress part. When I attacked you and killed the incubi, there was the warrior. Just now, I conjured that reflection."

"And you healed yourself as well. If you enchanted me, you've done five out of five."

When she nodded, the obvious hope in him grew dimmer. "Then what about the night of the Hie assembly?"

She frowned. "I did *nothing* that night."

"If you did nothing, then why could I no' take my eyes from you? There was a bloody vampire in the area, one I'd fought, and still I was struggling with everything I was to keep an eye on him and no' to stare at you." *And he's up* . . .

When he crossed his arms over his chest with a knowing nod, she blurted out, "The night we kissed, I did will you to want me as fiercely as I wanted you—I consciously did it, and even then I worried that I was *enthralling* you!"

Instead of looking discouraged, he appeared pleased with her. "So you wanted me *fiercely?*"

She felt her cheeks heating. "That was then, and this is now, MacRieve. And think about it, if I was ever going to successfully spellbind anyone, it'd be you—you're like a lightning rod for my powers."

"So I'm unique to you, too. Maybe I'm to help you in some way?"

She ignored that and heedlessly continued. "It might not even have been you I truly wanted. The night that you saw me without my cloak, the damage was done. Maybe I was just taking advantage of the situation—"

"What do you mean by *damage*? And why *did* you wear the cloak and glamour?"

Tell him everything. Let him make sense of it. She exhaled and muttered, "It was predicted that a warrior from the Lore would recognize me as his mate—"

"A *warrior* from the *Lore*?" *And he's up again!* "Then it's me!"

Gods, he has the sexiest grin. He always appeared so bitter, so grim, yet then, with one heart-stopping curl of his lips, his entire countenance changed, his amber eyes growing warm.

"It must be me, lass."

"But this could merely be a trick! You do recognize me as your mate, true, but that doesn't mean you should or even that it's real. I could very well have enthralled you. Some witches only have to recognize that they want something, and then, all of a sudden, it's theirs. That could have happened."

"And yet you believe that you could have left behind that enthrallment when you took the mortality curse away? You were weak and nigh out of your head with fatigue and injuries. You canna look me in the eyes and say you would be capable of removing one without the other."

When she pursed her lips, he raised his eyebrows.

She looked away and said, "Maybe not in the past—"

"Did you feel another of your hexes?"

After a moment, she shook her head.

"And you dinna do anything to me at the Hie. If you had no' had your glamour on that night, I would have recognized your scent then." *Way up*.

"You're reaching, because you want something definite. You want your black and white. And that's not what you're going to get with me."

He had a self-satisfied look on his face, a relieved one, that made her want to groan with frustration. "If you're telling me the truth, Mariketa, then there's a chance you truly are my mate."

"Why would you get two? Are you special?"

"You might be . . . you might be reincarnated." He frowned. "You doona look shocked."

"No. My friend Regin has a reincarnate, a berserker who's mad for her and keeps coming back. And he never misses an Accession."

"Aye, it makes sense that the Accession could fuel these events—*your* reincarnation as well."

She didn't feel that this was round two for her— wouldn't she sense it in some way? "Was your mate like me? Do we resemble each other? Act alike?"

"You're nothing alike, other than your names and ears. She was fey as well."

"How did you meet her—by entombing?"

He ignored the last and answered, "I'd known her all her life. After a five-year absence I'd returned to her father's kingdom, and she'd grown into a woman."

"Wouldn't you have known what she was the minute you met her?"

He shook his head. "'No' always. Females of different species often need to reach maturity to trigger the Instinct."

"I just don't sense this about myself. And that berserker always gets his memories of his previous lives. I don't remember anything like that."

"You're young still."

"Say all this is true—"

"It's true."

"—the fact remains that I don't want you. Even if fate decreed that we had a bond, I definitely don't recognize it. I don't even like you."

"If we had no bad blood between us, would you . . . like me?"

"I'd be attracted to you, but there's *no way* I'd want anything permanent with you—bad blood or not."

"What the hell's so wrong with me?" His eyes flickered, and the hint of uncertainty he'd just revealed was drowned out by a surge of arrogance. "I'm strong, I can protect you, and I'm rich. And I vow to you, lass, once you experience what it's like to share my bed, you will no' ever want to leave it."

His eyes bored into hers as he said the last, and despite herself, his utter confidence in this area affected her, forcing her to wonder what tricks a twelve-century-old immortal would've picked up over the years.

She inwardly shook herself. "MacRieve, when I settle down it's going to be with a male that has—oh, I don't know—a sense of humor, or of modesty. How about a lack of scathing hatred toward witches? Maybe a zest for life? Too much to ask that he's born in the same millennium?"

"Some of these things canna be changed, but know that I was no' always so . . . grave as I am now."

"It doesn't matter. We're just too different. I need a male who will get along with my friends, my witch friends, who'll be current enough to know the difference between emo rock and jangle pop, and who'll be able to get me through the ice world in Zelda."

MacRieve was no doubt speculating in what ice dimension this mysterious land of Zelda was. He finally said, "These differences are surmountable—"

"And the age difference? You keep talking about how young I am, but all you're doing is reminding me how old you are. Any minute now you're going to say something really lame like 'When I was your age . . . ,' and I'm just not going to be able to keep from laughing at you."

He scowled at that, but still said, "I'll change your mind about me. You'll warm to me."

"In two days? That's your plan? Forget it."

"Damn it, witch, are you no' even curious about where this could lead?"

"No, but I am curious how you can be when you despise my kind. How quick you were to tell me that when I suggested we work together in the Hie! I will never forget your disgust." Did his jaw clench? "Why *do* you despise us so much?"

He shrugged. "With witches you never know what you're in for. All false faces and deviousness."

"But with Lykae, what you see is what you get? Oh, wait, I totally forgot about the beast that lives inside you. And then by the time you see what you're in for, it's too late, isn't it?"

He narrowed his eyes. "I'm one among the most powerful species on this earth—none are stronger than the Lykae—and I've trained for war or fought it for my entire life. Yet you, with your wee body and utter lack of training, can still pin me by the throat. It's no' *natural*. Witches are no' natural."

"That can't be all."

"That's all you'll hear tonight."

"You know what? I'll play. If you answer one question correctly, I might consider possibly thinking about giving you a shot to maybe win me over."

"Ask it, lass."

"What if we somehow worked through all the obstacles between us and were together for a couple of years or so, and you were given another chance to go back for your mate? There could be another key. Would you ignore it if it was handed to you?"

Emotions seemed to pass over his face. He scrubbed his hand across the back of his neck. "I could lie, but I will no'. I'd use it."

Her lips parted. "Then why in the hell would I invest my time and my feelings when you won't be doing the same?" She stood, storming away from him. "Game over, MacRieve."

"But you have to understand why." He shot to his feet and seized her elbow. "I believe it would be you."

"I don't feel like I have a pre-owned soul. And furthermore, I like myself. Other than some late-blooming magickal powers and some sealed legal records, I think I'm pretty fucking nifty. Yet you would just wipe me out entirely?"

"You would no' be wiped out. Just different."

"What about my friends and family?" Not that Mari's family—being Jillian—would overly miss her. "What about the prophesy, of being Awaited? I have responsibilities."

"You'd have other family, another destiny—"

"If I'm a reincarnate and that soul's not available when I'm born, then I'm not *me*. You know that's true." She was shaken by how much this bastard was hurting her with this. "So just a hint: The next time you're courting a female, try *not* to divulge that you would readily wipe out her entire existence with the turn of a key—so you could be with another woman you preferred over her!"

22

Bloody brilliant, MacRieve, Bowe thought as he lay staring at the cavern ceiling. Drops of water traveled along it against gravity, before trickling down a stalactite. He exhaled. Not only hadn't he made progress with her, he'd likely deepened her hatred.

He was accustomed to doing as he pleased—and to having others do what he pleased as well. Yet when he'd wanted to talk to her more, to explain, the look in her eyes had said she'd been about to snap.

Bowe knew he shouldn't have answered as he had. Of course, she wouldn't view the situation the same as he did. But her question had caught him completely off guard. He was used to thinking along those lines but hadn't expected her to.

He should have just lied. As soon as the thought arose, he dismissed it because he didn't ever want to lie to his female. Except that she might not be his at all, and now he was farther away from the means to determine for certain.

He glanced over at her, lying on the other side of the fire with her back to him. Could Mariketa truly be a different version of Mariah? An utterly different version? Or was he seizing on reincarnation because it absolved him of guilt— for Mariah's death *and* for his undeniable lust for another?

The two looked nothing alike but for their ears. Mariah had been tall and lithe and so graceful, seeming to float when she walked. The petite witch rolled her hips sensuously until her every step sent blood rushing to his groin and away from his brain. For the thirtieth time tonight, he ran the heel of his palm along his shaft. He wanted to watch her walk naked to a bed he was in.

He told himself he wasn't comparing the two females to determine which was *better* but only to explore his reincarnation theory.

Hell, he didn't even know what he would do with a key now. Would he truly go back if he believed the witch would never live?

That was the crux of it, because if he knew for a fact that he would erase the witch, then he could be certain that she shared a soul with Mariah. And with that certainty, he could stay with the witch, even if there was a key, and there would be no guilt.

Wait. Why had he immediately decided on the witch in this situation? If he could just as easily have Mariah, wouldn't he prefer her? Mariah had been everything that was perfect.

Yet for the first time, Bowe admitted—with difficulty and reluctance—that she might not have been perfect . . . for *him*.

For most of his adult life, Bowe had said what was on his mind, and damn the consequences. Life was too long not to. But he remembered that his uttering even the mildest oaths would dismay Mariah—no matter that he and his kind had been using those words for millennia before they'd been deemed bad.

He'd often felt like he was walking on eggshells around

her. He'd striven to change for her, hoping to make himself a gentleman for her. Yet some traits were just a part of his nature.

He enjoyed his bed play dirty, and like all males of his kind, he was aggressive in bed. But Mariah had been a fey princess living in the eighteen hundreds and had been stymied with a very limited sexual mind-set. She'd never been aroused by Bowe—had never desired him as he did her. Bowe had known this, for she'd made no secret of it. With her violet eyes glinting, she would stroke him under the chin as she vowed that she would be the one to tame his beastly nature.

So he'd struggled to ignore his baser urges because she would have been horrified or even fainted if he'd acted on them. The sex words he'd wanted to use he'd stifled. The places he'd wanted to kiss her he'd tried to put from his mind. . . .

He'd never claimed her, and the one time he'd touched her between her thighs, his heart had sunk to find her utterly unaffected by his attentions. As cold as ice.

But when he'd stroked Mariketa, she'd been lush and wet, her body so ready to receive him. And the way he spoke? It *aroused* her. He knew the self-pleasuring witch would indulge in whatever would give them satisfaction. That night in the tomb, if he'd decided to taste her sex, she would have moaned with anticipation and spread her legs wide for him.

Maybe she hadn't been seething with power that night, but with passion, a passion stoked *by him*. Bowe hadn't realized until now how much Mariah's lack of desire had affected his confidence.

At once, he flushed at his uncharitable thoughts toward

her. She'd been a sweet lass, and she'd had much to offer a male.

She'd been a gentle fey of royal blood and good family, and marrying her would have brought about a valuable alliance between her kind and his. Elegant Mariah had chosen him to take care of her. Out of all her royal suitors—and there were many—she'd chosen *him* to marry. She would've been a good mate and a caring mother.

He frowned. Except that she'd told him she hadn't wanted to have children. No matter how long he'd always looked forward to a family.

But then she hadn't been a bloody witch either.

Bowe turned to his side away from Mariketa. This confusion wasn't as racking as the constant guilt, but at least with the guilt he'd known where he stood.

He heard Mariketa stirring and recognized that her desire was building once more. She eased to her side, then over again. Oh, bloody hell, she was not furtively grazing those sensitive breasts of hers. She hurt for what he would gladly kill to give her.

He palmed his shaft through his jeans yet again, hissing in an agonized breath. One hundred and eighty years had passed since he'd been brought to come by another. Not ten feet from him, a trembling bundle of lust in the form of a fantasy lay aching for a male's touch.

How much more could he take?

23

O verstimulation.

Being on the cusp of immortality left a lot to be desired. Literally.

Mari hadn't had a pocket rocket in her bag for no reason. She'd needed the thrice-daily release it provided like an ailing person needed medicine—she might as well have had a prescription for it. And now she craved an orgasm so badly that she'd briefly considered using MacRieve.

How could she still be attracted to him after his admission? She tried to ignore the need. *Think of other things.*

She *would not* think about how firm his lips were or how unyielding his erection had been when it had rubbed against her ass.

She wondered if she could work this out for herself right now, without him hearing. Two quick strokes and she'd be done. At least for a couple of hours. Maybe he was already asleep—

"Gods, Marike ta, I need to touch you."

Not asleep. "Go to hell."

"You think I canna tell how much you need a male? You keep forgetting what I am."

"I know *exactly* what you are. And what you're capable of."

He crossed to her so silently, she didn't even know he'd moved until he lay beside her. "Let me help you."

"Any closer, MacRieve, and I'll pin you to the ceiling and cackle at your expression like the witch that I am."

Her eyes must have changed, because he narrowed his. "This will only get worse. If you're truly transitioning, I canna imagine how you must be feeling."

Pretty damned bad. And by *bad* she meant *horny*. The need was unrelenting—how she would ever get used to this she couldn't imagine. She'd already been in love with sex even before she'd been on the verge of immortality and an eternity of superhuman lust.

And yet she hadn't had it—*in four years*. The timing of her breakup with the demon Acton had been regrettable—right at the advent of the cloak years. When she hadn't a chance in hell of attracting another lover.

Now she could enjoy sex once more. Now she yearned for this Lykae to stroke her.

"If you will no' let me pleasure you, then pleasure yourself." She'd begun to notice that the more aroused he grew, the more pronounced his accent became.

"Maybe I just will—if you leave."

"I canna leave you, no' alone in here. Just do it. We've established that you're no' shy."

He was so close that she could feel the heat of his body and smell his clean masculine scent. "I know your game. You think I'll get so lost that when you reach out, I'll welcome your touch—"

"I'd vow to the Lore that I would no' touch you. It will give you what you need and me a chance to earn your trust. There's no need for you to suffer just because you doona trust me."

"And what exactly would you be doing?"

"The same."

"Oh," she answered inanely. The idea of seeing him handling his thick erection until he came made rational thought leave her brain.

"I believe I'd go to my knees if I thought it would move you in this." His golden eyes were so intense when he gazed at her—as if there was nothing else in the world worth seeing. "Or I'd return the hand you gave me tonight." His voice husky, he said, "Mariketa, think of how good it will feel."

She couldn't seem to take her eyes from his, even when she amazed herself by skimming her hand down her front to her panties.

His brows drew together. "*Ah, you good lass,*" he rasped.

She swallowed. "You start."

His hand flew to his zipper. When he began pulling it down, the sound was surprisingly loud in the cave. He drew it open slowly as if he didn't want to spook her from what they were about to do. Her breaths came quick once he grasped himself in his jeans.

Yet movement out of the corner of her eye drew her attention away. A sizable cave spider crawled along his leg, but MacRieve was so absorbed in looking at her that he didn't even notice.

Rising to her knees, she reached for it. He must have thought she was aiming for his groin because he hissed an oath, and his hands seized her waist. After letting the spider take hold of three of her fingers, she brought it forward, displaying it to him. MacRieve abruptly released her.

When she returned from relocating it outside and lay back down, his eyes were narrowed. "You were *terrified* of that scorpion in the tomb, but no' of a spider the same size?"

"I'm not afraid of things like that anymore, not after I had insects crawling all over me . . ." *In the dark, for weeks.*

Her lips parted. What a timely reminder.

A bucket of cold water poured over her head couldn't have awakened her more sharply from this sensual stupor. Making her tone biting, she said, "And actually, I think the incubi varied my steady diet of blood with some, so I'm accustomed. As a *witch* I'm supposed to have a connection with all low creatures like that anyway."

His face fell.

"You *almost* made me forget what you're really like, *Bowen the Bitter*." She turned to her side, away from him. "But I'll be on my guard now."

24

Mari woke the next morning as surly as a bear roused in winter. She felt uncomfortable in her own skin, exhausted from the surprising demands that thwarted desire placed on her body.

Blearily rubbing her eyes, she scanned the cave but didn't see MacRieve. He'd gone, leaving behind fruit for her, which she regarded with a glare. Fruit was not her breakfast mainstay. She wasn't a coffee drinker, but she was an Eggo eater, and she hadn't had a single waffle in weeks.

He'd also left a change of clothes for her and had already packed up everything but her hiking gear and her toiletries. Did he think to dress her now?

One thing that was missing from the ensemble: a cloak. For the first time in years, Mari would get ready for the day without a cloak or glamour.

Was she worried about the prediction? Not really. She suspected she could handle the "immortal warrior." Her strategy? Throwing him.

In fact, she couldn't believe she'd dreaded this so much and for so long, and scowled to think of all the days at the beach she'd missed and the dates she'd failed to secure because males thought she was a hideous little troll covered in yards of scarlet cloth.

She could have resumed her glamour last night, but what was the point? The horse was already out of the barn in that matter. Besides, she hadn't realized how cumbersome and draining the glamour had been until she'd been freed of it—she felt like she'd shed a ten-pound parasite.

Once she rose and began motivating, she braided her hair into two plaits to cover her ears, as she hadn't had to do in years. Then she pulled her mirrored compact from her toiletry case—but *not* to check her hair or to make sure that her eyes weren't puffy from crying last night. No, she wanted to further investigate her new discovery.

Gazing into the mirror, she swallowed, then whispered, "My mother says I must not pass . . ." When she'd finished the rhyme, her own reflection was replaced by the visage with shining eyes and swirling hair. Mari was actually conjuring, using the power of yet another caste. Because . . . she was a freaking captromancer!

She decided to ask the mirror something she had always wanted to know. "What does the mark on my back mean?"

"In a dead language, it says, the Queen of Reflections."

"A queen?" A witch was considered a queen of an element when she was more powerful with it than any other witch. Mari had never met one before.

"What's the warning in the rhyme? What can't I know?"

"I'll show you." The hand broke the surface of the mirror, the glass becoming pliable to allow it—and the apple she presented—to fit through.

Mari stared at the shining apple, her mouth unexpectedly watering for it as though it were a waffle. She shook her head hard. "No, why don't you just tell me?"

"*All your questions can be answered if you come with me.*"

"Well, if you know so much, then tell me why Nïx gave the rhyme to me instead of Elianna. Or Jillian."

"*Take my hand.*"

"You're only going to answer so many questions at a time, aren't you?" Mari narrowed her eyes with realization. "And like a classic, frustrating oracle, you're rarely going to give me extrapolation or edification."

The reflection grinned coyly. Great. A glassy magick eight ball. Mari began to suspect that this reflection was going to prove to be like that little computer paperclip assistant—at first it helps, but after a while you just want the paperclip to die.

In any case, Mari had her own suspicions about why it had been Nïx who'd given her the letter. Valkyrie grew stronger as they aged, and some in the Lore had begun to whisper that Nïx had become powerful enough to *affect* the outcome of an Accession. Nïx had even mentioned it in the letter.

Mari told the reflection, "If that's all you have to say, then I'm going to log off."

"*Don't forget the apple.*"

As Mari accepted it, she mumbled to herself, "Don't forget the apple, meh, meh, meh," aware that she was making fun of her own voice.

Though she craved it, she was nervous, at once tempted to take a bite, but fearing to.

In fairy tales—which were almost always true—wicked witches proffered apples with evil intent. But apples were held sacred by all witches as symbols of knowledge and foresight. There was no more reason to think it evil than to think it good.

Holding it in both hands, she glanced around uneasily. Perhaps she shouldn't be alone in a shadowy cave the first time she made this leap. Yes, she would taste it . . . *later*. Decided, she slipped it into her hiking sack.

When she exited the cave, she found the morning mist was thick, the sky cloudy overhead. She blinked and lowered her face, disappointment settling over her that there was no sun to be felt. Vampires got more sun than she had for the last twenty-one days.

And she wasn't likely to get any in the hours to come. In preparing for this trip, she'd read about the jungles in the area and had learned that only a small percentage of the sunlight that hit a rain forest canopy made it to the floor. To catch the light, most of the trees were tall and spindly with an umbrella of leaves at the top. Which made for an odd environment—even as it was gloomy, the forest was open like a warehouse with intermittent pillars to support the roof.

She saw the others were gathered nearby, though MacRieve stood off to the side. All eyes were on her, with Cade's focus on her neck. Unnerved by their scrutiny, she wanted to blurt out, "We didn't do anything!"

Instead she turned to Rydstrom and casually asked, "Hey, top, what's the op?"

MacRieve grated, "Who made him the . . . top?"

"Rydstrom's like a *king*." She looked him up and down. "And you're . . . *not*."

"I'm third in line . . ." He trailed off at Rydstrom's amused glance.

Rydstrom answered her, "We're going to have to push hard to make it into Belize before you're to call in. But let us know if you need to rest." When she nodded, he continued,

"Cade's on point. I'll take the lead, with the females between the males." To MacRieve, he said, "You bring up the rear."

She knew the Lykae's eyes were on her ass when he huskily rumbled, "Any *day o' the week.*"

Then MacRieve stood right behind her, his toes to her heels, as if taking his job very seriously. "If you need help climbing, I'll assist you. And doona touch *anything*—moving or inanimate. Doona pull on vines—ever—and try to step exactly where the others do. Let them take the risk. There are snakes in this underbrush, some that'll go out of their way to strike. The fer-de-lance for one."

She'd read enough in her research to know that *fer-de-lance* equaled *bad*.

"And doona drink any water that has no' been boiled. I've a canteen in the pack that's already been processed for you. Just tell me if you need a drink."

"Are you done explaining to me things that are *not* counterintuitive?" she asked, huffily adjusting her knapsack.

Tierney laughed as he finished one banana and swiftly peeled another. "Looks like the werewolf struck out last night, huh, Scot?" he said between bites, seeming bent on regaining in one morning all the weight he'd lost.

Reminded that MacRieve preferred another *version* of her, Mari cast an overly pleasant smile over her shoulder. "He lost the entire series. All pennant hopes . . . *dashed*."

Cade cast a grin at her before starting off.

"Watch your step, witchling," MacRieve rasped at her ear, his temper obviously flaring. "I have no' even brought my A game yet."

* * *

Bowe was on edge after just a mile into their journey.

So much could harm her. While they were playing protect the mortal, it seemed everything out here conspired against them. Bad water, serpents, a certain *frog* could bloody drop her.

He felt as if he were carrying the most delicate crystal through a war zone.

"So are you planning on dressing me in addition to everything else?" she asked once they'd cleared a challenging rise.

"I planned to pack as much as I could this morning, so you could sleep later," he lowered his voice, "or take care of what went unfinished last night." He'd amazed himself by behaving so unselfishly as that. Her unfulfilled desire made it more likely that he'd get her into bed with him, and yet, he couldn't stand to think of her suffering. "I was attempting to be considerate. Though I've little experience with it."

"I'm not talking to you about this. I'm just *not*."

"I can feel your need as strong as my own."

"Maybe I do have these needs—doesn't mean you're the one I'll choose to help me work them out." Her gaze drifted to Cade, who was greedily chugging water.

His voice low and seething, Bowe said, "You regard him with an appraising eye one more time, Mariketa, and you're going to get that demon killed. All he wants is to 'attempt' you. Do you ken what that means?"

"In fact, I do *ken* what it means. *In the throes, you know.* One of my boyfriends was a demon."

"Boyfriends?" He frowned. "You mean *lovers*. How bloody many have you had?" He stopped. "Are you free with yourself, then? With other males? Because that'll be ending—"

"What'd you think?" she asked over her shoulder. "That I was a virgin?"

"You're only twenty-three," he said, sounding very stodgy, even to himself. "And I try no' to think of any male before me. But if you were no' an innocent, then I'd hoped it would have been once, in the dark, with a ham-handed human who was so bad you had to stifle a yawn or fight against laughing."

She shrugged. "I'm sure the number of notches in my bedpost can't compare to yours."

"Aye, but I'm twelve hundred years old! Even if I had one female a year, you'd understand how they could accumulate."

"Well, I am young." Just as he felt a flicker of ease, she murmured in a sexy voice, "But, baby, I've been *busy*."

His fists clenched.

"Jealous?"

She probably wouldn't think he'd admit to it, but in a low tone, he said, "Aye, I envy any man that's had his hands on you." She gave him an enigmatic, studying expression. "Now, if I guess the number you've taken into your bed, then you'll tell me if I'm right."

She hastily faced forward once more. "Not playing. Get bent."

He narrowed his eyes. "One. You've had one." Her shoulders stiffened barely perceptibly, and he wanted to sag with relief.

"Why would you say that?" she asked in a nonchalant tone.

"Because any male worthy of you would kill a rival who tried to steal you from him. I'm guessing the demon was your first and last. And how did you get him to let you go, then?"

"What if I told you I was still seeing him?"

Bowe shook his head. "No' considering the way you were with me that first night. Besides, if he allowed you to enter the Hie without being there to guard you, he does no' deserve you. When we return, I'll kill him on principle."

25

The deeper they went, the more *Land Before Time*–esque everything seemed to Mari.

Something growing on the tree trunks made them look furry—and creepy—in the mist. The squirrels she spied weren't gray but red, and many of the leaves on bushes were larger than she was.

Though most of the spindly trees had roots that forked out *above* the soil, looking like the veins they actually were, the ceiba tree's trunk was gigantic, its roots as tall as she was and as thick as her desk at Andoain—

"Duck." MacRieve reached over her with his machete to cut an overhanging branch. He continued to clear away even more than the others in front of her had—until there was twice as much room as she needed.

"Are my hips wider than I'd figured?"

"Doona want an animal near you. There's more danger here than you're aware of."

At that moment, howler monkeys roared from the canopy just above, startling her.

"Your hips, for the record, are faultless."

She experienced a small—trifling, really—thrill at his compliment, as well as an impulse to swish her hips at him.

Then she woke the hell up again and concentrated on navigating the jungle.

Trees fell where streams eroded the soil, so in the areas lining the banks, trunks were toppled over each other like Lincoln logs. The opportunistic underbrush shot up for its spot in the sun—an explosion of growth on the floor that was backbreaking to slog through.

Gradually, she and MacRieve became distanced from everyone—Rydstrom pushed hard with Tera right behind him, Cade scouted the trail ahead, and Tierney disappeared repeatedly to hunt for more food. This seemed to suit MacRieve fine as he took every excuse to touch her, wiping away a bead of sweat from her cheek or brushing a leaf from her hair.

At yet another pile of trunks, MacRieve simply picked her up and carried her. Then later, he did it again at a rivulet—and once more under a log pileup. Over or under and through the woods.

Over, under, over . . . under. At one point, he sat her on a high trunk, putting them face-to-face. "What're my chances of stealing a kiss from you right now?" His white shirt was unbuttoned halfway down and sweat sheened on his muscular chest. After last night, she now knew how breathtaking *all* of his body was—every inch of it.

Still she answered, "None point none. I don't want you to kiss me."

"I think you do a little." He brushed a damp lock over her forehead, then smoothly moved his hand just before she could bat it away.

"All I want is to get home, back to my Lykae-free life. Now let me down."

"I will no'. No' without a kiss for toll." He was easing

closer as if she were a skittish animal he didn't want to scare away. And though she dreaded losing her tenuous control over her *overstimulation*, she still was tempted to close her eyes and accept his lips on hers.

"*That's it, lass,*" he rumbled, gently cupping the side of her face with his big hand.

At the last second, Mari reached into her knapsack and snatched out her apple, bringing it between them.

His eyes went wide, then narrowed. "Doona dare," he said.

So, naturally, she did. Once she'd taken a hearty bite, he looked as if he'd just stifled a shudder and dropped his hand.

Around a mouthful, she said, "But I thought you wanted to make out!"

Stiffly setting her down, he turned from her and continued on, leaving her to roll her eyes at the succulent taste. It was like she'd eaten a super apple—crisper, more flavorful, and juicier than any before. She even felt more energized. As soon as she'd devoured it, she craved another and wondered when she could convene with the reflection again.

When she tossed the core, MacRieve glanced back at her. A thick lock of jet black hair fell over one of his eyes, making her want to sigh. Regrettably, Mari *did* find herself wanting him to kiss her. After everything, her attraction to him burned as hot as ever. Yet even if MacRieve was sexy—insufferably so—she wasn't going to be seduced into forgiving the hateful thing he'd said last night.

Especially not because he removed some foliage from her way.

He admittedly would be willing to forget her, and go

back for some perfect fey princess. If there was one thing that Mari despised, it was to be passed up. And yet it kept happening to her.

What is it about me? she asked herself for the thousandth time.

Both of her parents had found something they preferred over raising her. It wasn't as if she'd been a demanding daughter. Hell, if her father hadn't died he could've returned at any time and she would've forgiven the past. He could've shown up on her fifteenth birthday with some unwitting-absentee-dad gift like a tea set or a Barbie oven. Mari would've been so grateful she'd have held off getting her learner's permit to bake cakes with a lightbulb.

Yet he hadn't come back—he hadn't even called her. Not once. It was like he'd disappeared from the face of the earth. One day she had a father; the next day she hadn't.

But Jillian's desertion had hurt her the worst. If things had been bad between Mari and her, then her leaving wouldn't have been so devastating. But life with her had been *wonderful.*

She remembered her mother blindfolded and smiling on the beach, arms out, as she'd tried to catch Mari, who'd been squealing with laughter. *"Where's my little witch?"* she'd cooed, with her red hair shining like fire in the sun. When Mari had let Jillian catch her, she'd swung her up, and then they'd collapsed laughing onto the sand.

Elianna had explained that her parents were—or had been—Important People, and that they had—or had had—Important Things to Do. . . .

Acton, Mari's first love, had ditched her as well. For years, the young demon had been her boyfriend. He'd courted her when they'd been fourteen, taken her at sixteen, and then she'd taken him at every opportunity for the next three years.

She'd been happy with him until he'd thrown her over for a tall, willowy nymph with flowing golden locks. Well, not technically thrown her over. Because storm demons didn't have a single fated demoness, they often kept harems, and he'd still wanted a relationship with Mari as well as with the nymph. That was bad enough, but it was clear Mari would have been B team if she'd stayed in the game.

Of course she hadn't, but losing him had hurt so much and for so long. He was her first love and letting him go had nearly killed her.

Seemed Mari always was B team. Was that her fate?

She glared over at MacRieve. Ten-to-one odds said his fey princess was blond and tall.

And the Lykae wasn't merely choosing another woman over Mari—he preferred what he thought was another version of her.

As if reading her mind, MacRieve said, "Been thinkin' about the question you asked me last night."

"Oh, I have been, too," she said in a deliberate tone, her anger simmering. The werewolf had no idea he was sidling round a spring trap hungry for his paw.

"And what have you come up with, then?"

"No, no, you first." When he hesitated, she added, "I *insist*."

"I doona know that I'd answer it the same," he finally said. "The more I'm around you, the more I . . . the better you appear—even for a witch."

Suave, Lykae, melt my heart.

"Now you tell me."

She met his eyes. "I was thinking that if you don't come to a different conclusion, I'll be forced to protect myself."

He hesitated, clearly not presented with the answer he'd expected.

"It's a simple matter of self-preservation, MacRieve. If this reincarnation could possibly have taken place, then there's no way I'll allow you to go back and wipe me out. I'll destroy *you* first."

"Could you do it? You could no' kill me yesterday."

"You weren't intent on erasing me yesterday." She cast him a menacing smile, feeling very witchy. "Besides, I'd already killed my quota for the day."

26

I 've always wondered what goes on behind coven doors," Cade said to Mari when he'd returned from recon several miles ahead.

"I really can't speak for all covens, but mine is pretty worthless. Lots of soap opera and internet addiction." She was supposed to lead them to greatness, but then, Mari liked her soaps, too. "Have you pictured a slew of hoary old women cackling over a cauldron?"

He raised his brows. "Yes."

"If someone busted out a cauldron, we'd chortle with laughter and make fun of them for being 'old skool' for months. And you rarely see hoary old women because most witches use glamours of some sort."

She noticed MacRieve seemed to be listening intently. Even Rydstrom and the archers appeared interested in this topic.

"Do you really chant spells and make blood sacrifices?" Cade asked.

"We chant spells when they're new, but they quickly become second nature. It's like you wouldn't say to yourself, 'I am walking to the kitchen, and there I will boil water for tea.' You would just do it. But if it was the first time you'd ever walked to a kitchen or had tea, you might talk yourself through it."

"And the blood sacrifices?" MacRieve prompted.

Mari gazed around at everyone. "Do you guys really want me to talk about *witchery?*"

Cade hastily said, "Yes," just as MacRieve grated, "Aye." MacRieve in particular seemed absorbed in everything she was explaining. Could he really feign interest like this?

"Well, some witches still do the blood thing. But in our coven, we look at it like this—giving up whatever is prized and personal is a sacrifice. In the old days that was a lamb or a chicken because giving up food would be a great sacrifice. But now . . . if I wanted to call upon Hekate's altar, I could give up my iPod and feel the sting."

"What were you awaited to do?" Tera asked.

"I have no idea," she replied. "No one does—there's nothing but speculation."

Cade said, "Maybe you were supposed to destroy that tomb."

MacRieve gave a humorless laugh. "Do you think that's all the witch has in her? You've no' been on the receiving end of her powers as I have."

Mari was startled—she'd been thinking the same thing. She hadn't wanted to hit the high point of her life at only twenty-three.

"What enemies do the witches have that you could vanquish?" Tierney asked, plucking at the meat of a cracked-open coconut. Exactly how far had he run toward the coast to reach a palm tree?

She answered, "There are some wizards who went rogue, a sorcerer who likes to murder pregnant witches—"

"If you're to be the greatest witch," MacRieve interrupted, "then you've been put here to fight the greatest evil. Fate does no' blow her bullets for nothing."

"That's not possible," she said. "No mortal or even immortal can defeat our greatest enemy."

"Why no'?"

"Because she's a goddess." Mari drank heartily of the processed water, then wiped her mouth on her shoulder. "Or she was. Her name is Häxa, the Queen of False Faces."

"What's her damage?" Tera asked.

"Again, do you really want to hear this?"

MacRieve's "Aye" just beat out Cade's "Yes."

"Okay, then," she said slowly. "In the beginning of the Wiccae, there were three goddess witches, sisters. Hela was all good, Häxa was all bad, and Hekate was both."

"But you said you worship Hekate, right?" Tierney said, between chews. "That means you worship a goddess who was part evil."

"She was a balance of good and evil. We believe it's all about balance. All good is bad. The universe can't handle all creation without destruction."

"All sunshine makes a desert," Cade offered, and when she smiled and said, "Exactly," MacRieve shot him a killing look.

"When Häxa kept growing stronger, Hekate and Hela bound her powers—made her an immortal instead of a goddess."

"Why didn't they just kill her?" MacRieve asked. Naturally, that would be *his* first instinct.

"They can't. All three are witches at heart, and it's impossible for one of our kind to kill a member of her own family. And others have failed to take her out because

Häxa is still extremely powerful—she feeds on misery, seeding it in others, then harvesting it." It was even rumored that she kept living beings in her lair, frozen in eternal agony, feeding off their misery forever.

"What does she look like?" MacRieve quickly asked.

"She can assume the form of anything, or anyone, living or dead. No one knows her true face. She could be any one of us . . ."—Mari made her voice theatrically ominous—"*and we'd never know it.*"

"How does she choose her victims?" MacRieve asked impatiently.

"There's no discernible pattern. She'll strike out against a despot as easily as an innocent farm girl."

MacRieve seemed to mull this answer for long moments, then he said, "Is it true you witches will no' heal others without payment?"

She should have known MacRieve would cut straight to the heart of why witches could never gain the respect of other Lorekind. She swallowed, then admitted, "Mostly, it's . . . true." As expected, everyone grew quiet. "But you have to understand why." MacRieve raised his brows as if he couldn't wait to hear this. "A thousand years ago, witches gave freely, over and over, but we were always ultimately persecuted for it. My ancestors concluded that our kind needed the protection and clout that money could buy. The bottom line is that witches who live in mansions and have the ear of kings don't get *burned to death* as often as those who live in toadstool hovels at the edge of the forest."

MacRieve's expression was inscrutable, and she couldn't get a sense of what the others were thinking either. Should she try to convince them of the witches' plight? To point out that no other faction in the Lore was as persecuted as they'd been?

The opportunity was lost when the brush grew thick again. Conversation became difficult, which left her free to experiment more with the mirror.

She opened the compact in her roomy pants pocket. Merely touching the glass seemed to give her focus. Mari had long learned all the spells expected of her but had never been able to utilize them. Could she now, with the help of a focusing tool?

As she slowly rubbed her thumb in circles on the glass, magick rose up in her hand, but now it felt centered, concentrated. The mirror did in fact conduct her powers, steering them, almost like a ground wire for electricity.

While she was enjoying this heady control, she decided to test a few minor spells on the werewolf—because it would be good practice, and by *good practice* she meant *amusing for her*.

She caused a root to hike up directly in front of his feet. When he tripped, she folded her lips in, biting back a laugh.

Magick . . . *good*.

For the next hour, whenever his boots came untied just in time for the laces to collect bullet ants, or limbs whacked him across the face, or he scarcely dodged bird and monkey droppings, he always regarded her with narrow-eyed suspicion. She would casually glance over at him with a "*Whaa . . .?*" expression.

But he hadn't said anything, and as for her, well, she could do this all day—

Out of the corner of her eye she spied movement. What looked like a vine suddenly uncoiled from the ground and came flying toward her. With a shriek, she attempted a pulse of energy to ward it off. But MacRieve had already snatched the snake; her magick caught him and sent him flying, his body crashing through the brush, *felling the trees in his way.*

After landing one hundred feet away and angrily tossing the snake, he shot to his feet, charging back to her, eyes ice blue with fury. "*Goddamn it, witch, no' again!*"

27

⤜⤙⤚⤘

"I t was an accident!" the witch cried, and she might have been truthful, but Bowe was beyond caring.

"All morning you've toyed with me, have you no'?" He stalked closer to her, letting her see a good glimpse of the beast within.

Yet after swallowing loudly and retreating several steps, she seemed to force herself to stand her ground.

He was dumbfounded that she wasn't cowering. Battle hardened vampires recoiled in the face of a Lykae's werewolf form, but she'd planted her boots, and *she hadn't budged.*

She even raised her chin.

Cade had started hurrying down the embankment as if to protect her. The very idea made Bowe draw his lips back from his fangs. No doubt thinking his renewed fury was for her, she pulled magick into her hands.

Raising both of her glowing palms, she beckoned him with wiggling fingers. "Come on, then. I'll go another round. Though by now even an amoeba would've learned *not to fuck with me.*"

Everyone grew still, silent. Then Cade started back down for her, redoubling his speed.

"No, Cade, I've got this," she said evenly, never looking away from Bowe.

Meanwhile, Bowe had subtly pulled his head back, feeling as if he'd just been presented with a species of creature he had never seen. Then he caught Rydstrom's look of amusement—the demon was obviously loving this—and he found himself . . . grinning. "Kitten's quick to bear those claws, is she no'?"

Rydstrom ruefully shook his head at Bowe, as if sorry for his unavoidable and imminent demise, then got everyone, including a reluctant Cade, moving again.

As Bowe passed Mariketa, he leaned in close. Not bothering to hide his surprise, he murmured to her, "And damn if she does no' have them sunk into me."

Her gray-eyed gaze was wary. He noted that she kept her palms fired up for some time after they continued on.

Even after her blatant show of magick, he felt so proud she'd held her ground that he wanted to stand tall and point her out as his female. *That's my lass. Mine.* But his heart was also thundering because he realized that in the heat of the full moon, when he was completely turned, she might not run from him. He still intended to get her away from him before this full moon, but for the future . . .

Excitement burned within him, and he found himself closing in on her and saying, "You're bonny when you're about to strike."

"You would know."

"Come, then, sheathe your claws, kitten. And we'll be friends once more."

"We weren't friends to begin with!"

"You're warming to me. I can tell."

"True. I only throw guys I dig. And don't you dare call me kitten again!"

"You look like one with your wee, pointed ears."

"Are you done?"

"Canna say." He was silent for a few moments, then added, "Think you're the bravest lass I've ever seen. Though I doona care for your using magick against me so readily. Do you enjoy it?"

She seemed to mull this for a moment, then raised her brows. "I do. Besides, I think you need someone to threaten you now and again. To remind the great and powerful Lykae that you're not so unbeatable."

"Aye, I do." He clasped her hand in his. "Sign on."

She pulled out of his grasp. "I don't do temp jobs. And that's all you're offering."

Actually, he'd been reevaluating that stance all morning. . . .

On the trail, she'd never once complained or asked them to slow down, though he could see she was working hard to keep up with inexhaustible immortals. She obviously appreciated that these people were helping her when they didn't have to.

Besides having a bold heart, she made friends handily, with strong bonds. And she seemed to look at everything with wonder and curiosity. He'd noticed that she'd longed to stop several times to investigate some intriguing sight or another. Had it been only the two of them together, with no time limit, he'd have patiently followed as she explored. He knew that some of her wonder was due to her young age, but he believed she'd never grow out of it completely.

Today he'd learned that she didn't proffer blood sacrifices at an altar—always a gratifying detail to learn about a potential mate.

Not to mention that the witch looked like she'd been

plucked from his most fevered fantasy of a woman. Hell, she *was* a waking wet dream.

As if to illustrate his thoughts at that moment, she paused to wind up her hair and knead her neck. Each time she did this, he tensed in anticipation, rubbing his palm over his mouth, knowing she was about to draw up her shirt to wipe sweat from her brow. Once again she did, displaying for him the delicate marking at her back. Just below it, he spied the low edge of her black silk panties, which were visible enough for him to know she wore a thong—even if he hadn't picked it out this morning.

And with that teasing hint of a sight came an unwelcome realization. He was going to traverse the country of Guatemala with a raging cockstand the entire way.

Unless he could get her to relieve him of it.

When they began ascending a particularly steep trail, and she seemed to be flagging, he decided to cup her arse and push her up. Just as he reached for her, she said, "A fine way to lose a paw, MacRieve."

He grinned. "I have, and I doona recommend it."

"Then try keeping them to yourself."

Once they'd arrived at the trailhead, they came across a picturesque gorge. A slow-moving river flowed into terraced, limestone waterfalls. The water was aqua blue and clear.

Mariketa gasped at the sight, then turned to Rydstrom. "Can we stop here?"

He shook his head. "We need to keep going. You still have to make that call in time."

She looked so crestfallen, glancing out over the murky jungle they'd just emerged from, that Bowe found himself telling Rydstrom, "I need to boil water for her for the rest of the day anyway." He surveyed the area but found no dry wood, nor dry ground for that matter. He'd have to go back down into the forest. He scanned for Cade, and when Bowe didn't scent or see him or Tierney, he told Mariketa, "You've as long here as it takes for me to get your water ready."

She smiled brightly—the first real smile she'd ever cast his way.

Oh, bloody hell. She had a bewitching smile. *Aye, no shite.*

Then she dashed to the water's edge, raising her face to the sun. For three weeks she hadn't felt that light. Because of him. Trying to shake off his regret, he approached Tera. "I'm going to dry ground to make a fire, and I . . . I would ask you to keep an eye on Mariketa."

"I'll do it, but not as a favor to you," Tera answered shortly. Bowe had noticed the archers weren't as irate with him since they'd heard he hadn't meant to trap them so long. But they weren't eager to be buddies with a Lykae either.

He dropped his pack. "Her towel and belongings are in there if she needs anything." Then he lowered his voice. "But you canna let the witch go anywhere else. Just have her stay by the water. And doona let her touch anything. She'll likely get curious about something and wander off, so you canna take your eyes—"

"Lykae, enough! I won't let her get killed in the time it takes to boil water, okay?"

Mari nearly trembled with excitement. This place was . . . Eden.

Flowers with blooms as big as plates basked in the sun.

Their scarlet and yellow petals were so bright and flawless, they looked fake. Shallow pools cascaded softly down, one after the other. The water was turquoise, and each basin was surrounded by ferns or had islands of flowers dotting it.

She wondered if anyone had ever hoped for an oasis—not from the sun, but *of the sun*—and then been rewarded like this.

After MacRieve and Rydstrom had started off to make a fire, she and Tera had torn into the pack—Tera for soap and shampoo and a borrowed change of clothes, and Mari for her bathing suit.

Just before she'd lain out in her suit—a black string bikini—she'd had a moment of uncharacteristic wavering. Aside from MacRieve, no one had seen her dressed in so little in years. The triangles on top were narrow, and though the back was not quite a thong, it was close.

And she wasn't exactly svelte.

Before, she'd never been ashamed of the curves most women would aspire to aerobicize away. She'd made a deal with herself her senior year in high school. She'd diet the minute her bikini-clad body failed to stir the shorts of at least one of the hot guys at the beach.

If it ain't broke . . .

When the sun beckoned, she'd recalled MacRieve's reaction to spying her naked and shucked her towel.

Now as Tera lay out with her hair coated in conditioner, Mari unbraided her own hair, listened to her iPod, and enjoyed rays. In this place, her entire outlook from the morning shifted.

She still couldn't believe she'd been so worried about the prediction. *Seek to lock her away?* Nothing could hold her! Not an immortal warrior or a tomb of incubi.

Here she was free, when she'd thought she'd die in that place. Soon she'd see her friends again. She'd sing more really bad karaoke with Regin and Carrow at the Cat's Meow—and she'd do it without her cloak. Anonymous, cloaked karaoke just didn't hold the same thrill.

And on this trip, she had accomplished something monumental by taking out the incubi. She might not have won, or even finaled, in the Hie, but when she returned to New Orleans she wouldn't walk, she'd strut.

Everyone had been awaiting? Well, Mari had just annihilated a thousand-year-old source of evil. *Boo-yah for the captromancer!*

No one could ever take that away from her. She'd destroyed ancient evil; her regret for the incomplete in that Civics 101 class just didn't have the same bite.

Then, the best part of this whole scenario—she'd been paid for it. Many factions in the Lore shared collective property, but the witches were the opposite—everything in the covens was about private ownership. "Share and share alike" might be the Valkyrie's motto, but the witches' was "Mine is *mine*." Mari was expected to carry her own weight.

Now she would *in gold*.

She was officially a mystical mercenary, at last an earner in the House. Earlier, she'd rechecked MacRieve's pack just to make sure the headdress was inside, and had frowned to see he'd carefully wrapped it in a towel, as if to keep it protected for her. . . .

Though MacRieve continued to irritate, confuse, and frustrate her, the ego-building fact remained that he was one of the most gorgeous and compelling males she'd ever seen—and he couldn't keep his paws off her.

All morning she'd been treated to the sight of four choice males, and yet, if she fantasized about making love, it was MacRieve's face she saw above her. Last night, she'd gotten a glimpse of what he'd be like as a lover.

He'd be *wild*.

For Mari, making love to Acton had always been pleasurable, but not earth-shattering. He'd never seemed to get crazed by his desire for her, had never taken her with a furious lust. She'd been happy with him, and she knew that sexual relationships were never perfect, but she had long craved intensity.

Yet would MacRieve be *too* intense? Immortal males were known to be relentless lovers, but the Lykae were supposed to bite and scratch as well. And MacRieve was huge—in all respects.

Why am I even thinking about this . . . ?

She hadn't noticed how often she'd been sneaking glances at him until he wasn't available for her viewing purposes. How much longer would he and Rydstrom be?

Big males talking amongst themselves. She would kill to be able to listen in on their conversation—

Wait . . . She unplugged her earbuds and reached for her compact, easing it open.

Not just to hear it . . . but to *see*.

28

❦

"No progress with her, then?" Rydstrom asked as he sat on a boulder sharpening his sword.

Bowe paced beside his feebly growing fire. "None point none, apparently."

"Full moon's tomorrow night."

"Tell me something I doona know." Bowe was strung out from guarding the witch, from trying to keep his hands from her, from mulling what the hell she was to him. And always the shadow of the waxing moon haunted him.

Yet even as he worried for Mariketa's safety, he recognized that she was too full of life to go down easily. The witch was a fighter.

Unfortunately, he'd ensured she viewed him as the enemy.

"I'd wondered why you allowed the company on this trip," Rydstrom said. "I'm not just an extra sword, am I?"

Bowe shook his head. "If we don't get her out of here in time, you have to keep her from me. I will no' have had time to earn her trust or prepare her."

"You think she would run from you?"

"I canna take the chance—"

He stilled when a weird breeze blew, feeling crisp, even here in the jungle. Both he and Rydstrom peered around.

Bowe had the sudden uncanny impression that they were being watched.

Rydstrom asked, "Do you see anything out there that I don't?"

"No. And I'd scent anyone who came close." Shaking off the feeling, he resumed his pacing, considering what his path should be. *What's my next move with her?*

Challenge and kill Cade.

Of course.

"Stop thinking about it," Rydstrom said. "I will not let you kill Cade, so put it from your thoughts."

Bowe narrowed his eyes. "I thought you'd had your mind-reading ability bound along with your tracing."

"Don't have to be a mind reader in this case. Just so you know, if anyone is going to kill my brother, it'll be me. Besides, you don't have only Cade to worry about."

"What does that mean?"

"Mariketa will turn soon," Rydstrom said.

"So?"

"So, she's definitely ready for a mate." Rydstrom scrubbed his chin. "*Never* have I seen a female so ready."

"Doona speak about her like that!"

He shrugged. "You should have heard Tierney. I've been near her for three weeks—it's getting stronger every day. If you take her back to civilization without some bond between you . . . other males will seek to steal her from you."

"A bond? I doona see it forthcoming. She despises me." Bowe sank onto a stump. "I used to have it so easy with females." He had no experience with this. For a millennium, a crook of his finger had him anyone he'd wanted. Now he truly had to question if he could win Mariketa over.

"There is a pleasing sort of irony that you actually want a witch, and she doesn't want you back."

"Enjoyin' this, are you, then? She said we're no' compatible, or some such bullshite." He frowned. "Do you know what *jangle pop* is?" When Rydstrom shook his head, Bowe continued, "And she asked me if I would go back for Mariah."

"Discerning question."

"Whose bloody side are you on?" Bowe asked, but Rydstrom merely hiked his shoulders. "So she asked me, and I told her I . . . would."

"Ill-advised, Scot."

"That's the way I felt at the time. Should I have lied to her?"

"At *the time*? Twelve hours later, and it's different? Didn't I tell you to make a decision and stick to it?"

"It's no' that easy. Every time I realize how much I want the witch, I continue to feel disloyal. And I doona want Mariketa to think me disloyal—but then I'm really no' if she's truly Mariah." He raked his fingers through his hair. "One could go crazy thinking about all this."

"Just reason it out. What are the pros and cons with her?"

"Reason! Always with your bloody reason. Do you know what I'm going to enjoy? When you meet your demoness and she shakes to hell your unflappable demeanor. I'm going to laugh when you turn enraged, horns flaring ramrod straight every time she saunters by."

"Noted. Now, begin with the pros."

"Verra well. She's clever, she's brave, and, by all the gods, she's been graced in form. And I'm no' going to apologize for being a typical male—I *do* want the sexiest female

I've ever laid eyes on to be mine. I'll admit that I want her on my arm and in my bed. And I want to be smug over having her desire me, too."

"The cons . . ."

"Right back to the witchery. Would you no' be a tad unnerved if your female could unleash the force of an atomic bomb whenever she got nettled with you?"

Rydstrom nodded in commiseration, then said, "Take away the fact that she's a witch—"

"I will be taking away that fact," Bowe interrupted. "Practicing witchcraft is voluntary. I could see to it that she *never*—"

Out of the blue, a bee stung him. "Damn it," he muttered, slapping it away, then continued, "If I snatched her away from her coven and immersed her with the Lykae—"

Another sting. "Son of a bitch!"

When the odd breeze blew once more, Bowe narrowed his eyes. "The witch." He gazed up at the sky and all around him. "Playing with me *again!* I'll turn her over my knee for this."

When Mari had seen Cade and Tierney return, she'd hastily shut the mirror and returned it to her pocket. Yet even now, she was still reeling from everything MacRieve had said—and, naturally, she was dying to sting him some more.

She didn't know what had thrown her worse—that he'd so easily thought to take away her magick, or that he'd said she was the sexiest female he'd ever seen. *Sexiest* meant sexier than even his perfect mate. . . .

"Survived last night, I see," Cade said as he took a spot next to her on the rock.

"I was about to die of irritation, but that's about all I faced."

He drew off his sweat-dampened shirt. "I have to admit I thought things would be different." At her raised brows, he said, "Bowen used to have a lot of success with women. Or with 'wenches,' as he called them back then. A new one every night."

Wenches? "Is that so?" She wasn't jealous. Whatsoever. "Rydstrom seems to be friends with him, but you're not. Why's that?"

"We fought over a female, of course."

Maybe a tinge of jealousy. No males had ever fought over her. "What happened?"

"He knew she wasn't his mate, but she still could have been mine. He took her to spite me. After him, she had no time for a demon mercenary, though he never saw her again."

"Am I an attempt to get back at him?"

Cade ran his hand over one of his horns. "Maybe. Does that offend you?"

"No, because I might be using you to make him jealous."

"Because you want him?"

"No, because he wants me"—she smiled sweetly—"and I want to hurt him."

"MacRieve is long overdue for someone like you."

"I do my best." She tucked her hair behind her ear. "Cade, I was wondering about something. Rydstrom told me you two didn't grow up in the same household."

"I was fostered out. I rarely saw my family, but that's the custom."

"Oh, that must have been awful."

"Actually, it was great. I never wanted to return . . .

even refused to when Rydstrom summoned me to rule while he went to war. He blames me, you know, for losing his crown. Said if I'd been there while he was away from his kingdom for so long, he'd still have it. Hell, he blames me for all his troubles."

"I heard you two arguing about it in the tomb. Do you wish you had returned now?"

He nodded slowly. "At every hour." After glancing around, he leaned closer to her to murmur, "Mari, I wouldn't have said this in front of the others—because my reputation as a cold, selfish, and untrustworthy bastard suits me—but you sound like you've got a destiny to fulfill. And if you turn your back on your calling—maybe to be a Lykae's browbeaten mate and wife—fate will not just slight you." His expression grew grave. "She will *punish* you, over and over—"

A sudden roar sounded behind her. Out of the corner of her eye, she saw a huge fist swinging out at Cade.

It was MacRieve. In a killing rage.

29

Mari heard the crack of bone just before Cade flew across the rocks, landing in the brush.

She thought that his collarbone had snapped, but he still scrambled to his feet to face MacRieve.

As Cade snarled, his eyes and horns turned black. MacRieve's fangs and claws lengthened, but neither had fully turned to his beastly or demonic form—they both seemed just on the edge.

When Mari unsteadily stood, Tierney said from behind her, "Don't even think about getting in between them." Was he *eating* at a time like this?

Without looking away from the two, she said, "But they'll kill each other!"

"A single stray punch from one of them, and you're dead."

As Mari watched them fighting, she truly began to believe that. The two circled, scanning the other for weaknesses, striking out at intervals with fists like anvils. She caught herself flinching every time they smashed each other's face.

Like a shot, they both charged, their heavy, pounding steps punching through the brittle limestone ground. In a tangle of fists and claws, they crashed into the jungle, razing hardwoods with the impact.

MacRieve made another furious charge, barreling into the demon, sending them back toward the falls. They slammed into a rock face, pulverizing the outer layer to dust, then surged over the edge of one terrace, plummeting into the water of the next pool down.

Cade seemed to have the advantage, landing over MacRieve, but it was short-lived.

Shoving Cade back, MacRieve lunged for his throat with one hand; with his other, he slashed out with flared claws, ripping across Cade's torso. Blood poured from both, dissipating into the clear water.

MacRieve fought with such seething ferocity, just as he had the night at the assembly—when she could have admired him for hours. . . .

Without warning, Rydstrom lunged into the middle, throwing fists and elbows. Once he'd finally separated them, all three were out of breath and bleeding.

MacRieve turned his head, spit blood, then grated, "The witch is *mine*." Before she could react, he'd bounded up the rocks to where she stood. He snatched her tight to his side, laying his massive hand on her nape. His lips were drawn back from his fangs.

Cade gnashed his teeth in turn.

"Come near what's mine again, and I will destroy you." At that he simply swung her over his shoulder and started across the pools to the other side of the jungle.

She pounded her fists on his back and kicked to be freed. "What the hell are you doing?"

"Aye, thrash about. If anyone's foolish enough to follow me, the sight of that'd be sure to stop them in their tracks."

Reminded that her barely clad ass was jutting up for all

to see, she stopped her struggles. "Where are you taking me?" she demanded.

"Somewhere private." He leapt over an entire branch of the river, making her gasp, then added, "We've matters to settle between us."

Moments later, she squealed when pounding falls cascaded over her back. He shook his hair out without missing a step, so wolfy.

Not another cave!

One minute, she'd been sitting in the sun, chatting with a demon. Now she was being hauled about like a Neanderthal's prize into the dark once more.

But as he continued in, deeper and deeper, there came to be filtered sunlight shining down. How? She craned her head up. He'd taken her to a cenote—one of the sinkholes in the area, with a clear pool at the bottom. She knew from her reading that they were considered sacred to the Maya.

When he dropped her to her feet inside, he snapped, "Understand, you will no' ever go about dressed like this. As a matter of fact, if you doona put your glamour back on directly, then I'll be getting you another sodding cloak!"

Her awe at the beauty of this place was swiftly replaced by ire. "You are *crazed.*"

"Mayhap, but it's plain as day that you're no' like other females, and you canna dress as they do."

"What are you talking about?" she cried.

"Everything about you—from your curves to your red hair to that damned ring at your navel—makes a male lose his judgment. Cade knew what he risked from me, and still he courted my wrath to be close to you."

"One more time. I'm—not—yours. And hitting Cade

like that was so . . . so wrong! You could have killed him."

"Do you want me tae?"

She started away. "I'm going to check on him—"

"Then you *do* want me tae!" He seized her elbow and spun her around, a wild look in his eyes. His shirt was ripped almost free, displaying his sheening chest, still heaving from the battle. "This is a vulnerable time. I have no' claimed you, and the full moon nears. Yet you receive the attentions of another male? Witch, you play with fire!" He swiped the back of his hand over his bleeding temple. "Forget the demon. He knows you're no' his. If he'd truly believed you were, he would have put up more of a fight. He dinna even hit a rage state."

"You didn't change to your werewolf form for me!"

"I dinna want you to see it!" he roared, grasping her upper arms. "Doona ever doubt my desire for you—if I truly was in a contest for the right to have you, I'd have bitten his goddamned throat free, then laid it at your feet in offer!"

Her lips parted. She thought she'd just caught a glimpse of the inner workings of how a Lykae male thought.

And she . . . *liked* it.

He was breathing hard, with that muscled chest heaving. His eyes were still that lightest blue color, and were locked on her as if she was his most coveted possession—and one he'd feared losing.

MacRieve was fresh from the fight. Yes, at the assembly she'd realized she could watch him for hours, but now, she admitted that night had been when she'd first recognized how much she desired this Lykae.

That night she hadn't been able to kiss him as she'd desired, or stroke his powerful body.

Yet now . . .

Ferocity, the intensity. She'd craved it, always had—even before this uncontrollable, immortal need had begun to consume her. *Want it . . . want him.*

Her expression must have betrayed her hunger. His brows drew together, and he grated, "*Mariketa?*"

Her hand shot up and cupped the back of his neck, tugging him down so she could kiss him.

Obviously shocked, he stilled for a moment. Then, with a groan, he released his clenching hold on her arms. His hands landed heavily on her ass, kneading as if he'd only been awaiting a chance to feel her like that. Against her mouth, he rasped, "*Lusty witch.*"

"Kiss me really hard, MacRieve, like you mean it."

"Lusty *and* demanding. Gods, how you please me." He did kiss her then, slanting his lips over hers, slipping his tongue between them to sweep it against her own. Hot . . . wet . . . *hard.* She could do nothing but mindlessly meet him.

His big palms on her ass rocked her up to him, forcing her against his rigid shaft.

She was in heaven. . . .

Yet he broke away. Between breaths, he grated, "I doona share what's mine. No other males. *Only me.* It'll only be me for you."

She blinked open her eyes, becoming aware that at some point he'd begun holding her upright—her legs had given way under his kiss. Then she frowned. "And what about you?" she asked, trying to keep her wits about her when he began greedily kissing and licking her neck. "Telling me you're the only one for me—when you plan on ditching me for another female at the earliest opportunity?" With every word, her resentment grew.

He drew back and met her eyes. "I canna say for certain that I would now."

"Oh, because you think I'm about to give it up?"

He swallowed, then rasped, "*Are you, then?*"

She glared. Then her gaze flickered over his gorgeous face and muscle-packed body. She was so hungry for him. But she couldn't get past being passed up, which meant she couldn't enjoy his ferocity, which meant she was now furious. Her desire was thwarted again, blazing out of control, yet it remained fixated on a totally undeserving male.

"Mariketa, I doona know that I could part from you . . . for even as long as it'd take to go back." As if shocked by the realization, he murmured to himself, "It's true."

Good enough! "Okay, I'll give you props for that." She raised her face to snare another deep taste of him. Between kisses, she breathlessly said, "This is good bullshit—and it's *working*! Kiss me more!"

But he cupped her face, holding her away. "'*No*' bull-shite."

She blinked at him. She was burning for him and he was going to get chatty? "I'm not in a cave with you *again* for your scintillating conversation. Put up or shut up, Scot."

He raised his brows. "Wicked little witch." His brogue was so thick it gave her shivers. "I'll make you eat those words." He yanked off his ripped shirt and tossed it to the ground. With one hand cupping her between her legs from behind, he lifted her and set her on his shirt on the sand. "Sit that pretty arse down right here, and I'll give you what you're wantin'."

30

When Bowe yanked the triangles of her suit to the sides, she leaned up on her elbows. With heavy-lidded gray eyes, she watched as he bared her luscious breasts.

At the sight of her nipples, his cock pulsed, about to rip through his jeans. "I'm going tae suckle you so hard you'll feel me for the rest of the day. Do you want me tae?"

He groaned when she arched her back and fisted her wee hands in his hair to pull him down to one of her breasts. Sucking the peak in bliss, he felt it stiffen and bud under his tongue. As he moved to the other, he said, "Mariketa, you've the finest body I've ever seen. And I've a thousand things I want to do to it, but canna decide where to begin."

She moaned when he closed his lips on her other nipple. "Whatever you're going to do, do it quick! I'm close."

He leaned up, his brows drawn. She wouldn't last through him preparing her body to receive him. He decided to bring her off before he took her.

Eager to feel her between her thighs again, he plucked free the black string at her right hip. Would she be as wet as before? When he moved to untie the bow at her left hip, she wriggled over to give him better access, as if she couldn't wait to be rid of her clothes.

Still raised up on her elbows, she stared—rapt like him—as the V of material in the middle slinked down, revealing her auburn curls. He choked out the words, "Part your thighs. Show me how wet you've grown."

In answer, she whimpered and let her knees fall open. A groan broke from his chest when he saw her sex was glistening for him. His cock swelled to be inside it, the pressure in his heavy ballocks nearing pain. His hand shook as he lowered it to stroke her.

At his first touch, her head fell back; he sucked in a breath, thinking he might spend that instant. "So hot and slick. I canna imagine how you're goin' tae feel gripping my shaft."

She lifted her head once more, her brows drawn. "Oh, gods . . . *Bowen* . . ."

He spread her flesh with his thumb and forefinger, about to use his other forefinger to rub her tight little clitoris. Her short, soft moans grew louder with each of her breaths. So close . . .

The rising seed in his shaft made it throb for relief. Yet even as he was desperate to pin her hips to the ground and plunge it inside her, he wanted to savor the sight of Mariketa on the razor's edge.

Her reaction was the most erotic thing he'd ever seen.

Her piercing glinted in a filtered ray of sunlight as she began to shake. Her breasts were so plump, her swollen nipples jutting, as if begging to be sucked more. She looked from where he was about to stroke her, then breathlessly gazed up at him, meeting his eyes.

"Bowen, *please* . . ."

* * *

Mari lay back, lowering herself off her elbows so she could grasp his wrist, pulling his free hand down as she rolled her hips up.

MacRieve shook his head hard, as if he didn't believe what he was seeing. "Only with me, witch," he rasped, raking his gaze along her body. "This *must* be all mine."

At that moment, she'd have told him anything. Her voice sounding throaty, she murmured, "Only with you."

"Then come hard for me." One flick of his big finger sent her over. With a strangled cry, she arched her back sharply, undulating her hips to his hand in abandon. "*Good girl*," he rumbled in her ear as she helplessly writhed. "*You like that.*"

On and on it continued until the pleasure became too much, and Mari had to press his hand away. Finally, he allowed her to stop.

As he knelt between her spread legs, he yanked open his jeans, shoving them to his knees. His heavy erection sprang free, and he bit out a curse when her hands shot forward for it. She adored the feel of him, lovingly stroking his entire length up and down until he groaned and bucked his hips, shoving his shaft through her fists.

Then he slipped his middle finger inside her wetness, making her moan and him hiss, "*So tight.*" Gritting out the words, he said, "Doona want to hurt you. Need tae make sure you're ready."

The muscles in his neck were corded with strain, his chest slick from the falls and sweat. His gaze flickered over her body, but always returned to her eyes, as if he was as aroused by looking at them as he was by her breasts.

"Witch, if you doona stop with your soft palms, you're goin' tae bring me off."

She licked her lip but kept working his throbbing flesh. As he eased a second finger into her, she felt herself on the verge yet again. "*Bowen . . .*"

"I'm beginning to recognize that tone. You're no' near done, are you? I knew you'd be like this. I knew it."

Just when she thought he would hastily replace the fingers inside her with his shaft, she began to come in a wet rush and cried out.

"I can *feel* you squeezing me. S'*over.*" With his free hand, he enclosed hers in a fist, pumping their hands hard, rasping, "*I canna hold my seed, Mari.*" His body tensed, going perfectly still, then he gave a brutal yell. At the last second, he aimed away from her body. She gaped as he spurted out into the sand beside her, over and over, stunned by how magnificent this big male was in his wild pleasure.

When he'd finished with a shudder, she sank down again, and he sprawled on his back beside her, his penis still pulsing. Even as he lay there, seeming dazed, he reached over and seized her hand in his—just to hold it as they caught their breath. After the things they'd just been doing, he felt the need *to hold her hand.*

They stared up at the muted sunlight, side by side and hand in hand.

Mari, the water just got too deep, and you're in way over your head.

When he turned to her, his eyes were warm amber, and the corners of his lips curled. "You could no' please me more. Could no' possibly." He seemed in an elated mood, as if she'd just capitulated far more than she actually had.

And she knew that Bowen MacRieve was excited because, for probably the first time in nearly two centuries, he truly had begun looking forward to the future.

But she didn't want him to get his hopes up when she had no place in her life for him. Even if she forgave him for trapping her, and even if she knew encounters like they'd just shared would only get more cataclysmic, she also believed that she would have to radically alter her life to be with him. And she wasn't sure she'd be ready to do that for someone she loved, much less for someone she merely desired.

No matter how strong that desire was.

"Now, tae get you ready—"

She pressed his hand away and sat up. "No, I'm done."

"You're *done*? We're just gettin' started! Did I . . . did I do something wrong?"

With a shrug, she began dressing. "We need to get going."

His brows drew together. "Do you regret what we've done, then?"

"I'm not unhappy that we were together like this. But I'm not happy either."

He yanked his jeans up. "What would it take tae make you so?"

"Look, MacRieve, I wasn't giving you lip service before—you're not the guy for me. Yet you just assume that I'm on board for whatever you finally decide, and that's not how this will work. While you're trying to make up your mind, know that mine's already decided. There isn't any place for you in my life."

"Even after this?"

She rolled her eyes. "Oh, please, after all the 'wenches' you've nailed and bailed, you of all people should know that one hookup means nothing."

"Nailed and bailed? What in the hell are you talking about?"

"Cade told me about the female you two fought over."

"Damn it, she crawled into bed with me!"

"And now your cruel comment to him last night makes perfect sense. Of course, you couldn't kick her out of your bed for your friend?"

"I'd had some mead, and dinna even recognize her as the one he wanted."

She quirked a brow. "One wench among many, huh?" she asked, turning from him.

Mariketa was prickly, no doubt uncomfortable at the speed this thing between them was moving. But her coolness didn't daunt him in the least, because he now knew that he could win her. She had just cried out his name. *His.* He'd been prepared to fight for her; after this, he would only redouble his efforts.

Bowe had feared this witch could make all his sexual dreams come true—and he'd *dreamed constantly.*

Now he knew she could.

31

If the others hadn't already figured out that she and MacRieve had been intimate, they would have guessed by his behavior.

When the two of them had silently dressed and rejoined everyone, he'd had his shoulders back, sporting a victorious expression. His eyes kept straying to her, his gaze heated, and *proprietary*.

His obvious sense of satisfaction was a one hundred and eighty degree contrast from the glower he'd sported all morning. Now he was the epitome of masculine satisfaction.

She sighed. And damn, it was a good look for him.

Rydstrom and Tera cast her quizzical glances. Cade—with one of his eyes swollen nearly closed and his jaw already mottled with bruises—again focused on her neck. When she flushed under his scrutiny and glanced away, she heard him mutter to MacRieve, "Still don't see your mark."

His tone so smug, MacRieve said, "Day's no' over, demon."

At that, Cade flashed a look at her, then said, "I'll take point again," seeming to want to get away from them.

The group began following the riverside up the mountain, and again the terrain made for single-file going. Which was good. She needed to process everything that had just happened. Again, all she knew was that too much had.

From behind her, MacRieve said, "Doona worry about what they think."

"Of course, you can say that. They're not going to think you're weak. Or easy."

"No way they could consider you weak. They've seen too many demonstrations of your power. And no' easy either—all they'll believe is that such a young lass as you was no match for the seduction skills of a twelve-hundred-year-old Lykae."

Under her voice, she said, "Whatever—I jumped *you*! I started it."

"Aye," he began solemnly, "and that was a highlight of my long life."

"Riiight." Flustered, she stepped over an ant line, studiously regarding the leaves they carried.

"It's true, Mariketa. Though it is a shame I dinna get a chance to pay more attention to your pretty arse."

"Shh!" she hissed in a whisper. "They'll hear you!"

"Hear me? You worry about that now when you were just moaning so lustily? Do you always make so much noise?"

Her face flamed when Tierney, the next in line to her, glanced over his shoulder with raised brows. She slowed to let the others take more of a lead.

"Do you, then?" MacRieve asked again.

Fine, she could play. She turned to him, and in a monotone voice, she said, "Oh, baby. Oh, Bowen. It was you. Only you."

He grinned, and the sight made her want to grin, too. They were following the cascading river, and the sun was shining, and she'd just had two orgasms—her mood had definitely improved.

No! She couldn't get caught up in his palpable excitement, because she knew it wasn't due only to what they'd just done, but what he expected them to do.

Yet every time she tried to call up her previous anger toward him, she kept picturing him frowning as he asked Rydstrom what jangle pop was. Somehow, she knew MacRieve hadn't asked out of mere curiosity but because he was trying to learn, for her.

And the simple fact was that, Hekate help her, she *liked* being around him. Even when she'd despised him, she'd somehow been buoyed by his presence. Now that she *didn't* despise him, he excited her, gladdened her. . . .

From mere inches behind her, he said, "Was wondering, do you always come so quickly?"

"I don't know—do you?"

He gave a half laugh. "Demanding witch. You forget how long I went without. But I'm a swift rebounder." He furtively grabbed her hand and made her cup his growing erection.

If he was trying to embarrass her, he'd have to do better than that. Not missing a beat, she said, "Why, Bowen, I do believe you're flirting with me." Without glancing back, she rubbed with curiosity. After giving it a heft that made him rock his hips to her hand, she released him, blithely continuing on.

His voice rough, he said, "I must no' be any good at flirting if you doona know for certain." In a dry tone, he added, "Maybe I should be more direct?"

She couldn't help it—she chuckled, but covered it with a cough. She was supposed to be the one who could charm, but he was doing a damn commendable job, making her grin against her will.

Was she so easy that a mere two earth-shattering orgasms and her unwavering attraction to him could make her forgive their past? As she inwardly answered herself, she thought, *Then why fight it?* Mari had never been one to fight battles, much less losing ones.

He leaned over her and murmured at her ear, "Show me those bonny breasts."

"You just saw them!" she cried in exasperation, though she was secretly pleased by how much he seemed to appreciate her body.

"If I had my way, witchling, you'd never wear a top again."

She was biting the inside of her cheek to keep from smiling but didn't want him to see, so she quickened her pace. "Shouldn't you be concerned with getting me safely out of the jungle?"

"Come, then, remind me what I'm so happy to die for."

He was so . . . *wolfy*. So teasing. And Mari realized this was kind of *fun*. She half-expected him to play-trip her and start nipping at her ears. And she suspected she'd love it.

She waited, giving him enough time to drop back and assume she was ignoring him, then turned with her brows—and her top and bra—raised, flashing him. He took a stutter step, tripping over his feet. With his hands over his heart, he fell to his knees; she yanked her clothes down and whirled around, continuing on with a goofy smile.

But he was right behind her in an instant. "You good

girl," he rasped. "Give us a feel, then." She swatted at him. "Tease."

"Temptress," she countered.

"Aye, that you are. No' ten minutes ago, you made me come till my eyes rolled back in my head, and already you've got me randier than I was with my first milk-maid."

She turned and tapped her chin. "Hmm. Would you like me to wear a corset and bend over a pail?"

His jaw slackened. "Only if you want to see a man instantaneously spill his seed."

She gazed at his thick erection. "Sounds like a date, then."

He groaned, rushing up to her side again. "I'm a heart-beat away from taking you aside and bending you over the next boulder."

Ha! "Then keep an eye out for one that's about this"— she tapped her flattened hand at her hip bone—"high."

"Ach, I like this with you! I doona remember the last time that I felt something was . . ." He trailed off, as if he didn't quite recognize what they were experiencing.

"Fun?" she supplied.

"Aye, fun. And I believe I've discovered the key to you."

"What's that?"

"If I slake you, in return I get a smiling lass. I like this deal, kitten."

"Damn it, MacRieve, if you keep calling me kitten, then I'm going to start calling you something equivalent, like hound dog—and then we'll both be losers."

He grinned at that and asked, "So how much of my conversation with Rydstrom did you hear?"

She pressed her fingers to her chest. "*Whaa . . . ?*"

"Come, then. I know you were eavesdropping, witch. What did you hear?"

"I heard you say you think I'm sexy. The . . . sexiest."

"Aye, easily," he said, making her want to preen. "And what about you? You're more attracted to me than you were to your boy demon."

"*Boyfriend.* I said he was my boyfriend. And even if I was more attracted to you, I'd never feed your ego by telling you."

"How did you get him to let you go?"

"Why?" she asked, feeling herself softening even more toward MacRieve. "Do you think he had a hard time of it?"

MacRieve gave her an impatient scowl as if her question was ridiculous. And for the second time, Mari thought, *I might be in over my head with this male.*

But I'm thinking I like it.

"How long were you with him?"

She shrugged. "Almost seven years."

"That's nearly a third of your life!" he thundered. "Christ, I doona care for that. Did you . . . did you love him, then?"

"Yes," she answered honestly.

His voice broke lower when he asked, "Do you love him still?"

Over her shoulder, she said, "I guess a part of my heart will always be his."

When she realized MacRieve had stopped, she turned. She found his jaw clenched, his irises turning ice blue once more, and his claws shooting longer and darker. She was witnessing more of the beast even than before.

Mari swallowed, again reminded that this was an adult Lykae male. And one who thought she was the mate he'd ached for over centuries. She *was* playing with fire. No more teasing, no more toying with the sex-starved were-wolf. "Just forget I said anything—"

He pressed her against a tree, out of sight of the others. "I want to stab my claws into this demon's neck and rip out his goddamned spine."

"MacRieve, just wait. . . ."

His hand shot out, covering the back of her head. He leaned down to her ear. "Tonight, I'm going tae make you mine, Mariketa." His accent was thick, his voice rough, as if even his vocal chords were altered as he began to turn. "This other male might have part of your heart, but I will possess all of your body." He ran his other hand from her neck down to her breasts, cupping them both in turn. Under his hot, rough palm her nipples *were* still throb-bing—just as he'd promised. "Mark my words, I will claim you so thoroughly you will no' recall any other."

Intensity . . . Gazing up at him, she felt so small and vul-nerable and recognized that she should be afraid. Instead she was aroused once more—from his deep voice, from his hand fondling her, from the idea of his taking her hard, possibly within hours.

"After this night, you'll arch tae *my* touch and crave *my* kiss. When the heat is upon you, every inch of your body will recognize mine as its master."

She gave a shaky breath, shocked—and yes, excited—by his words and by his confidence.

"It's as good as done, witch."

32

Oh, no, no. I've seen this movie," Mariketa said when they came upon a wooden bridge hundreds of feet above a river gorge. The height was so marked, the river below looked like a thread. "And it wasn't a comedy!" She scrambled directly back into Bowe, then stiffened. Before she could retreat, he'd wrapped one arm over her upper chest and the other down to her waist.

He'd spooked her earlier—had known it was happening, even at the time. But he'd been filled with jealousy the likes of which he'd never known. And he'd been confounded that her revelation of loving another had felt like a booted kick to the ballocks.

Bowe didn't need to have Mariketa's *love*, he told himself. Just as long as he had *her*.

So why was he so envious of that faceless demon—the soon-to-be-dead demon who knew what it was like to be loved by Mariketa?

Now when she pressed back against him, as if for support, he gave her a quick nuzzle against her soft hair to praise her. "Mariketa, you're trembling."

"I'm petrified of heights."

"Rydstrom told me. Why this fear? Did something happen to you?"

"Yeah, sea level happened to me. As in, I'm rarely above it."

"Aye, then." Bowe asked Rydstrom, "Can we no' find another way across?"

Cade had just returned from scouting and answered, "Not without adding two more days."

Two days would be too late for him and Mariketa. He shot a look at Rydstrom.

"The bridge is sturdy," Rydstrom assured her. "These armies have been driving trucks over it. It's the way we must go."

Tera said, "All right, who's doing the obligatory thing with the rock?"

"What thing?" Bowe asked.

Mariketa said, "You know, someone drops a rock, and we all silently watch it fall while contemplating the plummet to our deaths?"

Oh, *that* rock thing. "Mariketa, there will be no falling. This will be safe to cross. There are even rope rails on the side. But we are doing this." She gave a muted whimper at his words. Knowing how important she found it to appear strong in front of the others—and rightly so in the world of the Lore—Bowe drew her aside. "How about I jog across the bridge to show you it's safe, then return to carry you over?"

She shook her head emphatically. "Y-you could be incrementally weakening it with every step."

He curled his fingers under her chin. "Lass, I will no' let you be hurt. Ever."

"I've got a bad feeling about this."

"Aye, you're acrophobic—there's no way you could have a *good* feeling about this. I'll just be right back."

"No, wait," she whispered, snatching his hand. "Don't go."

He waved the others on. "We'll catch up."

Tera said, "You okay, Mari?"

She gave a pained smile. "Ducky."

"Let me carry you over," he said again once they were alone. "Then you can keep your eyes closed."

"B-but both of us, together? You must weigh two hundred and fifty pounds."

"Look at the others," he said. Tierney was walking *on* the rope railing—and taunting her.

She narrowed her eyes. "Did he . . . he didn't just call me a skirt?"

"That he did."

She exhaled as if defeated. "Peer pressure always was my weakness." Glancing up at Bowe, she asked, "If I walk across the bridge by myself, will you follow me?"

Always. "I'll be right behind you."

"Really close," she said, then added in a rush, "but don't stand on the same board as me."

"Aye, noted. Now doona look down. Keep your eyes on Rydstrom's back. See, he's halfway across already."

"Okay." She gave a firm nod and reached for the railing. "I c-can do this. No looking down."

She was fear-stricken, her pupils like saucers and her hands shaking on the rope, but she still put one wee boot out onto the bridge. He'd known she was a brave lass, but when she took her first step, he wanted to howl with pride. Instead he said, "Was thinkin'. Maybe Lorekind would like you witches better if you were less mercenary."

"We *are* mercenaries!" she snapped without turning back.

"I ken that, but must you be?"

"For a thousand years, the House has been filled with mercenaries. That'd be like saying that people would like Lykae better if they were less wolfy. And let me tell you, you are *very* wolfy."

"Well, it's a good thing I'm rich so I can support you, kitten. I doona guess you've made too much money for the House."

Between gritted teeth, she demanded, "Why would you say that? And don't call me kitten!"

"Let's be realistic. I canna imagine you've been raking it in with your magicks, blowing up things the way you do. Does your coven have a money-back guarantee—"

"You're trying to goad me, to make me forget my fear."

"Aye. It was working. You're already halfway done."

"Tricksy, damned wolf—"

Birds shot from the canopy on both sides of the gorge. Moments later, the earth rumbled. Everyone on the bridge froze in surprise except for Bowe, who hooked his arm around Mari's waist, locking her tight against him.

"*Oh, gods! MacRieve?*" she whispered in a tremulous voice, her palms glowing with magick, as if in reflex.

"I'm right here, Mariketa." In mere seconds, everything had stilled. "It's over. Do you hear the forest quieting—"

Another rumble. With her bright hands death-gripped on the rail, her legs seemed to give out, but he held her upright. "No, no, Mari, I've got you. Come, then. We can even go back the same way, if you'll just let go."

She shook her head wildly, her eyes mirrors.

"Mari, you have to let go—I doona want to hurt your hands."

A sudden surge of pressure built in the air. When he

jerked his head up, he met eyes with Rydstrom, who had his brows drawn.

"Duck!" Rydstrom bellowed and Bowe just yanked Mariketa down before a boulder dropped directly over their heads. The force of it punched into the bridge, sending it rippling like a whip before rupturing it.

Looping his hand in the rope and locking his arm around her, he could do nothing but hold on as they swung like a pendulum straight for the sheer rock face.

33

～∞～

Mari screamed as they hurtled closer and closer to the mountain. MacRieve had a one-handed grip on the railing so they went spinning in the air. She squeezed her eyes shut, her scream cut off by his painful hold around her growing even tighter.

This can't be happening!

Just before they slammed into the rock, he twisted, keeping his body between her and the impact. They bounced off, and he twisted again.

When they finally settled, he said, "Are you hurt? Mariketa? Answer me!"

The rock slide had stirred grit and sand, and she coughed before she could cry, "Oh, gods, this isn't happening."

"Shh, shh. I've got you. Easy, then. I've got you now."

She ignored the urge to wipe her eyes, and instead tightened her grip on him. She clutched his arms so hard, her nails sank into the muscles, yet he said nothing. "A-are you okay?"

"Aye, fine. As soon as the dust clears, I'll climb straight up."

"What . . . what was that?"

"An earthquake. The area's known for them."

"The others? Are they safe?"

"Give me a second to see, lass. The dust is still settling over there as well. They're doubtless hanging on just like we are."

Bowe's jaw slackened. When the air cleared, he saw the bridge on the other side was . . . gone.

"Do you see them?"

"They're fine. They made it across," he told her. Not necessarily a lie. They might have leapt up before the bridge was lost—no matter how much more likely it was that they'd fallen.

Still, unless they lost their heads, a fall couldn't kill them. And until he got Mariketa down from this mountain, and safe from their present predicament, he didn't think it wise to tell her that her friends might have plunged hundreds of feet.

"Now, we've got to get ourselves to safe ground, too. I can use the bridge's wood slats as rungs. We'll just climb up. Verra well, Mari?"

"B-Bowen, wait! If you d-don't drop me on the climb up, I'll be nicer to you, and . . . and I'll sleep with you! I really will."

"Well, in that case, I'll be sure to hold you tight," he said, reaching above him.

"You're laughing at me."

"Nothing on earth could make me drop you." Almost to the top. "Even if you've been cruel to me."

"*I've* been cruel?"

"Aye, and toying with me."

"What are you talking about?" she demanded.

"About leading me to think you were going to 'give it up' then reneging."

"I never led you on!"

"Did you no' *jump me?*"

"You're trying to distract me again—" Her words ended in a shriek directly in his ear when he leapt from the bridge over the edge.

"There, we're on solid ground again. See, everything's fine." As soon as he'd gotten them back down under the trees, he set her on her feet, holding her shoulders until she was steady enough to stand on her own. But she launched herself right back at him, wrapping her arms around his waist, like she'd hug a tree.

He stared down at her. "Mariketa?"

"Th-thanks for not letting me die."

He dragged her arms up around his neck, then pressed her head to his chest, drawing her close. "I will never let anything happen to you." As she clutched him, he felt needed and strong—finally the protector he'd been born to be.

She whispered, "Bowen, I think you're quite possibly my favorite person in the world right now."

—*Yours.*—

I know. He did. For weeks he'd thought of her, dreamed of her. Her passion had awed him. Her bravery and beauty amazed him. Now he simply allowed himself to accept what he'd wanted so desperately.

She was his.

Her for him. Period.

"I can't believe you could hold on like that," she said. "You're really, uh, strong."

"I'm supposed to be, to protect you."

They both fell silent.

"Not *me*, MacRieve."

"I've made a decision, lass." He drew back and cupped her face. "If given the chance I would *no'* go back. You're mine. And I'm going to do whatever it takes, till I'm yours as well."

She made a frustrated sound. "Typical male! Because of what happened in the cave?"

"Aye, some. But also because of what happened after. We fit, you and me, and could make a life together. And, witch"—his gaze held hers—"we're going to have a bloody good time of it."

34

As they continued on, MacRieve grew quiet, seeming to carry the weight of the world on his shoulders. Mari couldn't read him and had begun to fear he regretted his earlier declaration.

To break the silence, she said, "You must be missing your clan. I've heard you're a tight-knit group."

He shrugged. "I'm no' much part of that—or I have no' been for some time." At her quizzical look, he said, "They question why I have no' found a way to die after my loss. I want to take you among them and say '*This* is why I kept going, you sods. And look at my reward.'"

Mari—alert—over your head!

"Have you been around my kind much before?" he asked.

"I've seen a couple of Lykae out on Bourbon Street—twins—but I've never met them."

"Ah, the infamous Uilliam and Munro. I wonder that they weren't all over you. Were you still with your *demon?*" He grated the word.

"No, we'd stopped seeing each other by then."

"Why did you break things off with him? Did he hurt you?"

"*He* left *me.*"

"Doona lie—"

"I'm not! He broke up with me."

When MacRieve nodded slowly, she said, "What? You can easily see that?"

"No, I was just thinking about a saying my clan has: 'Enjoy a bounty if one falls in your lap. Savor it if it was lost by a careless man.'"

Over my head. Maybe she *was* too young to resist. Maybe he was working her over like dough. Because right now, his prediction that he'd take her tonight was spot-on. "You see me as a bounty?"

"Aye." His eyes were so focused and sincere. "One I'm eager to partake of."

She grew flustered, and to break the moment, she said, "So, MacRieve, tell me five things about you that I didn't know."

He seemed strangely uncomfortable with her suggestion and said, "Why do you want this?"

"To break up the time while we're hiking."

"You first, lass."

"Well, I like to spin in office chairs till I'm nearly sick. My best friend thinks *"Laissez les bons temps rouler"* means "Plastic beads replace attire." I was a cheerleader—I know, the anti-establishment witch cheerleader. But it was the best way for me to get a scholarship." She sighed. "Until the cloak years."

He raised his brows. "A *football* cheerleader?"

"And some basketball, but mainly football."

"Happens to be my favorite sport."

"Mine, too! So how many is that?"

"Three. Go on, then. This is fascinatin' stuff."

"I like to play poker for cash, and pool-shark naive frat boys. Five things from you now."

"What about your family?" he asked. "Parents? Siblings?"

"Are you stalling?"

"I'm curious about you. Indulge me." He gave her a half grin. "Since I dinna drop you earlier."

Glancing away, she said, "Both my parents abandoned me at different times when I was a kid. Pops was a warlock—he ditched early and died soon after. My mother is a fey druidess—that's where I get the ears. She left me when I was twelve to go off and study druidry, or whatever it's called." Mari gave a self-conscious wince. "Wow. And I was really trying not to sound resentful."

"I'm sorry, Mariketa. I canna understand how any parent could leave a child behind."

For some reason, she didn't want Bowen thinking ill about her parents. "They must have had their reasons. They did care about me when they were with me." That, at least, she knew for certain.

When he didn't look wholly convinced, she said, "I remember when I was four, my parents took me to Disney World. My dad used magick to make sure I won all the prizes in the ring toss, even though he would raise his hands with an innocent expression every time I frowned at him. Both my mom and dad saw every mind-numbing musical and rode every ride, and all the while, they were weighted down with stuffed animals.

"By noon my dad had started carrying me on his shoulders. At the end of the day, the two of them had that bomb-blast look you see on parents in the final hours of an amusement park sentence. Even so, they'd stopped for one last treat for me. My mom was nearly cross-eyed with fatigue and almost tendered druid coins for ice cream. Then, when we were eating our ice cream in a plaza, my dad jerked up from a bench. 'Jill!' he yelled. 'Where's Mari? Ah, gods! I've lost our daughter!' Then my mother pointed out that I was on his shoulders."

The three of them had laughed until they'd cried.

Bowen cocked his head at her. "They sound like they doted."

Doted. What a fitting word. "I guess they did." After Mari's father had left, her mother continued to lavish her with attention—though Jillian would always appear saddened if they'd enjoyed themselves too much. Even at the end of that incredible day the two of them had spent on the beach, she'd seemed preoccupied—

Mari felt a sudden odd bite in the air and gazed up. She spied ravens circling overhead, making chills trip up her spine.

"What?" MacRieve asked, gently clasping her shoulders. "What is it?"

"I don't know. Probably nothing," she said, yet continued to peer around her.

"If you're having a gut feeling about something, I want to know. I should have listened to you about the bridge and will from now on."

But she couldn't voice what she was feeling, because she didn't understand it. "No, I'm fine," she insisted, forcing a smile. "You still owe me five things."

He rubbed his hand over the back of his neck, looking as if he'd rather deal with a mysterious threat than reveal five things about himself.

35

Bowe opened his mouth to answer her, but again drew a blank. Not surprising. He was on edge that she'd sensed a threat when he still scented nothing. Plus there was the fact that there was naught for Bowe to tell her.

Over the last many decades, his life had centered around his aim of bringing Mariah back. He wanted to steer clear of that subject—as well as that of the Hie. Yet aside from those pursuits, he hadn't had a real life in memory.

Bowe had known his existence was soulless and barren, but that fact had never been hit home like this.

He could tell her that he used to lead an army, a stalwart one. Yet the Horde had decimated it in the same war that Rydstrom had lost his, and Bowe would rather her not know of his failure. Today she'd begun regarding him differently, and he didn't want that to change.

He was good at killing. Also not helping his efforts with her.

And friends? Bowe didn't have many—or, rather, any—that he saw regularly. He'd let friendships wane, because it was always so uncomfortable for others to try to convey their sympathies to him. He'd rather save them the trouble—and besides, too often sympathy crossed over the line and became pity. Or they studied him like Lachlain did. Bowe put up with Lachlain's scrutiny because he was like a brother, but he didn't suffer it from others.

Christ, he was a cipher.

For the first time, he worried if he could be worthy enough for Mariketa. Did he even deserve her? Yes, she was a witch, but she was also stunningly beautiful and brave and clever.

"I like football, too," he finally said.

"You've already told me, so that doesn't count."

"I love the color of your eyes."

She tucked a curl behind her pointed ear, sliding him the bewitching smile that made his heart punch the insides of his chest. "What's your favorite place to visit?"

He absently answered, "Wherever you are."

"Bowen, five things about you can't all be about me."

But you're the only good thing that I've got. "Why no'?"

"Where's your home? I don't even know where you live."

"I have a place in Louisiana, but my real home is in the north of Scotland." Though he said *my* home, in his mind the large hunting lodge he'd had restored was already *their* home—but he didn't want to spook her further.

"What about your family? I bet you have a huge one, being a Lykae and all."

"My family was unusual. I'm an only child." Except for his male cousins, he had no one left.

Maybe that was why he wanted children so much, to grow his own family. Soon, he would reveal to Mariketa that he *wanted* that bomb-blast look parents had at an amusement park. And he and Mariketa would have brave children together—fearless even. He began to resent that patch of hers as a barrier to a prize he'd wanted for so long . . . a prize he now believed was within his grasp.

For the present, he cast about for something to say. "Tell me something about yourself that only your close friends know."

She scrunched her lips, then said, "It drives me absolutely crazy that I can't control my magick better. I act like it doesn't bother me, but it does. Just when I was about to leave for the Hie, these baby witches of six and seven came up to me and said, 'Mari, look what we can do,' and their little spells were more than I could manage."

"Maybe you were just a late starter at that age."

"No, more than I could manage—*now*."

He swiped his palm over the back of his neck. "Oh, then."

"Why am I granted all this power and then no means to control it? It's like giving someone a Ferrari with the horses under the hood raring to go, but then you get into the buttery leather driver's seat, and holy hell, there's no steering wheel. It's so frustrating."

"I know you will no' like to hear this, but it must be so with someone like you."

"What does that mean? And I caution you to proceed with care."

The corners of his lips curled. "You read about people like you in myths and in the Lore, struggling with their gifts. But it's the struggle that brings greatness. If your powers came easily to you, without incident, you would never appreciate them as you should. And you would no' be a good leader because you would be impatient with others who did have to work hard. It *never* comes easy to all the great warriors in history."

"It came easy to you."

He gave a half laugh. "And why do you think me a great warrior?"

"Rydstrom said you were frontline in every battle, and you're still alive. Therefore . . . great."

He grinned down at her. "My ego thanks you for that verra sweet stroke." His grin swiftly faded though. Reminded of Rydstrom, he realized that hours had passed since the bridge collapse, and still Bowe hadn't scented the others once. Though he couldn't detect them as well as he could his mate—he could find her a hundred miles away—he still should have picked up on them if they were within a quarter of that distance. But there'd been nothing.

Tomorrow would bring the night of the full moon, they'd been forced days out of their way, and as of now, he had no one to guard her—from him. Over and over, he'd deliberated if he should reveal to her how Mariah had died. He dreaded the thought that history might repeat itself, and feared that telling her would initiate a self-fulfilling prophesy.

If Mariketa ran from him out here . . .

He shook his head hard. Tonight, he would take her continuously, and he would mark her as he claimed her, revealing a good bit of the beast within him. Tomorrow, surely the others would catch up. But if not, Bowe would have accustomed her to his body, and then, when he inevitably lost control in the heat of the moon, maybe she wouldn't suffer from shock. He might prevent her from wanting to escape him.

When they heard the distant rumble of thunder, he dragged his gaze from her and said, "We need to start scouting for a place to make camp. It'll likely rain on the mountainside tonight."

"I could consult my mirror."

"Doona like that, Mariketa. I'd rather see you blow something up than that eerie apple bullshite again."

"I know."

"How do you know?"

"Witches believe the 'eerie' spells are the most powerful ones. What's more unnerving? A charging wolf or a non-poisonous snake dropping down on the back of your neck?"

"And you witches ponder these things?"

"We've kind of had to."

No longer. At least not *his* witch.

If Mariketa wanted to make bees sting, then that was one thing, but he would forbid the dark magicks, like the conjuring and enchantments. He would lay down the law, and by the gods, she would—

She turned to give him her siren's smile as she lazily trailed her finger over a boulder—a hip-high one. His heart raced, his previous thoughts unrecallable. This was truly going to happen—after twelve hundred years, he was going to claim his mate.

Yes, tonight.

36

By the time they saw the first strike of lightning that night, MacRieve had completed a platform and lean-to by a stream and had hunted for Mari. Once the nightly rain started, they were fed and clean. She was cozily dressed in his shirt once more—and nothing else.

And he'd just taken his first deep kiss from her.

When he drew back, it took her a moment to open her eyes. She found his were flickering from amber to ice blue and were intent on her as he studied her reaction.

She sighed, "I really like the way you kiss me."

"I hope you're going tae like more than my kiss."

"Bowen, you won't lose control, will you? It's been a while for me."

"No, lass, I will no'. But how long's it been?"

"Over four years."

He laughed without humor. "Try one hundred and eighty."

Her brows drew together. "Not a single female? Not a single encounter?"

"No' one. Hell, I might have forgotten how tae do this."

"Like riding a bike, right?"

"Let's see, then." He leaned forward once more to kiss her neck, flicking his tongue until she softly moaned. She found herself easing back under the firm weight of his hand as he rucked the shirt to her waist.

Then he laid his rough palms on her inner thighs and pressed her legs open. Though she began trembling, he didn't touch her bared sex. But his ice blue eyes were riveted to it, his growl rumbling low.

When he licked his lips, she shivered and grew wetter, knowing what he planned. "*Bowen . . .*" She bit the inside of her cheek to keep from begging for his tongue against her. Her body yearned for it.

He settled between her legs, kissing down her torso to nuzzle her ring. Then lower . . .

When he pressed his open mouth against her sex, slipping his tongue into her folds, she arched her back in delight, threading her fingers in his hair. He gave a harsh groan against her, and his hands clenched her thighs hard, as if he'd forgotten himself.

"Dreamed of tastin' you," he growled, his breaths hot against her. Through heavy-lidded eyes, she stared down at him. As he licked and teased, his brows were drawn, his eyes closed tightly, as if he was in an agony of pleasure.

She fought the building tension, wanting this to last forever. But under his hungry kiss, she waged a losing battle.

"Come for me, lass," he rasped, then gently suckled her clitoris, his strong tongue flicking over it.

She gave a cry out into the night, the deep knot of lust unfurling. As she began to come, she shot upright. Gripping his hair, she undulated her hips, rubbing her flesh against his tongue. He was snarling against her, lapping at her wildly. "*Witch . . . you drive me mad. . . .*"

When he'd wrung every last shudder from her, she had to push him away.

As if reluctant to leave, he kissed her thighs languidly, though she could feel his hands shaking.

"Bowen," she whispered. "I need you inside me."

"Anythin'," he grated, rising up to yank off his clothes, while she lay back and stared at him in awe.

This is actually going to happen.

Though he was in a lather from licking that orgasm from her—and still staggered from her wanton response—he somehow controlled himself to make sure she was ready to receive him. He delved his fingers inside her tight sheath until her nails bit into his shoulders with frustration.

At last, he allowed himself to lie in the cradle of her thighs. Again, his dazed mind thought, *I'm going to claim her.*

And he was . . . nervous.

He'd vowed to her that she'd never want to leave his bed, speaking with all the arrogance he'd used to possess— before he'd been celibate for nearly two centuries.

Yet even when he was on the verge of entering her, he somehow remembered the patch. He fingered it at her arm, making his voice as casual as possible. "Let's take this off, then."

Breathless, she asked, "Why would you want me to?"

"You've no reason to wear it. You'll have no other man but me, and I can only get my mate with bairns—no other female. So if you conceived, then all the better. We'll know without a doubt that you're mine."

"Whoa . . ." She stiffened beneath him, shoving his hand away. "I don't *want* to get pregnant."

His heart sank. *Of course not. Nothing's changed.* He rolled off her to his side.

"I'm only twenty-three. It's too early!"

He swung his gaze on her. "But you do . . . you do want to eventually?"

"Sure, but not now," she said, and he felt a welling of relief. "Not until I'm in my thirties or forties. Chronologically. That's the plan. I know I don't seem like the type of woman to have a plan, but I do."

"What's the difference between now and ten years in the grand scheme?"

"I've got a lot to get straightened out in my life. My powers, my place in the House. Right now I can't even take care of myself, much less someone else."

"I'll take care of you. Always." He cupped her face. "You've nothing to worry about ever again."

"*Wait* . . ." She went still. "That's what this is all about? So you can be sure?" His eyes widened when hers began to water. "The entire seduction. The full court press last night, today, tonight. So you can find out for certain whether I'm your mate or not."

"Do you think there's no other reason why I might want tae be inside you?" He shoved her palm to his aching shaft, but she yanked her hand back.

"Not one as important as your knowing for certain, as your black and white. Today, you said that you'd decided on me, so why this test?" She sat up, pulling the shirt to cover her. "I'll tell you—because you're still recognizing the possibility that I won't *pass* the test. You're trying to persuade me to throw all in with you, to accept you as mine—but *you're* not doing it!" A tear spilled down her cheek and she swiped it away with the back of her hand. "I'll become immortal soon, and I'll be impervious to most injuries, yet you couldn't wait for me to turn? Really, MacRieve, a mortal, giving birth to the offspring of a nearly seven-foot-tall werewolf? And Lykae conceive two and three at a time, don't they? Do you think I would survive the labor?"

"Damn it, I dinna think of that."

As *Lachlain always said,* "*Ach, Bowe, you've fucked up this time.*"

"You never considered these things?"

"Mariketa, I am a product of my times. For most of my life, males and females desired bairns and would do anything to have them. And since you doona act mortal or look it, each show of your power makes it easier for me to forget that you are vulnerable still. I would never want anything to happen to you."

"Because it would hurt *you!*" she cried. "Everyone thinks you were so selfless in your love for your dead mate. But the truth is, you're the most selfish male I've ever known. You ache for your mate because *you* don't want to feel empty or guilty over her death. Not out of love for her."

"You go too far, Mariketa," he said, even as her comment resonated within him—because at some level, he'd begun to wonder . . . if he *had* ever loved Mariah.

He'd been with the witch for mere days. Had whatever he was feeling for the lass already overshadowed what he'd experienced with Mariah?

"I don't think so. The tomb incident wasn't an anomaly. You really are a merciless bastard. Just get away from me."

"Mariketa—"

"Get away." She reached for her mirror. "Or I will put you away."

"Oh, no, no, bloody hell if you're doing that again." He'd be damned if he'd sit there and watch her whisper to a mirror in a conversation he couldn't hear.

* * *

"What is the appeal of that cursed thing?"

Mari was almost as furious that he wanted to take away her one true, dependable power as she was about his wanting *to knock her up*.

She felt like she was on the cusp of something big with her magick. The reflection was teaching her. Every time she did the conjuring she garnered more control over her power. And she suspected that with each bite of apple she grew physically stronger. "The appeal? I'm going to ask the reflection if the others are truly okay—because, for some reason, I find myself distrusting everything you've ever told me."

He crossed his arms over his chest. "No' near me."

"Then you better hurry up and leave."

"You think I will no'?" He shot to his feet and slung on his jeans, stomping into his boots. "I should leave you out here—to remind you how much you need me."

"Do it. Dare you to! And don't let a branch hit your ass on the way out."

"Oh, this is just great!"

"Oh, aye, this is '*juice grett*.'"

He pointed his forefinger at her, opened his mouth to say something, then snapped it shut. "I will no' watch this," he finally grated, before loping off.

Alone, Mari lay dazed by what had just occurred. She'd thought they were going to make love all night because he desired her. Not because he desired to impregnate her.

Or try to. MacRieve had to have his little test, because for whatever reason, he couldn't look at her, hear her voice, and be near her and know *she* was his.

What in the hell would it take for someone to say to Mari, "I choose *you*"?

She thought she would keel over in shock if someone got to know her, and then, based on her personal merits alone—not matehood, or *whatever*—said, "No doubt of it. You are the one for me."

And what would MacRieve have done if she didn't conceive after repeated attempts?

Left me, that's what.

That realization really blew, because now, when she thought of her future back in New Orleans, away from this other-world jungle, she kept seeing him in it.

She brushed another tear away. Damn it, what was it about her that made her so . . . disposable?

37

∽❦∽

Sometimes Bowe could tell in an instant when a memory would be as clear in a thousand years as the day he experienced it.

When he returned to the campsite after a hard run, he knew the scene before him would prove indelible, lasting through even an immortal's lifetime.

With flashes of lightning in the background, and soft rain falling, he found Mariketa lying on her side in the lean-to, one arm folded under her head. Her other arm was raised, with a huge spider lumbering over her glowing hand. She absently regarded it with brilliant, mirrored eyes. Her lips were a deeper red than he'd ever seen them— blood red—and three sinister-looking apples lay half eaten beside her. She looked like that preternatural reflection he'd seen in the water.

—*Be wary.*—

Those ominous vines grew in profusion, twisting in dense layers over the lean-to, as if defensively, and the entire platform was surrounded by beasties—iguanas, frogs, snakes, deer mice, and coatimundi made up a creeping moat. In the canopy directly above her, territorial howler monkeys sat unusually poised and watchful, sharing their limbs with owls.

In the witch's current mood, she seemed to attract them all.

—*Wary. Her power is unstable.*—

He got chills, shivering even as he sweated after his run, and still part of him wanted to charge over there and comfort her.

He could feel her sadness and her disappointment—in him. His own anger had turned to a weary realization. . . .

If he wanted her, *he* would have to change.

Weeks ago, he'd been disgusted to see that Lachlain had allowed his vampire mate to drink from him. Vampires had tortured Lachlain in unimaginable ways and had decimated his family. In turn, he'd killed thousands of their kind.

A vampire's bite was a mark of weakness, of abject shame among the Lykae; Lachlain wore Emma's bite like a badge. He had changed for her, had somehow overcome a millennium-long hatred.

Now Bowe understood why Lachlain had been moved to do so. But could Bowe accept the haunting female before him? Change an entrenched mind-set for her?

Bowe himself had advised Lachlain not to try to force Emma to their ways, but that hadn't meant that Bowe was saying to embrace her ways either.

He asked Mariketa, "Did you find out what happened to the others?"

Without facing him, she said, "They're safe."

"Are they coming?"

She shrugged. "I don't know—just learned that they're not in immediate danger."

When he remained silent, she murmured, "If you think I don't know what I look like, I do. No butterflies, fauns, and songbirds for me." She finally faced him. "It must be hard for you, going from a real fairy princess to the wicked witch who kills for money." She frowned to herself. "I think I'm supposed to be the villain in this piece."

"Maybe that's why we would fit so well." How in the hell could he expect her to tolerate the beast within him when he couldn't accept the power intrinsic in her? "If you're the villain, doona forget that I'm the monster."

Mari planted her hands on her knees as she sucked in air, her braids swinging forward with each inhalation. "You're doing this . . . to retaliate for last night." That morning, he'd pushed her for what had to be leagues, using his machete and his claws to thrash through the jungle at a break-neck pace. "Fine. Take the patch . . . knock me up with a litter . . . but just let me *stop*!"

"No' to retaliate." His mood, not exactly jubilant after having slept in the rain last night, had grown steadily worse as the day progressed.

"Then why are you pushing so hard?"

"I'd hoped Rydstrom and the others would have caught up with us by now."

She rolled her eyes. "A clue? You *slow down* when you want people to catch up."

"Their pace would be twice as fast as ours. They should've been able to rejoin us." He handed her the canteen. "Listen, Mariketa, I want you to know that I'm sorry for last night. Though I've long wanted bairns, I'd give up the chance forever if the alternative was your suffering. I doona know how to convince you of this, but it's true."

He appeared so earnest, and yet she wasn't sold. "I don't know how you can convince me either."

"Here." He held out his hand. "I'll carry you on my back, but we have to move. There might be a highway in reach. You could hitch a ride into Belize and get to the coast, maybe to an airport."

"Why am I the only one hitching a ride?" When he ran his fingers through his hair, she said, "What? Tell me."

"The moon is full this eve."

"Oh." Of course she'd noticed, but she hadn't thought the ramifications could be this dire until she'd seen his expression just now. *Oh, hell.*

"I've been debating the best way to get you out of my reach. If I run from you, I leave you vulnerable. If I stay with you . . ." He trailed off.

"You look like the apocalypse has arrived. Is it really so dangerous?"

Instead of reassuring her, he nodded. "Aye. I lose control over myself, and the difference between us in strength is just too vast. If given free leave to take you, I'd rend you in two."

She swallowed. "What exactly do you turn into, Mac-Rieve? Describe it to me."

He answered, "The Lykae call it *saorachadh ainmhidh bho a cliabhan*—letting the beast out of its cage. My face will change, becoming a cross between lupine and human. My body grows larger, taller. My strength increases exponentially."

"I've seen the fangs and claws."

"Sharper and longer. And flickering over me will be an image of the beast inside me. It is . . . harrowing to those not of my kind."

"What would you do to me?"

He looked away. "I'd take you in the dirt like an animal.

I'd mark your body with my fangs, and even after the bite healed, Lykae could still see it forever and know you'd been claimed." He rubbed his hand over his mouth, as if imagining it even then. "What does your gut feeling tell you to do with me?" he asked, facing her again. "Take away everything else—what do you sense?"

She thought for a moment, trying to digest what he'd just told her. She'd known Lykae bit and scratched each other during sex. But she'd never imagined that Bowen would want to sink his fangs in her skin, marking her forever—or that he'd lose control over himself so totally. "Honestly, I have no idea. But I could ask the mirror what to do."

He clenched his jaw, clearly struggling with the idea. "What can it tell you?" he finally said.

"I usually only get cursory answers. Classic oracular."

He hesitated for long moments, the conflict within him clear on his face. "Ask it, then. Would it be more dangerous to escape me—or to remain within my reach?"

38

Mari was out of breath, griping to herself, and pissed that because Bowen was going to get moon-ass-crazy, she had to do the jungle by herself, basically running for her life and all that.

And he was sprinting in the opposite direction. But if she didn't find civilization and some manner of vehicle for speedy travel, it wouldn't matter. He'd told her he could cover *hundreds upon hundreds* of miles to get to her on a night like this.

At a small stream, she knelt down to catch her breath and splash her face with water, careful not to drink any of it. As she unwound her canteen to knead her neck, she thought that if she could just get to a town, she could escape him *and* enjoy a hot shower for the first time in a month. Breakfast in the morning would be hot and waffly.

She froze when she thought she heard movement in a nearby copse of trees, then scanned the area. Probably just an animal. They tended to be in jungles. She turned back to the stream—

"Put your hands on your head."

Not an animal. As she slowly stood and turned, she recognized that these weren't locals. These were bad guys, three of them with machine guns aimed at her face.

In her present mood that equaled: *Why, I believe I'll turn them into frogs!* Just as she reached for the mirror in her pocket, they cocked their weapons.

The oldest man was clearly the leader, and his tone was deadly when he said, "Your hands on your head—or I'll put a bullet into it." He didn't have a thick accent. These must be the international narco-terrorists, the ones who made the cartel look mild. So much for the mirror's judgment.

Unless this was still better than Bowen.

Before she could even get close to working a spell, one soldier had a gun barrel shoved against her temple. She'd thought it would be cold, but it was uncomfortably warm.

Fear shivered through her, and she raised her hands. As the soldier bound them behind her with plastic ties like the ones the NOPD used, she said, "You have no idea what a mistake you're making—there are people who will be a shade irate about this abduction."

"We have never heard that from a hostage," the second soldier said as they started away. With a rough grip on her upper arm, he hauled her from the water, yanking her uphill and then down the next rise. She struggled against him, trying to think of some way to convince them to free her.

"For all you know, I could be CIA or DEA," she said when she heard an engine idling. Their vehicle was near—which meant the road had been close.

"Too young," the first lackey said. "You look like a lost environmentalist."

When they arrived at their army green truck, she resisted getting in the back. "Why haven't you asked me about my information?" she demanded. The man simply shoved her up into the truck bed, banging her knee so hard her eyes watered.

"Why would we?" the leader asked in an unctuous tone.

Her brows drew together as everything became clear. They weren't going to ransom her—at least, not at first. They were going to *keep* her. The thought made her retch into her mouth. She had to get her hands free.

Once the truck started down rutted roads, she determined that they were taking her right back in MacRieve's direction. "Listen to me, the only way you are going to live through the night is to release me this instant." She could already see the moon faint but full in the daytime sky. A portentous reminder. "You can't even conceive of what you're bringing down on yourself." They ignored her, having no idea that they were basically dragging bait back to their base.

She knew MacRieve would come for her, but that was the other half of the problem. She didn't want to be a sitting duck tonight.

When they reached a camouflaged outpost, the three hauled her from the truck though she fought them. After dragging her inside, they forced her down deep into a bunker, leading her into tunnels in the earth. *Cold and dark. Fancy that.*

One tunnel had a line of cells, all with solid steel doors, as if bomb-proofed. In fact, everything in this place seemed to be so. One of the men punched a code into a keypad, and an adjoining door slid open. The other soldier shoved her into a barren cell, with only a cot and a toilet within. She inanely remembered Carrow calling jail *two hots and a cot.*

"You have to untie me."

"You're in no position to make demands," the leader said. "Best accept your lot and prepare yourself for tonight."

"What's my lot?"

"It's very simple. We were out provisioning," he explained, raking her with his gaze, "and you are a provision." He turned to the doorway.

"Then there's nothing I can do for you," she murmured. "I vow you won't survive past midnight. And your last sight before you die will make you relieved to go."

One soldier laughed nervously. The second lackey scowled. The leader turned in a flash and backhanded her, his heavy ring catching her temple when she tried to duck. The force sent her spinning to the ground. Hands still bound behind her, she landed on her face.

Struggling to her knees, she wiped her temple on her shoulder. When she saw the blood, she cast him an evil smile. "You're going to die extra bad for that."

At dusk, Bowe couldn't resist the pull of his female any longer. Her scent was still in the jungle—she hadn't made it to the city and a flight out. Though he fought with everything he was, he felt himself changing direction, retracing his earlier footfalls to her.

He'd never run so fast . . . no, there'd been one other time. . . .

He shook off that memory. Mariketa's tantalizing scent called to him and nothing else mattered. Acres of treacherous terrain passed effortlessly beneath his feet. Just a mile or so more till he found her. *Closer.* He could tell she was near . . . yards away now, directly up the stream bank.

He jerked to a stop when he reached her scent.

She wasn't here.

He'd locked onto her bag, her clothes. So where in the hell was she? Her canteen lay off to the side—she'd never leave her boiled water. Other odors came to him—human males laden with aggression, gun oil, cigarettes. He sighted boot prints in the mud. Over the next rise were tire tracks. Soldiers had abducted her.

And Bowe knew why. His claws sank into his palms.

He barely detected another scent. Her fear.

—*Punish them*.—

They'd taken his female, frightened his vulnerable mate. *Turning . . . already*.

He would slaughter them, every one.

With a roar of fury, he let the beast free.

39

He'd come.

Mari knew when gunfire began to echo in the tunnels of the bunker. Men barked orders with authority, and machine guns popped in concentrated waves.

Yet soon the organized defense became erratic. The commands devolved into . . . screams.

These humans—along with herself—were trapped down in the earth with a monster. He'd begun to kill, and she could do nothing but wait with dread. With her hands still bound behind her, she rocked forward and back on the cot.

His onslaught of violence seemed to keep beat with the heavy drum of her heart. She heard hardened men yell out in terror before the sound gurgled from their slashed throats.

Had MacRieve used his teeth or claws?

Would *she* scream at the sight of him?

"*Dios mío!*" one soldier gritted out. Chills coursed through her when she heard another *weeping*—before being instantly silenced.

A split second after a wild clap of machine gun fire, an explosion sounded and the electricity flared. When the overhead light sparked and burst into fragments, she shrieked in the sudden blackness.

From somewhere out in the tunnels came his answering bellow of rage.

She swallowed with fear. Moments later red emergency lights hummed on. When she saw that chunks of glass had fallen out of the light cage above, she backed to the biggest piece, crouching down to collect it with her bound hands. Then she began clumsily sawing at the tie.

Just as she thought she was close to slicing free, she heard the keypad at her cell entrance. She didn't breathe as the door whirred open.

The leader slipped in, softly closing and locking it behind him. In a low voice, he hissed, "You'll tell me who's behind this incursion! Who's—"

He abruptly whirled around and jerked his gun up.

Harsh breaths sounded just outside her door.

MacRieve was here. And she couldn't imagine what he would do once he got past that barrier. Would he butcher the soldier, then shove her face into the cot? *Take you in the dirt like an animal*, he'd said.

Why was he hesitating? She heard the tips of his claws meet the steel of the cell door. He'd raised his palms to the door?

Yes, and then he rested his forehead against it, his claws beginning to sink in, in frustration. Her heart twisted.

Bowen didn't want her to see him like this.

Because sometimes monsters know what they are. She felt her eyes water with sympathy for him, experienced a sudden ache to comfort him—

With a deafening grinding sound, he wrenched the door from its groove.

The soldier turned his attention from her long enough

for her to finish cutting through the ties at her wrists. When she glanced up, she could distinguish only Mac-Rieve's outline in the shadows. His breathing was so loud it sounded more like snarls. His massive shoulders rose and fell with the heaving exhalations.

The man weakly raised his rifle and fired. Claws shot out from the dark to slice through the gun barrel as though it were paper.

Then MacRieve crossed the threshold. The red backup light finally caught him.

The soldier took one look at MacRieve and released his bladder; she swayed on her feet.

So much blood . . . MacRieve was covered in it.

Mari's thoughts began to register slowly, hazily. *Am I going into shock? Look at his face, his body. Had I thought I could handle this? Or comfort him?*

At once, his pale blue eyes narrowed on the mark at her temple, then flared with an unimaginable rage. *He truly is a beast, a monster from Lore.*

Panic bubbled up inside her, and she shook as much as the soldier begging for his life in broken Spanish.

MacRieve's harrowing gaze swung to the man then returned to her face. "*Struck . . . you?*" His voice was deep and raspy, his vocal cords altered.

She stared dumbly, unable to answer. MacRieve raised his hand above the man for the killing blow, his black claws glinting in the red light. A whoosh of air. She squeezed her eyes shut as jugular blood sprayed across her face, hot and thick.

What came next was a blur. The scream was hers. Light flooded from her eyes and hands. MacRieve flew across the room. As she darted for the entrance, she used magick to lift the onerous cell door, then slammed it behind her, sealing it like a plug.

His roar boomed off the solid walls.

The sound of a monster.

In pure terror, she ran through the smoky tunnels, absently working circulation back into her wrists. Everywhere dead soldiers lay mauled, their sightless eyes still wide with shock. Blood had splashed against the walls and pooled on the ground, looking like tar in the glow of the backup lights. She clenched her jaw against vomiting from the sickening odor, but she would spare no pity for killers like them.

She locked and sealed the next tunnel door, and the next, aware that she was only delaying MacRieve. Her only hope was to get a vehicle. . . .

Tripping up the last set of stairs to the surface, she used her hands to push herself up again and again. At last, she reached the outside. Running free into the rainy night, she sloshed in puddles, mud splashing up to her thighs. *Need a truck, need a truck . . . with keys.*

She stumbled, raised her gaze. *There . . . truck.*

Stolen truck. It didn't have doors or a roof and the rain continued to pound, but could there be . . . yes, *keys*!

She darted inside to the slick vinyl seat, pinched the ignition key, and twisted it hard. The engine rumbled and died. Once more, turning over, then dying. *"Come on . . . come on . . . start, you bitch!"*

Ignition! She stomped on the gas pedal—not too light on the clutch either—and the truck lurched into motion. Glad for once of the smell of burning clutch.

The roads were soupy. The rain was falling on and off, but in thunderous bouts. She fishtailed, attempting to get the wipers to work, but rain continued to pelt her eyes from above. She skidded along, driving too fast . . . too fast. *Have to or he'll catch me . . . .*

When she hit a dip and was almost bounced from the truck, she fastened her seat belt. Squinting, she recognized the area, remembered the sheer drop-offs lining these roads. *Way too fast.*

She shook her head. No, she'd risk a damn drop-off before she'd let him take her. She shuddered again at the image of him—the crazed look in his uncanny eyes, the blood spilling from the corners of his mouth and dripping from his fangs, his *size.*

And it wanted to . . . *mate* with her like that. To sink those bloody fangs into her skin.

No. Concentrate! She could do this, could get away. She swiped the back of her arm over her drenched face—

Eyes reflected back at her in the headlights. *His.*

She stomped the brake and yanked the wheel right, sending the truck reeling. The wheel spun wildly . . . until the back end lurched off the road's edge and jerked to a stop, the chassis sunk into a mud bank.

Have to run! With shaking hands, she fought to unlatch her seat belt.

The entire road began to creep away.

As she screamed, the truck slid sideways down a sharp embankment until it hit a stump and reared into the air. It slammed back to the ground with the front heading down at an almost ninety-degree angle.

She locked the brakes, and hardwood limbs stabbed at the front bumper, but the truck wouldn't be stopped. Broad leaves slapped the windshield as the speed increased. She screamed again when the glass finally broke.

Oh, gods, no . . . The edge would be close. Just as she raised her arms in front of her face, her body was catapulted forward, then snatched in place by her seat belt. Gasping, she lowered her arms and cracked open her eyes.

MacRieve was at the front—he'd *caught* the truck. She could hear his claws digging down into the hood as he grappled to hold her at the precipice.

The headlights shined over his bloody face and clothes, his straining muscles. The power in his changed body stunned her.

"Get . . . *out!*" he bellowed in that beastly voice. "*Higher . . . now!*"

Eyes wide, she fumbled with the seat belt. Wouldn't open. *No . . . no . . . this shit only happens in movies!*

The rain began again, a deluge. Beneath the truck, the ground moved, feeling loose, gummy, *loose* . . .

She froze, met his eyes.

In an instant, he leapt forward, stomping across the hood. With two swift movements, he'd cut her from the belt and tossed her over his shoulder. He lunged over the length of the truck to fight for higher ground, but the earth was collapsing under his feet.

40

❧

Bowe did the only thing he could when they began to plummet from the drop-off—wrapped his body around hers, praying he could protect her with it.

Falling . . . fear for her rioting within him as he squeezed her tight. Landing . . . in deep *water?*

He blinked his eyes, wanting to roar at their fortune. No time. Rapids caught them.

As they surged forward, he shoved her above him, letting her get air, twisting to shield her from any collisions with rocks or debris.

Just as before, she'd run, but he would not let her die again. He began battling the current to get to the shore. Freed of the river, he tossed her to the bank, feeling her for injuries. He found none.

—*She's safe.*—

His female . . . unharmed. Over and over she'd been in jeopardy—his heart about to burst from his chest each time—yet somehow, in all that chaos, he'd kept her from injury.

She went to her hands and knees, but didn't get far before collapsing onto her front. He dropped behind her, fighting to catch his breath. He'd been shot more times than he'd thought, but hadn't felt them before. Now the wounds were taking their toll.

How long they lay like this, he didn't know. Yet when the rain eased and the moon rose high, his female's scent became undeniable.

Resisting the need . . . the driving urges . . . struggling to ignore the Instinct:

—*Claim what's yours. She's strong.*—

Strong, yes, but she was also disgusted by what he was— he'd seen the undisguised revulsion in her dazed expression even before she'd risked her life fleeing him.

Again.

He closed his eyes, hating to the gods what he was—

She leapt up and darted forward, shocking him with her speed.

He labored to rise. The bullets lodged in his body stabbed like daggers. "No, doona run from me!"

Running from him . . . worst thing she could do . . . making him even wilder with her. He easily caught up to her, then tensed to spring. He lunged forward, his hand shooting out to clamp her ankle.

She screamed when he dragged her down to him.

In the mud, Mari crawled frantically, but he had a vise grip on her ankle.

"You canna run . . ." he grated with difficulty from behind her.

The hell she couldn't. Mari kicked back with her boot, the heel connecting squarely with the side of his face. Yet in retaliation he only growled low, smacked her on the ass, and spit out the back tooth she'd knocked loose. There was none of the fury she expected.

She slowed her struggles, so afraid to look back. . . .

When she chanced a glance, she found that the rain and the river had washed clean the blood from his mouth, his face, and his clenched hands and claws. His pale eyes met hers—the brutal rage she'd seen in him had ebbed.

His features didn't appear so gruesome to her. No longer did he seem like a monster—only a now unfamiliar male, one with an animal need to claim what he viewed as his to take.

"Doona run from me . . ."

She eased her body toward him, seeming to confound him. "I won't." At her words, his eyes lit somehow with both relief and anguish. "I've just . . . I'd never seen anything like you—and I was frightened."

"Should be . . . if you knew what I need, what I intend . . . tae do . . ." His hand shot forward to claw off her shorts.

"No, damn it! Just give me—give me a minute to process all this!"

When he forced her beneath him and began *biting* off her shirt, she screamed, "No!"

Light exploded. Power emitted from her hands and eyes, briefly blinding her. When she blinked her eyes open, they went wide. As if bound, MacRieve was pressed against a great ceiba tree, arms pinned back until his palms rested on the thick trunk behind him.

Holy hell.

He thrashed to free himself, his claws digging down into the striated bark. But whatever binding she'd used on him held firm. "Don't struggle—you can't get free. You'll just hurt yourself." When she realized he wasn't fighting only against her magick but against turning completely, she unsteadily rose and crossed to him. "Why do you fight it still?"

His eyes were so full of yearning. "*Want you.*"

When she could drag her gaze from his face, she saw his clothing was riddled with holes. "Oh, gods, you've been shot! How many damned times— How could you hold the truck? And get us out of the river?"

As though with pride, his chin jutted up just a touch. "*Keep you safe.*"

And her heart melted for this beast.

"You did, Bowen. You freed me and kept me safe." The carnage had all been to protect her—brought on because those men had planned to hurt her again and again. Bowen had killed so savagely only for her. Now she wanted to protect him as well, to heal the countless injuries he'd borne for her. "Can I use more magick on you?"

He eagerly nodded. "Knock me . . . unconscious . . . bash my head against a rock . . . know you can."

"That wasn't quite what I had in mind." She thought they'd been washed downstream far enough away from the bunker but still asked, "Would you scent if men got near us?"

"Aye. No one comes near you."

She nodded. "Bowen, I'm going to keep you like this for a little bit, okay?" she murmured as she began removing his clothes. When she stripped him of his bullet-riddled shirt, she realized that *she* could move his limbs and hands, positioning them at will—though he still couldn't.

This was some heady magick. She felt powerful and in control—such a change from how she'd felt fleeing Bowen, or when she'd been forced at gunpoint to that dismal bunker.

She removed his boots, then very carefully undid the

bulging zipper of his jeans. She could perceive his body quaking with anticipation, could hear low growls rumbling from his chest as his erection sprang forth. The crown was glistening, the shaft engorged and straining toward her. As she worked down his jeans, her hair slid over it, and he gave a harsh gasp.

Once he was unclothed, she began rubbing his skin with sweeping strokes, as she'd seen other witches do for a healing. Over each of the wounds, her hands turned hot. She knew that she was healing him, somehow melting away the bullets. Her eyes fluttered closed at the strange—but not unpleasant—sensation. When she moved her hand from an area, she left only smooth, unbroken skin behind.

While she ministered to him, she explored him, familiarizing herself with his new form. Without the rage and the blood . . . *I believe I can handle this.* As she continued to caress him, she even found herself aroused by him. His splendid muscles and towering frame were exaggerated, yet beneath the image of the beast flickering over him and the changes to his body, his skin was still much the same.

Reaching behind him, she felt bullet wounds on his shoulder blades and high on the back of his thigh. He licked and kissed her neck as she trailed one of her hands over his back, the other over the rock-hard muscles of his ass.

Only when he nipped at her neck did she comprehend that she had a naked, almost fully turned werewolf trapped by her power.

To do with as she wished.

At that moment, she realized her intent with him and was surprised by how strong her will was in this.

Somehow . . . Mari was going to have him, completely.

41

◈

She will no' run, Bowen thought in stunned relief, even as the pressure to claim her, to mark her, grew. He grappled to free himself from her hold, though he recognized that when he was pinned like this, she could explore him, study him—possibly lose her fear of him. "No' repulsed by me?"

"No, if you're not coated in blood and it's not dripping from your big fangs," she said matter-of-factly, as she rubbed her soft, soft hands over him. "I'm not going to lie to you—that scared the living hell out of me. But I think . . . I believe I'm getting more used to you now."

"Even when I'm like . . . this? After I killed?"

She nodded. "The world's a better place now that you've destroyed those men," she said. "But are you all right with what I'm doing, Bowen?"

She kept asking him to make sure *he* was comfortable in the midst of this. Though he felt no more injuries, she continued to touch him, but why?

Every muscle in his body shot tense when he caught the exquisite scent of her growing arousal. "Free me!" She wanted him, too. Even when he was like this, her body was readying for his, and he hadn't yet touched her.

"No, I can't do that," she said. "I won't. Just let me ease into this."

Naturally, she would be tentative. He could take wary over disgusted any day. "Then bare yourself."

Taking her hands from him, she peeled her sodden top over her head, yet hesitated with her bra. He jerked a nod at it, and at last she revealed full, creamy flesh for him. He could gaze at her breasts forever. Her nipples were the same ruby color as her lips—that attracting red that made him feel wild to have his mouth on them.

"Everything off." He gaped in delight, eyes following her every movement as she stripped down. Her misted skin was beautiful, and, he knew, would be so supple under his tongue.

When undressed, she returned to cupping and kneading him, her breasts slipping across his chest. But soon it felt like her hands kept rubbing where they'd just been, until his entire body was being stroked. He shuddered and his legs went weak.

"What're you . . . doin' tae me?"

A siren's throaty voice. "I don't know. It's just happening."

"Go mad . . . from this . . . feels so fucking good—"

His words died when she knelt before him. He stared in disbelief as she took his shaft in her hand and with her stunning face caressed the length. *Dreaming . . . must be.* She couldn't be real.

His female *was* straight from his dreams. And she was gazing up at him with her eyes filled with . . . *desire for him.*

He felt her warm breath just before she lovingly licked the slit of his cock head. Yelling out, he tried to rock his pinned hips, wanting deeper between those moist, red lips.

The hint of salt on her tongue made her hungry for more and aroused to the point of agony.

Bowen stared down at her as if in awe, seeming to memorize the sight of her pleasuring him. His body was so responsive. When she licked the underside of his shaft from the crown to the base, he bit out wicked oaths. Her tongue against his heavy sack stopped his breath.

And as she took the slick head deep in her mouth, he shuddered violently, his chest muscles bulging with strain. His flesh throbbed against her lips, making her moan around him.

She couldn't take all of his length, so she used her hand as well to fondle him. Under her palm, she could feel that the base of his shaft was swollen, thick with semen, and her sex clenched for him, wanting to be filled.

On the verge, he was struggling to thrust farther into her mouth. Then he seemed to shake himself. "*No' like this,*" he choked out the words. "*Need inside you.*"

Though she could kiss him all night, Mari wanted him inside her, too. With a final lingering lick, she released him and stood.

Studying the logistics, she debated the safest way to do this. Decided, she pressed her hands against his shoulders. As they both eased down to kneel, his arms slid along the trunk, still locked in position. Tilting her head, she worked his knees apart to bring him farther down. When he was more in line with her, she turned around and backed up to him, until her sex was resting on top of his jutting shaft.

"*Inside you.*" He sounded tormented that he couldn't penetrate her. "*Put it in.*"

She leaned against his chest and turned her head, pressing open kisses to his neck and murmuring, "I want to be ready for you. Be patient with me. . . ."

* * *

"*I'm bloody tryin'!*"

The witch took one of his hands and moved it for him, using his fingers to strum her nipples. His other hand she drew lower, past her flat belly, past the ring that aroused him so. When she pressed his whole palm between her legs, cupping the moisture, he yelled out.

Strangling frustration—to feel how wet she was but not be able to put his tongue or shaft between her thighs . . .

When she worked one of his fingers inside her and moaned low, he frantically rubbed his face against her damp cheek and neck.

Then a second finger. Torture. "*So tight.*"

As she began to fuck herself with them, readying for him, he roared with agony, about to lose control of his senses. His cock throbbed painfully, jerking up between her legs, pulsing with each wild beat of his heart. "*Inside you. Now!*"

She shakily nodded, drawing his fingers from her sex. Once she'd moved his hands to cup her breasts, she began working his cock head inside her. As she tried to take him, he could feel her body twitch and quiver, could hear the sharp inhalations of breath.

"*Deeper,*" he demanded. "*Take more.*"

But she couldn't seem to. "Oh, gods . . ." She was panting, undulating her hips on his cock.

All at once, the rain ended. The wind began to blow, rushing over his heated skin and clearing the clouds from the sky. Moonlight shot through the canopy.

He felt it like heat on his skin, felt it even on his shaft still waiting to plunge inside her. He saw the light bathe his mate's flawless skin—over the pure white of her shoulders, down to the riveting tattoo on her lower back, and over her plump arse as she rocked on him.

"Taste you."

When she touched herself and lifted her fingers to his mouth, he seized them with his lips. Sucking her taste from the tips, he growled with pleasure.

"Bowen! I'm *going*—" The words ended with her scream as she began to come. He was just deep enough to feel her sheath squeezing him, her body greedily seeking what his had to give.

He yelled to the sky, instantly joining her. With just his cock head inside her, he pumped hot within her, shuddering with ecstasy to be filling her with his seed.

He was still coming . . . when the moon's hold on him became stronger than hers.

42

When he threw his head back, Mari felt the vibration of his haunting roar tearing up from his chest to echo in the jungle. His ejaculation was palpable, shooting from the broad head wedged inside her.

Yet then the moon speared through the trees in a surreal silver, and she knew. Knew he was too powerful in this state to be contained by any magick she could conjure. And though he'd just come, he remained hard within her, his muscles still as tensed as before.

Mari had wanted intensity, ferocity. She swallowed and closed her eyes, bracing herself.

She was about to get it.

Seconds later, he broke from the tree, shoving her forward to her hands and knees. He reached over her to clutch her nape, then pressed her upper body down to the ground, pinning her there with his massive hand covering the back of her neck.

Holding her immobile, he slowly fed his shaft inside her, inch by inch, making her scream with pleasure.

When he was as far as she thought he could possibly go, he ground against her, his hips working, forcing her to take even more.

Seated so deeply, he somehow controlled himself, allowing her to grow accustomed to his size. Yet once she moaned for more, he wrapped both his arms tightly around her waist. He bucked once, hard and fast into her.

"Ah, gods!" she cried out. "Do that again. . . ."

He did, over and over, making her teeth clatter from the force, but she loved it, loved how unyielding he was, loved his rough beast voice wicked at her ear. "*Your sex is so tight . . . good and wet. Want to be here forever.*"

When she reached back between their legs to caress and cup his heavy sack, he growled his approval. But then he seemed to force himself to pull her hand away. "*No' goin' tae . . . make me come . . . 'fore I'm ready.*" He forced her arms back behind her. "*No stoppin' this, little mate.*"

This was the first time he'd called her his mate like that. If he'd accepted her as his completely, she knew there was only one way the night was ending. She could do nothing but surrender to the beast at her back.

Grasping her arms at her elbows, he drew her farther upright on her knees, then used his grip to pull her body down and back into each frenzied thrust of his hips. Her breasts quivered. Her skin was damp, and the wind rushed over it like a caress.

And it feels so good.

She tried to free herself to touch him, but he held her elbows firmly. "*Need tae . . . mark you. Mark you as mine.*"

Though she'd feared his bite, at that moment there was nothing she wouldn't give him. "Yes, do it!"

He hissed in a breath, his shaft pulsing inside of her as if with anticipation. "*Could no' . . . please me more.*"

She trembled in anticipation as well. Would it hurt? Would she cry? But she knew there was no stopping this.

She'd signed on for the full experience. This step was her due.

He placed his mouth between her neck and her shoulder and growled loudly against her, alarming her, yet thrilling her. She felt his strong tongue lick her there—

Fangs pierced the skin. She screamed with pain, and with shock because a violent orgasm raged through her. In total abandon, she arched her back beneath him, spreading her knees and mindlessly writhing her hips for more.

Even as he continued plunging between her legs, he didn't withdraw his fangs, seeming unwilling to release her now that he had her like this.

Just when she didn't think she could take any more, she felt his entire body tense over hers. He snarled brutally against her skin, then came in a forceful, searing wave, pumping on and on.

He finally released his hold and collapsed over her, still slowly thrusting, as though savoring their mingled wetness.

"Never lettin' you go."

"I need . . . to rest, Bowen." Late into that night, her body was sore, utterly spent. "I'm not strong enough for this hour after hour. Please, just a little rest . . ."

"Sleep." Without withdrawing, he moved them on their sides, with him spooning her. Still inside her, **he** reached his hand around to cup between her legs, pulling her close and holding her sex. Possessively.

Through heavy-lidded eyes, she saw vines growing over her. *Witch, nature, good.* Just as she relaxed, she felt him tense beside her, dragging her even closer, throwing his leg over hers protectively. He leaned up to scent the vines, hesitating. But he didn't move her, and his close hold on her meant he was enveloped as well.

About to drift off, she whispered, "It's okay, Bowen." And he allowed it.

When she woke it was still dark, yet the vines were gone, as were the scrapes at her knees and her palms and the aches in her muscles. Bowen was stretching his body over hers, holding himself up on his elbows. She saw the image of the beast was beginning to fade, the pale blue of his eyes just starting to darken.

Cradling her face with both his big hands, he gazed down at her with such questioning emotion, she felt her eyes water in answer.

He pressed gentle kisses to her forehead, her eyelids, her nose. If she'd seen the beast in a frenzy of lust earlier, now she was seeing it praising its mate for sating him.

Then his gaze flickered over her neck. She'd caught him looking at his bite throughout the night, appearing both proud and relieved to have it on her. "Your skin's healed. But the mark remains." His voice was returning to normal—yet she'd gotten kind of used to his beastly voice and raspy murmurs and was glad she'd hear them at her ear next month.

She frowned. Was she going to be with him for that long?

"Claimed you forever."

Well, at least one of them believed so. And who knew what would happen between them? He'd pushed her to new heights, demanding her body do things she'd never known it could. The affection she'd begun to feel for him surged strong within her.

Who knew what could happen?

"Need you again, 'fore dawn."

When she nodded eagerly, he reached down between them to grip his shaft, positioning it. At that contact, he threw his head back and she arched up to him, as if it were their first time joining. When he flexed his hips, gradually sinking into her almost to the hilt, he grated, "Canna get enough o' you."

Slowing the furious pace of the night, he lowered himself to his elbows once more, easing down until their skin just touched. As he kissed her, he languidly moved over her, with a skilled rolling of his hips that fed his shaft into her just as his body pressed forward to plunge it so deep. Never speeding up his rhythm, he did this again and again until she was panting. Against his lips, she cried, *"Bowen . . ."*

"I know my female's tone," he rasped. Even when she could feel how swollen he was and knew he was on the verge, he gnashed his teeth, continuing the measured thrusts for her until she climaxed. With a scream into the night, she arched her back, squeezing her legs around his waist.

"Givin' me . . . *so much!*" He yelled out as his body tensed, motionless, before he bucked uncontrollably between her thighs. As she smiled from the rapturous feel of his heat pouring into her, he groaned in her ear . . . *"Mariah!"*

43

Bowe woke to find his arms empty of warm, curvy witch. This displeased him.

When he had trouble shaking his grogginess, he realized she'd made him sleep, had cast another sodding spell on him. Damn it, why? He scented the air to locate her, and shot upright.

She was gone.

Had he been too rough with her? Frightened her again? Why else would she run?

Then he saw an area just to the side of him that she'd very purposely cleared of brush. In the mud, she'd written him a note with precise letters.

Fuckhead:

The name's MariKETA.

Go to hell,

The WITCH, doing a creepy spell somewhere right now.

He sank back on the ground, throwing an arm over his face as he swore low. Had he called her Mariah last night? *Oh, bloody hell.*

Ach, Bowe, you've fucked up this time.

She must be furious. Or worse, hurting. The witch had given him inconceivable pleasure, and this was how he'd thanked her?

He'd loved everything about Mariketa and the way they'd been together. The taste of her flesh was addictive, as was the feel of her wet little tongue lapping his skin as she boldly licked him all over. She'd bitten his shoulder in abandon, screaming against his muscles, and her nails had dug into the backs of his thighs as he'd taken her from behind . . . he hardened even now to recall that.

She'd given him the pleasure he'd waited for his entire long life. . . .

And I showed her my gratitude by calling another woman's name.

When he removed his arm, he blinked his eyes. Above him, he spied his jeans and boots hanging in the upper limbs of a five-story-high hardwood.

He rose, determined to find her, to make her forgive him. And then, gods help him, they'd start where they left off last night. He scented the air and might have caught a hint of her toward the southern coast.

Mariketa had magically covered her tracks—and her scent—well. But she didn't understand. He didn't have to have her trail. There were only so many places she could be. He'd run back and forth to the coast a thousand times, and he'd relish every step as one closer to her.

He looked up at his jeans again and was startled by his own deep laugh. He grinned in her direction.

Ach, he liked the games they played.

"Lemme get this straight. Getting hunted down in the jungle by a lust-crazed Lykae was one of the safer extracurriculars of your trip?" Carrow asked.

"That's what I'm saying." Mari adjusted the resort courtesy telephone against her shoulder, then took another gulp of her drink—a bourbon rocks with a pink, paper umbrella.

In seriocomic fashion, she'd somehow gotten herself to a Belizean beach resort, then actually enchanted the manager until he was all too happy to extend a hotel-wide tab.

Magick . . . *good*.

"I told you not to go by yourself, didn't I?" Carrow demanded. "What'd I say?"

As Carrow repeated herself, Mari obediently mumbled in unison, "*Darwin says people like you need to die.*"

"Yep, that's what I said. And after everything that's happened to you, I'm surprised you're still ticking."

Not only was she ticking, she was showered, dressed in beachy new clothes and sandals from the resort gift shop, and enjoying an unlimited bar tab as she awaited her flight home. "Well, let this serve as my call-in to the House to avert disaster. Only a day late. I hope you told everyone I've never been on time for anything in my life."

"Disaster averted. Already got a call from some dude named Hild. And then a demon named Rydstrom showed up here a couple of hours ago."

"Nuh-uh!"

"Yeah, uh-huh. I wasn't here, but I heard that wherever he turned his green-eyed gaze, witches dropped trou and proffered panties."

"Carrow, that's how rumors get started," Mari said in a chiding tone. "Did he say anything about the rest of his group?"

"Said everybody on his end came out okay." As Mari sighed with relief, Carrow added, "He left a number for you. You know *I* could tell him you're okay—over dinner and drinks."

She couldn't help but grin. Rydstrom would either love Mari or curse her for this, but she said, "Yeah, you call him. Tell him both MacRieve and I were standing as of this morning."

"So are you gonna fly out before the big, bad—with names—wolf finds you?"

"Damn straight." Bastard had called her . . . *Mariah*. Was that all Mari was to him? A substitute? A second choice? *Fucking B team!* The idea of that outraged her even more because last night . . .

Bowen MacRieve utterly ruined me for other men.

She almost wished she didn't now know that sex like that existed—or that what she'd thought in the past was great pleasure had been a mere toe touch in a vast ocean. She irritably rapped on the bar with her knuckles and signaled the bartender for another round.

"I don't suppose you found a big plane?" Carrow asked. "Or that you managed to score some Xanax?"

"No, and no," Mari was so sick of B team, she was actually about to fly out on a *baby plane*. "But I'm lucky to get a flight out at all. Besides, I'm self-medicating with whiskey. I'll land around seven, so come get me—if you still have your driver's license—and peel my drunk ass from the plane."

"Will do. But, Mari, I have to say that you might not be seeing clearly on the issue of the werewolf, because, well, you have *issues*."

"What's that supposed to mean?"

"Just that you get really chapped over stuff like this. Think about it, the very last time the Lykae was in the same situation—running around with a mate and cavorting or whatever *you people* do—it was with a female named

Mariah. Last night, when he was wolfy and moonstruck and getting laid for the first time in—what'd you say?—a hundred and eighty years, he basically forgot the *ket* in your name. You might want to cut him some slack. Or, I could cast a spell to make him fall in love with dryer lint. You decide. But if the sex was truly—"

"Cataclysmic?"

"Yeah, you already conveyed that like thirty times, you little bourbon lush. So you're telling me you don't want to get caught? Not at all?"

Mari sighed. "I might . . . if he wanted *me*."

"*I do want you, lass*."

She jerked around. *MacRieve!* He was dressed in new clothes, and looked showered and coolly collected. "How in the hell could you have gotten here so quickly?"

"Missed you, witch. Ran headlong. Now hang up the bloody phone."

"Oh, great Hekate, is that his voice?" Carrow cried. "*I just had an orgasm!* Fudge your name tag if you have to, but get you some of that *some-some*. Remember, friends let friends live vicariously—"

Click. "How long have you been here?"

"Got here an hour after you did."

"I'm that slow?"

"I'm that fast. Would've come to you sooner, but I had many arrangements to make." His gaze focused on her drink. "What in the hell are you doing?"

"I'm getting tee-rashed on some sizzurp."

"Why?"

She shrugged. "Small plane, big scared."

He sniffed. "That's bourbon? Who drinks whiskey on the beach?"

"Sounds like a great drink name to me! How did you find me?"

"You cloaked your trail well. But I'm a great hunter."

"And so modest, too."

"You should no' have left me like that. What the bloody hell were you thinking to put yourself in danger again? I believed we had an . . . understanding."

"We did. And then you called me by another woman's name." He looked like he'd barely stifled a wince. "And then I realized that I'd misunderstood our understanding."

MacRieve grasped her elbow and steered her to a private hibiscus-lined courtyard. "Damn it, witch, it will no' be possible for me to instantly forget someone who has played such a large role in my life. If you think of someone for so long, a couple of weeks will no' erase it."

She snapped her fingers and said, "Exactly. A couple of weeks won't. A year won't. An eternity won't. You won't ever be happy without her."

"I doona believe that any longer. And I can promise you this will no' happen again."

"I don't know what's more disturbing . . . the fact that you called me by another woman's name or the fact that now you'll have to make a conscious effort not to. You're still thinking about her either way."

"If you want to leave because you have misgivings or lingering fears about last night, then go. But you canna leave because you think I prefer another over you. It simply is no' so."

"How can I believe you after you yelled her name?" she cried.

"I need to tell you something"—he stabbed his fingers through his hair—"that I doona talk about, ever. But I will with you." He gazed to the right of her as he said, "When Mariah died, she died . . . fleeing me. Running from me as you did last night. Even as I was thinking of naught but you, always the guilt for her death lingers at some level."

Mari gasped. "Why didn't you tell me?"

He finally faced her. "I feared it would only hurt you to reveal this, that it would set up the same situation. I dreaded that."

"It was an accident though. Right? You can't carry that guilt forever."

"Sometimes, lately, I feel it's worse, because . . ." He trailed off.

"Because what?"

He scrubbed his hand over his face. "Even if I do believe you're of the same soul as her, I *never* wanted Mariah like I want you." He seemed shamed by the admission, even as she felt herself softening toward him—as ever. "And what does that say about me? How could you choose for yourself a male so disloyal? When I *want* to surrender this bloody guilt?"

"Of course you do—it's been nearly two freaking centuries! Enough's enough."

"Gods, I was hoping you would believe I've waited long enough." He exhaled a relieved breath. "I want to look forward."

"As you should. Cut yourself some slack."

"Done—if you will do the same for me as well."

She made a grated sound of frustration. "Oh, you sly—"

"Lass, we're going to have problems between us sometimes. We'll both make mistakes and forgive them. This is one of those times."

"You're acting like I've signed on for the long-term deal. And I haven't."

"What would it take to get another shot with you?"

"Nothing you have. My time here's getting short—"

"Nothing? But you have no' seen everything that I have. What if I told you I've an olive branch that the mercenary in you should appreciate?" He curled his finger under her chin. "You've never shied away from anything else, and you will no' regret this now."

She *needed* to stay strong, to stay furious. But all she *wanted* to do was get back to being with him.

"Take a chance on me, witchling."

It was then that she made a fateful observation.

Bowen MacRieve was holding his breath.

Damn him! And there went strong and furious, gone with a whimper. Still, she met his eyes. "Don't call me by her name again, Bowen. It hurt."

"Shh, lass." He wrapped those big arms around her, drawing her against the warmth of his chest. "I will no', I promise you." When she finally relaxed against him, he nuzzled her ear. She could feel his lips curl just before he said, "And doona hang my clothes in tall trees."

44

Bowen's olive branch for her was a private island just off the coast of Belize, replete with a boat and a mansion in the middle of a breezy palm forest.

And the two weeks she'd stayed there with him had been the happiest of her entire life. Tonight they sat on a blanket on the beach, lazily regarding a driftwood fire. The breeze soughed through the palm fronds, and the stars glittered feverishly. As she lay against his chest, she mused over her time here with him.

At first, she'd thought he'd merely spent a fortune to rent this property, but then he'd said, "If you want it, it's yours." Apparently, he wasn't just wealthy but obscenely rich. So she answered as any self-respecting witch would: "Gimme . . . deed."

After their first night here of nonstop sex, she'd woken in bliss, unable to stop grinning stupidly. Had she actually believed that sexual relationships couldn't be perfect? He'd appeared surprised by her reaction, then had done that jutting-chin show of pride. "The aging werewolf's still got it, eh, lass?" He'd tickled her till she'd screamed with laughter.

Then later, once they'd decided to stay for a few weeks, they'd set some parameters for their cohabitation.

She wasn't to do the "mirror thing" while they were here, because, as he'd said, "Every time I see you do that spell, I get a sharp sense of foreboding. My Instinct tells me that it's wrong . . . dangerous, even."

As for magick in general: "If it slips because you're startled by something, that's one thing, but to willfully chant to your reflection disturbs me greatly."

All she'd asked from him was not to disparage her kind—or to sound like he was planning to take her away from witchery and the House.

Oh, and she needed clothes.

During the day, they swam the Caribbean, and he caught lobsters that they cooked at night over their beach fires. They explored colorful towns on the mainland, shopping, sightseeing, and necking in back alleys.

Just today he'd pressed her behind a row of fruit stands. With the sultry air redolent with sugar cane, and his hot, possessive hands fondling her breasts, he'd taken her, stifling her cries with his kiss—

"Lass, what are you thinking about that's affecting you like this?"

"Hmm? Oh, nothing."

"You always say that. I canna help but feel that you're holding some of yourself back from me."

Maybe she was holding back, likely afraid that yet another person she cared for would leave her. And in the back of her mind, she feared he would always doubt that she was his until she conceived. Still, she asked, "How?"

"I doona like that you have your secrets."

"Secrets?" Her tone was innocent, but she did keep secrets from him—many of them.

For instance, she couldn't seem to give up going to the

mirror, no matter that he'd told her how much it bothered him or how happy he made her. She'd figured out that if the reflection answered only so many questions in a session, then she needed to have as many sessions as possible.

And she hadn't told him that night after night she'd experienced bizarre dreams, so vivid and realistic that when she woke she had trouble differentiating between what was real and what was not.

In one dream, she stood in a shapeless plane of unbroken black. Mari saw her mother, weeping with the palms of her hands pressed against her eyes. Her father was lying on a stone slab, motionless, his eyes closed, his hands in fists.

Other times, she dreamed of a thousand voices begging her to hurry—but to do what, she didn't know. And sometimes, on this balmy, breeze-kissed island, she dreamed of a snow-covered forest with no leaves, the limbs thick with ravens. . . .

Yet even with her misgivings and her secrets, Mari continued to fall for her strong, proud werewolf more and more each day. She had a good feeling about Bowen.

So why don't I get a good feeling about us?

"You're holding back from me, too," she finally said.

He was. Bowe hated that she'd had a first love, and feared she'd never be completely his because of it. And always there was the apprehension that he would somehow lose his mate again. She couldn't turn immortal quickly enough to suit him.

"Maybe I'm suspicious of this because it is so good," he answered honestly. "I suppose I'm so used to being miserable that any deviation unsettles me."

"Is it so good?" she asked quietly.

Even with lingering doubts, he'd never known contentment like this before her—hadn't known it existed. "Aye, lass. It is for me."

Aside from the witchery, he liked everything about his new mate. He liked the fact that, for some reason, when they went *lobster* fishing, she would exclaim, "We are on the crab, baby!" He liked that she ate, drank, and played with gusto. Her sense of humor had him laughing every day.

Making love to her fulfilled him in ways he'd never imagined.

He was even growing used to her small magicks. When she slept, if she was content, light thrummed in her wee palms as though she purred, and sometime during their stay here the sight had gone from unnerving him to . . . charming him, making him grin down at her.

And occasionally bizarre things *occurred*. Last night he'd woken to find that everything in the room, from curtain to wall clock, had briefly turned blue. He'd shrugged, tucked her close, and gone back to sleep.

Yet though she'd promised not to chant to the mirror, his Instinct continued to warn him.

—*Her power is unstable. Be watchful.*—

He shook off his misgivings. "It is good. And I think it will only get better. For instance, I believe you'll like visiting"—*living in*—"Scotland." He hoped she would approve of their home, but if not, he'd buy her whatever she needed to be happy. And he hoped she would get along with his cousins and the clan—though if anyone so much as contemplated slighting her because of what she was, he'd throttle them.

"What's your place there like?"

"It's a renovated hunting lodge with oversize fireplaces and immense beams in the ceiling. In the winter the snow comes, and it's surreal. Some nights it falls in silence, and some nights the storms howl and throw down blankets."

"It sounds wonderful. I've never seen snow."

"*What?*" he bit out, astounded. "Never?"

"There's not much snowfall in Nola. And the only time I've been out of the country before this was to Cancún for spring break. Guatemala was the first time I'd ever seen mountains."

"Do you want to see other countries?"

"If I can get there by big plane, with proper sedation, then I'd love to."

"I could take you places I've been. Show you things."

"Like where?"

"We could drink wine across Italy and go diving off the islands of Greece. We could watch the sun rise over the Indian Ocean."

Eyes wide with excitement, she nodded up at him.

"I want to show you everything, watch your expression with each new sight." Over the last two weeks, when he'd realized how many things he wanted to do with her, he'd found that the need to have bairns was dimmed. Now he had a thousand places to take her before they settled down. "I'd be an excellent guide for you."

She grinned. "My man's so *modest*."

"But in the winter, I want to take you home to Scotland." He gazed at her and he knew he would see her in his country, walking the land beside him. And his heart was glad. "Snow would become you, lass."

45

Do you remember where I put the cast net?" Bowe called to Mariketa. He wanted to catch her favorite fish for tonight. If she was to turn soon, he had to keep her well fed, ensuring she didn't lose a single ounce of her curves. He could admit that he was developing a wee obsession with her shapely little body.

She always knew where he put everything, from his boat keys to his wallet to his favorite lure. He was beginning to wonder what he'd done without her for the last millennium.

Just as she rushed around the corner and said, "Not in there!" he opened the hallway closet door.

Inside, a garbage bag turned over; apples thudded to the floor, the area thick with them.

He backed away, chilled to his bones. "What's the meaning of this, Mariketa?"

She rubbed her foot against the back of her other ankle. "I wish I could say this isn't what it looks like, but . . . it is."

"How many times have you gone to the mirror?"

She shrugged. "Count the apples if you want to know."

"You lied to me. You hid this, sneaking around."

"You forced me to."

"What does that mean?"

"You want me to give up magick, but it's a part of me that I can't deny."

"No, you can shed yourself of it if you try. Practicing is a choice."

"Then sacrifice something dear for me," she said, a challenge in her tone.

"Like what?"

"Like . . . *hunting*. Never hunt and run the night again."

"You're mad."

"It's equivalent!"

"No, it's no'. Hunting does no' harm other people."

"Yet you assume I'm going to?" She narrowed her eyes. "I know Lykae are mistrustful of witches, but there must be more to this deep a prejudice."

"Aye, there is." He ran his fingers through his hair. "Long ago, a witch . . . killed five of my uncles. The guilt of their deaths destroyed my father. He was never right, no' up to the day he died."

She gasped, her face paling.

"My da was just a lad at the time and wished that he was stronger than his brothers. She killed them all, granting his wish."

Oh, great Hekate.

"Bowen, I am so sorry that happened to your family. But you should have told me this sooner."

"Why?"

"Because you're not going to just *get past this*." After this revelation, she had to question if she'd ever had a shot with him. "And we dance around the issue, but now I *know* you will never tolerate my coven. And they won't accept you because you won't respect the responsibilities that I have."

"Let someone else bloody take care of them."

Oh, the idea of surrendering all that responsibility was tempting. When Bowen acted as if the sun and moon revolved around her, Mari caught herself dreaming about doing nothing but traveling the world with him.

Why should she have to be saddled with something she never asked for—and had displayed no talent for?

Yet now, seeing Bowen like this, she recalled Cade's words: *"If you turn your back on your destiny—maybe to be a Lykae's browbeaten mate and wife—Fate will not just slight you. She will punish you, over and over."*

Mari thought of the prediction once more. Maybe the warrior's seeking to keep her away from the House wasn't *physically*. Perhaps she would be so afraid of losing yet another person she cared about that she would sacrifice anything—*taking herself* out of her coven, away from her calling, from her old life. . . .

"I might like to relinquish them, but I can't turn my back on my destiny. And it's not like I'm saying 'Look at me, I'm such an important badass.' It's more like I'm scared not to assume the mantle. Either way, it has to be done."

"Damn it, what you do is a choice! And I will abide it no longer."

Browbeaten. Her outrage building, she snapped, "Who the hell are you to order me around? Or to make me doubt what I am and what I was put here to do? It's obvious to me that if you can't accept what I am, then I can't be with you."

"Verra well, witch," he grated, his own anger flaring. "You will no' pressure me to change my mind in this!"

"I understand that!" With perfect clarity. He would *never* change. And she'd be damned if she'd fight a losing battle. "That's why I won't even try," she cried, storming to the bedroom.

Long after she'd passed by them, the pictures in the hallways rocked on the walls from her turbulent emotions.

With a vile oath, he stomped down the stairs, outside to the beach, then ran for hours, until sweat dripped and the sun had set. Could magick possibly be this integral to her? Was it as critical as hunting and running was to him?

When he returned she was deeply asleep, but her palms were dark, and she looked as if she'd been crying. Brows drawn, he felt her pillow. When he found it still damp, he might as well have had a sword plunged through his chest.

Was he doomed to hurt his female again and again? To make her miserable because he was so unlike her—and so resistant to change?

Maybe this entire experience, this reincarnation, was to teach him to be more tolerant. That night in the jungle Bowe had recognized that he would have to change to have Mariketa, and had wondered if he could accept such a haunting female, fully—to learn everything about her, about her kind, and even go among them.

Tonight, he determined that he was going to . . . try.

He showered, then joined her in bed, pulling her close. In sleep, he dreamed that the field adjacent to the lodge in Scotland had been planted with an orchard of apple trees.

When he woke, Mariketa was up and rushing around the bedroom, though it was still early morning. He rubbed his eyes. "What're you doing?"

"Leaving. I need to get back."

"The hell you are." He shot out of the bed. "Not without me!"

She always ogled him when he was unclothed. Now she turned away as if impatient with him.

When a horn honked outside, Bowe crossed to the window. A water taxi awaited her. The boat driver picked up the bag she'd already set at the end of the pier.

She truly intended to leave him?

"Just give me five minutes to get dressed." He hastily slung on his jeans, then glanced around for his shoes. She always knew where he'd put them.

At the bedroom doorway, she said, "This really is for the best. It's obvious that neither of us can change, and I don't want to spend eternity hiding what I am just to please you."

"Five goddamned minutes, Mariketa!"

"Toxic goddamned relationship, Bowen!" She whirled around, darting from the room. As he charged after her, he spied her flick her hand in his direction. When he reached the threshold of the door, he ran directly into an invisible barrier that shot him back on his arse. "Little bloody witch!" He scrambled to his feet, lunging from one window to another. But she'd sealed all of them and all the doors as well.

Leaving him? He sank to his knees and stabbed his claws into the wood floor. *Never.* As he ripped, he smiled menacingly. "Ah, witchling, you underestimated your male."

46

⁕

$\mathfrak{M}$ariketa rolled her eyes when Bowe ducked inside the cabin after taking the steps to the plane two at a time.

The pilot, a short, nondescript—nonhuman—male, drew the door closed behind him, then promptly readied for takeoff. Apparently, they were to be the only passengers.

Bowe loped down the aisle to where she sat, then dropped into a seat beside her. "You ken the pilot's a demon?"

"Yeah, so? Oh, wait, you're prejudiced against them as well."

"With demons you have a fifty-fifty chance of them being rogue."

"He's the one who was supposed to take me back two weeks ago—when I *should* have returned." Her demeanor was icy. "I thought I made myself clear earlier. Nothing's changed since I left you behind."

"Maybe no' with you."

"What does that mean?"

When the pilot lined up on the runway and revved the twin propeller engines, the plane began to rattle.

"There's something I need to tell you. . . ." Bowe trailed

off with a frown at her death grip on the armrest. "Mari, I can hear your heart's going wild—you've got to relax. The noise is normal." This was a typical Carib aircraft—a puddle jumper, and likely, in some runway instances, a goat dodger. "There's nothing to be scared of."

As they gained speed down the runway, the rattling and the whine of the engines increased. "They put wings on a lawn mower," she muttered.

"The trip will only be two or so hours, a mere jaunt." He made his tone confident, but the fact that a demon was in the cockpit vexed him. Perhaps he *was* prejudiced.

During takeoff she squeezed her eyes tight. He took her hand, and she let him.

Once they'd reached altitude and leveled off, Bowe reluctantly peeled her hand from his and rose. "I'll be right back."

He could tell she wanted him to stay, which heartened him. Maybe he hadn't blown his chances with her. He crossed to the cockpit, opening the cabin door. "Everything all right up here?" he asked the pilot.

"Yessir." His manner was casual, even bored.

"What breed of demon are you? Aye, doona look surprised. I can tell."

"I'm a Ferine."

They weren't the *least* peaceable demons.

Bowe returned to Mariketa. "Do you have that satphone we got on the mainland?"

She took it from the purse at her feet and handed it to him with a questioning glance.

He dialed his cousin. When Lachlain answered, Bowe spoke in Gaelic, expressing his unease about their current situation. "Can you have some men meet us at the executive airport?" he asked. "We could be flying into trouble. Better yet, can you get Emma to help you track this phone? The pilot might not be planning to land in New Orleans at all."

"Why no' take the controls?" Lachlain asked.

"I canna fly a plane—but believe me I'll be able to within a week."

"We'll be there, ready for anything."

Bowe said, "It might be nothing." But if something was happening, he could think of no one he'd rather have in his corner than Lachlain.

"If so, then the worst that happens is that I'll get to meet your witch. I canna wait to regale her with embarrassing stories about you."

Bowe frowned. Lachlain had never offered the same with Mariah.

When he hung up, he saw Mariketa had closed her eyes. She seemed to be doing her damnedest to block out the situation, so he put the phone back and let her be. . . .

Other than a minor squall cropping up, the next hour was uneventful and passed with the same heading. They were closing in on the mainland, yet *still* he couldn't stem this sense of apprehension.

"Mariketa, I need you to help me with something." When she opened her eyes, he continued, "I dinna want to scare you for no cause, but I canna get past the feeling that the pilot means one or both of us harm."

"Are you *trying* to push me over the edge?" At that moment, lightning struck just off the port wing, and she jerked with fright.

"No, no, it's probably nothing."

"Then wh-what do you want me to do?"

"I canna believe I'm saying this, but ask that witch of

yours, the one in your mirror, if the pilot intends us harm."

"Oh, now you *want* me to use magick?" she asked, nervously glancing out the cabin window as the storm intensified.

"Just do it."

With shaking hands, she drew a compact from her purse. Once she began whispering to the glass—"*Must not pass . . . red mouth to whisper low . . .*"—the reflection turned dark. Bowe just stifled a shudder.

"Does the pilot mean us harm?" she finally asked it.

A moment later, the blood drained from her face; the compact cracked in her grip.

"Mariketa, tell me! What's the answer?"

Eyes blank, she whispered, "The pilot's . . . *gone*."

Bowe stormed to the cabin, tearing down the now locked door. Empty inside. The bastard had traced, leaving the yoke mangled and the instrument panel shredded—everything except the fuel gauge.

He'd dumped the gas. *Fucking demons!*

"Wh-why would he leave us?" Mariketa cried from her seat. "Can you drive a plane?"

Bowe ran his fingers through his hair. *Think!* He searched through every compartment but found no parachutes, which meant there were no alternatives. They were going down unless she could do something.

Bowe could do nothing.

Making his demeanor calm, he returned to her, and in as even a tone as he could manage, he said, "He's bailed on us, lass. And, no, I canna pilot this plane."

Her eyes were glinting, her body trembling. "We're gonna crash?"

"No, no, it does no' have to be," he said, even as rain pounded the windshield when they began to lose altitude in the storm. "You said the reflection teaches you things? Spells and conjuring?" When she nodded, he said, "Somehow we've got to get you off this plane. Do you think you could ask that mirror how to teleport yourself out of here?"

"What about you?" she cried, having to raise her voice over the growing whine of the engines.

As an immortal, he might live. She didn't have a chance. "Worry only for yourself—"

She cried out when the plane dipped sharply, flinging him across the aisle. Her seat belt was the only thing keeping her in place. He scrambled back to her. "Focus, Mari, and ask it how you get off this plane."

"I'm trying!" Tears began streaming down her face, each one a knife to the heart.

He rubbed her arm. "Come on, lass, focus for me."

"I can't hear her whisper over the engines! I don't know what she's saying!" When Mariketa gazed up at him, her pupils were dilated beyond anything he'd seen. "*Bowen, I-I can't hear her.*"

Her heart pounded so wildly, and her breaths were so quick and shallow, he wondered how she remained conscious. She was growing nearly catatonic with fear.

Should he push her? Or accept their lot and pray for mercy? He pushed. "Witch, listen to me!" He shook her shoulders—hard—until her head lolled. No response. Another dip sent him reeling, and he lunged back to her. "Mari!" *Nothing*.

The sat-phone had fallen from her overturned purse and skittered by him in the aisle. He snared it, hit the redial button, and flipped on the GPS beacon.

Through the windshield, he could see the water rushing toward them. Not enough time. He couldn't break through her fear to reach her.

So he sliced open her seat belt and scooped her up. Sitting on the floor between the back aisles, he held her in his lap, arms wrapped around her. "Think of something else," he murmured, rocking her as gently as he could with the death grip he had on her body. "Think of your home. Or of the snow I'm goin' tae show you. Think of blankets of white."

Ah, gods, please let her survive this. Please . . .

She shook uncontrollably. "Come here, baby," he said against her hair. "I'm no' goin' tae let you be hurt."

If I lose you, I'll follow this time without a second thought.

Salt rushed his senses. *Close.* "There's my good lass. Now, close your eyes. . . ."

47

Roaring in her ears . . . churning under the water . . . the force of bones shattering. A terrible pressure built on her thigh till she felt the flesh and bone giving way.

Can't swim—can't move. Sinking deeper. Drowning.

A grip under her arm?

Bowen. He was dragging her to the surface.

As soon as she felt the rock of waves, she heard him, indistinctly at first, then louder. "Mari! Ah, gods, wake up!" He was running his hands over her body, shuddering at each injury. When he touched her leg, an agonized yell broke from him.

The stench of an oil fire on the water was overpowering. She heard flames hissing in the rain.

"You doona dare leave me, witch!" His voice was heartrending. With his whole hand at the back of her head, he pulled her against him, tucking her into his chest. *"You stay with me."*

She wanted to nod, to reassure him—she'd never heard anyone in such pain before—but she couldn't speak, couldn't open her eyes. . . .

In and out of consciousness. How long they stayed like this, she didn't know. She woke to a hazy drone, growing louder—the rhythmic whoosh of a helicopter's blades. She thought he murmured, "Lachlain . . ."

When she felt wind on her face, he rasped, "You're goin' tae be safe." She thought he kissed her temple. "You will no' get away from me this easily."

After Bowe had lost Mariah, he'd been destroyed. Lachlain had witnessed it, had known his cousin understood that all dreams of a future or of a family had died with her, gone forever. And the guilt over her gruesome demise had tormented him.

That time was nothing compared to these last four days, when the little witch's life had hung in the balance. She lay broken, seeming so small in Bowe's bed. Her skull had been fractured and her leg torn free from her body. Casts and bandages covered her.

Now Bowe's voice broke low as he smoothed her hair from her bandaged forehead. "She called me selfish on more than one occasion—and she was right. If I'd made the smallest effort to understand her and her skills, she could have practiced her magick, honed it. She might have been able to save herself from this. But I was too stubborn, too prejudiced."

Bowe had been injured gravely as well, but he'd healed even though he didn't eat, didn't sleep. Hour after hour, he sat beside her, with her hand swallowed by his shaking ones, his eyes going wet whenever she whimpered in pain. "She accepted my nature, my needs. And because I dinna do the same for her, she lies . . . dying."

From what Lachlain understood, the only thing keeping her alive was the magick of united covens and sorcerers, feeding her energy.

Her kind had wanted to take Mariketa back with them, but no one in the House would dare challenge the crazed male werewolf guarding her so fiercely. So since then, Bowe's home had been overrun with witches, coming and going at will, bringing food, some of Mariketa's clothes, and special potions. Bowe didn't seem to give a damn about any of them, when two months ago, this would have proved a special kind of hell for him.

But the donated magick couldn't preserve Mariketa forever. She was too powerful. Her entire being was used to power and demanding of it. She was draining the others, and it was only a matter of time before they either let her go or followed her down.

And for these last four days, uncanny things had occurred at the compound. Lachlain shuddered to recall them. The first night, hundreds of black cats had prowled around the house, mouths open but silent, watching intently. Another night, frogs had seemed to rain from the sky, hitting the tin roof, without injury. . . .

At sunset, when Emma traced to Lachlain, he left Bowe and joined her in the hall outside the bedroom. "Have the covens found the demon who did this?" He had his own men looking, too.

"Literally thousands of witches are scrying for him," Emma said. "He doesn't stand a chance of escaping a net like that. He was probably working for someone, but the witches can't figure out who would want to hurt them."

"Mariketa had booked the plane and the pilot before Bowe rejoined her. There are dozens who would want to take her out before she reached immortality."

Emma glanced at Bowe's door. "What will happen to him, if she doesn't . . . come through?"

"Once he's meted out retribution to whoever is behind this, then Bowe won't live the week out. Unfortunately, he now knows exactly where to go to die—"

Without warning, Bowe burst out of the bedroom with the witch in his arms. Lachlain winced again to see her leg missing. "Bowe, you canna move her." As Bowe strode out the back door into the night, Lachlain called, "They said it could kill her! Where in the hell are you taking her?" At the doorway, Lachlain turned back. "For once, Emma, you stay inside!"

When Lachlain reached Bowe, he became convinced his cousin had lost his mind.

Bowe was painstakingly setting Mariketa into the green ivy at the foot of an oak. He seemed to await something, and when it plainly didn't happen as he'd expected, he tore at the ivy, trying to bury her in foliage. "Too late," he rasped, sinking down to his knees. "Brought her too late."

Lachlain ran his hand over the back of his neck when the air began to grow oppressive, and yellow lightning flashed out horizontally across the black sky. He scanned around them and spied unblinking, glowing eyes staring out from the nearby swamp.

His hackles rose when vines began to grow over the witch, enclosing her. Biting out a curse, he lurched back.

Bowe should be shuddering with unease; instead, once she was covered, he closed his eyes with relief.

When Mariketa sighed, as if comforted to be among the vines, Bowe had to swipe his sleeve over his face. Then . . . her skin began to pinken and heal. As she regenerated from her injuries, Bowe ripped off bandages and sliced through casts. He gently unthreaded unnecessary stitches.

Within a quarter of an hour, the witch was healed . . . completely healed.

Mariketa blinked open her clear gray eyes, gazing up at Bowe.

"Lass, are you all right?"—his voice broke an octave lower as his throat tightened—"Say something tae me."

When she whispered, "What'd I miss?" he just kept his emotions in check.

He'd almost . . . lost her.

With shaking hands, he tucked her against him and absently murmured an explanation about where she was and what had happened. When she shivered, he lifted her and hurried back to the house, passing a visibly stunned Lachlain.

Inside, Bowe took her to the bathroom, then ran a bath. Gently setting her in the tub, he scooped water over her back and shoulders with an unsteady hand. He wanted to apologize for everything, for being so stubborn and stupid, but didn't trust himself to speak about something so important. Not yet. Every time he tried, his voice broke.

"Bowen, did I hear my friends outside?"

He coughed into his fist, then said, "Aye, they come by all hours of the day and night. Carrow and Regin are here now."

"Could you tell them that I'm okay? And that I'll be out in a minute?" Mariketa asked.

"Will you be all right by yourself?"

She nodded. "I'm fine. Back to normal via greenery."

"Aye, then, of course. I'll be right back."

In the sitting room, he found Lachlain and Emma, Carrow, and the Valkyrie Regin. After he delivered Mariketa's message, her friends hugged each other.

"I told you people she'd pull through," Carrow said, then cracked open a bottle of champagne—for herself.

"Aye, she's a clever girl," Bowe told them, feeling like his chest was about to burst with pride. "Healed *herself*." His lass got the very earth to give to her. How many mates could do that?

Lachlain and Emma were clearly delighted for him. "*Now*, I'll get to regale her with stories about you. . . ."

Suddenly, everyone grew silent, and all eyes fell to the front door behind him.

"What?" Bowe asked, turning. "What is it?"

At the doorway stood . . . Mariah.

48

What trickery was this? He still scented Mariketa in the bath.

This must be another being. This was . . . *Mariah*.

"I . . . I . . ." He couldn't form words. There'd been no reincarnation?

In her tremulous voice, she said, "I can see I've shocked you, Bowen."

"How . . . how can this be?" For so long, Bowe had ached for this, had imagined their reunion in a thousand different ways. He'd gone to his knees and begged fate for one more chance.

Apparently, he'd been given it.

"I was brought back to you," she said, gliding over to stand before him. "Resurrected by a sorceress."

Bowe scanned the room as if hoping for someone to explain this. Everyone appeared as dumbstruck as he felt. "How did you come to be *here?*"

Her tentative smile was rapidly fading. Of course, she would have believed he'd be overjoyed. And two months ago, he would have been.

"Once I was revived, I was sent to wherever you were."

"Why *now?*"

"B-Bowen, you sound almost angry." Her violet eyes watered.

He'd gotten so used to his witch going toe-to-toe with him that he'd forgotten how timorous some females could be. "I mean, why no' sooner? It's been nearly two centuries."

"The sorceress needed the energy that surrounds an Accession to be able to bring me back." Just as Mariketa had said about another reincarnate. "As I lay dying that night in the forest, I wished that I could have had a life with you, wished it with everything in me." She lowered her voice to say, "I wished that I hadn't run from you."

He winced at the memory.

"The being heard my cries, kissed me gently, and took my pain away."

"A sorceress would no' do this out of kindness to you. What did she demand of you?"

"She demanded my eternal soul. But I gave it up gladly, Bowen, just to have another chance with you." Mariah smiled softly. "Though you're going to have to protect me so that I may never die again."

The sacrifice she'd made staggered him.

Yet instead of feeling joy at her return, or gratitude for what she'd given up, all he could think was how much he just wanted to get back to help his witch with her bath.

Why hasn't Bowen returned?

Mari hoped he wasn't having words with Carrow, though she could definitely see that happening—the most pro-witch female Mari knew versus the most anti-witch male?

Once she found a bag with her things in the adjoining bedroom, she hurriedly dressed, determined to douse any conflict. When she entered the sitting room, her friends stared at her, seeming stunned.

"What?" Mari asked Carrow and Regin, but they remained motionless by a wall. "I know I look like hell, but damn, I *was* in a plane crash this week. . . ." No, they were staring over her shoulder.

Mari got chills on the back of her neck, and she slowly turned. Somehow she knew what she would find. The female standing there was . . . Mariah.

There'd been no shared soul between them.

The blond princess stood, tall and graceful, by Bowen's side, resplendent in a long, white gown. And they looked *perfect* together. Her violet eyes glinted with emotion as she glanced from Mari to Bowen. Bowen's own eyes burned with some inscrutable light.

Stay standing . . . stay standing. "She's returned?"

"Aye. Resurrected by a sorceress. You knew what I believed about you and her. So tell me how this is possible, Mariketa."

He wasn't outright accusing her of an enchantment again, but there was a suspicious note in his tone. Faced with this scene, even she began to doubt herself. "How would I know?" She pinched her forehead between her thumb and her forefinger. Though she'd just come from a healing, her head had started to pound.

"Because you're a witch—"

"A witch, Bowen?" Mariah sidled even closer to Bowen as if for protection. "But you despise them!"

As he absently patted her hand, he said to Mari, "This is your area of expertise."

"Resurrection is *not* my area of expertise. I only know that there are a very limited number of beings on earth that can do it. Most of those *won't*," Mari answered. "Look, I don't know what's going on—I'm fresh from a plane wreck and a shade bewildered here. But I do know we can figure it out." She met his eyes and held out her hand. "Together."

Just when she thought Bowen's body tensed to move—to cross the ten feet to Mari's side, the princess said, "Bowen, who *is* this woman? Did you . . . did you find another? You told me I was the only one," she added softly. "You vowed to me that you'd *never want another* as long as you lived."

He didn't walk the ten feet.

Mari exhaled a breath she hadn't known she'd held and dropped her hand. She could read the writing on the wall. Just what in the hell would it take for someone to look at her and say "I choose *you*"? "If I leave here today, MacRieve, I leave for good."

Seeming as though she'd faint, the princess whispered, "I gave up my soul to rejoin you. Was this sacrifice for naught?"

He put his flattened hands out as if motioning everyone to slow down. "Just give me a minute . . . to think. . . ."

Her soul? How can I compete with that? Mari wanted to loathe her, needed to, but she only pitied this other female who'd made the ultimate surrender to be with the male she loved. She found herself murmuring, "To think I'd worried about you going back for her, when she was already on her way forward."

Hope flashed in the fey's violet eyes. "You were trying to go back for me?"

"For nearly two hundred years," Mari told her. *Relentlessly. Mercilessly ridding any obstacles in his pursuit of this exquisite princess—a fairy-tale princess.*

Mariah was the name he'd called out the night he'd believed he'd claimed his mate.

"Then you must still care for me," Mariah said. "And you wear my pendant after all this time."

Mari swung her gaze to the medallion he wore at his neck—the one that he never took off.

Even when he'd made love to her. *Bastard!*

He glanced down, seeming surprised he wore it. "I just need to think for a few bloody minutes. Just . . . just let me *think*."

B team. Why am I even surprised?

"What's there to think about, Bowen?" Mari demanded. "You've got a choice—make a decision." *But choose me!*

His eyes narrowed. Maybe she was being unreasonable. Maybe he wouldn't take her hand not because he no longer wanted Mari, but because he wanted to spare the princess any unnecessary hurt. Yet Mari needed him to walk to her side and pronounce her as his *so badly*—longed for him to. "MacRieve?"

"Doona push me, witch."

Witch. Her heart fell. *He'll never see past that.* At his words, Mari was reminded that she and Bowen hadn't resolved the obstacles between them—because they *couldn't*. The fey princess suited him far better, and probably deserved him more for the sacrifice she'd made.

Suddenly, Mari became aware of the group witnessing this scene—Emma and her Lykae husband gazed at her and at Bowen with sympathy, while Carrow and Regin looked alternately sorry for her and incensed with him. Mari recognized that arguing with him here like this wouldn't get him back. She could think of nothing that would. And Mari wasn't known for fighting losing battles.

It was time to take herself out of the game—again. "I'll go get my bag." With her shoulders shoved back, she turned toward the door, refusing to cry.

Which was proving difficult—since she'd already fallen in love with Bowen MacRieve.

Damn that witch for pressuring me like this!

Bowe knew why she felt she had to leave. She thought herself passed over yet again. Both parents had deserted her, and then her first love had thrown her over.

And I've told her there'd never be another female for me— then my mate showed up on my doorstep.

But he hadn't made any bloody decisions, hadn't chosen Mariah over her.

Regin hissed at him and followed Mariketa, with Carrow right behind them. As Carrow passed Bowe, she said, "*Prick.* You and Twice-Baked here deserve each other."

Clasping his forehead with frustration, Bowe turned to Mariah. "You remember Lachlain, do you no'?" he asked, as if speaking to a child. "He and his new wife are going to sit with you for a few minutes. Everything will be fine."

Lachlain stepped up, his arm wrapped tightly around Emma's waist. "Aye, I'm sure you've questions—"

But Mariah seized Bowe's hand with both of hers. "Please don't leave. I'm so confused by all this. By this place and time I've been brought to." Tears streamed. He'd nearly forgotten how fragile she was. "Ah, gods, please, Bowen."

Bowe glanced from her to the doorway Mariketa had

just exited. The witch was only going back to the bedroom. *I'll stop her before she tries to leave.*

As she stared into the dresser mirror, Mari wiped at tears with the back of her hand. She didn't have to bid the reflection to come. Knowing she would likely get just one answer, she decided to ask, "Am I his mate or not?"

"*You are.*"

She gasped. Apparently Mari was his—and he still passed her over! "Then what in the hell just happened?"

The hand breached the glass with an apple. "*Come with me.*"

"Damn it, if there was ever a time to answer more than one question, it's now! Tell me how this is possible!"

"*Are you ready to know the truth?*" the reflection whispered.

"The truth about what?" Mari snapped.

The reflection smiled. "*About—everything.*"

Mari frowned, recognizing that she finally *was* ready to go. *I have nothing to lose.* She was going to journey into that mysterious world of the mirror.

She nodded. "I am." Mari took the apple and set it on the dresser, then grasped the offered hand. She climbed up and through the portal, entering another dimension. Here it was soft, a place veiled in mist and sublime silence.

The reflection was gone—because Mari *was* the reflection now? Doubt over her action immediately suffused her. When she glanced over her shoulder, she saw Carrow and Regin rushing into the room, bewildered by what they were seeing.

Behind them . . . ravens gathered on the windowsill.

Ravens? Had she just gone willingly to her own doom?

* * *

As Bowe tried to disentangle Mariah, his heart felt like it sank to his gut—for the second time in minutes.

Mariketa's scent was utterly gone.

He tore away toward the bedroom, but of course, she wasn't there. "Where the hell is she?" he bellowed at Carrow.

Eyes wide, Carrow hiked her thumb at the dresser. "In the mirror."

A single red apple sat beside it.

❧❧❧

49

"Elianna?" Mari whispered when she spied her mentor waiting for her here. "Are you . . . real?"

She patted her wrinkly skin with a frown. "The last time I checked."

Mari pinched her forehead. "Am *I* real in this mirror? Or was the reflection fake?"

"Everyone's real." Elianna chuckled. "The reflection is merely a facet of your being. A bit like an astral projection. And before you ask—yes, you do look that diabolical when you are using strong magick."

Somewhat reassured, Mari hugged her. As always happened, pungent scents from the powders and dried leaves in Elianna's infinite apron pockets wafted up between them. "I missed you! I'd wondered why you weren't with Carrow holding vigil."

"Well, don't think I wasn't watching over you."

Mari gazed around her. This was the plane of unbroken black from her dreams. "What is this place?"

"This is your new home. Your very own dimension." She smiled brightly and waved her hand around. "You can decorate it however you like."

"Um, why would I need a new home?" Mari asked.

"Every great sorceress has her own dimension."

"I'm not a sorceress."

"Do you want to be?" Elianna asked in a strange tone.

"I just want to understand what is happening."

"This is where you need to be for now," she said. "You're safe here from the magick of others. And no one but your family and other members of the Wiccae can ever come here—unless you expressly invite them."

"Was I in danger?" Mari asked.

She nodded. "Come with me." As Elianna crossed to a *cauldron*, Mari followed, apprehension pricking at her. She hadn't seen witchery like this in years.

Elianna stirred the bubbling brew inside it with a staff, clearing the smoke to reveal a scene. In a dimension much like this one were two marble altars.

Mari's parents lay atop them.

Her father was on a slab of cold rock, with his fists clenched, just as Mari had dreamed. Her mother lay beside him, her beautiful face frozen in pain.

Mari bit back a cry. "Oh, gods, what is this? Are they alive?"

"Yes, but they were struck down by a powerful sorceress. Ensorcelled by a dark power."

"Who? Who would do this to them?"

Elianna hesitated, then finally answered, "Häxa."

Mari swallowed. "She *does* feed off trapped souls."

Elianna nodded, then continued, "Your father succumbed first."

"He didn't . . . he didn't just ditch us?"

"No, leaving his family nearly killed him, but he is a powerful warlock, and his destiny had always been to fight Häxa. He was ruthless in his preparation for battle. Black magicks, sinister pacts for spells of greater power. He dealt with devils and rogue wizards. Yet still he was unable to smite her."

"And Jillian?"

"Häxa froze your mother when she went to beg for his life. Jillian knew the futility, but she couldn't live without him."

Mari felt like she was choking. No wonder Jillian had always seemed so sad—she'd been *missing her husband.* . . .

"Druid *sabbatical*, Elianna?" Her father lived? Her mother hadn't remained away by choice? "How could you not tell me about this?"

"Jillian wanted you to have a normal life for as long as possible."

"Normal? I thought I was unwanted! That they both chose to leave me."

Elianna looked baffled. "But they adored you—surely you remember that?"

Mari pointed an accusing finger at her. "You should have told me about what happened to them!"

"When should I have? When you turned eighteen, should I have said, 'Your parents are frozen in eternal pain and agony—and you can't do a damned thing about it for many years.'? Then wish you luck on your SATs?"

Her parents had loved her. "How do I wake them?"

Elianna glanced away. "You have to kill the one that did this to them."

Häxa was one step down from a goddess, the most powerful sorceress ever to live. "*Fate does no' blow her bullets,*" Bowen had said. He'd been right. Mari was to fight the witches' greatest enemy. She feared the idea, but the fury churning inside her wouldn't be denied. Elianna stared at her eyes, and Mari knew they'd changed.

"I'm going after her. Tell me how to find her."

"You will know how to find her when you are prepared to fight her."

"For once, stop this witchy, mystical bullshit, Elianna! I want to kill her *now!*"

"You're not ready," Elianna insisted.

"If you think I'll sit around here waiting to turn immortal—"

"That won't matter," Elianna quietly interrupted. "Häxa can turn any living being to dust. Immortality or mortality will make no difference."

"Then do I even have a shot at winning against her?" Mari demanded. "What do the seers say?"

"Anyone who tried to read the battle between Mariketa the Awaited and Häxa . . . was struck mad. We doubt Häxa has even been able to see this."

"Doesn't matter. I'm still going after her, with or without your help."

"If Häxa defeats you, she will usurp your powers. We can't risk that—or she will become unstoppable."

"I'll figure it out!"

"Your parents are not the only ones in this state. There are thousands more, taken from all Lorekind and accumulated over time. Think of others suffering. You have responsibilities to them as well."

A thousand voices calling to her in her dreams.

"How do I prepare, then?"

"You are a captromancer. You'll use the medium given to you to learn. No longer will you be given hints of information or power. Because you are the Queen of Reflections, knowledge will flow from the mirror straight to your being. You'll learn everything from how to coax fire from water to how to shield yourself from another's magick attacks, deflecting damage."

Mari thought over all Elianna had revealed, struggling to remain calm. "Does Häxa have any weaknesses?"

"It's been reported that her eyesight is poor. Her animal familiars see better than she does."

"Familiars? What kind?"

"Trolls, some kobolds, ravens, and—"

"*Ravens?*" Mari bit out. When Elianna nodded, Mari said, "Häxa's already been watching me! I saw them in the jungle, and in my dreams. Even just now when I stepped into the mirror, ravens were on the windowsill."

"It makes sense that you've had foresight about her. And I figured she would already be spying on you. But remember, she can't get to you here."

"Were you watching the scene when the fey princess showed up?" Mari asked.

Elianna gave an emphatic nod. "Was I ever."

"Mariah said a sorceress brought her back—it has to be Häxa that's done this. What better way to create misery than to return a male's mate precisely when he's decided to move on." To herself, she thought, *What better way to hurt me? First take my parents from me, now separate me from the man I love.*

"It's certainly possible. This is how she operates."

"If I actually succeed in killing her, what will happen? Will the world be changed?"

Elianna answered, "Aside from freeing so many souls, your act won't change anything about *today*. But if Häxa is not stopped now, she will continue to grow more powerful. Soon there will come a time when she will enslave the entire world in misery. Hell will reign on earth."

"But if Häxa's destroyed, what will happen to the balance between her, Hekate, and Hela?"

"This balance might be disrupted already because Häxa is no longer a goddess. And some are saying that Hela isn't as *beneficent* as she once was."

Mari exhaled a long breath, wondering if she'd have to do battle with Hela one day as well. Had Mari actually dreaded the idea that her career highlights would peak when she was twenty-three? "How do I begin?"

"I suppose you'd best conjure a mirror. Just imagine one you've seen and a facsimile will appear here."

Mari pictured her oval antique mirror, framed in oak in a spindle stand. Within a nanosecond, a copy manifested itself. "I just stand in front of it?"

"Yes, but be cautious with it," Elianna said. "The knowledge is potent and addictive. You'll receive an understanding no mortal has ever experienced. If you feel yourself getting in too deep, then you must pull back."

Mari nodded and faced the mirror. *Beautiful glass.*

Her eyes flashed, reflecting back. To infinity, Mari's eyes seemed to reflect. No more tedious questions and answers. Knowledge had begun to funnel directly into her, spells and magicks becoming part of her.

It was exquisite, but now she had only one thing she wanted to know.

How to kill a sorceress.

"You always stand outside," Mariah said as she joined Bowe at the porch railing. "Is it to scent *her*?" Over the last few days, Mariah had settled in here, as best as she was able.

"I want to know she's safe." Bowe had just returned from another failed attempt to locate Mariketa. Though he could scarcely believe it, the witches in her coven had allowed him to come and go into Andoain at will. But none could—or would—tell him how to find her.

Bowe had found that to the naked eye, the property had a proud-looking mansion surrounded by laden apple trees with shockingly green leaves. Butterflies flew everywhere.

Yet when he'd blinked for a fraction of a second, he'd seen an entirely different landscape. Hot stones choked up steam and smoke around a dilapidated manor house. Serpents wound along rotting balusters. That was the true Andoain—Mariketa's home.

"You are so miserable, Bowen. It's clear to me that she's cast a spell on you. What's unclear is why you seem not to care."

"Mariah, the years after your death were . . . harsh."

"I know. But I want to get past those times and look to the future. I need new memories. My last memories are of my death, and it was a . . . horrific death. But you know I don't blame you."

Then why bring it up? he thought, then flushed. She'd never irritated him like this before. But everything about her was different from the witch, so that meant everything about her was . . . wrong.

"I see so many things differently now. I want to learn your ways, and give you the children you've always longed for."

"What changed?"

"I was so selfish before and couldn't be more sorry for it. Death brought my priorities into focus. I want to create life." She smiled shyly up at him. "With you."

Here Mariah was, offered up to him as he'd begged the gods for decades. All the difficulties he'd had with her seemed erased. She wasn't a witch of unspeakable power, but a gentle fey.

She was everything he'd thought he could ever want.

And he wasn't even certain that the witch would take him back. They'd fought before the plane wreck and hadn't overcome the difficulties between them.

Yet none of this mattered.

Whether the witch was his mate or not didn't matter—because what he felt for her was stronger even than that pull. He'd already fallen for her.

For the first time in Bowe's endless, lonely existence . . . he loved.

50

Mari was shamed to realize that although the fates of the earth and of a thousand tormented lives and those of *her parents* were dependent upon her defeating Häxa, she still couldn't get Bowen out of her head.

She did assiduously study and train in her new home—the imagined shelter on her plane had become a melding of the cottage where she'd grown up, her room at the Andoain manor, and the island house where she'd fallen in love with Bowen. Elianna and Carrow spent every day with her here at—as Carrow had dubbed it—the "Cottanorouse."

Yet in between the times when Mari had learned how to attack and deflect and how to bind others' powers, she'd used the mirror to try to uncover more about how the princess was resurrected. Every time Mari consulted the glass about her, it grew blurred, giving up no information—which only convinced Mari further that Häxa was behind the resurrection. . . .

And sometimes, Mari found herself wanting to use her mirror simply to gaze at Bowen.

Like right now.

Mari furtively checked for her friends, peeking around the corner of her bedroom door. For some reason, she thought they might frown on her taking the time to stalk her ex-lover when the future of the world rested in her hands and all.

The two were in the cozy den before a fire. The coast was clear.

Apparently, Mari was not above spying on him—even though she knew she couldn't watch if he kissed his princess, or worse. So far, she'd rarely seen them together. In fact, Bowen spent more time at Andoain, or searching for Nïx, than he did at the Lykae compound.

Yet sooner or later, she knew she was going to see something that she wouldn't be able to handle.

Do I really want to do this . . . ?

With a nod, she whispered, "Show me . . . Bowen."

The mirror image shifted until she saw him pacing the sitting room of his house, looking as if he hadn't slept in days. He also appeared to be intent on voicing something, yet couldn't seem to bring himself to do so. Mariah patiently sat on the sofa, hands folded in her lap. A perfect lady.

"Mariah, I was true to you," he finally began. "For so many years, I was."

"I know. You're a fine male. I couldn't be prouder."

"Damn it, I doona want to hurt you, but I have been with Mariketa, and I have feelings for her. Undeniable ones."

Mari's eyes widened. *He was telling her this?*

"Bowen, I understand how difficult all those years must have been for you. And I forgive you for your . . .

indiscretion. But can't you see that the witch has tricked you? Enthralled you?"

"I canna believe that what I feel for her is no' real." He raked his fingers through his hair. "Would you want me, knowing I will never love you?"

The princess stood and crossed to him. "I can change how you feel about me. If you'll take me to your bed, in nine months you'll welcome our first child to the world."

If? So they haven't *slept together?*

"Think of it, we'll start the family you've always wanted—the family that you can only have *with me.* Things will be wonderful. I'll make you happy, and you'll keep me safe. Just as providence intended."

Gods, she's good.

"I'm sorry, Mariah, truly sorry for all you've been through. And I will help you find another male, a good protector—one who would love you as you deserve. I'll help you in any way I can."

He *was* truly telling the fey this!

Of course, Mari had known that leaving Bowen hurt, but she hadn't acknowledged how utterly devastated she'd been, until there was hope of being with him once more. Mari could help Bowen find someone for the princess— setting her up with another male was the ideal solution! Mari would be on the horn to Rydstrom and Cade directly. Hell, the princess was tall and blond—*Acton* would love her.

Mari frowned to herself. Would she actually set up her first love with another female just so she could have Bowen?

In a freaking heartbeat.

But Princess Mariah wasn't giving up yet. . . . "I surrendered my soul for you." She'd begun softly crying, and her tears were obviously killing him. "And you made an oath to me before you did to her. Can't you at least give us a chance? Don't you think you owe me that?"

"I do owe you that."

Mari's heart fell.

"But I canna live without Mariketa," he said, and Mari's eyes widened. "I *will* no'."

The princess was now openly weeping, and Bowen's expression clearly told how agonized he was about this.

"You—a loyal Lykae—would break your vows to your mate and give up your only chance for children, all for something that isn't even real? For a *witch*?"

Though he looked as if he was about to double over with guilt and shame, he still said, "Mariah, I will no' be moved from this. If I canna live with that *witch*, then I'd rather no' live at all."

Mari gasped. At once, Mariah's head whipped around, her eyes narrowing on the mirror.

There was no way she could have heard, and yet even now she seemed to be staring directly at Mari.

Impossible. Unless . . .

Mari broke away from the mirror. "Oh, great Hekate!"

Or rather, the great Häxa—wearing a false face. Mariah had never returned, had never been resurrected. This was all Häxa, and the sorceress was . . . *feeding*. Expertly building Bowen's misery, then seizing it.

"Elianna, Carrow, I'm going!" When they hurried into her room, she was yanking on a pair of canvas pants, with pockets along the sides—to be filled with as many mirrors as she could carry. "I've found her, found Häxa. She's wearing a false face, as Mariah. She's right through that mirror—currently feeding off my male!"

Wide-eyed, they gazed through the mirror.

Then with a sigh, Elianna said, "It figures—it's always either the butler or the resurrected mate."

As Mari frowned at that, Carrow asked Elianna, "Is Mari ready for this fight?"

Elianna seemed to force a smile. "Mari will never be more prepared to battle her than she is now."

Carrow was too jacked up with excitement to notice how cryptic Elianna's answer was, or how sad her eyes looked now.

But Mari got chills. *I might die tonight.*

"Here, Mari," Elianna said as she dug into her seemingly infinite apron pocket and pulled out a small, mirror-covered box. "Your parents wanted you to have these. They were made by druid weavers."

Mari took the box. Inside was a pair of fingerless gloves fashioned of a jet mesh. "Um, thanks?" They were striking, but maybe not so apropos just now. Mari's mentor was as befuddled as ever.

Elianna scrunched her lips. "Just turn them over."

When Mari did, her eyes widened, and she breathed, "*Things—just—got—interesting.*"

Lining each of the palms was a *mirror*—made of spunglass threading. The mirror mesh was perfectly flexible, smooth, and resilient. She slipped the gloves on, stunned by the fit, the soft fabric seeming to conform to her hands.

Elianna explained, "These gloves will be like megaphones for your power. And you'll always have them at hand, so to speak, if you want to rub them for focus."

"Lock and load, babee!" Carrow cried, more than ready to engage the sorceress. "Marines, we are *leav-ing!*"

But Häxa wasn't like a rogue demon or a malevolent phantom, where one additional spell could mean the difference between success or failure. The sorceress would simply use Mari's friends to wield them against her.

Just as Häxa would do with Bowen if she discovered how deeply Mari had fallen in love with him.

"I'm going alone."

"Alone?" Carrow blinked. "What did I tell you about things like this? It starts with 'Darwin says.' Come on, Mari, how many chances does a witch like me get to rid the world of ultimate evil?"

Knowing Carrow would continue protesting, Mari said, "I'll tell you what, let's compromise. You guys watch the fight through the mirror. If I get into trouble, then just crawl through and come rescue me. That's fair, right?" She said this even as she planned to block the portal to them.

Carrow seemed whipped with disappointment, but when Elianna said, "That's for the best," Carrow agreed to stay. "For now."

With that settled, Mari gazed out at her enemy. Any fear and doubts she'd had fired into outrage. This evil being had already devastated Mari's family, and now she seemed bent on using Bowen's feelings for Mari to torment the proud, stalwart warrior—the warrior who had chosen Mari over . . . *everything*.

Häxa was as good as dead.

"I'm going." Mari might not live through the night, but if she went, then she was taking Häxa down with her. She turned back. "I've got a wicked bitch to destroy."

Carrow stared at her eyes with a look of something like awe. "Mari, I think . . . I think you *are* the wicked bitch."

Bowe rubbed the back of his neck, sensing that he and Mariah were no longer alone. He turned, scanning the room. Had the wall mirror just moved?

Suddenly, the glass bulged out. Two small, gloved hands broke the surface in the middle, drawing the now pliable glass to the sides.

Mariketa.

His heart leapt at the sight, even as he knew Mariah studied him. He didn't want to hurt her needlessly, but he couldn't hide his excitement. He'd begun to fear he'd never have the opportunity to talk to Mariketa, or to tell her how he felt about her.

Yet the witch didn't spare a glance at Bowe. With magick growing in her strangely gloved palms and a murderous look in her glassy eyes, she made straight for Mariah, who retreated, visibly frightened.

"Witch! What in the hell are you doing?" Bowe lunged after her, absently realizing he was more worried about Mariketa's hurting an innocent than he was about Mariah's safety.

Had she lost her mind? Over the spells or over Bowen's perceived betrayal? Was *she* under some kind of spell?

Mariketa peered over her shoulder, eyes brilliant.

"Don't fight me, Lykae." The coldness in her stunned him as much as any of this. . . .

With a wave of her hand she shot him against the wall and froze him there. True fear coursed through him.

He was unable to move, unable to speak, forced to do nothing but watch as the witch closed in to kill.

51

ari wondered how long the sorceress would keep up the charade. Now that Mari knew Häxa's real identity, the cloying and the play were so obvious.

Still in disguise, Häxa finally stood her ground. "Come to fight me for him?"

Mari gave a bitter laugh as they began circling each other. "No, Häxa. He matters not at all," she lied baldly. "If I wasn't about to destroy you, I'd wish you two well."

"Destroy me, is it? I was musing when you'd finally find the courage to come face me." Her voice began to change, becoming raspier as she sneered, "Or when you could drag your pretty gaze from the glass."

Mari could *feel* Bowen's confusion, heard him struggling. To him, this still appeared to be Mariah talking.

"Yes, I know all about you," Häxa continued. "The vain witch. The Queen of Reflections." Her eyes darted in Bowen's direction. "Does the Lykae's heart beat so madly for you or me? I wonder."

"Before I kill you I want to know why you seized on him. Why use Mariah?"

"Kill me? Oh, you fanciful child."

Her amusement rankled.

"I'll tell you. Eighteen decades ago, a spoiled princess bade me enchant him."

Mari's lips parted. There'd been an enchantment—but it hadn't been Mari's.

Behind her, she heard Bowen's struggles abruptly cease. This revelation had no doubt confounded him.

Häxa continued, "Seems Mariah hadn't appreciated that when all other males fawned after her, begging for her hand, Bowen had absolutely no interest in her, even seemed to disdain her—Mariah, a *princess*. For years, she loved him from afar, or at least she fancied herself in love with him. No other would do. She *had* to have him. So I granted her wish, knowing that this situation would be replete with pain and suffering—and that if I grant a wish, I get to reap the misery from the outcomes of *all involved*.

"I gave him to her, and her to him, then killed her within weeks. On the night I caused her death, I realized that the wolf would lead me *to you*, the Awaited One. I merely watched him until you came into his life." She turned to Bowen. "Thank you for removing her cloak for me. The red made my vision irritatingly blurry."

"And the plane wreck?" Mari said. "The earthquake when we were on the bridge?"

"That was merely playing. Every time this one thought he'd lose you again, I got an infusion of despair. Besides, the demon pilot begged me to unfreeze his family, volunteering to do anything for me. How could I resist?"

Mari's animosity toward the pilot left her in a rush.

Häxa continued, "Since I've returned as Bowen's dead mate resurrected, he's given me a veritable feast of misery, seasoned with guilt. Delectable. I could have killed you at any time. But you hadn't used your magick against me, so I couldn't siphon it from you. And captromancer, I do so want your unique powers."

Häxa? Bowe struggled to comprehend what was happening.

She can assume any form, Mariketa had said. And Häxa was revealing that he had, in fact, been under an enchantment—but long before he'd ever met Mariketa.

Mariketa held out one of her hands in his direction, displaying a strange mirror in the palm of her glove. Suddenly, his medallion began tearing from his neck, shooting pain through him. It was as though the thing had planted deep roots in his skin that were now being stripped away, tearing as they went. In the past, every time he'd decided to remove it, he'd always forgotten to. Now he knew why, and now he understood why Mariketa hadn't sensed another curse on him—because it had been a *part* of him, like a cancer.

Once freed, the medallion flew across the room to her. She caught it, then melted it in the heat of her mirrored palm, until it resembled a lead ball.

When she dropped it to the ground, a thick haze seemed to be lifted from Bowe's vision. Now when he gazed at the image of Mariah, he felt nothing but . . . *fury*.

For so long he'd suffered immeasurable grief. He'd walked around like the living dead in an existence of nothing but longing and pain—and it was all because of the *whim of a spoiled princess*.

Mariah had invited this sorceress into his life, had ensured that Häxa found Mariketa, and had driven a wedge between Bowe and his true mate. Mariketa hadn't even seemed able to stand the sight of him earlier.

"Vain witch, did you see your parents' bodies? My handiwork is so beautiful."

What had been done to her parents?

"You won't feed off me, Häxa. I feel only hatred."

"No loss. I've had a surfeit from that Lykae and am as strong as I've ever been. Are you certain you wish to battle me? When I take your powers, I'll be a goddess once more."

"When I take yours, I'll be a sorceress," Mariketa said, sounding confident and as brave as ever.

"You have no idea what you toy with, child. But tonight, on another eve brimming with purpose, I'll teach you one last lesson."

Häxa finally began to shuck her disguise, like a snake slithers from its dead skin. The windows exploded and wind rushed in, howling over them. Curtains flew and furniture skidded across the wooden floor. Pictures on the walls went flying like discs.

Her true form was hideous. The whites of her eyes grew black, the pupils a filmy yellow. Her skin was waxen and gray. She stood at least eight feet tall, with claws as long as his fingers.

In comparison, Mariketa looked so small and frail with her hair whipping, buffeted by the wind and struggling to remain upright.

Häxa raised her hands; Mariketa's eyes went wide. She opened her own palms and tossed a table in front of Häxa's beam just before it hit her. The wood disintegrated *into dust.*

Another two beams flashed out. Mari dodged one by shooting up on her toes and arching her back. The other hit her, sending her spinning into the wall.

The Instinct screamed inside Bowe for him to protect his own, yet he could do nothing.

Mariketa lurched under yet another beam, but she was

getting slower, weaker. At last, she fled, ducking behind a wall across from where Bowe was trapped. She slid down to the floor at the corner. He saw her swallow with fear, peek out from the edge of the wall, then squeeze her eyes shut as she barely missed a sudden blast by her face. Leaning her head back, she stared at the ceiling. He barely heard her whispering, "*Shit, shit, shit.*"

Run! He wanted Mariketa to escape. Instead, she brought magick to her palms. Then, as if testing, she glanced around the corner . . . and finally threw a beam at the sorceress.

Häxa was shot across the room.

With her brows raised, Mariketa dropped her gaze to her gloved palms.

The sorceress shrieked with pain and rage. Smoke began to swirl in a tempest around her, growing thicker and thicker until she was concealed. Mariketa stood and crossed the room to face her, her eyes glowing feverishly, looking like she'd bloody follow her into the haze.

Doona go in there! Doona go . . .

He finally managed to roar his fear for her. At the edge of the tempest, Mariketa turned to him. But he didn't think she even saw him. A gruesome gray hand slithered out from the smoke and palmed her entire head. Just as claws dropped down like a cage over her forehead, Mariketa put her forefinger against her red lips to quiet him.

Then she *smiled* as she was yanked into the chaos.

He fought against his invisible bindings, grappling with all the strength in his body. *Arms free.* He had to get inside to her. The smoke choked him, blinding light sparking inside it—

Suddenly, *Häxa* was thrown from the tempest.

When Mariketa followed, her feet didn't touch the ground. She looked like nothing he'd ever seen—a killer ready for annihilation.

Mariketa kept her mirrored palms up, delivering a continuous beam at Häxa. Bowe could see Häxa's neck begin to stretch and heard bones snapping. Shrieking, she tossed frenzied beams at Mariketa, but they were useless. "Give me another, Häxa," she sneered. "I didn't quite feel that."

Take her head! Do it!

As if his frantic thoughts called her attention, Häxa raised her head and cast a beam at him.

The hit struck him like a battering ram to the chest. Bones shattered under the force.

52

Her concentration was interrupted just long enough for Häxa to grasp her beams and pull. She yanked Mari into her like a pitched ball, then batted her away, sending her flying.

Mari landed on her back, with such a crushing force that blood sprayed from her mouth. Even prone, she tried to attack, raising her gloves, but Häxa had somehow bound her outgoing magick.

"Just stay down, child," Häxa said, rising to her towering height to close in on Mari. "Your father didn't even make it this long. I yawned while I froze your mother."

Häxa loomed over her, building magick in her eyes, her mouth, her hands. Building . . . building. She was going to use everything she had to finish this, to render Mari to ash.

The Queen of False Faces was just too strong.

The kill shot neared.

Coughing up blood, Mari lolled her head to the side, wanting to see Bowen a last time. . . .

The bone in one of his legs was broken, jutting up, piercing his jeans. His chest was bleeding profusely. The blood had spread out across the front of his shirt and was sopping a trail along the floor as he still struggled toward Mari.

All at once Mari understood why people fought losing battles—because if you want something badly enough, *you can't do anything else but fight for it.*

Mari would fight.

The mirror she'd climbed through lay on the floor between her and Bowen. She met his eyes, furtively opening her palm for it. Calling it to come to her, she might have budged a corner. Gnashing his teeth, he lunged for it, spinning it across the wood floor to her until her magick could seize it and draw it close.

The sorceress blinked her eyes at them, then shrieked with fury, letting loose her power. At the last second, Mari shoved the mirror upright, huddling behind the glass like a knight behind a shield against the fire of a dragon.

The beam reflected, trapping Häxa with her own unstoppable power.

So hot . . . hold on . . . fight!

Häxa's screams echoed, piercing the night. In a circle all around Mari, the force of the beam's overflow splintered the floor as though a jackhammer had broken through. Shards of wood flew upward. Stakes embedded themselves in the ceiling.

Just have to hold on longer than she can.

Häxa's screams grew dimmer.

Hold on. . . .

Bowe watched as Häxa's body seemed to rupture from within, cracking open into thick fissures. With her claw-tipped fingers clenched in pain, she began to shift—and a thousand forms flashed over her.

In the midst of them, Bowe spied a witch with raven hair and draped in a black stole.

Then . . . light exploded inside her, incinerating her.

Like an atomic bomb, a flat line of energy cast out before erupting straight up. The force blew the roof off the house, searing it to instant ash. Cinders wafted down as the walls groaned and collapsed.

Mariketa shakily set the mirror away. He saw her drop her head as if she were staring at her stomach.

"Oh." She grasped something in her front, then yanked. Her fingers went limp and a spike of wood, dripping with blood, rolled from her grasp. Holding her side, she tried to stand, but fell back on her hip. Another unsteady attempt, and she finally made it to her feet.

When she faced Bowe, he winced at her bloodied face, the bruises already emerging. Her hair was coated with soot. As she limped to him, her eyes began returning to normal.

"Mari," he grated, "you've got to heal yourself."

"Bowen, your legs . . . your chest."

"I'll be fine—"

Another sudden wind rushed over them, scattering debris. Mariketa cried out as an invisible force assailed her, seeming to strangle her from inside.

"What's happenin' tae you?" he yelled. "What is this?"

Grueling moments passed. When the wind eased, and she was released from whatever had gripped her, she appeared confused. "I think . . . I think that was Häxa's power. . . ."

If what Mari had said earlier about destroying a sorceress was true, then she'd just had an infusion of a near godlike power.

As she started for Bowe once more, the whites of her eyes and her irises seemed to become flooded with black, as though ink had spilled inside them—like Häxa's had been. As if possessed, Mariketa swung her gaze from him until her uncanny eyes locked onto the glass on the floor.

Her expression was as if she were starving, even *lustful*, and she hurried to it, stepping directly atop it. The ground seemed to fall out from under her, and she dropped down, disappearing.

Bellowing with fear for her, Bowe dragged himself to the mirror to reach her. But she was gone.

He raked his claws down the glass, desperate to follow.

53

~~❦~~

Somehow Mari had managed to enthrall . . . *herself*.

For days, she'd remained in her dimension, standing motionless in front of her antique full-length mirror. Though she was conscious and rapidly healing, she was unable to move, to look away. She couldn't even part her lips. If anything was placed between her gaze and the mirror, her eyes—fully black from Häxa's power—burned it away.

Mari had already been walking a razor's edge with her new captromancer abilities before she'd been saddled with Häxa's power. Though not inherently evil, the power was greedy, ravening for the knowledge the mirror helplessly ceded. Mari couldn't free herself. . . .

Once her parents had awakened and made their way back home from Häxa's plane, Mari couldn't even hug them back, couldn't even cry with her frustration, though her dimension had become drenched in rain. They'd looked so worried for her, yet so proud of what she'd accomplished.

With the help of the coven, the two planned to bind Häxa's power within her, letting Mari get accustomed to it gradually over decades. But they couldn't bind the power when it was in active use—like when it was freezing unwitting witches in front of a mirror. And Mari's eyes constantly glowed like two LED lights.

At least her coven was stepping up to the plate, witches motivating like crazy. Apparently, the wake-up call had been when Häxa, one of the world's most ancient and evil powers, had risen, only to show up—directly in the parish next to their Andoain Animal House. No longer did they feel insulated and protected by the law of *laissez les bons temps rouler*.

The world wouldn't know what hit it when that crew got it together.

As her parents did every day, Carrow and Elianna visited with her at the "Cottanorouse." Knowing Mari could hear them, they chatted, and brought her tea as if she would drink it. They also urged her to unenthrall herself, as if Mari might not be totally convinced that she wished to do so. She wanted to point at the new power and say, "Take it up with stupid."

Because Mari was on a plane of the Wiccae, and she couldn't speak to invite Bowen, he couldn't come to her. Her friends and family had deduced that it snowed whenever she missed him; the plane had become a constant whiteout.

Today at Mari's place, Carrow played solitaire, bundled in blankets. Elianna looked to be sorting dried frogs' legs by size, and then by toe webbing. Mari's parents were out consulting seers for the answer of how to rescue Mari. Today they would meet with one of the most powerful oracles in the world—Nucking Futs Nïx.

"Damn, Mari, it's cold!" Carrow chafed her arms. "I dig the whole Narnian vibe you've got going on, I do. And I've been dutifully keeping an eye out for talking beavers wearing armor—but come on, this is getting ridiculous! If you miss the Scot so much, then just break free."

Elianna said, "Do you know he's bought the property just next door to Andoain so he can scent you the minute you come home. And, well, because his house got blown up."

"Look, Mari, you have to come out of this and do something," Carrow said. "Put him out of his misery—or—allow me to make him fall in love with dryer lint. You decide." She shrugged. "I know you'd worried about Bowen not wanting to come near the coven—but we can't get him to leave. Apparently, some of the witches admitted to him that you're on a different plane—he can be really dogged with the questions—and now he's determined to reach you here. Interestingly, he believes the information about the plane's existence—but not about the fact that he can't travel to it."

"He returns to Andoain daily, sometimes hourly, researching witchery," Elianna said.

Carrow glared. "Well, maybe if you and the others would stop sneakily setting out food for him, he wouldn't keep coming back!"

Crossing her arms over her chest, Elianna said in a mulish tone, "He wouldn't eat otherwise."

"Whatever. But seriously, Mari, he's having such a hard time with all this that even *Regin* feels sorry for what he's been through."

Elianna added, "He's watched your graduation video so many times, I'm sure he's memorized your school's alma mater."

"I don't know what he does with the videos of your college cheerleading he brings back to his place"—Carrow waggled her eyebrows—"but I have suspicions."

Elianna coughed delicately.

"Now that you've done what you were Awaited to do—well, part one at least—everyone's grasping about for a new name for you," Carrow said. "If you don't kick this enthrallment, then I'm going to campaign for Mar</br>iketa the Glass Witch, or 'Glitch.' Come kick my ass if you don't like it, otherwise . . ."

Elianna squinted at Mari and sighed. "I think she wants to be called Mariketa MacRieve."

Mari did. She wanted to go to Bowen and tell him she loved him, she wanted to visit with her family and friends, she wanted to . . . blink. But the knowledge flowed through her veins; the power demanded.

It seemed that she would be forced to stay here until she knew . . . everything.

Which meant she'd never leave.

Because everything is the very thing I cannot know.

When Bowe tracked down Nïx at last, she was perched like a gargoyle on the roof of a building on Bourbon Street. He climbed up to her, feeling only a lingering ache in his healing leg. "Nïx, you have to help me."

"What's put you all in a dither, werewolf?"

"You were right about everything, about the Hie, about me finding my mate. All your predictions came true—though you might have bloody told me exactly *who* had put a hex on me."

She finally faced him. "I said you'd been *ensorcelled*, not enchanted, and everyone knew Mariketa wasn't yet a sorceress." She rolled her eyes. "Really, pet—*duh?*"

Keep a rein on it.

She added, "Though I am truly sorry that you had eighteen decades of unadulterated misery."

Bowe compared the princess's actions to those of the witch who'd hurt his father. The only difference was degrees of pain. But he had little time to think of what she'd done to him—to all of them. "I need to find Mariketa." Gods, did he need to find her. The longing for his witch was a thousandfold more powerful than what the strongest sorceress on earth could engender in him.

"Have we lost her again? Bowen, you must keep up with your captromancer better than this!"

"Nïx!"

"Oh, I know already, of course. She's gone off to a witch's plane, in a different dimension. Before you ask, I'll tell you that they're held sacred, and I can't give you directions to it. There are some laws even the proto-Valkyrie won't break."

"After all this, you will no' tell me how to reach that place?"

She tilted her head at him. "You, Bowen MacRieve, want to go to a world where only witches and their kindred live? Where magick is in everything from a raindrop to a bird's feather?"

"Nïx, I want to do whatever it bloody takes—"

"I wish I could help you. I do." She quirked a brow. "Especially since you're keeping yourself up a bit better." She clawed the air in his direction, and he scowled. "And actually, there is a simple way for you to reach her. The means is so obvious it hurts me—*hurts me*, I tell you."

"Damn it, what is it, Valkyrie?"

"You have as much right as anyone to be on a witch's plane."

"But I'm no' connected by blood to the Wiccae. And I'm no' Mari's husband—yet."

"Figure out why you've the right to be there, and I'll help you with the logistics."

Her gaze locked on something below them. Her small form tensed like a predator's. She appeared to be stalking *Regin*. Or at least someone stalking Regin. "Must go." She finally met his eyes. "Do not come to me again without an answer. . . ." Then, like a blur, she leapt to the ground, disappearing into the crowd.

54

The next night, Bowe had been asleep for only an hour—after dropping exhausted onto his mattress on the floor at his new place—when he sat up in bed, his heart thundering. The answer was on his tongue.

Once he'd hated to the gods what he was. Now he realized it was the answer to reaching her.

Bowe dragged on jeans . . . couldn't find his shoes so he went without . . . was still throwing on a shirt as he charged out into the night to find Nïx.

Luckily she was at Val Hall—and lucid, he saw, when she met him outside the Valkyrie's home.

"Nïx, I figured out how I can join her," he told her at once. "You said witches and their kindred can reach that other place. From what I've been reading, that means *familiars* as well."

"Um, Bowen," she began slowly, "familiars are . . . *animals*."

He raised his eyebrows in an "*and your point is*" expression. "I read that familiars can be protectors—*I* am Mari's protector. One witch had a tiger—another even had a bear. Why no' a Lykae?"

Nïx beamed proudly. "I'm impressed!"

"So how the hell do I get to her?"

"Go to her room at Andoain."

"I was just there this . . ." He trailed off, having learned not to question these things endlessly—or, in some instances, at all. "Verra well."

At Andoain, he bounded up the stairs to Mari's bedroom three at time, ignoring the growing pain in his leg. From the corner of his eye, he spied witches blinking at him from behind their doors. He dimly noted that candles were lit throughout—they seemed to be expecting him.

He swung open Mari's door. And was suddenly in another house, with buckets of snow falling outside. He glanced around, battling his sense of disquiet. Was any of this real? Was he dreaming?

Easing farther inside, he found a woman within who resembled Mariketa. Beside her stood a man who crossed thick arms over his chest, raising his brows at Bowe.

At that moment, Bowe realized that he was meeting Mari's parents—and that, in addition to his bare feet and unshaven, rough appearance, his shirt was on backward. And inside out.

"*This* is the male she's been seeing?" the man muttered. "He can't even dress himself."

Bowe just stifled the urge to point out that though he might not be able to dress himself, he sure as hell could perceive when a bairn was on his shoulders. Instead he bit his tongue. This warlock, though arrogant, was Bowe's future father-in-law.

"A werewolf, Jill? Really."

"*Hush.*" The woman slapped the back of her hand against his stomach, then said, "I'm Jillian. And this is my husband, Warren. We are Mari's parents. And we know you're Bowen MacRieve of the Lykae clan."

He gave her a nod.

To Bowe, Warren demanded, "Aren't you a bit old for my daughter?"

When Bowe scowled, Jillian blithely continued, "We've been waiting for you. Mari's been waiting. She needs your help."

"Where is she?"

"Follow me." Jillian showed him to a room that looked like a cross between the bedroom in Belize and Mari's at Andoain.

His breath left him. Mari stood in front of a full-length mirror, utterly still, dark eyes unblinking. His voice broke low when he asked, "What's happened tae her?"

Jillian answered, "Once she received Häxa's powers, she basically enchanted herself. And no one's strong enough to combat her magick."

"None can fix what they can hardly touch," Warren said.

Jillian added, "But we think *you* might be able to talk her from this. Nix told us this morning that you intend to be her protector—"

"He's a beast familiar," Warren scoffed.

"Which makes him a werewolf protector. And that's why he's been allowed here."

"Can she hear me?" Bowe asked, disregarding the fact that he hadn't spoken to Nix until minutes ago.

"Mari's aware of everything we're saying," she answered.

"How do I free her?"

"You persuade her to somehow find the power to pull away. Talk to her, make her fight," Jillian said. "Reflections are Mari's strengths, but they're also her weaknesses. She can be hurt by them if she draws too much on them—once you succeed in freeing her, then you have to make sure she doesn't lose herself in the mirror like this ever again."

No wonder he'd had such a strong reaction to her chanting to the glass.

Warren added, "Tonight, *if* you succeed, we're going to bind Häxa's power within her. For a few decades, Mari will need to use the mirror for knowledge sparingly—only in the *direst emergencies*. She can travel through mirrors and use them to focus spells, but the knowledge is what Häxa's power will always crave—and bindings are not infallible."

"Can we trust you to see to this?" Jillian asked.

Bowe gave a sharp nod. "Aye, I can see to it."

"Don't try to put anything in front of her eyes," Warren said. "She'll burn away whatever blocks her gaze. And whatever you do, do *not* break the mirror."

Without looking away from Mari, Bowe asked, "Why no'?" This seemed an ideal solution to him.

Jillian murmured, "The shock could . . . it could kill her."

No' ideal.

"I want to be alone with her," Bowe said.

She nodded. "We're going to the binding ceremony. Good luck, Bowen."

After they closed the door, Bowe could still hear Mari's father say, "Jill, why are you so confident in MacRieve?"

"Because he won't ever rest until he has her back with him," she replied before they descended the stairs.

Alone with Mari, Bowe said, "Lass, we're about to take a break from the mirror for a bit. How am I to marry you in front of all those witches in an eerie, embarrassing cere-mony if you will no' look away?"

No reaction.

He put his arms around her waist and leaned down to kiss her neck, closing his eyes with pleasure just to be close to her once more.

"Doona wish to turn from your glass? Verra well. Then ask it some questions while you're here. Ask it how much your Lykae's missed you."

Had she blinked?

At her other ear, he murmured, "Ask it who Bowe loves."

Her lips parted. Her body seemed to begin thrumming, as if she was struggling with everything she had in her to be free.

"Aye, that's right. Ask it who's the only one Bowe's ever been in love with." He brushed the back of his fingers down her cheek, willing her to meet his gaze in the mirror. "And the last question we're goin' tae have before you come away with me . . . ask it how damned good our lives are goin' tae be together, just as soon as you turn tae kiss me."

Her brows drew together, and her stiff posture tightened, then relaxed. Her eyelids slid closed.

"There now, that's it, beautiful girl," he rasped, easing her face toward him. Behind her, he pressed the mirror until it flipped over, revealing the back of the frame. "Now, kiss me, witch."

When Mari opened her eyes once more, Bowen's warm, firm lips covered her own. Then he was lifting her and carrying her to the bed.

Once he settled her in his lap, she laid her hand against his unshaven cheek. How she'd missed him! She felt a sharp pang at how exhausted he looked. "I can't believe you made it here."

"I'm your familiar." He jutted his chin up in that proud way. "I'm tae guard you. Besides, you canna lose me this easily." His gaze held hers as he said, "I'll follow you anywhere, Mari."

"I'm so— Whoa," she abruptly whispered, her hand flying to her forehead. The ponderous weight of Häxa's power was lessening. "Are my eyes clearing?"

"Aye." He exhaled with relief. "The binding's working."

"I can feel it." She bit her lip. "Bowen, about earlier—I'm sorry that my dad was rude to you. And I'm so sorry for everything that happened to you. The enchantment—"

"I'm no' sorry about that." When she gave him an incredulous look, he amended, "At first, I was furious. Then I realized that if we can be together, then everything's brought me to you. Think of it—I've even got to thank that damned vampire for beating me in the Hie. If not for that . . ." He trailed off with a shudder. "Besides, I doona mind the struggle, when the prize is so worthy."

"But it must eat at you that you went so long, and it was so agonizing—"

"If you doubt what I'm saying, then you have no' grasped what I'm feeling for you. I would do *anything* to be here with you like this. If you'll have me." His brows drew together. "You know how I feel about you, but I'm no' certain you love me ba—"

"I love you," she said quickly.

"Doona wish to ponder this? Be certain of your feelings? Play coy?"

"No way." She shook her head emphatically. "I've been a goner for you since the island, and was whipped since the first night we were together, together. But can you handle all this . . . witchery?"

"I wanted to tell you the day of the plane crash that I'd made up my mind to do whatever I had to in order to keep you—and that included accepting everything about you. I doona give a damn about all the variables as long as the constant is *us*—together." He squeezed her in his arms, tucking her into his chest.

He was holding her tightly—as if he'd never let her go.

And this struck her as tremendously good. Then she frowned. "Bowen?"

"Aye, love?"

"Why's your shirt inside out?"

55

Scotland
Winter Solstice, six months later . . .

"So that's how we're tae play this, wife?" Bowen said, when her snowball beaned him squarely in the face. He shook the snow from him in that wolfy way she loved. "You challenge a master at your own peril and have been duly warned."

She wiggled her gloved fingers at him. "Bring it on, Father Time."

But her eyes widened as he began piling up the biggest snowball she'd ever seen. She took off, darting back toward the lodge.

Playing in the snow—what an incredible way to end an already wonderful day. They'd arrived in Scotland just this morning. The jet ride was forgettable—literally, with proper sedation. And last night, just before Mari and Bowen had flown out, her parents had told her *they were having a baby*, which delighted her, though she promised them she'd "act out" due to the new sibling—

Bowen's mammoth snowball smacked her on the ass,

nearly knocking her down. She gasped, looking over her shoulder.

"*That's* how you throw a snowball." Grinning, he took a bow, then loped after her.

Bowen grinned a lot now. And damn, it was a good look for him.

Playing with him like this, she recognized that her own chance of making it to forty without having kids with her Lykae was nil.

With a squeal, she let him catch her, and he dragged her down into the snow with him. "Dinna hurt you, did I?" he asked as he eased her beneath him.

Even though she'd turned immortal over three months ago, he still asked her that. She thought he always would and loved him for it. "Not at all."

"So you like it here?"

"*Adore* it."

"You're no' just saying that? Because I can—"

"I want to live half the year here." They'd stay the other six months in their place next to Andoain. "If I'm needed by the coven or for a freelance job, I can commute to the coven via mirror." She'd been working hard these last few months, organizing the Andoain coven with her parents' help and selling spells on her own. Did she hit it out of the park with each magick job? No, but at least she continued to get referrals.

"In addition to the apple orchard I had planted here over the summer," he began, "I also bought a six-foot-high, full-length mirror. So *we* can commute. You'll take me through with you. Since I'm your familiar."

He took the position of "protector of his witch" very seriously, going with her to all her jobs, and grumbled when she suggested he was more of an *accountabilibuddy* for her magick. "Sounds good to me."

"So what do you think about *real* snow?" He'd razzed her without cease because apparently, her dimension's imagined snow had been like the stuff they used on movie sets.

"It's *beautiful.*"

"Aye, beautiful," he said with his gaze locked on her face. "I knew snow would become you. I canna quite believe I'm finally enjoying my favorite season, and I'm doing it with you—my favorite sight."

He cupped her face and leaned down to give her a languid kiss. But when she wrapped her arms around his neck and hugged him tightly, he slanted his mouth over hers, deepening the contact until she was trembling beneath him.

Against his lips, she murmured, "*Bowen . . .*"

He drew back. "I know my female's tone. I'll be takin' you tae bed now."

When she nodded eagerly, he gave her a sly grin. "Your werewolf's still got it, eh, lass?"

Breathless, she smiled up at him. "If by *it* you mean *me,* then you'll never lose it."

Dark Needs at Night's Edge

A vampire warrior consumed by madness,
trapped in the lair of an otherworldly temptress
only he can see.
The beauty wants him gone—the warrior can't leave.

Let the games begin . . .
May 2008

S*tay sane, act normal*, he chants to himself as he strides down the rickety pier. On either side of him, water black like tar. Ahead of him, muted light from the bayou tavern. A Lore bar. A lone neon sign flickers over flat skiffs below. Music and laughter carry. *Stay sane . . . need to dull the rage. Until the endtime.*

Inside. "Whiskey." His voice is low, rough from disuse.

The bartender's face falls. Like last night. Others grow skittish. *Can they sense that I ache to kill?* The whispers around him are like metal on slate to his ragged nerves.

—". . . madder than any I've seen in all my centuries."

—"A killer for hire. If he shows up in your town, then folks from the Lore there'll go missing."

Missing? Unless I want them found.

—"Heard he drains 'em so savagely . . . nothing's left of their throats."

So I'm not fastidious.

—"I heard he eats them."

Distorted rumors. *Or is that one true?*

Tales of his insanity spreading once more. *I've never missed a target—how insane can I be?* He answers himself: *Very fucking much so.*

Memories clot his mind. His victims' memories taken from their blood toll inside him, their number always growing. *Don't know what's real; can't determine what's illusion.* Most of the time, he can scarcely understand his own thoughts. A grenade with the pin pulled, they say. Only a matter of time.

They're right.

Stay sane . . . act normal. Glass in hand, he chuckles softly on his way to a shadowy table in the back. *Normal?* He's a goddamned vampire in a bar filled with shifters, demons, and the sharp-eared fey. Christmas lights are strung up in the back—through the eye sockets of human skulls that frame a mirror. In the corner, a demoness lazily strokes her lover's horns, visibly arousing the male. At the bar, a massive werewolf bares his fangs as he tosses a small redhead behind him.

Can't decide if you should attack, Lykae? That's right. I don't smell of blood. A trick I learned.

The couple leaves, the redhead all but carried out by the Lykae. As they exit, she peers over her shoulder, her eyes like mirrors. Then gone. Out into the night where they belong.

Sit. Back against the wall. He adjusts the sunglasses that shade his red eyes, dirty red eyes. As he scans the room, he resists the urge to rub his palm over the back of his neck. *Watched by someone unseen?*

But then I always feel like that.

He swoops up his drink, narrowing his eyes at his steady hand. *My mind's decayed; my sword hand's still steady.* A ruinous combination. He takes a deep swallow. *The drink.* The whiskey dulls the need to lash out. Not that it has disappeared.

Small things enrage him. An off look. Nearing too quickly. Failing to give him a wide enough berth. His fangs sharpen at the slightest provocation. *As though a living thing hungers inside me.* Ravenous for blood and a throat to tear. Each time he acts on the rage, others' memories blight more of his own.

He still has enough sanity to stalk his targets—his brothers. He will mete retribution to Nikolai and Murdoch Wroth for doing the unspeakable to him. Sebastian, the third brother, was a victim like him, but must be slain—simply because of what he is.

And my time grows nigh. Like an animal, he recognizes this. He's found the three in this mysterious place of swamps and haze and music and has seen them with their wives. He might have felt envy that his brothers laugh with them. That they touch them possessively, with wonder in their clear eyes. But hatred drowns out any confusing jealousy. Murdoch and Nikolai have no right to a future.

Offspring will follow. He'll kill their females as well. *Destroy them. Destroy myself.*

Endtime. His brows draw together. A whisper of regret. The thing he regrets most. He tries to remember what he covets so dearly. Another's memories bombard him, exploding in his mind. His hand shoots up to clasp his forehead—

Nikolai enters the bar, Murdoch behind him. Their expressions are grave.

They've come to kill me. As he expected. He thought he could draw them out by returning here again and again. He lowers his hand, and his lips ease back from his fangs. The bar empties in a rush.

Then . . . stillness. His brothers stare as if seeing a ghost. Insects clamor outside. Rain draws near and steeps the air. Just as lightning strikes in the distance, Sebastian enters, crossing to stand beside the other two. So he's allied with them? That he hadn't expected.

He removes his sunglasses, revealing his red eyes. The eldest, Nikolai, seems to stifle a wince at the sight, but shakes it off and advances. The three seem surprised that he'll stay to fight them, that he hasn't traced away. They are strong and skilled, yet they don't recognize the power he wields, the thing he's become. He can slaughter them all without blinking, and he'll savor it.

They walk to their doom. *Can't keep them waiting.*

He lunges from his seat and clears the table, knocking Sebastian unconscious with a blow that cracks his skull and sends him flying into the back wall. Before the other two can raise a hand in defense, he snatches them by their throats—one in each hand as they grapple to free themselves. "Three hundred years of this," he hisses. Their struggles do nothing; their stunned expressions satisfy. Squeezing . . . clenching—

Wood creaks behind him. He shoves back and hurtles his brothers at a new enemy. Too late; that Lykae's returned and slashes out with flared claws, ripping through his torso. Blood gushes.

He roars with fury and charges the werewolf, dodging claws and teeth with uncanny speed to barrel him to the ground. Just as his hands are about to meet around the Lykae's corded neck, the beast claps something to his right wrist.

A *manacle*? Clenching harder, he grates out a rasping laugh. "You don't think that will hold me?" Bones begin to pop beneath his palms. The kill is near, and he wants to yell with pleasure.

The werewolf cuffs his left wrist.

What is this? The metal won't bend. Won't break. *They goddamned mean to take me alive?* He leaps to his feet, tensing to trace. Nothing. Sebastian on the floor, pouring blood from his temple, has him by the ankles.

He kicks Sebastian, connecting squarely with his brother's chest. Ribs crack. He whirls around—in time to catch the bar rail the Lykae swings at his face.

He staggers but remains on his feet.

"What the fuck *is* he?" the Lykae bellows, swinging the rail again with all his might.

The brutal hit takes him across his neck. A split second of faltering. Enough for his brothers to tackle him.

He thrashes and bites, snapping his fangs. *Can't break free . . . can't . . .* They attach the manacles at his wrist to another chain. He kicks viciously, choking with rage when they trap his legs as well. He strains against his bonds with all his strength. The metal cleaves his skin to the bone. Nothing.

Caught. He roars, spitting blood at them, dimly hearing them speak.

"I hope you came up with a good place to put him," Sebastian says between rasping breaths.

Nikolai grates, "A long abandoned manor—place called *Elancourt*."

Chills seize him even through his fury. He can never go to this Elancourt. He doesn't understand why, just knows he can't—knows this with a savage certainty.

If they take him there, they won't take him alive. . . .